A SAUCERFUL OF SECRETS

A SAUCERFUL
OF SECRETS

Jane Yardley

Doubleday

LONDON · TORONTO · SYDNEY · AUCKLAND · JOHANNESBURG

TRANSWORLD PUBLISHERS
61–63 Uxbridge Road, London W5 5SA
a division of The Random House Group Ltd

RANDOM HOUSE AUSTRALIA (PTY) LTD
20 Alfred Street, Milsons Point, Sydney,
New South Wales 2061, Australia

RANDOM HOUSE NEW ZEALAND LTD
18 Poland Road, Glenfield, Auckland 10, New Zealand

RANDOM HOUSE SOUTH AFRICA (PTY) LTD
Endulini, 5a Jubilee Road, Parktown 2193, South Africa

Published 2005 by Doubleday
a division of Transworld Publishers

Copyright © Jane Yardley 2005

A catalogue record for this book is available from the British Library.
ISBN 0385 609329

Typeset in 11½/14pt Adobe Caslon by
Falcon Oast Graphic Art Ltd

Printed and bound in Great Britain by
Clays Ltd, Bungay, Suffolk

1 3 5 7 9 10 8 6 4 2

Papers used by Transworld Publishers are natural, recyclable products made from
wood grown in sustainable forests. The manufacturing processes conform to the
environmental regulations of the country of origin.

DEDICATION

The Questors Theatre portrayed here looks and functions pretty much like the real one in 1969, but I've played fast and loose with all the people and all the productions. Although this enables me to make the traditional claim that any resemblance to characters living or dead is purely etc., it also means I've expunged from the history of the Questors the man whose name was synonymous with it for more than half a century. That won't do. So, with apologies, I dedicate this to the late Alfred Emmet. He was an extraordinary man, and his theatre is extraordinary still.

There are worse things than not finding what you are looking for; there is finding them so different from what you had hoped.

J. M. Barrie, *Mary Rose*, Act III

The London suburb of Ealing is not a ski resort or far-flung hilly outpost, and wasn't in 1969 either – though admittedly it has always been a bit of a slog out of town. All that happens is the land rises two hundred feet above sea level and suddenly half the street names sound as though they were somewhere up an Alp. Kim had spent most of an hour tracking down a Mount Hill Crescent among the Mount Park Crescents, Mount Avenues, Hillcrest Crescents and Hillsides of the 'Queen of the suburbs'.

The other thing about Ealing is that this used to be an affable little town in its own right until it was co-opted into Greater London, when the suburb instantly picked up another bad habit to do with street names, a hooligan habit from the metropolis. It hid the bloody things. Kim, who was used to the relative orderliness of an English countryside where even the cows are labelled, wasn't merely lost but mystified.

She was also cold. Her street map had evoked images of an uphill trek all the way from the train station, so Kim had decided to travel light and avoid arriving sweaty and puffing. Among the dozens of commandments her mother Peggy had added to the usual ten was 'Never arrive at a stranger's house sweaty and puffing.' Besides, it was a sunny morning in April. But a chilly wind sniped at unexpected angles along these respectable empty daytime streets; by the time she found somebody to ask, Kim was frozen and wretched. She was thirteen, but the despondency that now dragged at her spirit was a child's, black and absolute.

Hanging forlornly from her small left hand was a paperback book entitled *Starched Linen*, by one Imogen St Clair. Her street map dangled from the other. Overhead droned the passenger planes, climbing, climbing, from London airport to the clouds. When Kim eventually trudged up to the door of number 154 she was just a heartbeat away from sitting down on the tiled path and crying for her mother.

Except that Kim never cried. Kim had not cried since earliest childhood, not even when she was five years old and the neighbour who offered them a car-ride home from the shops slammed the door prematurely with Kim's small thumb hooked around the frame. The child turned the colour of cheesecloth and Peggy thought she was dead, but her only response was a brief spasm of gulping, hardly louder than the chattering of teeth.

Now she stood at the door of this middle-class residence with its Gothick embellishments, and half of her hoped she had the wrong address. To its credit, the place was more than twice the size of Kim's home with Peggy. There was also a vintage Rolls-Royce parked in the driveway, vanilla white. Unfortunately, slap bang across the paintwork someone had added a peace symbol in a shade of orange loud enough to distract the jumbo jets. The house had the only scruffy front garden she had seen all morning, and in the window was a sticker demanding 'BURN DRAFT CARDS NOT PEOPLE'. Kim's interest in the Vietnam war was desultory but she was sure that if President Nixon had extended the draft to Ealing she would have heard.

At least there was a proper doorbell that chimed. Kim watched a shadow lurch and swell behind the stained-glass panels of the door, and then it was opened by a man wearing horns on his head.

'Oh,' he said when he saw her. He was tall, clean-shaven, with a strong lean face. Apart from the Norseman's helmet he was dressed in tight black leather trousers and a frilled white shirt, the ensemble topped by a pair of heavy-framed glasses, like Michael Caine. He had uttered only that one vowel, but from the sound of it Kim had a good idea how he would respond to her own.

'Is this the right house for Imogen St Clair?' she asked, carefully aspirating the *h*.

'It's pronounced Sinclair,' he said dispiritingly. 'And who might you be?'

Instinctively Kim glanced down at the paperback. It was a gesture of nervousness, and now she watched the man register it.

'Oh *no*,' he said. 'Not another one!'

That she wouldn't be the first hadn't entered Kim's head. But it did now. Of course, she thought, Imogen St Clair has had children my age turning up at her door like refugees off of the telly for the last four years.

'Aren't you too old?' demanded her interlocutor with irritable weariness, and rubbed his nose. The glasses twitched and his horns jiggled.

'I'm thirteen and a half,' Kim told him. 'I only look older because of the eye make-up.'

'Ah yes,' he replied after a pause. 'The eye make-up.'

'I was born Friday September 2nd 1955,' she continued with a precision she had rehearsed on the train. The man's response told Kim instantly that this was the right day. It gave her the strength to plough on. 'So can I see her please?'

'Not a chance,' he said. 'Who are you, anyway?'

'I'm Kim Tanner. And who are you?' she added, rallying. 'Noggin the Nog?'

He blinked at Kim uncomprehending and then crossly pulled off the helmet, muttering something about the theatre. 'It beats me how you people manage to get hold of this address.'

In fact, it hadn't been difficult, St Clair wasn't a common name. A friend's father had unearthed an old London telephone directory, pre-dating the publication of the best-seller now drooping from Kim's hand. When the phone number didn't work the operator said Miss I. St Clair was unlisted, not that the name and address didn't match.

'I'm not letting any more of you in, it only upsets her, so I suggest you turn round and go back where you came from. And if it's your mother who put you up to this, tell her to find some other scheme for making a dishonest dollar.'

'My mother's dead,' said Kim. 'Six weeks ago.'

Whether it was the fact itself or the stricken look in Kim's eyes, this did at least shut him up.

'Miss St Clair's book never said the birthday,' she persisted. 'So—'

'So you could have searched at Somerset House for the birth certificate. Plenty have.'

'What's Somerset House?'

'The Public Record Office.'

'I didn't know it was allowed,' said Kim, not defiantly, merely noting a fresh and interesting fact: ordinary in-dividuals were entitled to look up other people's birth certificates somewhere called Somerset House.

'I'm not after anybody's money,' she continued doggedly. 'I just want to see Miss St Clair.'

He gave an extravagant sigh, a descending chromatic scale whose theatricality fitted with his earlier remark. 'You are not Imogen's long-lost daughter,' he said. 'If you insist, I'll explain how I can be so certain, but it's extremely un-flattering so I advise you just to accept the fact and go on your way. You're not Charlotte.'

'I know what you're going to say,' responded Kim. 'Imogen's posh and I'm common. You're going to say the home for unmarried mothers would never've let a baby go to people that spoke like me.' Kim saw from his reaction that she'd hit a coconut. 'But it isn't that simple. My mum that brought me up never adopted me. That was another couple. They did it legal and christened me Linda, but then they had one of their own and didn't need me any more so they gave me away. To Peggy Tanner, who I called my mum. That's who changed my name. Then when I was ten the book came out and Mum had this joke about me being the spitting Imogen. So we thought probably I was born as Charlotte before I was adopted as Linda and then given away as Kim.'

'*Her name was Magill and she called herself Lil, But every-one knew her as Nancy*,' quoted the man.

A female voice from somewhere within the house asked, 'Who is it, Sebastian?'

'Rocky Raccoon apparently,' he called lazily back. And to Kim, 'I sense a certain tenacity in you. I suspect we have a tiresome time ahead.'

Behind Sebastian in the hallway stood the subject of the book cover. She was in her late twenties and dressed in a lot of lace and Indian cotton; her hair was the same flaming red as Kim's but in place of Peggy's uncompromising crop was a phenomenon of tendrils falling nearly to her waist – and now most obligingly backlit by sunlight from some further window. It wasn't lost on poor Kim, the absurdity of her assertion that she was the spitting image of this beautiful woman. Nevertheless, with the last iota of her failing courage she was past Sebastian and into the house.

'Watch where you're jabbing your bloody elbows!' complained her defeated gatekeeper.

'I'm Kim Tanner,' announced Kim to the loveliest face she had seen in her life. 'And it's ever such a long story.'

2

Imogen St Clair's kitchen was big, warm and lightly grubby. Its windows were pebbledashed inside with the splashes of an inadequately cleaned sink, so the yellow sunlight reaching Kim had been smeared in transit, its stripes falling across the room bleary at their edges. This wasn't the medicated light of Peggy's kitchen. *And before you let the sun in, mind it wipes its shoes*, the two of them used to repeat cosily to each other, from Kim's classroom copy of *Under Milk Wood*. And cosily was right: despite the fastidious hygiene, the drilled sense of order, the concrete underpinning of work ethic and church ethic, about Kim and Peggy's shared life there had been a snugness, a big, soft, marshmallow comfort.

Imogen's windows looked on to a garden long and walled, through whose unmown grass twinkled bluebells and the tossed petals of prettily misshapen apple trees.

'I bet you've got the sort of neighbours that complain about your weeds,' suggested Kim, and she was right. They also complained about the posters in the window, the music, and a certain sculpture of Admiral Lord Nelson with a massive erection that had stood (proud) by the front door until removed by police. No charges were brought and it was last heard of in Marylebone police station sporting handcuffs and a doughnut.

The kitchen confused Kim; it seemed to have a split personality, apparently carried through from the front of the house with its odd juxtaposition of anti-war defiance and ding-dong doorbell. Gadgetry straight from the Ideal Home Exhibition shared its space with incense burners and an op-art collage full of clashing aggression and four-letter words. Beside a silver teapot were sprawled some handbills in blobby lettering and saturated colour. '*Shash Books*,' read Kim. '*Underground press, imports etc*'. Everything was alien, but the aroma of percolator coffee warmed her spirits like embrocation. As did the proximity of Imogen. She was perched beside the girl at the table, her knees drawn up to her chin, the tautened skirt outlining her thighs, turning them into a Henry Moore sculpture, all curvature and womanhood.

'Your mother was perfectly right,' said Imogen. 'You do look like me.'

'I know I'm not pretty.'

'Who says so? Prettier than me at your age. I was a carthorse.' She smiled and shook a heap of chocolate fingers on to a plate to melt stickily in the sun. 'I would be really proud if you were Charlotte, but unfortunately I don't think it's possible. I never go into details in case they're bandied about, but often I can tell at first sight.'

Kim heard the words with pain but not shock: the horrible morning had been driving her headlong towards disappointment – the cold wind, getting lost, the obnoxious Sebastian. 'You're sure, then?' she said eventually.

'I'm so sorry.'

Kim nodded in a transparent parody of deep thoughtfulness. Clearly this wasn't the sort of girl to make a fuss, plead her case, burst into tears. The publication of *Starched Linen* had led to far more fuss, tears and case-pleading than

Imogen had bargained for, mostly in this very kitchen. Kim's dignity touched her.

'If you can tell at first sight,' said Kim, 'does that mean the father was—?' She hesitated. Peggy was always particular that you didn't use derogatory language about your fellow man. 'Was the father a coloured gentleman?'

Imogen's smile twitched at the corners. 'No, it isn't as dramatic as that; only that two people with brown eyes can't have a baby with blue ones.'

'I thought it was the other way round.'

'No.'

'Oh. Well, not to worry,' continued Kim with bleak resignation. 'I wasn't certain I was Charlotte. That was Mum's idea. If she hadn't died, I would never have . . . you know.'

'It was sweet of you to come all the way over here from Essex. It's been lovely to meet you.' And then, recognizing that this sounded like a dismissal, Imogen moved on hurriedly. 'Your own history sounds extraordinarily exciting. When did you first learn of it?' Even Kim's downbeat delivery couldn't dispel the impact of her bizarre tale. Imogen was a writer. Her authorial antennae quivered. But Kim only shrugged.

'I've always known. Mum said little kids accept things easy enough if you don't make a big kerfuffle. Anyway, it sounded quite romantic – how I was probably born to some poor girl that wanted to keep me but wasn't allowed. And then this couple adopted me, and it made them so happy they managed to have a kid themselves straight away. And there was Mum desperate for a baby but no husband to do the deed, so God made sure she was on the spot when I was up for grabs.'

'I like the sound of Peggy,' said Imogen. She lit a cigarette, tilting her face and breathing deep. Kim was disquieted to discover anyone could look beautiful smoking a cancer stick. Peggy had never let Kim wear red with her ginger hair, but Imogen in crimson looked like strawberries and cream. There was no ring on her wedding finger, and given what Kim had seen of Sebastian, she was delighted. He had taken himself off to another room, mumbling something about 'motivation for my reluctance to murder Macduff', at which Kim wondered whether she had been conversing with a psychopath.

In truth, Kim was trawling the situation for drawbacks to mitigate Imogen's rejection. If the boyfriend is horrible and potty then it's for the best, she told herself, though without conviction. Ever since Peggy's death, the one light to shine through the chaotic configuration of Kim's grief was the thought, I know my real mother wants me, she wrote a book on the subject. And the disappointment was aggravated by Imogen's heart-rending beauty. There was nothing remote or dazzling about her looks: Imogen's eyes smiled, she looked shy, you wanted to put your arms around her. Sebastian or no Sebastian, Kim wished she were this woman's daughter. Her senses ached.

'So how many people know about your origins?' Imogen was asking.

'Nobody. Well, I told my best friend but that's all. I always understood not to talk about it in case the couple got into trouble. Mum called herself Mrs Tanner instead of Miss – which is completely legal, you can call yourself Madame Pompadour if the fancy takes you – but questions about a Mr Tanner weren't welcome. She always said if people drew their own conclusions that was their dirty mind, not hers.'

'So you were raised without a father. Was that awkward?'

'Kids at school used to rag me a bit when we were small. Said I was a little b. You know. But Mum told the teachers and got that stopped mostly.'

'Still, it must have been a struggle to get by.'

The girl's clothes were clearly home-made – black bell-bottom trousers and a blouse in a shade of blue that might have been quite fetching had it not found itself in a losing battle with the eye make-up.

It was only in the last couple of weeks that Kim had discovered the transformation that could be brought about by blackening not only her lashes but her white-fair eyebrows with a mascara brush. Features emerged from the hinterland of her pallor and she looked sixteen instead of about nine. Kim's schoolfriends loudly approved, and there was no Peggy to ease her away from the startling wet ebony towards a tone more in keeping with her complexion. As it was, her face looked like a picture somebody had doodled on, and next would come the moustache.

'Things weren't as hard for us as for some,' replied Kim to the question. 'Mum was a Treasure.'

'Treasure?'

'Cleaning lady. Charwoman. In the beginning she just did for Mrs Murray the doctor's wife,' expanded Kim, sounding like a game of Happy Families, 'then word got about. You could do with a bit of help yourself,' she added, running a professional eye over the kitchen.

Imogen glanced vaguely around her. 'I do have a cleaner but I'm utterly hopeless at laying down the law.'

'Want me to give your sink a scrub before I go?'

'Good Lord, no!'

'I don't mean I'd charge you.'

'Absolutely not, you're a guest. Please!'

Kim recognized she had made a faux pas, and turned back to her coffee. She wasn't a child prone to fidgeting, but when she first sat down she had scratched nervously at her neck. Imogen watched the girl's skin react like a developing photograph, the tracks of Kim's fingers turning white then red, and finally deathly white and embossed. It was a reaction Imogen had seen before.

'Does your skin stay like that for hours?' she asked.

'Yeah. It's got a name, which means "skin writing".'

'Dermatographia,' said Imogen surprisingly. She had

been ambushed by a memory of Douglas lying naked across the bed of his theatrical digs, the pale skin of his belly bejewelled with the word IMOGEN that she had sketched herself by a gentle drag of her thumbnail. But perhaps the condition wasn't so rare, she thought. Most of the girls who turned up here had some evidence in their favour. Heaven knew, this poor child had little else.

'May I ask how Peggy died?'

'Accident,' replied Kim shortly. 'She got knocked down crossing the road. Nobody's fault. Some cars hit one another and this motorbike had to swerve. She didn't linger, I have that to be grateful for. Grateful for small mercies.' The hackneyed phrases hung dolefully in the air.

Imogen gave the girl a moment to collect herself. Then she said, 'One day you will be glad you could grieve for her. I never forgave my parents for forcing me to give up Charlotte. Mother and Pa both died when I was in my early twenties, and I was still angry.'

'You said in your book they packed you off to Hong Kong straight after the baby.'

'And told everybody I was already in Hong Kong when actually they'd had me incarcerated in that terrible mother-and-baby home, in case my condition caused house prices to crash in Mount Hill Crescent.'

'Was this their house then?'

'Oh yes, I grew up here. See those handbills advertising a bookshop? The friend who owns it says I only stay to spite Mother and Pa's memory.'

Peggy and Kim had read *Starched Linen* together, comfortably discussing the iniquity of Holbridge Manor: the rustling linen of the book title; the smell of disinfectant and reek of disapproval; the grounds with their damp melancholy where Imogen spent her early days as unpaid garden labourer until advanced pregnancy qualified her for promotion to unpaid indoor skivvy. But Kim had been most affected by the descriptions of Hong Kong, the harbour emerging through a gauzy mist as Imogen's ship hooted into port. She saw future adventures of her own there, with silk-wearing tradesmen scurrying through typhoon rain to hail rickshaws. 'The world is my oyster,' Kim told herself with the unconscious arrogance of extreme youth. 'I'll strike as soon as the iron is hot.'

Imogen was asking her, 'You don't intend to go out cleaning for a living, do you?'

Kim shook her head. 'Mind you, the tax man doesn't see a penny of the money. I bet you get fleeced for those books of yours.'

'Actually I believe in taxing the rich,' said Imogen gently. 'Think of Robin Hood,' she added with a smile.

'Labour governments aren't Robin Hood,' said Kim, scandalized. In Peggy's view they were robbin' bastards.

'For example,' continued Imogen quickly, 'because of our taxes, people from your background can get student grants to go to university. Have you considered that?'

'Yes, probably Cambridge,' answered Kim simply. 'It's called the natural sciences tripos. I thought of medical school and my teachers say I should try, but those places take less than ten per cent girls so you can just guess what they'd think of me. I'm not having some toff in a bow tie looking down his nose like—' Kim was going to say 'like your Sebastian', but stopped herself. 'Anyway, I fancy the Cambridge NST so Mum had this meeting with the head-master and he got me some past papers for the entrance exam and I could do a lot of it already.'

Imogen tapped the ash off her cigarette and uncoiled in her chair. She was aware of a fine electricity of excitement, of an overhaul in that part of her mind where, for all these years, her lost daughter had dwelled and walked and smiled; of a prickling desire to reconsider Kim point by point against the Charlotte criteria – and take a chisel to those that didn't fit. Eye colour, for example. Was she wrong after all? It was what she had been told, but her baby's eyes were

still newborn-blue when Imogen gave her up at six weeks
. . . The waif-and-stray raised by an Essex charlady had just
been transmogrified. Even the deplorable voice could be
excused, the way one did for rock musicians. Imogen knew
her sentiments were shameful and her turnabout suspect.
But from the emotional hullabaloo that had regularly
capsized her life since the publication of *Starched Linen*, she
also knew that although you can choose how to manage
your feelings, you can't choose what feelings to have.

Imogen had sat at this table gently sounding out pretty
little things whom she wanted to believe though they didn't
even have the right birthday, or plain, podgy, pudding-faced
little things who had various correct credentials but against
whose claims Imogen had fought with every fibre of her
mind. It was not true that Imogen had ever been a carthorse.
'This is *not* my flesh and blood,' her instincts would cry, as
if the real Charlotte would trigger recognition like a flare
going up. But one by one every child had failed (Imogen's
word), the pretty and the plain. They failed when she dug a
little into their background. Though the mother-and-baby
home had withheld the names of adoptive parents as a
locked-filing-cabinet secret, an on-pain-of-death secret,
there was something Imogen knew that she hadn't
published in *Starched Linen*, and it would eliminate every
couple but *the* couple.

And the children themselves? Some had come here seeking a vicarious fame, and others came from mercenary
motives that shocked Imogen, but there was one whose
intentions were clearly genuine and disappointment agoniz-
ing. Imogen had asked her, 'Are you unhappy with your
adoptive parents?' and the girl replied, surprised, 'This isn't
about finding out who my parents are, it's about finding out
who *I* am.' This was a revelation to Imogen, who, whatever
her insecurities, grew up knowing who she was.

Now Imogen asked Kim, 'Are you living with relatives?'

'There aren't any. When Mum died I was made a ward of

court. The bit of money she left went into a trust fund. Me and the furniture were put into store,' added Kim drily.

'Surely you're not in a foster home?'

Foster homes carried for Imogen that starched-linen reek of institutionalization. But Kim was never one to rail against fate and anyway she was entirely comfortable with totalitarians. It was liberals Kim distrusted. She replied easily, 'It isn't that bad. I got given to Mr and Mrs Antrobus, and I already knew them. They go to our church.'

Imogen poured more coffee and Kim added milk from the bottle. The Antrobus family also allowed milk bottles on the table, which had outraged Kim's sensibilities as Peggy's daughter.

'It isn't that I'm unhappy as such,' she clarified. 'It's just there's seven kids and no peace and quiet. Plus I do miss my mum.' Her voice faltered.

'Would you like to talk about Peggy?' suggested Imogen gently.

'I do, to Mr Antrobus,' responded Kim, 'but I won't here, if you don't mind,' and Imogen was surprised to feel her own small visceral pang of rejection.

'Was it easy to get your book published?' Kim asked her.

'Lord, yes. A decade later, having babies out of wedlock was extremely trendy. The confessions of an unmarried teenage mother from the upper-middle-class suburbs? – well! Five publishers bid against one another.'

'Nice for you.'

'Then I turned to fiction on a similar theme and here I am now, the uncrowned queen of literary illegitimacy.' It was an expression coined by her friends in the London counterculture and meant as entirely derogatory, but Kim just nodded. 'And *Starched Linen* is to be made into a movie, did you know? They've cast Julie Christie as me. Won't that be something?'

'I think you're prettier than Julie Christie,' said Kim. 'I think you're prettier than anyone.'

'Get away!' Imogen turned pink and gave Kim the sort of buffet she would get from her best friend Denise. Kim was astonished and hot with pleasure.

From a distant room, a well-modulated voice declaimed that Macbeth could not be vanquished until Birnam Wood be come to Dunsinane. Now behind it rose a different declaiming voice: Jim Morrison of the Doors. Kim heard rather a lot of the Doors via Denise, who played 'Light My Fire' day and night until her father shouted despairingly at the heavens, 'Will somebody give that man a bloody match!'

'The couple that adopted you,' began Imogen cautiously, keeping her voice steady, 'have you been in touch with them?'

'Can't. Don't know who they are. Mum and them were living in Ilford, but afterwards they moved away, that's how everyone could pull it off. Mum changed her address, too, to stop the neighbours poking their noses in. Made it easier. The less questions asked the better.'

'Does your adoption birth certificate have their original address? I don't know how the system works.'

'No idea. Never seen it.'

'Your birth certificate?'

'No.'

'But you do know their name?'

'No.'

'Surely Peggy must have told you? Legally it's your own. In the eyes of the law they're still your parents.'

'Mum said I was hers now and the rest was history.'

Suspicion seeped through Imogen's excitement and short-circuited it. She asked, knowing it was clumsy, 'Did Peggy have your colouring?'

'Well, she was nearing sixty, but she'd been ginger once. As soon as she set eyes on me, Mum knew I was the daughter she should of had.'

Imogen was aware of a sad sliding away of something that would have changed her life. 'Back in 1955,' she said, 'it was a terrible disgrace to—'

The doorbell rang. They heard Sebastian wearily swearing, and then his steps across the hall. 'Imogen!' he called a moment later. 'Insurance man. Money.'

Imogen patted Kim on the shoulder and drifted from the kitchen. Kim could see down the hall. Another Doors track, 'The Unknown Soldier', was now belting out at a volume that rattled the teaspoons. And from the startled look on the face of the insurance man Kim guessed he probably wasn't a fan. The house was apparently full of the military manoeuvrings of a firing squad.

'Well now,' said Imogen brightly as the shot rang out. 'How much do I owe you?'

Kim had heard her tell Sebastian, 'There's coffee on the stove, darling,' as they murmured past each other in the hall. There wasn't, however. He lifted the percolator from the livid electric ring, swore, and dropped it with a clatter. A dark dribble ran disparagingly from the spout.

'Fuck, that's hot!' he said, sucking his hand. 'Fuck it!' Sebastian seemed to feel Kim's disapproval needling the air. His heavy glasses flashed. 'So you're still here. Oughtn't you to be at school? Or should one conclude you're bunking off?'

'Our teachers are on strike.' Peggy had taught Kim that it's no sin to hold your own under attack. 'Oughtn't you to be at work?' she countered, hoping he would hear her unspoken 'Or should one conclude you're unemployed and sponging?'

Perhaps he had. 'I am an actor, you impertinent child. I'm playing the lead in *Macbeth*, if you know what that is.'

'Wearing horns. Should go down nicely.'

'I need something heavy to practise with and the battle helmets aren't ready yet. Satisfied?'

'And how about the bicycle on your nose? Is that a prop?'

Any reply Sebastian might have made was doused by bright goodbyes floating in from the hall. Sebastian waved a hand from Imogen to the upturned percolator.

'It was empty and on the verge of melting. Make some

more, sweetie. And when the coffee's ready, be an angel and leave it by the door. Oh, and keep the noise down, would you?'

'I do try, darling.'

'I know you do, darling.'

On his way out, Sebastian smiled condescendingly at Kim. 'I don't imagine I'll see you again,' he said. 'Bye-bye.'

Imogen was back at the greasy sink with the percolator. As cold water *hish*ed against the red-hot metal she lit another cigarette, having forgotten she'd left one balanced against the ashtray; Kim had caught it rolling off towards the kindling of those handbills. The bills themselves were grubby with dust. If my mum had spent half an hour in this kitchen, decided Kim, she would no more have suggested I was born to Imogen St Clair than that I might be half Vulcan like the man with the ears on *Star Trek*.

Imogen turned back to her. 'We were talking about your extraordinary origins. Have you ever wondered—?'

But there was a new voice in the hall, Imogen having forgotten to shut the front door properly. 'Ginny?'

'We are doomed never to get through this conversation!' said Imogen. 'In here, Monique.'

The new arrival marched in, smiling, until she caught sight of Kim. Her eyes flickered to the paperback on the table. She looked from its cover to the girl, and from the girl to the cover.

'Oh Ginny, you've found her,' she said. 'You've found Charlotte!'

3

Peggy would have liked Monique. She cut straight through Imogen's ditherings, told her she had never been right about brown eyes, and demanded, 'Where's that photograph of darling Douglas – bedroom? Bring it downstairs.'

Her dramatic announcement had kicked the props from under Imogen's rickety composure. Imogen said something tearful about Kim's background and not being able to bear yet another disappointment, at which the businesslike Monique simply handed her a length of kitchen roll to blow her nose and said, 'Go and get that photo.' Then she turned her attention to the percolator, plopping aromatically on the stove.

Monique was older than her friend, short, dark and wiry. A magnificent Afro haircut shimmered around her small face like some halo derived from a black sun. 'Here we are – coffee,' she said to Kim. 'Do us both good.'

Kim reached for the mug. This was her third, and there had been a pot of tea all those hours ago at breakfast. She was becoming quite desperate for the lavatory, but flinched from the idea of running into Imogen in the socially unstructured context of a staircase and a loo door.

'So who first noticed the resemblance?' asked Monique.

'My mum. But she died and the whole thing's ever such a rigmarole, so I'd rather not go through it all again if that's all right.'

Monique looked hard at her. 'Well, I expect everything will sort itself out,' she said eventually. 'Ah, Ginny!'

Imogen had returned. Monique held out her hand for the photograph, a glossy studio portrait in black and white. She screwed up her eyes. 'Kim's got Douglas's mouth and bone structure,' decided Monique and handed the photo to Kim. 'See what you think.'

A powerful and handsome face looked out at her. Its jaw was strong like hers, as were the ears which Monique had politely omitted from the comparison, but Kim would never have picked out this man from a line-up of fathers. Neither could she see herself in Imogen, not any more – though it had all seemed obvious enough when Peggy compared Kim point by point with the author photographs. Now, Imogen with her face teary and smudged didn't look much older than Kim.

'Is it a secret who he was?' she asked.

'Only on account of his wife and children.'

'Yes, all right, Monique,' interrupted Imogen. 'He was a stage manager, Kim, with a repertory company.'

'It was really sad in your book, where you left the father's name blank on the registration papers to stop your own parents punishing him.'

'He got Ginny pregnant at fifteen,' responded Monique briskly. 'Douglas deserved to be punished.'

'Perhaps he loved me so much he couldn't help himself,' said Imogen in a small voice, to which Monique responded with a hail of explosive *tut*s that reminded Kim acutely of Peggy.

Imogen seemed shy of looking at her. Because she doesn't want me to see the doubt in her eyes? thought Kim. Or because she thinks it might seem like she's accepted me as Charlotte when she hasn't? Or because—

'Oh God, I've forgotten Sebastian's tray!'

Monique tutted again. 'For heaven's sake, Ginny, make him do his own tray for a change.'

'But he's working on his speeches.'

'So?'

But Imogen was already rattling china and pouring coffee. As she carried it to the door her hair bounced across Kim's shoulders. It's the same hair as mine, realized Kim. It only looks better because it's up against a better face.

'I need the toilet,' she blurted out on a wave of physical pain, and fled upstairs while Monique was still giving her directions.

The spacious hall was even more peculiar than the kitchen, bright with hanging rugs and cluttered with kinetic sculpture that swung and clunked as Kim scooted past. Silk embroideries clotted with snags were tacked up on the wall, their sumptuous colours volatile in the shifting light. Reaching the bathroom, Kim locked the door and tore at her clothes. Her bones tingled and she quietly whimpered.

Afterwards she took her time washing her hands, sick with reluctance to return downstairs. The implication of Imogen's unfinished questions had settled on her, cloying like the sticky dust on the lime-encrusted bathroom tiles. Everybody's going to say I was Mum's illegitimate kid, she realized, and I can't prove them wrong without papers.

It was the view across the suburban gardens that calmed her. Kim's one consolation during the miserable morning trudge was that she found Ealing surprisingly lovely, particularly Mount Hill Crescent. This was despite its house numbers running in two apparently unrelated mathematical series (those few you could find at all), as if, thought Kim, accustomed to Peggy's war reminiscences, to baffle enemy parachutists who might still have their sights on residential London. Nevertheless she thought it beautiful, this crescent of interlinked turn-of-the-century houses in aged red brick uncoiling in front of her with their fanciful gables, and every line softened by the spilling and climbing vegetation in spring colours and a hundred shades of green. As Kim tramped round and round, the textures and geometries had unfolded before her like an artfully constructed mosaic.

Most people would have considered that her home village of Crowhurst Green – open countryside, hedgerows and country lanes – had the edge on this, but to Kim, suburbia's ordered streets with their implied hearth-and-home warmth were infinitely superior to unpeopled fields anywhere. The village comprised a small core of pretty old houses and the accretions of recent and less picturesque expansion. Kim had taken one look at suburbia and dismissed Crowhurst Green for ever as an unruly sprawl.

When eventually she returned to the kitchen, creaky with shyness, Kim was saved having to make conversation because the peace immediately exploded into obscenities. Sebastian. He stormed in waving a velvet jacket. Brown fluid dripped from its expensive sleeves.

'This was over the chair and it's bloody ruined! Your stupid coffee tipped up.'

'What, all on its own?' demanded Monique.

'Just give me a hand, will you?'

While managing to convey the impression that Imogen was hampering him at every turn, Sebastian rubbed at the sopping material with a handkerchief. The velvet chafed and squeaked. Kim was on her feet.

'You're rubbing velvet!' she bleated, sucking her teeth. 'Velvet!'

'Ginny,' said Monique. 'Look!' She shook Imogen's elbow, which was locked tightly into her side. Her fists were balled like a baby's.

'Stop it!' Imogen was imploring as she sucked her teeth. 'Not velvet!'

*

'I have never come up against anything like this,' said the social worker, whose name was Miss Unsworth. 'Not in all my born days.'

It was almost verbatim what her boss had said, and her colleagues, and the lawyer. 'Mind you,' each of them had put in as a codicil, 'it'll turn out to be all my eye and Betty Martin. That girl's the illegitimate daughter of the woman who raised her.'

The meeting wasn't in Ealing but at the house of Mr and Mrs Antrobus. The social worker was middle-aged and overworked, and the continual need to make decisions with far-reaching consequences had given her a bossy appearance. This didn't faze Kim, who at thirteen inhabited a world stuffed full of bossy appearances, but it had profound effects on Imogen. Miss Unsworth was not of the new breed trained in child-care theory, but grew up in the old school of Moral Welfare Officers. Faced with Miss Unsworth, Imogen was once again a teenage girl with a baby in her arms and a grown-up at her bedside.

'Don't go getting attached to it. Baby will have its new mummy to love any day now.'

'Please don't call her It. Her name is Charlotte.'

'Not for much longer. Anyway, whyever did you pick on something so old-fashioned?'

Because Imogen's favourite book was *Jane Eyre*.

Kim had read it.

'And what did you think?' Imogen had asked later that day in the kitchen.

'It was OK,' replied Kim, 'till the story got far-fetched. I reckon Charlotte Brontë should've ditched the stuff about the mad woman in the attic.'

And now Kim was the eponymous heroine of Miss Unsworth's daunting file. She had refused to go to school while everybody decided her future in her absence.

'Even a murderer gets to hear the verdict first-hand,' complained Kim.

'But not the deliberations in the jury room,' retorted Miss Unsworth.

It was Mr Antrobus who settled it. A big, round-faced hearty man with a smile full of goodwill and gingivitis, he weighed in on Kim's side. The family had four boys of their own and up to three foster children at any one time. It was a happy place. Though his wife popped her head round the door periodically between bouts with the twin-tub washing machine, it was always Mr Antrobus who dealt with officialdom. His house was certainly used to social workers. Known locally as the Antrobus Motel, the building was a long, wandering single-storey construction, backed by a vast hide-and-seek garden kept in check by a goat. Kim had already decided this could be a solution in Mount Hill Crescent as Sebastian was clearly too idle to get the mower out.

Mr Antrobus had no opinion on whether she and Imogen might be mother and daughter, but he recognized how desperately Kim wanted it to be true — this despite the off-hand manner with which she had explained the situation on her return from Ealing.

'It's a long complicated doo-dah,' she had announced, fiddling with the cutlery drawer, 'but Mum wasn't my real mum, I was adopted, and there's this author living in West London that probably is my mother, and she wants me to live with her.'

Mr Antrobus and his wife had stopped dead, stared, and said, 'Come again?' all in perfect and comic unison.

Now, Mr Antrobus was faced with the author herself: those brown eyes with their oriental slant and a mouth so wide her smile disappeared into the edges of her hair. And that exceptional hair. Given Kim's raw grief and the fact that the arrangement had Peggy's implicit approval, it was not surprising that this exotic creature tugged at the child's heartstrings.

The relationship certainly wasn't impossible. Kim's

features might be Imogen's expressed in smaller dimensions and their effect hardened by that jawline. And looking at the two together, Mr Antrobus recognized that Imogen wanted this as much as Kim. They sat side by side with careful decorum, sharing the occasional world-containing smile, both ginger heads up-tilted with anxiety. And he could see that whereas Kim's nose-in-the-air nervousness was being interpreted as commonplace teenage truculence, Imogen's radiated an aristocratic disdain that was doing her no good at all with Miss Unsworth; Imogen was behaving like the lady of the house facing down an impertinent out-burst from her cook.

'None of us has come up against anything like it,' responded Mr Antrobus to the remark that opened the proceedings. 'But it can't be unprecedented. Nothing new under the sun, Miss Unsworth.'

'I dare say, Mr Antrobus. But the plain fact is, when Miss St Clair gave up her daughter for adoption it was final and irrevocable.' She turned to Imogen. 'You must have been told you had no right ever to trace your child.'

'I was a frightened young girl bullied into it,' said Imogen.

'Be that as it may.'

'And legal or not, I have traced my daughter – she's here!'

'There isn't a shred of evidence that Kim Tanner is the daughter you gave birth to. But even if she were, you would have no legal relationship. You could not have a say in her upbringing.'

'But the adoptive parents can,' said Mr Antrobus. 'If we find them, we can seek their permission for Kim to live with Miss St Clair. Given the circumstances I think it unlikely they'd refuse, don't you?'

'Mr Antrobus, neither have we a shred of evidence Kim was ever adopted.'

'Well, I came from somewhere,' put in Kim. 'I wasn't hatched out of an egg in a barnyard.'

'The most likely explanation remains that you are Peggy Tanner's natural daughter.'

'That at least can be verified,' pointed out Mr Antrobus. 'If Kim was born to Peggy, there will be a birth certificate at Somerset House.'

'And I bet you anything there won't,' said Kim. 'Mum wouldn't've lied to me.'

'I thought it was your contention she'd been lying to all and sundry for most of your thirteen years,' said Miss Unsworth caustically.

'Even so, I'm rather inclined to agree with Kim,' put in Mr Antrobus. 'Remember, Jill and I knew Peggy Tanner. If Kim were her illegitimate daughter I believe Peggy would simply have told her so.'

'Oh, Mr Antrobus,' said Miss Unsworth jadedly, 'I could find you a hundred cases where neighbours were mistaken about the integrity of a child's mother. And another hundred where wild tales were invented to cover up an illegitimate birth.'

'Would a blood test help?' suggested Mr Antrobus. 'I mean, to establish a relationship between Kim and Miss St Clair. Does anyone know?'

'Kim knows,' said Imogen brightly, giving the girl a playful nudge.

'I know,' agreed Kim, nudging her back. 'Imogen's blood group is A. Basically her baby could be anything. We'd need to know about the father, or know what else Imogen got in her genes from her own mum and dad. But we don't.'

'Clever clogs,' said Imogen, nudging her again.

'Smarty-pants,' retorted Kim and walloped her on the arm.

Imogen squealed. At this, Miss Unsworth's settled distaste was stirred to a fizzing irritation.

'Perhaps we could return to the matter in hand,' she snapped. 'When Peggy Tanner died, Kim was made a ward of court. Whether or not Miss St Clair is her natural

33

mother is an unfortunate irrelevance. As a single woman she would not even be allowed to foster Kim.'

'May I return us to Mr Antrobus's earlier point?' asked another voice. The speaker was elderly and the only other man in the room. His name was George Massingham and he also lived in Ealing, where he was a magistrate. An army man originally, he held on to his rank in civilian life, perhaps his only conceit. That and the handlebar moustache. He was also Imogen's godfather. 'If the adoption story *is* true,' he said, 'the couple can be traced.'

Miss Unsworth now turned to him. 'Colonel Massingham, even if the adopters actually exist, how on earth are we expected to put the girl in touch with them? She has no name, no address—'

'Linda. Ilford,' said Kim.

'Linda. Ilford,' repeated Miss Unsworth. 'And according to Kim, Ilford was only where they lived when they gave her up. Where they were living at the time of the adoption is a mystery. And they moved away *again* immediately after handing her over to Mrs Tanner.'

'It cannot be beyond the wit of Social Services—'

'Can't it, Miss St Clair? Do you know how many children were adopted that year? Thirteen thousand and five. And no doubt most of them called Linda; it was an extremely common name.'

Colonel Massingham said mildly, 'However, it would be a straightforward matter to establish whether Miss St Clair's baby was given the name of Linda after adoption. Of course, if she was, that wouldn't constitute proof. But if she wasn't, it would be safe to conclude that the link does *not* exist. One could start from there, couldn't one?'

There was a general murmur of agreement, through which Miss Unsworth brusquely sliced.

'Colonel Massingham, with respect, you know perfectly well that adoption records are a matter of secrecy.'

'Not from Social Services, surely,' said Mr Antrobus.

'Even from us. Absolute confidentiality is enshrined in adoption proceedings. The records don't even use names but serial numbers. The information that bridges the two is kept under lock and key, and there can be no access to it without a court order.'

'Then perhaps we could get one.'

'Never. The 1950 Adoption Act was brought in specifically to prevent interference of this sort, especially from the relinquishing mother. The law is adamant that once the court order goes through it signifies a clean break and a fresh start. The former mother has no further place in Baby's life with its new parents.'

'But Kim *isn't* with—'

'The law is still the law and the legal mechanism you require does not exist!'

'What about when I need a birth certificate?' said Kim. 'One day I'll want a passport and . . . What other things do you need it for? Getting married? Having a driving licence?'

'All of those,' confirmed Mr Antrobus.

'What about going after a job, even? Don't you need it so they can give you a number and take tax off of you?'

'Undeniably,' agreed Colonel Massingham. 'You need a birth certificate to get a national insurance number.'

'Well then, what does a person do who hasn't got one?'

All eyes turned to Miss Unsworth.

'That is a matter for the Public Record Office,' she said. 'Nothing to do with Social Services.'

'Not my department,' paraphrased Imogen scathingly.

'Exactly, Miss St Clair. We have an agreement – the PRO promises not to foster out children if we promise not to issue certificates of birth, marriage and death.'

Colonel Massingham said pacifically, 'I'm sure the last thing Social Services want is a long-drawn-out dispute. I have a suggestion.' It was a suggestion that had been taking shape from the moment he arrived at the Antrobus Motel. His reaction to Kim had been as immediate as Monique's.

Though he couldn't gauge the girl's resemblance to the unnamed father as he had never met him (and would have horse-whipped him if he had), Massingham immediately saw his goddaughter in Kim, in her burnished hair, the angle she held her head, the shape of her nose, the tiny wrists and ankles. At Kim's age Imogen's small bones gave her that same air of fragility, reminding him of a little lamb. Also Imogen had explained about Kim's skin, the dermatographia; a visit to the medical section of Ealing library quickly confirmed this was usually inherited. Here in the Antrobuses' utilitarian sitting room Colonel Massingham would have bet his pension that Imogen and Kim were mother and daughter. 'I'm a magistrate,' he reminded everybody. 'Suppose I offer to act as the child's legal guardian?'

From looking collectively fraught, the company now perked up.

'It's a big step,' pointed out Mr Antrobus, and Colonel Massingham knew this was mild compared with what his wife would say when he got home.

'Quite,' he responded, 'but on this matter I trust Miss St Clair's judgement.'

'Thank you, Uncle George,' said Imogen.

'As legal guardian I could give permission for Kim to take up abode in Ealing. How does that sound, Miss Unsworth?'

'It is highly irregular. What about the child's schooling? We're far too late in the academic year to enrol her in a new school, with different syllabuses and exams at the end of term.'

'So all you're saying is the proposal will have to wait until the end of July.'

'Possibly,' conceded Miss Unsworth, cornered.

'What if,' said Kim, 'I go and live with Imogen *and* carry on going to school in Warley till the summer? If somebody pays for a taxi between the train station and school, I can do the journey in two hours, easy.'

'Four hours' travel a day is entirely unacceptable. The courts will never agree.'

'Let us ask them,' said Colonel Massingham.

So they asked them. And the courts said yes.

'By the way,' Kim told Imogen as she made arrangements to move to Mount Hill Crescent, 'there's something I forgot to mention. I've got a dog.'

4

Jack Robinson

It was Ursula who had kept me together, Ursula with her County Cork obstinacy and loyalty thick as a blood tie.

'Charlotte needs her mother, Ginny. Don't let 'em tell you it's in her best interests.'

But from the day she took her baby son and left I could feel my resolve dribbling away like air out of a punctured tyre. Even so, I might have withstood the psychological batterers: my mother ('If you think you're bringing an illegitimate baby into the house you've another think coming'); the wardresses ('If you had exercised a bit of self-denial you wouldn't be here in the first place. Now you are, behave with some penitence'); the clinic doctor who checked us all for venereal diseases ('Come along, lassie, open up. You weren't this shy a few months ago!'). But now Ursula was gone I could hear quieter voices that her ebullience had blotted out. Well-meaning voices.

I shall call her Mrs Atkinson. 'Real love means caring

more about Charlotte than about your own feelings. Think what sort of life she'll have: you've nowhere to go, she won't have a father. The grown-ups will whisper behind her back, schoolkids will throw it in her face: "Your mum had you when she wasn't married. You're a little bastard." What life is that for the poor thing?'

What life indeed?

There was one piece of advice that was advanced by voices on both sides of the divide, pertaining to Collection Day:

'Go and sit in the recreation room with a good book. Turn on the wireless or put a record on the gramophone. The other girls will know today's your Collection Day. They'll understand. But don't wait at the window.'

Good advice, I'm sure. Had somebody put a gun to my head I could not have taken it.

Mrs Ormond took Charlotte from my arms at three o'clock on an afternoon full of low October sun and violet shadows. It was nearly four by the time they arrived. I had been weeping for an hour and my head throbbed.

The other girls had taken themselves off with their babies as we always did: 'You know where we are if you want us,' so I was alone in the top-floor dormitory. Sunlight dazzled the windows, rimed the cold metal of our regimented beds, each with its cot. The metal shone because we polished it. It was our duty and our punishment to polish everything, scrub and polish, down on our knees for choice. The allusion to supplicants at prayer was no accident; though Holbridge Manor was not formally owned by the Church, Church money went into running it and that presence was everywhere: the endlessly visiting vicars and Anglican nuns, and the philosophy of earning redemption from sin, undermining our dignity as relentlessly as death-watch beetle in a bell tower.

The car came swinging in through the iron gates shining like a suit of armour, and grated to a halt by the beech trees. The cognoscenti had explained about the beech trees. 'Mrs Ormond makes them park there so nobody manages a look at the licence plate. That's why we're all herded inside for the afternoon.'

But this couple hadn't got it right. They had parked short of the regulation area. Both doors opened together, the couple emerged, both doors closed together. From my position three floors above, the black car with its flapping doors was an elephant's head, an African elephant giving one angry threatening beat of his ears. The man and woman righted themselves and started across the gravel. They were hurrying; they were late, that was why they were carelessly parked.

How could they be late? cried my head. I was told Charlotte's new parents yearned for her, were counting the days. Why weren't they hopelessly early, pulling up round the corner an hour before the appointment? I'd been standing an hour at this terrible window.

I saw them in foreshortened view like the car. Both wore dark suits, both wore hats, the woman's a stylish affair with a feather. As they hurried across the drive their shadows preceded them, clean-edged and aetiolated, caricatures of their own long-limbed elegance, sweeping over the dazzled gravel with an unstoppable authority. Then the hats bobbed up the sandstone steps, beneath the canopy of rambling roses, and were lost to me. I stayed at the window and indecision raged through me like bushfire.

I was frantic, half-mad with vacillation. I was also in various sorts of pain, the sun-seared headache and jaw that hurt from crying, and also the soreness of my leaking breasts. My summer dress shone wet across the front. The last time that happened I had been sermonized by the staff, lectured and threatened; we were not allowed to nurse our babies after the first month; we weren't keeping them so they must be bottle fed. But I would wake at night and pick her up, her cries, her urgency, her sweet wet sucking mouth, my aching love.

I ran to the door. I ran back to the window. I ran to the door. I could feel the censure of the unforgiving dormitory, the serried ranks of its bedsteads with their silk-bound blankets and hospital corners, their reek of boarding school and army barracks. I knew the very essence of panic, a bleaching out of normal thought, a blind-and-deaf convulsion like some bitter orgasm. And I knew that if I was to change my mind I must do it right now.

The knowledgeable had explained, 'All the formalities are sewn up already. On Collection Day the parents are not encouraged to hang about. You know what old Ormond's like – she has them in and out faster than you can say Jack Robinson.'

And suddenly my indecision vanished. Suddenly the very idea was ludicrous, that strangers could be sanctioned to walk out of this benighted place with my baby.

I was through the door, across the landing, on the steps of the marble staircase. My stockinged feet skittered on the stone. Only six months ago a girl named Lilly had skidded down an entire flight, bounced all the way on the base of her spine, fracturing her coccyx.

As I tore round the turn of the stairs I heard Mrs Ormond's voice moving across the hall, and the murmur of other voices, a man's and a woman's. I hurtled across the first-floor landing, driven by burning whips of absolute panic. I saw Mrs Ormond closing the front door.

And she saw me.

'Doctor!' she called in a voice of routine emergency. 'Restraint, please!'

'*No!*'

I flew down the last flight and was across the hall. I was at the front door. I had it open. I was out.

The couple were halfway down the drive, the man putting on his hat. Against the navy wool of the woman's costume, a great splash of white trailed across her right arm – the standard crocheted shawl.

They turned round. No doubt they had been warned by Ormond never to turn round but I was flying at them from behind, a panicking madwoman, hair everywhere and my unshod feet already bleeding on the pointy stones. The man stepped between me and his wife, between me and my baby.

'Miss St Clair!' The duty doctor was at my back. He pinioned my arms. 'Go,' he implored the couple. 'Leave this to me and go.'

'I've changed my mind!'

'This will do you no good, lassie.'

The couple hurried away then, shoes crunching like an outgoing tide on shingle.

'I said I've changed my mind! They can't have Charlotte, I'm keeping her!'

'You silly girl, have you no decorum at all?'

I heard the car doors slam. After a moment the vehicle revved and then rasped away from the trees. I watched it turn, shoot forward, drive out through the gates. I watched it go.

'It's over,' said Mrs Ormond as I was dragged back across her hellish threshold. 'Baby has a new life with decent people. You should be exultant, not standing here snivelling. You should rejoice.'

5

Kim's best friend Denise sat on the end of the bed, which was a bunk bed, and watched her pack. Denise had been crying on and off ever since Kim announced she was leaving Crowhurst Green for the London suburbs. Now they had reached what she called 'The Point of No Return' (the capitals were Denise's), her air of burning martyr was enough to set off every fire alarm in Warley High School. While Kim folded her clothes conscientiously into a couple of suitcases, Denise bewailed her abandonment.

'And another thing,' she sobbed with the ready lucidity of a seasoned arguer. 'What about our pact to meet up in Trafalgar Square on my forty-fifth birthday? I suppose that's all out the window too.'

Kim's dog watched them miserably. Named Welly because his feet were the size of wellington boots (it was widely said his ancestry included a sheepdog, a polar bear and a yeti), he lay with his enormous woolly white head on his paws and a pleading look in his upturned eyes. Having grown up with Peggy and Kim, Welly had no experience of weeping women. What he really wanted was to clamp those paws over his ears.

Mr Antrobus left them alone and demanded that the other children did likewise. He needn't have bothered. Their view of Denise was not substantially different from Welly's.

'And what about being each other's chief bridesmaid? I suppose your new mother will stand between us for that, as well.'

Kim was holding a stuffed toy called Tiger Tim. She couldn't remember whether she'd brought him here packed under her clothes in the suitcase or carried him by the tail.

'Imogen's really looking forward to meeting you,' said Kim absently. She knew her friend's jealousies of old; they were easily soothed with the right words. 'Imogen keeps asking me, "When am I going to see this Denise you're always going on about?"'

Which wasn't entirely true; Imogen was being almost as tearful as Denise, and heard very little of anything said to her.

'We have to sort out your bedroom!' she had suddenly announced through a disintegrating Kleenex.

'No, Imogen,' said Kim, surprised, 'I'll just make up a bed in one of your spare rooms.'

'Look, look, our room is biggest. You take that and we'll move into the back.'

'No, Imogen,' responded Kim and Sebastian in unwonted unanimity.

'Look, look, Monique knows Ken Partridge who did John Lennon's place. How about a replica of one of the Beatles' rooms? Or I might be able to get Peter Blake to do a mural or—'

When the proposals progressed to Andy Warhol, Kim explained that what she'd really like was floral wallpaper and a poster of the Bee Gees.

'And think of the fun we'll have with that Sebastian,' Kim continued to Denise. She had seriously considered inviting her entire class round for the sheer pleasure of pissing him off.

Sebastian had been enraged by the court's acquiescence and could not comprehend why for once he was unable to bend Imogen's will by bullying. Luckily he would be at rehearsals for *Macbeth* evenings and Sundays, but once the show finished the summer ahead would be a long one.

Of all the astonishing conversations that day in Ealing, the most staggering was the one in which Monique explained that Sebastian was her husband.

'Yes, he's living with Imogen,' said Monique breezily. 'And yes, he's a lot younger than I am. Ten years, if anyone's counting. I'm forty.' Seeing Kim's expression she added hurriedly, 'Ginny didn't steal him from me, dear. I booted Sebastian out long ago. And now he's moved in here. Like some upwardly mobile tomcat. At least I had the sense to get rid of my married name – even though my own is unpronounceable. Monique Shashkova, that's me. Half French, half Russian émigrée. Terribly exotic. Except I was born and raised in East London.'

'What was your married name, then?' asked Kim.

'Duck,' said Monique.

'Duck?'

'He's Sebastian Duck.'

'Good,' said Kim after a tiny pause.

Now Denise continued dramatically, 'My mum will never let me go to Ealing. What with Imogen being a hippie and an unmarried mother and now living with a man in sin.'

'I bet you'll talk her round,' said Kim, who knew perfectly well that Denise came from the least censorious household in Crowhurst Green. 'You're just brilliant at persuading people, Denise. Anyway, I'll still be at school for ages yet, and afterwards I'll need you more than ever. Who else can I trust to help me find my legal parents?'

'I thought officials had to do the tracing.'

'How? They'll never manage it by themselves. But you and I will.'

Denise looked down from the height of the bunk bed, at

the neat, carrot-red head bent over the stripy toy. Denise's own hair was deep brown and styled in a bubble cut that set off the babyish prettiness of her round eyes and little snub nose. Her complexion was already tan from the spring sunshine. Black mascara suited Denise.

'Do you know something you haven't told them?'

'Of course I do.' Kim sat back on her heels. 'I'm not having people like Miss Unsworth poking around in my mum's life. If there's nosey-parkering to do, it's a job for me and my best friend.'

Denise's tears dried up like a blocked spout. 'But what is it you know?' she demanded, gratified and mollified.

'I know who else Mum was doing for in Ilford at the same time as my legal parents. I know because she kept in touch at Christmas and things. They're called Hazel and Bob Barber, with a daughter a bit older than me. And they knew the family that adopted me. I know because Mum said we couldn't ever meet up again. She never told them about me, on account of they'd guess who I was the minute they clocked my hair.'

Denise hopped down off the top bunk. 'And you know their address?'

'Yep.'

'So when are you going to see them?'

'Small problem,' said Kim. 'When I was little they emigrated to Australia.'

*

The day Kim moved into Mount Hill Crescent, Colonel Massingham's wife Frances said, 'Well, George, I only hope you know what you are doing.'

They were a faithful repetition of the words she had used to him the night he returned from the Antrobus Motel.

'It is highly irregular, George,' she had said then.

'Oh, not that deuced word, Frances, please. I have been hearing it all day.'

Her husband had looked tired. Nevertheless, Frances Massingham pushed on. 'My concern is for the child. What is it that's convinced Imogen she has found her daughter? The evidence sounds flimsy to me.'

'They do look alike,' said Colonel Massingham. 'Despite the fact that the girl is a plain little thing and Imogen is . . . well, we know what Imogen is.'

'Mmmm,' said Frances.

'I haven't seen her so happy since she was a girl herself, Frances, before Hong Kong. Her eyes shine,' he added. 'She looks radiant.'

'I dare say,' said his wife in a further unconscious imitation of Miss Unsworth.

They had children of their own, she and George, three boys, grown-up now, respectably professional in the law and married with boys of their own. And as the colonel often reminded himself, the whole lot together had never succeeded in giving a *fraction* of the trouble caused by his wayward goddaughter.

'Pregnant at fifteen!' Colonel Massingham had so often complained, bewildered.

'Yes, ours spared us that,' responded his wife.

And then publishing those embarrassing books, and now cohabiting with a theatrical layabout in leather trousers. 'It isn't as if her parents were lax,' he would invariably add. Imogen's father had been a schoolfriend at Harrow. 'And yet one can't help being fond of her. Would it be very wrong of me, Frances, if I said I probably forgive Imogen because she's so beautiful? Though I suppose if she hadn't been, none of this awful business would have happened in the first place.'

'Don't be silly, George,' responded his wife with vigour. 'If the sex impulse only attached itself to exceptionally beautiful people, the human race would have died out by now.'

Frances Massingham was short, plump and pretty, and had always been pretty. To Frances, Imogen's looks did not excuse her the duties of ordinary folk. She had overheard their eldest describe some young woman as 'dippy'. Frances hadn't met the word before but guessed what it meant. It meant Imogen. And not merely dippy in a general sense but seriously defective in judgement when it came to men. First there was the father of her baby, who had clearly deserted her, and now, heaven help them all, Sebastian. Frances had rapidly got the measure of Sebastian: the careless good looks, the arrogance, the casual air of ownership, of power. An attractive rotter. And no doubt supremely demonstrative in bed. Oh dear, oh dear.

'But how can you be sure Imogen's commitment will last?' she said now. 'Motherhood is hard work, George, and teenagers particularly so. Suppose she tires of the girl. Are we to take her on, we in our late sixties with a youngster who's a stranger to us?'

Colonel Massingham thought of Kim and smiled. 'She's a plucky little lady,' he said. 'Kim could probably bring herself up. Truly, my dear, I don't think Imogen will tire of her; remember, there have been dozens of children who claimed to be Charlotte, none of whom convinced Imogen. On the contrary, I think that with Kim she has achieved her heart's desire. There! I'm not often given to poetics. And with luck,' he added, nose-diving, 'that lazy damn actor will be ousted from Imogen's affections, and she'll throw him out on to the street!'

6

By midnight of Kim's first evening as a resident of Ealing, the house had yielded up the responsibilities of the day and taken on its nocturnal personality.

Until recently, Kim had unthinkingly assumed that night time was pretty much the same from one end of the earth to the other. Then she moved into the Antrobus Motel and discovered that it wasn't the same from one end of Crowhurst Green to the other. At home with Peggy, their sleep was seldom offended by anything more intrusive than the cry of neighbouring babies and the infectious barking of distant dogs – much as she imagined it might be in a village in the Andes or sub-Saharan Africa. By contrast, the Antrobuses' house stood beside the sharpest chicane of a meandering country road, upon whose hairpin bends speeding night-drivers would happen unexpectedly in a scream of brakes and rubber, swearing the air blue.

'Whoops, there goes another one!' the children would holler across the house in the small hours as Mr Antrobus sleepily pulled on a dressing gown preparatory to giving aid or calling an ambulance.

Now, in her new bedroom, Kim sat up in the bed with its

squeaky nylon sheets ('But you must have Egyptian cotton at the very least. Satin if you like.' 'But nylon's what I'm used to, Imogen, if that's all right'), shifted the sleeping Welly off her numbed legs and dissected the sounds and patterns of the peri-urban night.

The occasional car cruised past en route to Eaton Rise or pulled into a neighbour's drive, its doors clunking shut with well-bred restraint. Indoors, the fabric of the air had none of the threadbare monochrome Kim was used to, the patchy blackness punctuated by a sharp triangle of silver at the top of the curtains; Mount Hill Crescent's version of darkness had an ochrous cast, stained sodium orange by the street-lamps. Kim's bedroom would never be properly dark; she would have no need to turn on the light when she got up to go to the bathroom. When she did get up she found the stairs dappled with harlequin shades of the stained glass above the front door. Peggy hadn't liked stained glass in a house, she said it made the place look like a funeral parlour.

Back in bed again, Kim got down to business. She said her prayers and then talked to Peggy's photographs, giving her a run-down of the latest turn of events in a businesslike tone, as one dictating a memo. Mr Antrobus had encouraged her in this. 'And don't feel bad about getting everything off your chest. There will be moments when you're feeling guilty about finding a new mother. And times when you blame Peggy for leaving you. Go ahead and tell her all about it.'

To Kim, the idea of blaming Peggy for the motorbike that mounted the pavement and knocked the life out of her was sufficiently irrational to count as barmy. Nor did she feel disloyal about her affection for Imogen, as Imogen had been Peggy's idea in the first place. However, Kim did take enthusiastically to the idea of updating her with bulletins.

'But you're sure it's not blasphemy?' she'd first demanded of Mr Antrobus. 'Talking to the dead? I wouldn't want to rub God up the wrong way at this stage of the proceedings.'

And Mr Antrobus had assured her that she wouldn't be rubbing God up the wrong way.

'The more things that come to my notice,' Kim told Peggy's smiling image, 'the more I'm inclined to think you were correct about me being Charlotte. Like the father's skin had that same writing thing as I've got. And I've him to thank for my sticky-out ears. Also they say he was an organized sort of bloke and practical. Imogen can't remember if he might've been double-jointed in just the one arm, like I am. Which is a pity, cos that would have clinched it, I reckon.'

Kim was holding an entire fistful of photographs fanned out like a poker hand. Peggy always kept the family snaps in a chocolate box. It was her own mother's from years back, and had two beribboned Scottie dogs on the lid. After Peggy died Kim was thankful for every picture. Many of them pre-dated her, and showed Peggy in outmoded clothes and an Ilford garden, the date and location confirmed by soft-pencilled notes on the back, 'Wingfield Drive, Easter 1951', 'Wingfield Drive, August 1939' and so on. Kim had been persuaded to give the full address to Miss Unsworth to pass on to whoever, though without a scrap of faith that it would help track down her adoption papers. Now, she reshuffled the photographs and talked to a later one, taken on Kim's thirteenth birthday.

For reasons lost with the passing of the years, they had a tradition of celebrating her birthday with a picnic in the garden. As this applied come rain or shine, and as a downpour required so much more organization and therefore ritual, this was the one day of the year Kim prayed for wet weather. The last two Septembers had failed her, but on her eleventh birthday she had got her wish.

'Now, which of you is taking the golfing umbrella, and which of you's taking the one with the sunflowers?' Peggy addressed Kim and Denise as she tucked peanut-butter sandwiches into the side of the traditional birthday hamper.

'Please can I share the golfing umbrella with you, Auntie Peggy?'

'You're not sharing with Mum! I'll share with Mum and you have the sunflowers.'

'Nobody's sharing with anybody,' Peggy told them calmly. 'Now put your gumboots on, the pair of you, and pick an umbrella without arguing.'

Responding to the general excitement, Welly whirled round and round in ecstatic circles like some demented spinning top. He still hadn't quite grasped the concept of space. Until rescued by the animal cruelty people, Welly had lived in a two-foot cage.

'Are we having sunshine sandwiches as well as peanut butter, Auntie Peggy?'

'Yes, and treacle ones too. But only if there's no arguments.'

Sunshine sandwiches were another wet-day treat: bread and butter coated with 'hundreds and thousands' – sugar-sweet and rainbow-coloured, crunching like some delicate eggshell.

'Right then, I'm done,' announced Peggy. She snapped shut the hamper's metal clasp. 'Ready for Rainy-Day Inspection?'

The girls, dutifully booted and coated, giggled.

'Boots on? Raincoats buttoned? You too, Welly, are you ready? Best feet forward, then. No, wait a tick, I haven't counted them yet: two and two is four and Welly makes eight – *off we go!*'

The picnic hamper was now over in the corner beside Kim's serviceable new desk, with Tiger Tim lolling on it. Their very familiarity was unsettling in this strange environment.

'It seems like Imogen's quite sure in herself that I'm Charlotte,' Kim told the photograph. 'When she looks at me her eyes go all swimmy and lovey.'

Peggy had not been a kissy sort of mother. There was a

bedtime kiss after they said their prayers, and there were always hugs, but none of the touching and hair stroking that characterized Imogen's ideas of affection.

'She can't help it,' Kim explained. 'It's all that flower-child stuff, it's turned her head.' But even as she said it, the memory of Imogen's buffeting and nudging made Kim's heart beat faster. It was lovely. Imogen was lovely. Yet she wasn't . . . it wasn't as if . . . She might be my mother but she's not my mum, thought Kim confusedly, knowing Peggy would have understood. Then with cruel certainty she thought, I'll go on missing Mum for ever and ever. Kim immediately pulled herself up. A threat of tears had tickled her throat. She staunched it as if tears were her life blood, in danger of seeping fatally across the bedlinen. Kim never cried.

Imogen, who cried a great deal and had spent much of the last week teary from excitement, had nevertheless pulled herself together sufficiently to dish up an edible celebratory meal of macaroni cheese followed by chocolate cake. Kim's choice. They'd eaten in the kitchen, and lit candles when the April evening turned to a crepuscular grey. Kim had obviously never heard of people lighting candles when there wasn't a power failure, but Imogen explained how they often did it for fun. And Kim found it fun, too. Even Sebastian behaved himself – which took some self-control when he was faced with the excitable Welly slobbering over his trousers. Imogen had been surprisingly warm to Welly. It was Sebastian who walked wide around him and jumped each time he barked. But tonight Sebastian suppressed his exasperation even when the high-flown tone to which he was accustomed plummeted to the level of the playground.

It began with Imogen, another cigarette in hand. 'Can you give me a match, Sebastian?'

'Your face and Marianne Faithfull,' put in Kim.

'My face and Boris Karloff, more like.'

'Marianne Faithfull with knobs on—'

'Boris Karloff with double knobs and no return—'

'We were discussing Macbeth,' interrupted Sebastian loudly, 'and the witches' prophecy about Birnam Wood.'

Kim had refused Sebastian's suggestion of a glass of wine.

'It isn't illegal,' he told her with commendable patience. 'Not in your own home with a meal.'

'I'm grateful for the offer,' Kim replied politely, 'but alcohol pickles your brain cells, we learned it in biology.'

'Know what I remember most poignantly about you as a baby?' asked Imogen in one of her numerous reminiscences as sugary as any rainy-day sandwich. 'The soles of your little feet. All rosy and vulnerable. My heart still turns over at the thought. For more than thirteen years I've had to avert my eyes from the feet of babies!'

But their celebrations didn't go undisturbed; halfway through the macaroni someone hammered on the front door, and then roared into the kitchen protesting at how far Ealing was from the rest of the world. Kim would soon learn that people turned up at this house all day and half the night: writers and artists, and the hangers-on of writers and artists. All of them harangued Imogen about the distance, even those who had come from no further than Ealing Art College.

'Why d'you guys live out here, anyhow?' demanded this one. 'What is it, on a ley line?'

'Nope, the Central and District Lines. Kim, this is our favourite literary experimentalist,' said Imogen, whatever that meant, and she added a name Kim heard as Lenny Hanky-Panky.

He had been pulling up a chair. Now he stopped dead. '*Jesus*, what the fuck—? It's a dog? You're kidding me.'

'Sebastian darling, would you like to take Lenny—'

But Sebastian was already taking him, fleeing from the talk of babies and the baby-talk. A couple of minutes later Kim could hear the Doors playing in the other room.

One thing was certain, Denise was going to like it here.

Strangely, with Sebastian's egress Imogen's conversation suddenly grew up. She dropped the juvenilia and began to draw Kim out, asking about her interest in sciences, probing, getting her to expand on the answers. This wasn't whimsy – though Kim's language and delivery were those of a don, her awe and eagerness were like a child on Christmas morning, and Imogen wanted to understand. By the time the plates were cleared, Kim had filled her in on the implications of the second law of thermodynamics and was moving on to Einstein, and Imogen was visited by an image of the girl in a glowing cocoon: a glittering aura of numbers and formulae sparkled around her, dividing and multiplying, and making sense out of mystery and chaos. A sort of truth. It wasn't a sort of truth that would cut much ice with Imogen's friends, most of whom believed the secrets of life were best dealt with by the poets, but Kim's impassioned articulation gave it a validity Imogen trusted.

In the excited lead-up to Kim's moving in, Imogen had drawn up a list of Do's and Don'ts, at the head of which was 'Don't let her think you're trying to usurp Peggy.' But it was rapidly clear that the girl's sensitivities didn't run along those lines; Kim's relationship with Peggy being unassailable, there could be no usurpers and therefore nothing for Kim to resent.

In her turn, Imogen was relieved to find that her own resentments were not aimed at Peggy for bringing up Charlotte; they remained where they had always been, directed at 'Baby's new parents', they of the hateful black car on the gravel of Holbridge Manor.

Perhaps because Imogen's head had been reeling ever since Kim first turned up in her life, it wasn't until this evening that the full implication sank in, about the couple's treachery: that haughty pair with their fast clipping footsteps had given her precious baby away the moment they had their own, like a stopgap that was now redundant. The pain sickened Imogen, fury screaming through her entrails. Kim saw, and stopped in mid $e = mc^2$. But she didn't turn tactfully away, she asked what was the matter, and when Imogen sketched a diffident explanation Kim said, 'But it was better than keeping a kid they didn't want, Imogen, and it's not like I was abandoned in a cardboard box – they gave me to this completely brilliant mum.' And Imogen reached across and hugged her till she blushed.

'Why didn't you have another baby to replace the one you gave up?' probed Kim once she was free.

'Babies can't be replaced,' replied Imogen, smiling. 'But I did try to get pregnant a couple of years ago. Nothing came of it. And Sebastian certainly doesn't want a child.'

No, I bet he doesn't, thought Kim and added 'husband and baby' to her inventory of tasks to accomplish in Mount Hill Crescent.

And now it was approaching midnight and the start of Kim's first weekend in a greatly changed life. As she finished her recital to Peggy, a quiet footfall drifted through to her room from the stairs. Imogen coming up. As Kim listened to the steps across the landing, soft as a dancer's, a small thrill tickled the lining of her stomach. Doors opened and closed, a rustling recrossed the hall, and Kim could make out the muffled echoes of bathroom sounds. Minutes passed, and a heavier tread mounted the stairs, generating a darker spectrum of vibrations. Sebastian. A new and dis-likeable emotion pricked at Kim's senses, which she immediately blocked from her mind.

'Night night, Mum,' said Kim to Peggy's photograph. 'And don't worry about Welly. He isn't pining for Crowhurst Green. I think he's the sort that accepts whatever hand he's dealt.'

Like me, thought Kim, and kissing Peggy goodnight she snuggled down in the bed and pulled the bedspread up to her ears, determined to fall asleep before Welly started snoring.

7

'But Kim darling,' said Imogen for about the ninth time, 'for all I know, Mrs Newman relies on me.'

'Then she should take a bit more care,' reasoned Kim, one index finger quivering indignantly at Imogen's sink like the Ghost of Christmas Yet To Come. 'I mean – look! If your books were as slapdash as her cleaning, do you think your publisher would pay you?'

'Good point, Ginny,' said Monique, who was enjoying herself.

'But not a good analogy. Authors are ten a penny and cleaners are gold dust. Besides, Mrs Newman is famously temperamental. She'll give notice.'

'All the better,' said Kim. 'That'll save you firing her.'

Monique laughed, and put a hand down to scratch Welly's tummy. He had talked her into it; Welly was sprawled on his back with his legs out like something tied at the four corners. Monique called him Mr Bigfoot. She liked seeing Kim confident instead of the faltering, shy child of that first morning in the kitchen. Clearly, the girl approached the task of organizing the household with a missionary zeal. Monique also suspected Kim viewed it as her contribution, a repayment of Imogen's generosity, almost like rent. But what of that steely, unyielding bossiness? Was it an echo of the capable Peggy or simple genetics? Because God knew, it was so like Douglas as to be shocking.

'This is how I see it,' continued Kim steadily. 'You're rolling in money, Imogen. And you haven't got masses of ornaments around the place, fragile china shepherdesses and stuff.'

'I don't see what—'

'Loads of young mums would be glad to earn a bit extra if only they could bring their kid along on the job. No reason why not, here.' No reason except perhaps the presence of that op-art collage on the kitchen wall screaming its four-letter words at all and sundry. Perhaps I can hang a tea towel over it, thought Kim. 'I reckon five hours a week would do the trick, if she puts her back into the job.'

It was Monique's turn to shake her head. 'Even so, attracting a good cleaner won't be easy. It will take more than the perk of bringing her child to work.'

'Course it will,' agreed Kim. 'It'll take twenty-five shillings an hour.'

'*Twenty-five shillings an hour?*'

'Good God,' said Imogen.

'It's give and take,' reasoned Kim. 'She gets the dosh, you get a clean house for the first time in donkey's years. What day does Mrs Newman come?'

'Thursdays,' answered Monique.

'Good. Don't fire her till she's ready to clock off, will you, Imogen? By then there'll be adverts in all the local shops. Denise and I did them lunchtime today, on postcards. The instructions say to phone here no later than Saturday. And only one child. It's not a kindergarten.'

'You'll be mobbed,' said Monique. 'What will you do – interview them?'

'Well, of course I'll interview them,' said Kim, surprised.

'And try them out on the kitchen and bathroom. I mean to say, there's no shortage of grime.'

'Kim darling,' said Imogen with her first show of actual defiance, 'it's no good asking me to fire somebody. You must have realized by now I'm not capable of it.'

So she didn't. The following day Imogen took herself off to the library while Mrs Newman sauntered in and out of various rooms with a fluttery duster.

'I won't disturb you, Mr Goose,' she said sweetly, interrupting Sebastian halfway through an immortal rhyming couplet.

'Mr Duck!'

'That's right, dear. I'll leave this room for today if you're practising your acting. Are there any other rooms you'd rather I didn't do? Just say. It's no trouble.'

So when Kim came in from school she got Mrs Newman's address out of Monique and went round there herself.

'That's the situation,' said Kim, summing up on the woman's doorstep. 'Nothing to stop you applying for the job yourself. Everybody judged on their merits.'

'Is this a joke?' demanded Mrs Newman. The girl, still in school uniform, had turned up in the middle of *The Man from U.N.C.L.E.*, announced that she was Imogen St Clair's long-lost daughter, and rattled off a catalogue of derelictions of duty, from a written list.

'Hairs clogging up the plughole,' read Kim, 'basin *and* bath. Cobwebs, average 1.66 per room. Splattered fat across the eye-level grill.'

'You cheeky bugger!'

'And enough dirt behind the kitchen appliances to silt up our school's newt pond,' Kim concluded. 'It isn't a joke, it's my area of expertise,' she explained politely. 'And I was brought up to know what's fair and what's not. The interviews are Saturday and Sunday.'

'I'll interview you in a minute!'

'Saturday and Sunday,' repeated Kim equably. 'If you think you can hack it.'

Kim had no need to hang tea towels over the op-art. Her embarrassment infected Imogen, who relegated it to the attic. 'And what's next?' demanded Sebastian. 'Censor the bookshelves, do we? Burn the William Burroughs? Plaster black stickers over the erotica? This is all so plebeian, Imogen.'

The uneasy truce with Kim had not endured. With her advent Sebastian had actually been forced to make a cup of tea for himself. ('And then what?' he'd demanded of Monique as she talked him through it. 'Do the teabags go in the kettle?')

Then Sebastian finally lost caste with Kim when she discovered the local theatre where he was doing his Shakespeare was non-professional.

'Well, he should've said it was just amateur dramatics!' Kim had responded, crossly. 'We've got them at home, doing *Finnegan's Rainbow*.'

Imogen turned pink. 'The Questors Theatre is not am dram, Kim. We've a brand-new playhouse in the round, the first flexible-stage theatre in the country. Our president is Michael Redgrave.' Other names followed including Alec Guinness, but Kim had never heard of him either. But she caught the word 'we'.

'So are you an actress, too, as well as writing books? I bet you look good on a stage. I bet you're a star.'

'That's sweet of you, but I'd die the death. At school I couldn't even read to the class without bursting into tears. I'm just a stagehand. Sebastian is the star.'

Kim's initial assumption had been correct: he was indeed unemployed. And as for sponging, it went far beyond bed and board.

'How long have you had the white Roller?' Kim had asked Imogen.

'The—? Oh, the Rolls-Royce. Rather ostentatious for my taste. It was my gift to Sebastian when I sold the film rights to *Starched Linen*.'

At this, Kim had been aware of a twinge of intense pain. Before she could put a name to it, she forced her mind away from Sebastian to more manageable domestic problems. But she was growing less successful at this, and there was a name. It was jealousy.

As Colonel Massingham said, Imogen had never looked better. And Kim, too, was improving; the hair that Peggy had kept as tight as a bathing cap was growing out and softening, kiss-curls forming curly commas on her cheeks. Even the Cleopatra eye make-up had lost its asp-like sting.

One drizzly Saturday Imogen offered to do Kim's make-up for fun, and they spent the afternoon playing in front of the mirror in a slew of spilled powder and rouge and demi-lashes.

'You can't make a silk purse out of a sow's ear,' Kim warned Imogen, and so they conversed in oinks and snorts, ending with the pair of them in eye-streaming giggles that came close to negating the entire project.

It was a form of intimacy, and one far less shy-making than sitting before the mirror with eye contact and touching and close-up breath. But when the hilarity subsided they did return to the mirror. Imogen picked up her make-up compact, and was aware of Kim's creeping bashfulness.

'Hey, let's put the radio on,' she suggested, thinking to dissipate tension by singing along to the top twenty. It was a good ploy. Kim's posture lost its stiffness and her laugh its edge. When Imogen's fingers stroked a forgiving sage-green into the pale eyelids and brushed a soft leathery brown across her eyebrows, the physicality was coped with. And successfully contained: Imogen defeated the urge to snuffle Kim's hair and Kim, for her part, pretended impassivity to Imogen's intense scrutiny and the various caresses of fingers and breath on her cheeks. So by evening not only had an important hurdle been overcome but Kim's face now looked as if it belonged to a girl instead of a panda.

Their relationship was watched over by two interested observers, one more sympathetic than the other.

'I don't think you need worry,' Monique told Frances Massingham reassuringly. 'They behave as much like teenage sisters as mother and daughter.' Monique especially welcomed the slapstick, which she saw as tempering Imogen's tendency to mawkishness.

'But I do worry, Miss Shashkova,' said Frances.

The conversation was one of many in the kitchen. This time Frances's lecture on the duties of motherhood was interrupted when Imogen excused herself to do some shopping. Not a pretext; the vegetarian Imogen was required to go to the butcher, get Welly his meat for the week, and lug it back up the hill. This was a duty of motherhood with which Frances was seemingly unfamiliar. And one which mystifyingly doubled the food bills.

On the table in front of Frances and to her clucking disapproval was a letter from a Mr Thomas who lived at number 150, citing the delinquencies by which Imogen and Sebastian were lowering the tone of Mount Hill Crescent. Frances was on his side. In her opinion this household was barely fit to be entrusted with a caged gerbil, let alone a vulnerable teenage girl. And the vulnerability was of real concern: Frances suspected the child's feelings for Imogen weren't in the least sisterly: she was love-struck.

'The fact remains that Kim is thirteen,' she reminded Monique, 'and Imogen nearly thirty. I do hope she keeps in touch with her own friends.'

'There's a Denise,' said Monique appeasingly. 'They are obviously close. Come summer I suspect we'll have two thirteen-year-olds in residence.'

But in fact Denise's first visit was not a success. She turned up at Ealing Broadway shiny with excitement, and proceeded to recount her journey from Brentwood stop by stop, to Kim who did it five days a week.

'And then this couple got in at Holborn,' gushed Denise as the girls walked up Eaton Rise, 'and didn't stop snogging till Notting Hill, never mind how much the carriage was swinging about!'

'Yeah?'

'Like they were in training for the *Guinness Book of Records*. Then this man got out and left his book on the seat and I picked it up, but there was a nude woman on the front. So I put it down again,' added Denise simply.

Kim wanted Denise to stop talking and look around her. It was now May. The horse-chestnut trees blazed like candelabra, the lilacs were coming out, every front garden was a smoky haze of forget-me-nots. Kim sometimes left for school even earlier than her usual six thirty in order to take the long way round via the District Line, from whose slow-trundling carriages she could gaze at the backs of houses, at the gardens and tennis clubs and occasional abrupt vistas of shops clustered around a neat green, all the way to Hammersmith before the walls closed in.

Though an infrequent daydreamer, Kim had imagined this walk from the Broadway with Denise, herself dropping names and her friend gasping in admiration. Five minutes down the road were Ealing Studios, the oldest film studios in the world and home of British comedy films, now owned by the BBC. 'They're probably filming *Doctor Who* as we speak,' she had intended to say. Even more impressive, given that this was Denise, just yards from the station was the site of the Ealing Club, heart of the blues and R&B revival of a few years back, a revival taken across the Atlantic to white America by people like John Mayall and the Rolling Stones, the rest being history. Kim knew because Monique had told her. But Kim couldn't care less about blues and R&B, the point was to *tell Denise*. And now she was here Kim couldn't get a word in.

But if Denise was uninterested in Kim's suburbia, her first sight of Imogen knocked her for six. It was mid-morning, which meant Imogen was in the kitchen sorting out a breakfast tray for Sebastian. Toast bounced unwatched from the electric toaster. She wore a floor-length Victorian nightdress, all tucks and pleats. With her pale skin and that mass of titian hair, Imogen looked like several of the Pre-Raphaelite Ophelias, including the drowned one.

While struggling with breakfast she did her best to provide coherent responses to Denise's feverish babble, a random interrogation that touched on Imogen's books and how many famous people she'd met. It fell to Kim to retrieve the butter dish from Imogen's distracted placement of it in the oven, and generally rescue and salvage. Even when Imogen left them and Kim could coax Denise up to her bedroom, it was heavy work to involve her in the real business of the day. They were supposed to be drafting the letter to Mr and Mrs Barber in Perth, Australia. Denise was far more interested in Kim's colour TV set.

'It makes sense,' Imogen had said, 'and will save clashes downstairs.' Meaning Sebastian.

'But *colour?*'

'The whole country is in colour,' replied Imogen. 'At long last. Of all things this decade has achieved, the greatest is to kick the drab out of Britain.'

Denise was enchanted. 'You got a colour telly! I've never seen one. Can we switch it on?'

'Most stuff is still broadcast in black and white,' said Kim.

'I know, but still. Can we switch it on?'

'There's nothing at this hour except the test card.'

'I know, but still. Can we switch it on?'

By the time the day was done and Kim walked Denise back to Ealing Broadway ('Come *on*, Denise, you promised your mum and dad to be home before dark.' 'Imogen, have you ever met the man that wrote the Beatrix Potter books?') Kim was exhausted and miserable. I'm outgrowing my childhood friends, she thought. My unusual experiences have prematurely aged me.

At least the letter had been completed.

Kim spelled out the facts concisely, concluding with:

> I apologize that this letter is so long but I want
> you to know the whole story, which is complicated
> and very surprising as you did not even know
> Peggy was bringing up a little girl.
>
> If you can help put me in touch with the other
> lady she was cleaning for, the one that adopted
> me, please do. My address is at the top. (It is not
> Essex but Ealing, which is another long story.)
>
> Thank you in advance for your kind
> information,
>
> Yours sincerely
>
> Kim Tanner

She would post it on Monday after school. The man in the post office had said airmail letters to Western Australia took about a week.

*

'We in for a lot of this, do you think?' said Denise's father to Denise's mother.

'Which do you mean – pestering us to move to Ealing, or badgering me to grow my hair long and dress in a caftan?'

By way of reply her husband rolled his eyes to heaven.

'Take no notice. I give it a month until the next craze comes along.'

'Well, she's messing my head up,' complained Denise's father.

It was dinnertime. His wife was at the sink draining the potatoes. The splashing water, the metallic clang of the saucepan lid, all were muted, mopped up by the droning extractor fan. These were broad-minded people, easy-going about rules, restrictions, mores. Nevertheless, Denise was an only child, and as such she lived in the glittering cone of a day-long spotlight, the inexorable follow-spot of parental fixation.

'Maybe if we can't beat them we should join them,' suggested her mother. 'You first. Kit yourself up in a pair of tight leather trousers. She would be mortified.'

'She wouldn't be the only one,' said Denise's father. 'It's a curious business all round, wouldn't you say?' he continued. 'Frankly I don't know what astonished me more, Kim's story or the fact that Denise knew for years and never let on. I would have said our daughter couldn't keep a secret to save her life.'

'But she's always been a bit in awe of Kim, remember. It's Kim has the upper hand. Whenever they've fallen out, Denise is the one who has to go crawling because Kim can get along on her own and Denise can't.'

'I suppose. You don't think it might be right what that social worker suspects, and Kim really was Peggy's and the story is all moonshine?'

'Wouldn't make any sense,' objected his wife. 'As there was never a Mr Tanner on the scene, a lot of people assumed Kim was her illegitimate daughter anyway. I know the kids in her class did. So what would be the point of spinning Kim a fairy tale? Particularly one that includes a living author. It was bound to come to the crunch one day. Anyway, Peggy was always down to earth. I think if she'd had Kim out of wedlock she'd have said.'

'Yeah.'

'Not worried, are you?' asked his wife. 'Mr Antrobus assured me it's all above board and he should know. Broaden Denise's horizons, was how he put it. There's a retired colonel overseeing the whole show, remember.'

'That's not what worries me. What did you used to

think?' he asked. 'I mean, before Peggy died and all this came up?'

'Me? I always wondered if there was a bad marriage somewhere in the background and Peggy had taken Kim and left him. Just my gut feeling. Because she was so reticent about the past.'

'And now it looks like she was reticent because she took on some other couple's adopted kid. I don't know, it seems unnecessarily devious,' continued Denise's father. 'It isn't illegal to raise somebody else's child if you've got the parents' permission, so why the secrecy? Where I come from it happened all the time. That was the standard way to hide an illegitimate birth, pass the offspring over to someone else. And not only illegitimate kids, the same thing went on in any big family with one baby too many.'

'Just because it was common doesn't mean it was legal. They were supposed to inform the authorities.'

'Really?'

'Yes. And you're talking about natural parents. Kim's had adopted her, remember, and signed a heap of papers about Baby's welfare; maybe they thought they'd get in serious trouble. Anyway, that's apparently how Peggy got her, so who are we to argue?' When her husband didn't respond she turned to look at him. 'Something's really eating you. Tell me.'

'We're sure . . . we're sure Peggy did have permission?'

'Well, she didn't steal Kim, if that's what you're thinking. Peggy wasn't a criminal or a lunatic, and you know it.'

'Yeah.'

His wife trickled milk into the pan and picked up the potato masher.

'I keep thinking, though,' he persisted. 'I mean, children do disappear. There was that bad business back in the '50s. The Jarman kid. Was that before or after Peggy and Kim came to Crowhurst Green?'

'Why?'

'Only that the Jarman kid was adopted too, and they had a baby of their own straight afterwards. Just like Peggy told Kim. And wasn't she a redhead? And Denise's age?'

'A few months older.'

'Yeah? How old is Kim?'

'A few months older.' His wife turned round again from the steaming pan. 'And no, I'm not thinking what you're thinking, and I suggest that's the end of the conversation. Can you call Denise down for me? Tell her dinner's on the table, and to change out of that Indian dress or she'll trail the sleeves in it. I have enough washing and ironing as it is.'

8

Frances Massingham was right; Kim's feelings for Imogen were now intense. She was besotted.

Wednesday was Imogen's thirtieth birthday; with Denise as adviser Kim chose an elaborate necklace of cowrie shells. Before leaving for school she had it delivered to Imogen's room wrapped in glittery paper and strung round the neck of a springing Welly. Kim then hid behind the door trembling with coy excitement.

'Darling, it's fab!' called Imogen sleepily across the lifeless body of Sebastian. 'I bet it's the best present I get.' And Kim wouldn't be surprised; the usual literary friends were due round this evening, and they struck Kim as a tight-fisted lot. 'Hey!' said Imogen. 'Come here!'

Kim crept over to her side of the bed and into Imogen's arms.

Imogen was warm, sleepy and aromatic. The smell of humid skin mingled with other scents: the shampoo zest of her hair, an acrid rumour of tobacco, other, sweet-sour tangs that wafted up from the bed, secret smells floating in body heat. Kim, inside the force field of Imogen's intimacy and dizzy with love for her, was aware of several massive emotions clamouring in her head and heart, exquisitely painful. She was exultant and triumphant, and desperately embarrassed. Kim knew she was scarlet in the face, and was self-conscious about emerging from Imogen's bear-hug. When she did, Kim said sniffily, 'That nightie isn't very practical. All those pleats to be pressed.' And Imogen laughed. Beside her in the bed Sebastian shifted. A deep caveman grunt rose from the pillow.

'Better be off or I'll miss my train,' said Kim in a grunt of her own, and left the bedroom within a tinkly cloud of Imogen's thank-yous. But it was the sound of Sebastian that would hang around Kim's head like tinnitus, the pressing memory of his presence, there with Imogen, seigniorial. In her bed.

*

Mid-afternoon and seated at the typewriter, Imogen finished feeding the new ribbon through, set the spool in place, wound up the slack, snapped the plastic casing back on, wiped the ink from her fingers, and then with her right hand clicked the wheel of the roller clockwise until her last lines of type emerged clear of the mechanism and she could more easily read them back. For once she took some care. All too often, when Imogen came to the bottom of a page she would spin the wheel to roll the paper up, and catch her hair in it. Last week she did this with such panache she was half an hour with her head on the desk disentangling herself strand by strand.

> The dust was golden, kicked up by the hooves and heels of the herd, and hovering – hanging in the air between Amelia and the sunset like some beaded curtain, phosphorescent in the low-leaning light. She had heard the villagers call this 'the hour of cow dust'. Now, through her tears, Amelia

Can you have a beaded curtain that's phosphorescent? wondered Imogen, her confidence undermined by thoughts of alarm-clock dials. And then: surely Amelia ought to be a tad more cheerful faced with this spectacle? Most of Imogen's acquaintances would give their eye teeth to be standing in an Indian village in a warm enchanted sundown, and there's Amelia whining with homesickness and blubbing into a hanky.

The trouble was, having heroines who blubbed into hankies was an occupational hazard of writing one book after another about unmarried mothers, whether you set them down in the Punjab or the middle of Penge. A vast and ungovernable impatience overcame Imogen. She ripped the paper from the machine in a highly satisfying mechanical rattle, and tore it to pieces.

Behind the typewriter squatted a large crystal, heavy and dark – sodalite, for mental clarity. On a nearby table were candles, rose and gardenia for creativity, peppermint for stimulation, their little flames pallid, cancelled by the streaming sun. Imogen's study was formerly the smallest bedroom of the house. It faced the garden. Across the mossy buttresses of her wavering walls trailed the pink-tissue-paper blossom of late-flowering cherry trees, and yellow droplets of laburnum that tumbled from next door's pergola. It was uncared for, disgracefully bedraggled and utterly charming. Sunlight painted the room's far wall the colour of butterscotch, an image taught her by Joni Mitchell.

'I can't be doing with this,' she told her manuscript, an expression taught her by Kim. 'I'm too happy to tolerate Amelia's misery.' And not merely because it was her birthday. Her watch said three o'clock. Kim would be home by six. A thrill shivered through Imogen's skin.

The whole strange business not only had an excitement more usually associated with falling in love, it also had many of the epiphenomena. For example, everything to do with Kim was suddenly everywhere: the names Kim and Tanner, villages in Essex, the Cambridge tripos. Imogen couldn't turn on the TV or radio or pick up a newspaper without at least one of them looming at her, and often one after the other. And like in a brand-new love affair, Imogen wallowed in every trait of Kim's that was different, unusual, special. The very foreignness of her background and aspirations felt exotic and wonderful.

And being in love, Imogen had both more and less affection for everyone else in her life. More in quantity, far more – love brimmed from Imogen like hot jam overflowing a skillet. But she took a great deal less care dispensing it. And that won't do, Imogen reminded herself.

Last night after Kim went to bed there had been a snappy argument with Sebastian. Wary of talking to him about Kim directly, but incapable of straying far, Imogen found herself meandering on to the topic of stage management by way of Douglas. But not for long.

'Imogen, does the advent of Douglas's daughter mean I have to be subjected to these continual homilies to him?'

'I hardly think that's fair!'

'No? Maybe you should listen to yourself. The guy was a shit. He knocked up a chick and dumped her.'

Imogen coloured and shut up, but in her head she heard Monique. 'Oh Imogen, no, darling, no, the guy is a shit.' But that wasn't Douglas, it was Sebastian.

In fact, at the time it hadn't seemed to be true; back then Sebastian was being incessantly sweet to Imogen, a behaviour he scrupulously maintained until he had her, until she worshipped the ground he walked on – hardly even a metaphor: once, walking on a beach, Imogen had found herself following Sebastian with her feet in the prints left by his in the sand. And of course when a man is a god, his casual cruelties fall outside the moral realm of lesser mortals.

'I hope you are bloody joking,' Monique had responded to that particular insight, Monique who had married

Sebastian on the crest of an early wave of his self-serving charm, allowed him just one bad lapse, and then slung him out. Three years later he was making a play for Imogen, who was saying, 'Oh but Monique, he's *changed*.'

'And as we're speaking of lovers,' Sebastian had continued last night, 'a little more of it in this direction wouldn't go amiss. I haven't been getting my greens lately.' That was deliberately crass, a crude jab to taunt Imogen's middle-class propriety. He watched her wince, and added, 'If a man can't get a balanced diet at home, don't blame him if he starts eating out.'

'You do that anyway!' she responded, rattled into imprudence.

'Oh?' retorted Sebastian dangerously. 'I thought we'd been through this, Imogen. I thought we agreed never to go through it again.'

'I was only saying—'

'Is that what love means to you, that we must own each other's bodies, like property rights? That we deny each other the natural pleasures of sexual recreation with other beautiful people?'

'Of course not,' she had insisted hurriedly. 'Please stop. Please, Sebastian.'

He did stop, and they talked about something else – but only after a long, bitter pause in which various implications sparked like some ominous static. Unfortunately Sebastian had learned early in their relationship the erotic effects on Imogen of sexual jealousy carefully stirred up and then left to simmer.

9

The cleaning job was eventually awarded to a Mrs Harris after a tie-break playoff between her and a Mrs Ross, who, humiliatingly for both, was Mrs Harris's next-door neighbour. In the middle of it that experimental poet turned up again, whose name Kim heard this time as Lenny Dumper-Truck. He decided the pinafored women scrubbing in synchrony were great as performance art, and suggested asking his friends round. In the end, Kim judged that Mrs Harris's plughole work was of the higher quality, and that plughole work was the more highly to be prized.

'Though I thought Mrs Ross had the edge regarding behind-the-cooker grunge,' put in Monique, who had rapidly got into the swing of things.

'It was a difficult decision,' agreed Kim solemnly, 'as I don't mind admitting. Time alone will tell.'

The winner would be starting next Thursday morning, and bringing her baby, who, to Kim's further approval, was just three months old. 'Gives his mum time to settle in before he's old enough to go falling down the stairs,' she said. 'Cause no end of trouble.'

'And what's the next step?' asked Monique. 'Finding a gardener?'

'All in good time,' said Kim. 'We don't want to run before we can walk.'

'Is this child programmed with clichés?' demanded Sebastian. 'I haven't heard one single, solitary original phrase issue from that girl's lips since the day she first fetched up here.'

' "Single solitary" is tautological,' said Kim with a deliberate yawn. 'And if I were you,' she added, getting to her feet, 'I'd be a bit more friendly. This snarling at me – can't you see Imogen doesn't like it and you're putting a strain on your relationship?'

'Oh, and you'd know about relationships, would you? A thirteen-year-old school kid?'

'I know when somebody's pissing on his chips,' said Kim.

Originally, Imogen had been deputy stage manager for *Macbeth*. But that was before Kim moved in.

'*One night a week?*' the stage manager repeated as Imogen imparted the news of her slashed commitment.

'Plus Sundays, Daphne. And once it comes to the actual show, of course I'll do every performance,' Imogen heard herself add, entirely against her intentions.

'And what possible use are you going to be to me then? You will barely know the show.'

'But, Daphne, my daughter has come back to me.'

'Well, all I can say is, it's a pity her timing wasn't a little more considerate!'

To Kim's further astonishment it was Monique who was playing opposite Sebastian as Lady Macbeth. In what she called a former life Monique had been a professional actress. One autumn Saturday in 1954 she was playing Nora in *A Doll's House* when a fifteen-year-old Imogen came to the stage door for autographs.

'This was in Richmond,' Monique told Kim. 'The pubs

were closed so we were all going off to a coffee bar. In the most wrong-headed impulse of my life I invited Ginny to join us. Our stage manager was Douglas.'

'*You* introduced them?'

'I know, I know – first Douglas then Sebastian. I'm the kiss of death.'

The two women kept in touch, even during the years Imogen was hidden away in Hong Kong.

'I expected to stay in theatrical rep until I was too infirm to totter across a stage, but suddenly London changed. Things began to buzz. I was meeting people who talked about music imports and American beat poets. One evening in 1965 I went to the poetry recital in the Albert Hall. Half London was there. I found out afterwards it had cost £400 to rent the hall and the main guy behind it earned £13 a week. Suddenly, things could be made to happen just because people wanted them to. Six months later I was running a bookshop from decrepit premises near the fruit and vegetable market at Covent Garden, and living in the attic.'

She named it 'Shash' for Shashkova. The shop was now one of the landmarks of Swinging London. You went to Shash to browse, to buy books you couldn't get elsewhere, to pick up the latest issue of the underground papers *IT* and *Oz* and back-copies of *East Village Other* or mimeographed magazines with a circulation of fifty. You dropped in for a smoke and a chat, and then hung around because John and Yoko were upstairs and two members of Pink Floyd in the basement.

The place heaved. It should have been a gold mine. It wasn't. Shash was plagued by shoplifting. Despite the fact that Monique ran the business with a small staff as a workers' cooperative, London's youth stood by the slogan 'property is theft', and merrily thieved it back from her.

But even worse than the lawbreakers were the law enforcers. The police would seize half the stock on the pretext of obscenity, and keep it for months without bringing charges – or issuing receipts. They would play havoc with business by walking off with the accounts and invoices.

'The real porn shops are round the corner in Soho,' Monique told a disbelieving Kim, 'and they don't get busted. It costs them up to a thousand quid a month but they don't get busted.'

It was rapidly clear to Kim that Monique was a member of a new elite. Everyone who turned up in Mount Hill Crescent was either revered in the arts or actively running something: a rock band, an experimental theatre, a sit-in, or the sort of publication where production costs were higher than the selling price, so the more copies they sold the more desperately into debt they went. These people would fall in through the door with a diatribe about Ealing, and then talk into the small hours, 'about anything with a Z in it', Kim told Denise: Nietzsche and Frank Zappa. The zodiac, the zeitgeist, Zoroastrianism. And Kim was surprised to see that Imogen, floating between them with her poetic vagueness, was actually a fairly competent hostess: the filling might fall out of her sandwiches but nobody had an empty plate or glass all the long night.

Kim herself would sit on the floor with a Butterick dress pattern and her mouth full of pins, thinking about Shash. Monique was a friend; protecting a friend's business from light-fingered hippies was the least Kim could do. She added it to the list.

*

Towards the end of May came a sparkling blue Sunday, all feathery cirrus cloud and flag irises. After a lunch of nut cutlets and gooey gravy ('Macrobiotics,' said Kim approvingly to Denise; Peggy's daughter was in favour of any food that kept you regular), the others left for rehearsal. But not Kim, who was loath to go anywhere Sebastian was the centre of attention. Today she walked Welly until he was dropping and then took herself off to the Royal Botanic Gardens at Kew. From where she came home with one of the gardeners.

The name was Joan, a hearty person in her late twenties with a predilection for tally-ho imagery, and a tendency to hoot. Kim's first view of her was a large corduroy rump angled into the air in the sort of ungainly posture appropriate to a friend of Winnie the Pooh. She was bending over a trench.

'Excuse me,' ventured Kim. 'I'm looking for a bit of help.'

The hefty body, apparently hinged and cantilevered, swung itself upright and swivelled to face her. 'Lost?' barked Joan.

'No, not lost,' said Kim. 'Just on the lookout. For a gardening expert with a bit of time to spare and no particular aversion to getting paid cash in hand.'

Joan gave Kim a long look, and then rubbed at some soil on her nose with a soily hand. 'Say on,' she said. 'I'm listening.'

So Kim said on.

It was evening by the time Joan clocked off and the two could leave Kew for Mount Hill Crescent. But first, Joan had to retrieve her dinner from the compost heap.

'With a mound that size the temperature inside is as good as an oven,' she informed Kim. 'Wrap a bit of foil round your baking potatoes, and by the time you take 'em out they're done to a turn.'

At which Kim knew the two of them were going to get along.

'Do you often work Sundays?' she asked as she hopped into the passenger seat of Joan's elderly car.

''Fraid so. I need the bally overtime. Firing on all cylinders, are we?' she demanded of the car. 'Then home, James, and don't spare the horses.'

Joan too lived in Ealing ('with Mother and a couple of

seriously eccentric poodles'), so she knew Mount Hill Crescent. 'Terraced, aren't they, the houses?' said Joan thoughtfully. 'No side-path. Have to trundle wheelbarrows through the place. Awful mess.'

'That's all right,' Kim promised. 'If our cleaner doesn't like it I'll sack her and get a new one.'

Joan gave Kim a startled glance and botched the gear change. The car kangaroo-hopped up the hill. By the time they came to a halt outside number 154, Imogen and Sebastian were home. In fact, they were in the garden, chilling out in the wilderness of grass. Sebastian was reading aloud an essay entitled 'Birnam Wood Be Come to Dunsinane: Macbeth's Last Stand'. They weren't in the best frame of mind for confronting a beefy, corduroy-clad land girl with a turn of phrase like Bertie Wooster.

Sensitized from previous encounters, Kim had schooled Joan in house etiquette so she would know not to call Imogen Mrs Tanner or make the catastrophic solecism of thinking Sebastian was Kim's father. Now she led Joan through the house ('Well, who's this?' she demanded of the overjoyed Welly. '*What* a big boy!') and out through Mrs Harris's sparkling kitchen.

'Hiya!' called Kim.

'Hullo!' added Joan, striding towards the surprised couple on the ground. 'Golly, isn't the place a jungle? If Charlie went to earth here, the poor old hounds would have a tricky job sniffing him out. Joan Bolton-Harding,' she informed them, adding, 'No, no, don't get up,' though far from being inclined to rise, Imogen and Sebastian appeared to be frozen on to the grass. Joan's meaty hand grabbed Imogen's and pumped it up and down.

'Gardener. Kew,' she added. 'Kim called me in to cast an eye over your plot of earth with a view to making something of it. And at first glance, I'd say the job will need as A1 a practitioner as ever wielded a spade and a vat of paraquat.'

They stared at her. '*What?*' said Sebastian eventually.

'Good size though,' continued Joan. Welly had come bounding up. Joan waved an arm at the garden and elbowed him in the eye. 'A hundred feet, is it? I thought Kim's tale of woe was an exaggeration, you know, how the garden looked like somewhere Stig of the Dump might want to see tidied up before he'd agree to move in. But now I'm here – well, I can't fault the girl!'

Sebastian was on his feet. Imogen struggled up with him. 'Gardener?' she said. 'You mean . . . Kim, you've brought someone home to—?'

'Joan's just giving us the once-over free, gratis and for nothing,' Kim said reassuringly as Joan took herself off to examine the garden's shaggy edges.

'For fuck's sake, Imogen!' hissed Sebastian. 'Get her out of here!'

Joan had found a choked lilac bush. 'Bindweed,' she called across to them. 'Pretty flowers, but it's a persistent little blighter and will stifle the life out of your borders.' She tugged at handfuls of throttling convolvulus.

'Imogen – do something!'

'Oh bloody hell. Joan! Miss Bolton-Harding?' Barefoot, Imogen picked her way through the weedy grass. 'Unfortunately this really isn't a good time.'

But Joan had taken off again, followed by an admiring Welly. He wasn't used to companions who had as much joie de vivre as he did.

'Dear me,' Joan commiserated brightly, stamping a path through rusty dock leaves with Kim at her boot heels. The bottom of the garden housed a hunched greenhouse and shed, guarded by the barbed wire of tangled brambles. 'Can't have the dog catching his coat in this lot,' said Joan and turned casually to Welly. '*Stay!*' she commanded and Welly, greatly surprised, froze with one paw in the air.

Kim indicated the greenhouse. 'It was Imogen's dad's, but all weeds now.'

'The greenhouse isn't safe!' implored Imogen in desperation. 'The glass—!'

But Joan, inexorably smiling, had already dragged open the door. She took another step forward and came to a halt as if she'd slammed into a post. Kim edged to one side of her and stared in at a surprisingly orderly arrangement of shelving and tables. Bushy little plants with palmate leaves trembled prettily from the vibrations of the door, a massed collection of delicate five-fingered hands.

'Well, well,' said Joan quietly.

'Yeah, I know,' tutted Kim, who clearly didn't.

Imogen herself had reached them by now. She was saying something about seeds carrying on the wind. 'They blow across from our neighbours,' she said weakly.

'Really?' replied Joan, the joviality quenched like a doused flame. 'How sickening of them.'

A bag of fertilizer was slumped on the ground beside the door, and next to it watering cans and spray-cans. 'That's litmus paper,' said Kim, pointing to a pile in protective wrapping. She felt Welly's wet nose at her ankles.

Joan turned away from the vegetation and addressed Imogen. 'It's getting late. Too awful if Mother were to worry and phone the police. Haul in the constabulary. That sort of thing. Mmmh?'

Imogen didn't reply. From somewhere within the house came the sound of doors slamming and what might have been a teapot hurled against a wall.

'I have a notion you're not entirely convinced about landscaping the grounds,' continued Joan. 'But when you've slept on the idea I wager you'll fall in with it.'

'Do you?' said Imogen.

'Under the circs. I could turn this garden into a jolly little oasis. Very jolly indeed. I charge a hundred guineas.'

There was a longish silence. 'A hundred guineas?' repeated Imogen faintly.

'Cash,' added Joan. 'Doesn't include the cost of materials,

of course: paving, shrubs, bedding plants and so on. Say one-fifty all told. And when we've got the place spruced up and tickety-boo, we can talk about doubling your harvest.'

'What harvest?' said Kim. 'I thought the apples were too old.'

'Oh, you'd be surprised what can be reaped from a well-tended suburban garden,' said Joan vaguely. 'Given green fingers and the right frame of mind, one can have a cash crop in no time. I'll leave you to think it over, Miss St Clair. And then I'll give you a ring.'

10

115 Sandy Point
Perth
Western Australia

20 May 1969

Dear Kim,
We received yours of May 10. It was a great
surprise as you can imagine, and we were upset to
hear Peggy had passed away so sudden as we were
always fond of Peggy.

You asked for information. I'm sorry dear, but
my husband does not want to get involved and
says I shouldn't either. We have our own daughter
Cathy to think of. That is the end of the matter so
please don't write again as you will not get a reply.

Yours,
Hazel Barber
PS: It was Peggy that lived in Ilford, not us.

'Thanks a bunch!' shouted Kim, the letter crackling in her
pale hands. She reread Mrs Barber's line dissociating herself

from Ilford. 'I suppose you were Barkingside or Fairlop – rotten snob!' added Kim, and tore up the thin paper with the ferocity of an industrial shredding machine. Around her in the packed carriage, commuters swayed and lurched and pretended, embarrassed, that they hadn't heard.

*

Kim's only acquaintance with Shakespeare had been *Twelfth Night* for the school syllabus. Now she lived among people who talked *Macbeth* day in day out, surrounded by texts devoted to the subject. The seriousness of this pursuit both surprised and impressed Kim, the seemingly endless discussions of every nuance of the play, even if some of it was a load of old rubbish about witches. Monique kept up explanatory asides:

'It's his wife who persuades him to murder Duncan the king as a career move. She manipulates him with taunts about his manhood. Therefore it works best if the audience can feel their sexual chemistry. Our production has the further slant that he's a young man and his wife is forty, so there's the suggestion that she's the more experienced of the two and taught him all he knows.'

'I think it's a bit off,' Kim complained to Denise, 'talking about sexual chemistry when Monique and Sebastian used to do it together for real and now he does it with Imogen.'

'Perhaps it's different for theatre people,' suggested Denise. 'Perhaps they're more tuned in to the difference between what's real and what's pretend.'

But there was one facet of interpretation Monique could never recount to Kim. An early rehearsal, back in March: she and Sebastian, on their feet for Act I, ran into the actors' perennial problem with the Macbeths' marriage. Mocking her husband's qualms, Lady Macbeth suddenly throws out a reference to a baby.

'I would, while it was smiling in my face, Have pluck'd my

nipple from his boneless gums, And dash'd the brains out, had I so sworn as you Have done to this,' she proclaims apropos of nothing remotely to do with nipples. But Macbeth has no children and an heir would tear holes in the plot. On a showery Sunday afternoon at the Questors Theatre this issue was thrashed to within an inch of its life, one half of the cast deliberating round in circles while the other half contended with skyrocketing exasperation that it didn't matter a fuck, could they please just get on before everyone *expired*?

Eventually Monique and Sebastian decided they did have a baby – that died. Here was a couple whose terrible bond was cemented not only by sex but by tragedy; when his wife throws that line at him, it is the vilest form of manipulation. At which point Imogen stumbled from the rehearsal room in floods. It had not previously occurred to Monique that as far as Imogen was concerned she had had a baby that died.

Now, just a few weeks later, that dead baby had appeared on her mother's doorstep. A sudden terror gaped in front of Monique like an untimely opened trapdoor. What if something went wrong? What if Imogen was left to grieve a second time? What then?

11

The Rabbit's Foot

Our children didn't have names, they were called 'Baby'. 'This is how to keep Baby's bottom dry.' 'Never let Baby sleep face down . . .' 'Baby should not be at your breast, young woman. Bottle! Now!'

And all of us who passed through the doors of Holbridge Manor were told that when Baby went to its new mummy and daddy we could leave one keepsake of our own for it to take forward into this new life: a lucky charm or piece of jewellery, something small, no bigger, we were told, than a rabbit's foot.

None of us was from a poor background; we had money to spend, guilt money from the parents who put us here. We went into the nearby market town and visited jewellers; we agonized; we shelled out huge sums for tiny jewels and then changed our minds and handed over a long-held trinket of our own that was of sentimental value. Something we loved.

After Mrs Ormond's death in 1961, Ursula wrote to me in Hong Kong. When the new managers opened the office safe they found a treasure trove. Literally.

It was all a sop; nothing went away with our sons and daughters except a simple set of clothes and the crocheted shawl. Our keepsakes stayed in the locked darkness of Mrs Ormond's safe, where they would have stayed for ever, the tokens of love from heart-broken young girls, the bracelets and crucifixes and pearl drops. The rabbit's-foot charms.

To most people, this particular fiction will seem to be the least serious of the insults perpetrated against us; certainly not as bad as the lie, promulgated by Mrs Ormond, that once Baby left Holbridge the adoption was final. I was to learn years later that the court proceedings take a further three months and the mother can contest the order. But a totemic significance attached to the little gold chain with a horseshoe charm that I bought for Charlotte one Saturday afternoon. To discover that it had been taken from her and locked away in a metal box was like watching the last flame of hope smothered by the careless blunder of a jailer's hand.

12

The highpoint of Kim's Sunday was Matins.

Ealing was well provided with churches so she had a choice. ('What will you do,' asked Sebastian sarcastically, 'interview them?' 'Well, of course,' responded Kim.) In the end she settled for a cluttered red-brick building in what Sebastian called 'the Dog's Dinner school of ecclesiastical architecture', where in lieu of the traditional organ there was a guitar to which the congregation sang and clapped their hands. For Sebastian, this constituted a final refutation of any possible blood link between Kim and Imogen.

'I can accept that a baby of yours might be raised by an Essex washerwoman,' he told her, with too little care about whether Kim was in earshot.

'Cleaning lady!' corrected Imogen.

'I can also accept, at a pinch, that a baby of yours might grow up to be homely looking and underdeveloped for her age.'

Kim, who could indeed overhear, registered the word 'underdeveloped' in its schoolyard connotation. She pulled open the neck of her T-shirt and had a stare.

'What I *cannot* believe is that you gave birth to a

right-wing happy-clappy God-botherer, and a bigot into the bargain!'

This last was unjust, but had been brought on by a chance reference of Kim's to one of their Questors friends. He was male but apparently had a lover named Philip. Kim knew the word queer was offensive, but not . . . 'Is he a homo, then?' she asked.

'A *homo*!' Sebastian repeated with relish. 'Yes, Kim, Gareth's a *homo*. But not any of your other insulting appellations. He isn't, for example, a coon, a darkie or a yid.'

And Kim, to everyone's astonishment, went off like a rocket on Firework Night. 'I never called anybody those names!' she screamed. 'You made it up!'

'Kim!'

'I never, Imogen! I promise I never!'

Mostly, those of Sebastian's side-swipes that Kim actually registered she treated with contempt: 'I can give as good as I get,' she assured Peggy's photograph. But this particular allegation defamed her at the very heart of her Christian tolerance. Sebastian had lit a touch paper; Kim was instantly incandescent.

'You're lying,' she yelled at him.

'*Kim!* Leave it! And, Sebastian, shut up for God's sake.'

Kim was flailing at him. Imogen grabbed her, wrapped her arms round the girl's waist and hauled. Welly, in the garden but hearing the commotion, howled and pawed at the kitchen door. Kim squirmed free and launched a dimpled fist inexpertly at Sebastian's chest.

'It's not my fault I don't always know the right names! But I never said the *y* word or the *d* word or—'

'Oh, and another thing, Kim,' threw out Sebastian as he dodged. 'People from China are Chinese, not Chinamen. And people from Japan—'

'Sebastian, stop tormenting her. Go into the kitchen and give me some space! Kim, *calm down*!'

'I'd say we've seen her true colours,' Sebastian called over his shoulder. 'She went for me like a mad dog.'

'Because you goaded her into it, for God's sake. No, Kim, stay here! Sebastian, she gets it from Douglas. He would suddenly go up in flames and there was nothing you could do with him.'

'What fun that must have been at dress rehearsals,' replied Sebastian, closing the kitchen door behind him.

Kim opened her mouth to yell something back.

'Don't even try,' said Imogen wearily. 'Sebastian always has the last word, haven't you realized that by now?'

'I'm going to my room!' shouted Kim. She had one consolation: the noises off suggested that Welly was now taking run-ups before he hurled his weight at the kitchen door. Sebastian, a coward if ever Kim met one, must be staring at it expecting the animal to come torpedoing through the wood leaving a dog-shaped hole like in *Tom and Jerry*.

A few minutes later Imogen tapped on Kim's bedroom door.

'May I come in?'

Kim sniffed. 'If you want.'

Imogen expected to find the aftermath of hot weeping, but the girl was sitting on her bed tense and white, with her dry eyes burning. As Imogen lowered herself gently on to the quilt, her mass of hair bounced. There was always something autumnal about Imogen's hair, its sun-streaked multi-tones; the way its tendril-untidiness fell across her shoulders in sections, like the foliage of October sycamores.

'Doesn't it get on your nerves?' said Kim ungraciously. 'Always falling in your face and tickling?'

'I don't have your itchy skin; that was Douglas again. I should have been more careful who I chose as the father of my daughter.'

'Where's Welly?' demanded Kim, suddenly realizing he had gone quiet. 'Sebastian killed him, has he?'

'With his bare hands,' replied Imogen cheerfully. 'You should have seen him, Kim, wrestling the animal to the ground. I was so proud. There, that's better,' she continued as Kim snorted. 'Kiss and make up?'

'But Sebastian's *horrible*. He's really awful, Imogen. You don't need him. You could have anyone.'

Imogen sat quietly for a moment. Then she said simply, 'I love Sebastian, Kim.'

'You *can't.*'

'Darling, I'll stop him bullying you, I promise. We won't have any more shouting matches. He'll behave himself. And you know I'll stand up for you always. But I can't discuss our relationship. It's the one area beyond negotiation. Can you accept that?'

'No,' said Kim.

Imogen was wearing the birthday necklace; it clinked every time she moved. She smelled of burnt incense and baby powder. Her face was reflected and reflected again in the triple-winged mirrors of Kim's dressing table, an infinity of diminishing Botticelli angels in caftan and cowrie shells. Kim loved her so much she carried a copy of *Starched Linen* in her schoolbag and left it in view all day just to have Imogen's name there in embossed letters. And Peggy's daughter, who had never needed to know jealousy, was toxic with jealousy of Sebastian.

There had been an incident, brief as a cloud blowing across the moon, the memory of which Kim avoided, squirming. It was the usual crowd in the sitting room, Lenny and friends, Sebastian on a beanbag with a lazy arm around Imogen's shoulders, music on the hi-fi. Glancing about him Sebastian's attention lit on a blond girl, pretty and pouty. She raised her eyebrows and put out the very tip of her tongue. Looking the young woman straight in the eye, Sebastian cupped his hand around Imogen's breast and ran a finger round and round her nipple. It swelled against her Indian cotton. Imogen blushed and cuffed him, and the world moved on.

The memory seared through Kim because . . . because this was her first direct glimpse of sexual power. That this power was regularly exercised over Imogen was bad enough but there was worse. Kim sensed from her own reaction, part revulsion and part something hot and tempting, that such casual command might be part of adulthood; that one day sexual submission might encroach upon Kim's own life and blow her precious autonomy to smithereens.

Unfortunately there was a further dimension. That casual, loose-limbed carelessness as Sebastian deliberately excited Imogen's breast to provoke an onlooker, it reeked not merely of power but . . . arrogance. And it was this that linked the incident to another in Kim's recent experience, and opened up a world dark with the possibilities of the bedroom.

Sebastian was not the first example of a monstrously arrogant male to come striding across Kim's mental horizon all leather thighs and testosterone: after all, her best friend was a Jim Morrison fan. One lunchtime at school Kim found herself caught in the crossfire of an appalling exchange of secrets; a gathering of the boys in her class, seething with knowledge about the Doors' track 'Back Door Man'. They spelled out its significance to Kim with eye-watering stories related by Jim Morrison's long-suffering girlfriend.

If men do that, Kim's unsilenced imagination taunted her, what else do they do? Behind Sebastian, she saw a ghastly mental montage of conceded demands and orifices invaded.

'Hey,' said Imogen, giving her a squeeze. 'When the run of *Macbeth* has finished and sanity returns to the world, we can explore London together. I know you're not into the counterculture scene, so let's do the tourist thing: King's Road, Carnaby Street, watch them changing guards at Buckingham Palace. What do you say?'

'All right,' said Kim.

Imogen kissed the top of her head. 'May I translate that as Kim Tanner language for "Wow, terrific, that's a gas!"?'

'If you want.'

'Good. But in the meantime I have a rehearsal to go to. Over the course of this afternoon Sebastian will be taunted by apparitions, haunted by a ghost, frightened half to death by the sight of an entire forest apparently coming at him, and finally put out of his misery when a man worth ten of him runs Sebastian through with a sword. Keep that at the back of your mind,' suggested Imogen, standing up and straightening the quilt, 'and the rest of the day will just fly by.'

13

On the Monday Colonel Massingham got a phone call from Miss Unsworth. Somerset House had tracked down Kim's birth certificate. She had been born to Peggy Tanner.

'Oh no,' he said. 'Oh no.'

'Naturally, they will be sending a copy to your good self as legal guardian,' Miss Unsworth told him with a chirpiness not evident in that meeting at the Antrobus Motel. 'But because of the peculiar circumstances I'm taking the liberty of telephoning ahead.'

No, you're taking the opportunity to gloat, thought Colonel Massingham bitterly. 'You are entirely sure of your facts?' he barked down the phone.

But Miss Unsworth's triumph was beyond his ability to spoil it. 'The matter was simple enough for the PRO to establish,' she replied with an infuriating airiness. 'After all, the rest of the girl's information was perfectly correct: Peggy's full name was indeed Margaret Mabel Tanner, and she was living at the address Kim gave us, 93 Wingfield Drive, Ilford. It was only the facts about the actual birth that were a complete fiction. A complete lie,' added Miss Unsworth to hammer it home.

'Well, if it was that simple a matter,' he snapped, 'what a pity it took them so long to unearth the blessed thing!'

'The PRO does have other priorities, you know,' responded Miss Unsworth, at which Colonel Massingham realized he could take no more. He demanded to know how soon the document would be with him, and when he got his answer put the phone down.

'I'm so sorry, George,' said his wife.

'Is that how officialdom always sounds?' he challenged her, Miss Unsworth's stilted language echoing in his head. 'Is that how I am in court? Do I adjust my vocabulary and pontificate?'

'Yes, dear, I'm afraid so.'

'Oh Frances, what a mess. I would have sworn Kim was Imogen's child. Now she not only loses Imogen but discovers Peggy lied to her all her life. Poor girl.'

'Two poor girls,' amended his wife. 'But they simply won't believe you, George, not until you have the document itself. How will the PRO send it, do you know?'

Miss Unsworth had told him second-class post. 'But they've addressed it to me,' she explained, 'and from to-morrow I will be away on a course. Still, there's no urgency now the facts are established.' This final jab had made him want to cry.

'So that could mean a couple of weeks,' calculated Frances.

'It's insufferable! And that damn actor will do some gloating of his own,' added Colonel Massingham with vitriol, Sebastian being almost as much of a thorn in his side as in Kim's. 'And meanwhile we still have to face Kim and Imogen. Frances, I need advice from someone who knows the girl.'

The Massinghams had found it difficult to get to know Kim. She made regular duty visits with Imogen only to sit in their drawing room stiff and silent, all her natural vivacity quelled by the bone china and the tick-tocking clocks.

There would follow strained conversations about Cambridge University, the Massinghams' careful treading mistaken by Kim for condescension. Frances alone could see precisely what these visits meant to Kim. 'We make her feel like a donkey at a pony show.'

'I need advice,' repeated her husband. So he phoned the Antrobus Motel.

'I am surprised, Massingham,' said Mr Antrobus. 'Though it was always the simplest explanation to fit the facts, I confess I'm taken aback.'

'As am I. You know the child best. What will she want to do?'

'Kim is fearfully proud. She would rather be flogged than live with Miss St Clair if they both know she isn't really Charlotte.'

'I was afraid you would say that.'

When he came off the phone, Frances watched her husband's hurt gaze turn to the whisky decanter. 'I suspect it will make you feel worse rather than better, George,' she advised him. 'But if you do pour yourself one, pour a second for me.'

14

Letters of Referral

It was a school day, a morning in late January and bitter. According to our science mistress the last two weeks of January are statistically the coldest of the year. I came shivering out of the unheated bathroom and found my mother waiting.

'Into your bedroom.'

'But I need to—'

'No arguments, Imogen. Into your bedroom, and don't let your father hear.'

I sat on the bed. She stood.

'Sick again,' she said. 'Five mornings in a row.'

'Something has upset me.'

'So I surmise. You had better give me his name and address.'

I was silent.

'I should have known you were up to no good. Spinning us that yarn about drama lessons, yet there were no extra charges at the end of term. Alarm bells should have rung then.'

So should mine. I simply had not allowed myself to confront the truth, not even as I dashed from the breakfast table to the lavatory bowl and then lay like death on the linoleum of the bathroom floor.

She was a slim, elegant woman. Strong. People liked my mother, friends and neighbours, Pa's colleagues at the bank, tradesmen, the daily help: 'You know where you are with Mrs St Clair.' Impossible to imagine her frightened as I was. I could see myself in the dressing-table mirror, the school uniform with its pitiless bloodshot maroon making my pallor worse, making a ghost of me. Downstairs the radiators were on, but not upstairs. Mother believed central heating was unhealthy in bedrooms. My white legs were goose-flesh above the ankle socks and flat heavy lace-up shoes. From the waist down I looked twelve years old. But I wasn't, I was a young woman. I was pregnant.

And the 'him' of my mother's abrupt demand? Gone, the week before. We said goodbye at the station and caught our separate trains, mine to school in Kensington, his to another town, another job of work. He had never lied to me, I knew there was a wife, children, a life. And there on the station platform both of us cried, not only me.

'What are you going to do, Mother?' I asked.

'What any self-respecting parent would do. I'm going to see the boy responsible, then I am taking you to Dr Bayly.'

'To . . . to confirm that—?'

'*Confirm?*' she snapped. 'Do you imagine it takes medical training to diagnose this sorry state? I've no doubt your headmistress knows a pregnant girl when she sees one, too. The day cannot be far off when she demands that I remove my daughter from her school. Well, let us hope this mess can be cleared up in time to take the wind from her sails. Dr Bayly will put us in contact with a psychiatrist. It shouldn't be difficult to establish that you are suffering some debilitating nervous breakdown.'

'I don't understand.'

'Then let me spell it out for you. You are to have an abortion. This unfortunate condition is imperilling your sanity. You can say you have hallucinations and hear voices in the head. I will back you up. It can all be taken care of in a matter of days. I see no need to upset your father at all.'

He was downstairs at the breakfast table with the toast and *The Times*, ready for his train and his office, the safe routine behind which he scrupulously camouflaged a mouse-like timidity. Weakness of spirit that might, in some other marriage, have made a kind man of him, forgiving because he understood human failings, had instead been exploited by my mother and turned into a spiritless acquiescence. It suited them both, his being under her thumb. She nurtured his unflagging feebleness.

'Dr Bayly should be able to see us at ten o'clock. You can keep your school uniform on, it adds to the impression of helplessness.'

Abortion. I was to have an abortion. Clearly it made no difference that this was supposed to be illegal. Mother would explain things to Dr Bayly who would write a letter of referral and I would be examined by a psychiatrist. I must simply pretend I was crazy, so far round the bend that having a baby would precipitate frank disintegration. The doctors would write more letters culminating in my admission to a clinic where they would flush out the pregnancy and pack me off home again, a fully documented mental case with psychotic delusions. No need to upset Pa. He would merely pay their fees.

'Mother, I'm sorry but I shan't give you the man's

name, and I'm not pretending to be insane either. If you make up tales, I shall tell the psychiatrist so. I shan't do it.'

'Then what do you imagine is the alternative? If you think you're bringing an illegitimate baby into this house, Imogen, you've another think coming.'

Well, in that she succeeded – I never would bring my baby into her house. And she did recruit Dr Bayly to tell lies on her behalf: he signed me off school with fictional glandular fever, and I was kept at home until my embarrassing condition began to show. And then? Mother-and-baby homes do not take girls earlier than six weeks before their due date. So she promptly found one willing to have me as an unpaid labourer in return for some undisclosed financial donation from Pa. I worked in the gardens of Holbridge Manor, digging and hauling wheelbarrows until even their callous rules brought me indoors out of the rain. But Mother failed to have my daughter aborted against my will. I had never fought before but I fought over this.

Was it out of love for my unborn child? No. She wasn't Charlotte yet, just morning sickness and calamity. But if they could declare me psychiatrically unhinged for the purpose of procuring an abortion, if they could do that on a Monday, what was to stop them locking me in an asylum on a Tuesday? The next time I contravened the rules of society, what cure would they come up with – drugs? Worse? Frontal lobotomy? I might be alone and in a very great deal of trouble, but I wasn't declaring myself insane for the convenience of my mother.

I wasn't feeble.

15

Kim finally made the trip to the Questors Theatre the first Sunday in June.

She didn't intend to: Imogen had rushed out leaving behind a folder across whose cover was scrawled in uncompromising black 'REHEARSAL NOTES: DO NOT REMOVE FROM SHAW ROOM'. It was nearly five o'clock before Kim came in from walking an exhausted Welly all over West London, and found it lying there. So she went after Imogen.

Kim already had a map, sketched by Monique when she first moved in: 'Everyone's heard about you. They'll be thrilled.' Kim ambled across Ealing, found an alleyway intriguingly named Barnes Pikle, and turned right down Mattock Lane until the big houses gave way to the great open site of the Questors.

Despite everything, Kim had never shaken off her impression of clunky amateurs in church halls. The sheer scope shook her. There were loads of buildings, all of them serious: a substantial Georgian house, some recent constructions in classroom style, the Playhouse itself, a huge round edifice with a plaque that referred to the Queen

Mother. Elsewhere were less reputable captions: a foundation stone cited the Moscow Art Theatre and an unpronounceable sign read 'The Constantin Stanislavsky Room'. Beyond them all was a kind of stable block from which issued the shriek of sawn wood.

Everywhere was busyness. Tinkly piano drifted into a multi-layered soundscape. From somewhere else a voice shouted, 'No, no, you're supposed to be *drunk*, Gerald! Don't *mince* across the floor, man, *stagger* over there and throw a punch at him – he's just deflowered your fiancée!' A woman in paint-ruined overalls strode past carrying bagpipes and a stuffed whippet. Kim stepped forward nervously.

'Excuse me. I'm looking for Imogen St Clair.'

'Which show?'

Kim paused. Monique had warned her, 'Don't ever use the word *Macbeth* within theatre grounds or you'll cause a dozen walkouts and at least two fatal strokes. There'll be grown men in tears.'

'She's doing the Scottish play,' remembered Kim. 'Backstage.'

'They're in the theatre. Today's the get-in.'

'Get-in?'

But her adviser only pointed and was gone.

Kim made her way between the buildings until just short of that screaming workshop she came to a pair of barn doors wedged open; two men trundled enormous sheets of hardboard up a ramp. She followed them.

She was in a huge space dominated by blackness and dust, and ringing with the noise of construction. Despite the gaping doors daylight didn't seem to enter. The black slab-walls were prison-high. A dusty curtain tied into an enormous knot hung from a metal pole, swinging drunkenly as every passing wooden plank and A-frame ladder slugged it in the midriff.

Behind Kim was a vast chest of drawers like something that might belong to a giant in a fairy tale. Surreal labels were gummed to the drawers: *Black legs. Old grey legs. 12-foot legs*. Kim sniffed the air. Wood, glue, paint and something else that she couldn't define, that was actually made up of sawdust, general dust and the ghosts of other productions.

A woman in overalls was shinning up a vertical metal ladder into the black dark of the flies.

'Excuse me!' called Kim. 'I'm looking for Imogen St Clair.'

'Ginny? Off-prompt vom,' responded the woman and carried on climbing.

Baffled, Kim crossed over to the slab wall. Beyond it, the space opened out into something recognizable as a theatre: a great arc of seats, upholstered in purple plush and steeply tiered. The area towards which they were angled was a kind of pit; men and women lugged steel decking into it and shouted to one another. Twenty feet above their heads, along a great criss-cross of walkways, other figures were doing their own lugging and shouting. Shouting at Kim.

'Oy – you!' Kim looked up. Staring down were two women balancing some kind of massive lantern. 'Any idea what one of these weighs?'

'I'm sorry, I'm new here,' said Kim.

There was a burst of unfriendly laughter.

'All right, joke over.' This was another voice, a man's, middle-aged. Though he was dressed like a sweep who'd fallen down a chimney, the accent was the Massinghams'. In fact, so were all the voices, right across the chatter and bustle: educated, cut-glass, not a dropped *h* or glottal stop in the place. But at least this one addressed Kim kindly.

'They're rigging lights immediately above your cranium,' he explained, leading her away. 'See? That's a follow-spot. If one of those falls you'll know nothing about it but un-happily we will – and we'll have the devil's own job washing splattered blood off the cyc.'

'Psych?'

'Cyclorama.' He indicated a sweep of gauze behind them. 'I'm Benjamin Sacks. Stage director for the theatre, and in charge of safety. My name is on notices everywhere forbidding people to do things. What is it you're looking for?'

'I'm trying to find Imogen St Clair,' complained Kim, 'only I keep asking people in English and they keep answering me back in Martian.'

He stared at her. 'My God. You must be Kim!'

'She forgot this book.' Kim indicated the folder under her arm.

'Did she really? How very unlike her.' Which was sarcastic, but not nasty. 'Come with me,' suggested Benjamin Sacks.

A semi-circular tunnel ran behind and below the auditorium. They found Imogen round the other side, teetering on a heap of filthy old carpet to tie up a curtain. At the sight of Kim she came skittering off the rugs, all dust and dither.

'Ben, it's my daughter! Hey, everyone,' she shouted into the din. 'Come here a minute! Meet my lovely Kim!'

'Imogen, they can't see if I'm lovely or not – you've got me in a headlock!'

'Where there's no sense, there's no feeling.'

'No feeling? I feel like an absolute . . .'

'Right!' interrupted Benjamin Sacks. 'I'll leave you both to it.'

'No, Ben, wait. I've a question for you.' Imogen loosened her grip on the wriggling Kim. 'You're not a fisherman by any chance?'

'Nope,' he responded. 'Why?'

Imogen's voice dropped. 'Daphne's given me every filthy job she can find. You know the banquet scene with the ghost, played by Reggie, dripping blood and cobwebs?'

'Of course.'

'Well, the moment he pops out looking like a bad joke on Hallowe'en, I come up through the trapdoor under the table, open a flap and swap the fruit bowl that's up there for a different one, under cover of an actor's cloak.'

'Why do you need a fisherman?'

'Anglers' bait. Think of all that imagery of putrefaction. There's an earlier banquet, remember, but we've had a lot of bloodshed since then. So for the second of them we start with the same festoons, until I swap the fruit for a hideous rotting mess – covered with maggots. Real maggots. Writhing around inside this whacking great glass vase.'

'Tell me this is a wind-up.'

'Sadly not.'

'A bowlful of maggots?'

'You know how tricky it is handling props up and down ladders, in and out of trapdoors.'

Both of them turned instinctively towards the steps that led to a crawl-space under the stage.

'I'm down there with live maggots encased in real breakable glass.'

There was a thoughtful silence. 'Well, good luck,' said Benjamin Sacks. 'I'll be thinking of you. Nice to meet you, Kim,' he added brightly. Then he waved a hand and was gone.

16

'George, it is two weeks since you had a decent night's sleep. At this rate you will be ill.'

Colonel Massingham looked quite dreadfully ill already.

'It's iniquitous that you should be put through this torture. Use your influence to hurry the proceedings along. Phone Somerset House.'

'Frances, this isn't the fault of the PRO. That damn woman Unsworth is off on some perishing course while Kim's birth certificate lies on her desk.'

'Then phone and demand a second copy.'

'Much as I dislike Miss Unsworth, that would breach professional etiquette.'

'Fiddlesticks!' said Frances.

So her husband put through a call to Somerset House.

*

The following evening Imogen and Kim sat subdued in the kitchen. Welly lay at their feet, both women distractedly stroking him, one ear each. 'Imogen, I know it's horrible, but I'm in this too, remember.'

'I keep thinking of her revelling in it. I knew she'd taken against me.'

Imogen looked so crushed Kim hardly had the heart to suggest they weren't defeated yet. But Imogen smiled weakly and said, 'Go on. Let's hear your plan to show her she can't grind me down.'

'Yeah? Well, Denise's dad is a fisherman and what he doesn't know about maggots isn't worth knowing. So I said, "Do you buy them by the dozen?" and he said, "Don't be daft, you buy them by the pint." Then I checked your bowl with a milk bottle and you'll need eight pints in total. Imogen, it's no good looking like that.'

'OK. Go on.'

'So then I asked how much a maggot weighs and Denise's dad said, "In the entire history of coarse fishing nobody's ever asked what a maggot weighs," so when Denise's mum wasn't looking he bunged some on the kitchen scales and he reckons the whole caboodle will weigh in at just under 6 lbs. Now, the point is, left to themselves maggots hatch out in a couple of days.'

'Hatch? Into what?'

'House flies or bluebottles, of course,' explained Kim in surprise. 'Anyway, Denise's dad says they'll last nearly a week if we keep them in the fridge.'

'You can't be serious. *This* fridge?'

'Have they got one at the theatre?'

'Yes! In the Grapevine bar. Good thinking.'

'And will they let you store eight pints of live, maturing maggots in it for nine performances and a dress rehearsal?'

Imogen shut her eyes.

'That's what I guessed. Now, the glass bowl is too big for this fridge, so each night you'll have to scoop them into something that fits. Plastic bag should do the trick.'

'This is *foul*.'

'We can share the job. You scrape them into the bag for the night, the next evening I spoon them back into the bowl for the performance. Of course, mine's the easy job because the larvae will be dormant from the cold, whereas by the time you stir them up with a ladle they'll have done a turn under the stage lights. The whole lot will be squirming about like worms in a beak.'

Imogen put a hand across her mouth.

'Oh yeah, and Denise's dad said before you seal the plastic bag, suck out the air. That'll slow 'em down and make the supplies last longer.'

'I can't believe we're having this conversation,' announced Imogen. 'I am not ladling maggots. I am not keeping maggots in my fridge, and if anybody thinks I'm holding a plastic bag full of maggots up to my face and *sucking* they must need their head examined. Daphne can do it. I resign. I am out of there. I quit.'

'Yeah? So what happened to "I won't let Daphne grind me down" and "The show must go on"?'

'I've come to my senses,' said Imogen. 'It's only a bloody play. I've finally seen the light.'

*

The birth certificate arrived by that morning's post: a long, thin document in red and cream that claimed, with off-putting grandeur, to be a certified copy of an entry of birth pursuant to the Births and Deaths Registration Act, 1953.

The name and address were consistent with Kim's information, but the mother's name in its entirety was given as 'Margaret Mabel Davis formerly Tanner', Tanner being her maiden name before she married one Sidney Davis, who was in Column 4 as 'father'. These complications accounted for why the PRO could not immediately track it down. Another column gave the baby's name as Patricia Kim. She was born at the King George Hospital, Ilford, on 23 September 1955.

Imogen's baby had been born on 2 September. Colonel Massingham's first suspicion was an unworthy one – that

Kim's claimed birthday was an invention, a ploy, to fit with Charlotte's. That she or her mother had been to Somerset House themselves, as many others had done who were contenders for Imogen's acceptance.

'You're not thinking clearly,' objected his wife. 'Kim's date of birth must have been known in Crowhurst Green long before *Starched Linen* was ever published – the school would have it, and the local doctor. This can't be the same child, George. This isn't Kim Tanner, she's Patricia Kim Davis.'

'It makes no sense,' he had said, staring nonplussed at the copperplate handwriting of the registrar. But it started to make sense a couple of hours later when the second post brought another envelope from Somerset House. In this one was a death certificate.

Patricia Kim died on 24 September, the day after she was born. Under 'Primary Cause' were the words 'hyaline membrane disease'.

'I've met that term before,' Colonel Massingham told Frances. 'In court. I think it applies to premature babies.'

'So Peggy had a daughter in perfectly respectable circumstances,' said Frances thoughtfully, 'and lost her, poor little thing. And by the time she took on Kim, Peggy had left her marital home and reverted to her maiden name.'

'I wonder why she left.'

'Yes. And didn't merely leave. It seems Peggy never mentioned her husband's existence while she was living in Crowhurst Green. It must have been a terrible marriage for her to expunge him from her history. George, would you like me to phone our doctor and ask about that cause of death?'

'Please, my dear. But first, I have another call to make.'

'Miss Unsworth,' he said, his voice cold as a box of knives, 'you understood the implications. Yet you had not the foresight to check . . . I am not losing my temper, on the contrary, I am being remarkably civil!'

But he wasn't. The voice of the Social Services continued

with imperturbable efficiency. 'Our instruction,' said Miss Unsworth, 'was to ascertain through the PRO whether there existed a birth certificate from September 1955, consistent with a particular name and address. And there was.'

'You had a duty to be rather more careful than that. You knew precisely what distress your news would cause to—'

'I am surprised you passed on the news at all,' interrupted Miss Unsworth, goaded by an acrid intuition. 'In your place I would not have informed either Kim or Miss St Clair until I had the actual document as evidence.' She paused. 'Did you do so?'

'That is hardly the—'

'Did you do so, Colonel Massingham?'

'Luckily I did not,' he said in a voice so deep it seemed to roll out of his shoes, swinging punches as it came.

When he put down the phone and there was nobody else he could reasonably shout at, Colonel Massingham had to decide what use to make of the unhappy information. He was now at a loss.

'What should I tell Imogen? I do feel disinclined to expose Peggy Tanner's sadness, which she obviously went to enormous trouble to keep secret from Kim.'

'One moment, George.'

'On the other hand, Kim is bound to find out sooner or later during her own dealings with the PRO. We're still no nearer tracking down her papers.'

'George dear – stop for a moment.' Frances Massingham rested her hand on his arm. 'We have to think about this. The poor woman has a premature baby that doesn't survive. Shortly afterwards she acquires another child to replace her, under circumstances we know were secretive. And she names the girl after her own lost baby. George, I think we have to consider the possibility that this isn't all it seems.'

'Frances, please don't talk in riddles, my dear. Whatever do you mean?'

'Suppose it was a secret because Kim wasn't given away voluntarily.'

'You can't mean stolen! Antrobus gave the impression Peggy Tanner was an upright woman!'

'George, it is all so very odd. The secrecy has always struck me as out of all proportion. Don't we at least have to consider a more murky explanation?'

He closed his eyes.

'George?'

'All right, Frances, all right.'

'I presume you can make discreet enquiries?'

'I'll talk to Gordon. He plays golf with some pretty senior coves at Scotland Yard.'

'It shouldn't be difficult to find out whether Kim could fit the details of a baby girl stolen at some date after September 1955—' Frances Massingham's voice suddenly gave out.

'What is it? What is it, Frances?'

The Jarman case, she thought. The Jarman child. 'Nothing,' she replied after a moment. 'A touch of indigestion. What was I saying? Yes, until we eliminate that awful possibility you certainly shouldn't talk to Imogen. I know you love her dearly, George, but Imogen is the last person in the world I'd impart delicate information to. That girl could no more hide this from Kim than beat Apollo 11 to the moon.'

17

Kim began to understand why Imogen had flinched when Kim mistook the Questors for am dram. So did the entire London counterculture.

When they talked about theatre it was the Arts Lab, or they would tell Kim more than she wanted to know about a Frenchman called Genet masturbating in a prison cell, but non-professional theatre was an embarrassment and a taboo. Monique could get away with it because of Shash, and Sebastian could get away with it because he could get away with anything, but Imogen was already deplorably Establishment, with her mass-market books written in plain English and properly punctuated. The Questors, with a Playhouse opened by the Queen Mother, just put the tin lid on it.

'First it's true-life teenage pregnancy in the suburbs,' complained Lenny Honky-Tonk, lying across Imogen's cushions, eating her food and browbeating her, 'then fictional teenage pregnancy in Hong Kong. And now it's teenage pregnancy seeking enlightenment in India. It's all so bloody *bourgeois*, Ginny.'

Which stumped Kim. Although the crowd included the occasional bohemian aristocrat or Madison Avenue sophisticate, the overwhelming majority were suburban-born, comfortably off, and indisputably middle class.

Kim had identified the central characteristics of the underground scene: they all knew one another, and they all had two independent claims to fame. Lenny, for example, had posed nude for Francis Bacon, and it was his story of setting fire to a girlfriend's flat that had inspired John Lennon to write 'Norwegian Wood'. A sculptress named Chi-Chi had once stood bail for Timothy Leary and was descended from the Marquis de Sade. And so with them all.

Between the get-in and the opening night of *Macbeth*, Joan began landscaping the garden. Sebastian had been strangely averse to the idea. 'It's extortion!' he'd shouted at Imogen. 'I'd sooner bulldoze the whole bloody lot!'

Kim had been driven to the end of her patience. 'If you want a cheaper quote than Joan, let me get hold of a couple of gardeners from Hampton Court and let *them* give the place the once-over,' she'd said, at which Sebastian's behaviour had become completely unreasonable. It was then that Kim launched her campaign for finding Imogen a husband.

She didn't carry the burden alone; Denise came to stay for the weekend and they worked on it together. They would even have some men to choose from: the girls were off to a fête given by one of Kim's Christian organizations. By contrast, the grown-ups' day would be spent at a technical rehearsal.

Monique explained the form to Kim: 'It's where you check your doors don't stick, the firelight flickers, cats meow on cue, and the wind machine doesn't blow all the wigs off during your storm scene. Unhappily, more often than not the doors meow, the cats catch fire, and you spend all night picking hairs out of the lighting gantry. A bad dress rehearsal runs until midnight. A bad tech runs all day, all night and half the following morning.'

Cast and crew had been called – but not the maggots,

which wouldn't be going live until the final dress rehearsal. Imogen had not thrown in the towel, of course. The show must go on.

Kim and Denise's demands that weekend were slight. The fête was somewhere called Little Banton on the Hill; all Imogen had to do was find this on the map, hop into the white Rolls, and drive them there before ten o'clock Saturday morning.

'Don't worry about us getting home later,' Kim assured her. She was confident this would be taken care of by some Ealingite or other – though admittedly sometimes people agreed to give her a lift and then welshed when they saw Welly.

'However did you get him here?' one particular vicar had demanded.

'In the back of a Rolls-Royce,' said Kim, to which the vicar snapped, 'And don't you be sarky to me, girl!'

But for once Imogen said no. 'I'll have to organize a taxi this time, darling. Sebastian and I need to sleep in on Saturday morning. God knows when we'll get another full night before the show finally comes down at the end of the month.'

'But you'll be up by half eight anyway,' said Kim.

'No, darling, we will not.'

'Yes you will,' insisted Kim. 'At half eight Joan's bringing the builders in with a pneumatic drill and half a ton of paving slabs. Didn't I tell you? Even Sebastian can't sleep through that.'

The South-East England Branch of Christian Mothers Against the Permissive Society Summer Fayre ('In association with "Literate People Against Spurious Spellings and Indigestible Syntax"?' suggested Sebastian) took place in the grounds of a very grand house. Denise and Kim were in charge of the white-elephant stall. This provided an excellent vantage point for checking out potential husbands.

'Here's what we're looking for,' Kim summed up, counting off on her fingers. 'He's got to be single, obviously. And older than her, so he's somebody she can look up to. When I say older, I mean within reason; I don't just want Imogen married off, I want her to have that baby she's so desperate for but doesn't know it. No good landing her with some codger who's too old to manage the necessary.'

'So what's the outside maximum?' asked Denise. 'Thirty-nine?'

'At most.'

Denise was thoughtful. 'But won't you mind if Imogen has a baby?'

'Me? Why?'

'Not being an only child any more.'

Denise tried to imagine her own parents suddenly producing a rival sibling. I would die, thought Denise. It would kill me. A momentary panic seized her and Denise had to remind herself that she had just made it up. Surely even Kim's sang-froid would be rocked by the appearance of a *baby*. Denise was well aware of her friend's jealousy of Sebastian, you couldn't miss it. But that was unsayable. 'Won't you mind?' repeated Denise.

But Kim only shrugged.

'Is it cos Imogen's more like a big sister than a mum?' Denise persevered, but she was wasting her time. Kim just wasn't given to self-analysis. Besides, she had neither experience of nor interest in babies, and saw them as something akin to getting a puppy. Kim certainly wouldn't be jealous if Imogen had a new puppy, even if she loved it to death.

'Imogen wants a baby, so a baby would be good,' said Kim impatiently.

'OK,' agreed Denise. No point in stirring up trouble where there was none. 'So, what about the guy's looks? She's going to be fussy. Imogen's such a looker herself. And I know Sebastian's a complete bastard and everything, but he is a dish. Yes he is, Kim,' maintained Denise. 'That dark moody face. Husky brown voice. Sean Connery eyes.'

'All right, all right.'

'Slim, wiry physique,' continued Denise. 'He might be a grot-bag but he's no bow-wow, Kim.'

Kim reminded herself that Denise's taste in men was idiosyncratic. Long before Jim Morrison, in the days when 'Wild Thing' was in the charts Denise had dreamed of snogging a Trogg.

'And obviously we got to find someone religious,' said Kim, dragging them back to the point. 'If ever there was a person that needs a firm grounding against moral turpitude,' she said, incorporating a phrase being bandied about in Little Banton on the Hill that afternoon, 'it's Imogen.'

With the white-elephant stall Kim proved a good sales-person, milking the extra penny out of her customers for such unlikely money-spinners as a home-made mechanical hair-drier and a sickly green urn 'big enough to take an aspidistra'. And the lift home had been booked: Kim had tracked down a different Ealing vicar, with a station wagon and a soft streak.

Late in the afternoon, when the donkey derby finished, the girls presented themselves to their chauffeur. 'Ah,' he said as Welly hurled himself against the vehicle's paintwork, 'all things bright and beautiful. Well, hop in.'

Already hopped in was a man Kim had seen at church, now introduced as Barry. In his late thirties perhaps. There was not a hint of a flair to his trousers, his jumper was hand-knitted in a diamond pattern, and as the car sped along the London road he led them in a singsong of 'He's Got The Whole World In His Hands'. I know every prayer is answered, thought Kim, but that wasn't half quick.

Denise recognized her friend's reaction, and her heart sank. Sitting immediately behind Barry she watched the pale reptilian neck, of which there was a great deal more than there should be, and tried to imagine what sort of woman would climb over Sebastian Duck to get at him. An unhinged sort of woman was Denise's answer. Wearing a paper bag over her own head in case the one over his head broke.

'Kim,' she whispered urgently under cover of the high notes. 'He's a bow-wow, Kim.'

'Shush up or he'll hear you.'

'Kim, he's a woof-woof.'

With hair that short, how can anybody manage to have dandruff? marvelled Denise, who being downwind of it was speckled like a plover's egg before the car reached Northolt. And not even her position in the back protected her from his halitosis – was it ricocheting off the windscreen?

'It's been so nice to meet you,' Kim told Barry as she hauled Welly out of the car.

'Hurry up, Kim,' rang out Denise across her, 'or we'll miss *Lassie Come Home*.'

'Can I ask you round to tea one evening? I've got somebody who'd really like to meet you.'

And Barry said he'd love to come to tea.

'Say Tuesday week?' suggested Kim. 'About six o'clock?'

There was no Questors performance and she happened to know Sebastian was doing some sort of experimental naked improvisation at an arts club.

'I'll bring my guitar,' said Barry.

Denise sighed. 'If I were you,' she said, smiling into his face and trying not to whimper, 'I'd leave off the community singing till you get to know her better.'

It was one in the morning before the technical rehearsal finished and Imogen and Sebastian came rolling home, as Kim put it.

They didn't roll alone. Monique wasn't with them but another man was; from the crosstalk being carried on from room to room, Kim and Denise gathered his name was

Gareth. Sebastian's voice reached them from the kitchen. 'What an un*conscionable* bloody shambles!'

'Drunk!' snapped Kim in a tone the Mothers would have been proud of. But Denise didn't agree.

'I don't think they're drunk,' she said. 'I think they're just knackered and hysterical.'

Below the girls, shouts of laughter seemed to confirm Denise's diagnosis. It was now Imogen's voice that rose up to them. 'Even with bad techs, we can usually see light at the end of the tunnel.'

'I'd rig one for you, Ginny,' responded the stranger's voice, 'except at this rate John will never have the fucking stage finished for me to focus it on!'

Shrieks greeted this. Sebastian's voice had lost the timbre of the kitchen; the girls followed its progress across the hall and into the sitting room. 'I said to Daphne, I said, "If I were you, Daph, I'd shift those scaffold poles and the rope. We only need a hint like that to bloody hang ourselves!"'

Screams of laughter buffeted from room to room, the chaos of sound swelling and dimming, swelling and dimming. Doors slammed, and at last the racket tightened into a single hot knot of noise in the sitting room. Meaning directly below Kim and Denise.

Kim got out of bed intending to stamp downstairs and ask them what sort of time they called this, but Denise talked her out of it. 'They're the ones that'll suffer in the morning,' she reasoned. 'It will do them good to learn the hard way. Anyway, if you go, it'll only wind Sebastian up.'

So they compromised; Denise did it. With her bubble-cut hair in curlers and a vast candlewick dressing gown adding twenty-five pounds to her physique, Denise materialized among the bean-bags like a caricature fishwife and suggested to the trio that a bit of consideration wouldn't go amiss. Into the resultant stunned silence Imogen's voice ventured that they were extremely sorry, and in fact she was coming to bed in a minute.

'They're running out of cigarettes,' Denise told Kim as she shrugged her dressing gown on to the quilt and slid back into bed. 'They're passing the same one round. I think the party will break up shortly.'

But the party showed no signs of breaking up. After Imogen came upstairs Sebastian put a record on. By two o'clock, Pink Floyd's *A Saucerful Of Secrets* was belting up through the ceiling, all woofers and tweeters.

'That's it!' said Kim. 'I'm going down myself.'

'To tell them off?' asked Denise sleepily. She had a soft spot for Pink Floyd and was enjoying slipping out of consciousness to the drones of 'Set The Controls For The Heart Of The Sun'.

'No,' said Kim. 'It's just this thought I've had.'

The name Gareth had finally rung a bell with Kim. He was the one with the boyfriend. Just suppose . . . She had a vision based on a cartoon sketch doing the rounds at school. Kim's image of Sebastian as a slavering sex monster might encompass that too. And if so, surely it would put the kibosh on Imogen's love for him? Kim was down the stairs and at the door of the sitting room.

Her hopes were dashed instantly; the two men were not in each other's arms, they were sprawled in separate chairs.

'Not a bar open in the whole of Ealing,' Sebastian was saying. 'I felt like a desert dog looking for trees.'

'We can't have drinks near the lighting console anyway,' complained Gareth. 'Ben Sacks put up a notice. "Due to the cost of equipment" etc.'

'Yeah, well, he'd know all about cost, wouldn't he, Benjamin Sacks?' said Sebastian. He blew two grey tusks of smoke from his nostrils, and handed his cigarette over to Gareth. 'Bloody yid,' said Sebastian.

Kim stood a moment at the door, stupefied. Then she slipped away, and crept back up the stairs to the bedroom.

18

On the Monday morning Colonel Massingham's contact came back with an answer – and the answer was negative: there were no unsolved cases of child abduction that could reasonably fit with Kim's age and description, not in Ilford, not in Great Britain, not even abroad, added Gordon, delighted to drop the word Interpol into the conversation: there was no unclosed file on a female child that remotely fitted with Kim. This came as a vast relief to Colonel Massingham. What he couldn't understand was why it seemed not to come as a relief to his wife.

'George, you know more than I do about the girl's background. Does she say Peggy always lived in Essex?'

'I believe so. Dagenham originally, then Ilford. She was at the Wingfield Drive address for about twenty years. Though of course Kim doesn't know Peggy lived there as a married woman.'

'Which means we can't necessarily trust Kim's other information. For example, according to her understanding, when Peggy took her over from the adoptive parents, she moved to a block of flats. In Kim's words, Peggy changed her address so the neighbours wouldn't ask difficult questions. But you and I know that when Peggy left Wingfield Drive she was walking out on her marriage.'

'Kim's version could still be partly true,' argued Colonel Massingham. 'It is feasible that Peggy left with the baby Kim because the husband refused to bring up another couple's child. Entirely feasible.'

'Yes, you are right, George. That could be what happened. Either way, you told me Kim doesn't have an address for these flats, so why is she certain they were in Ilford?'

'She remembers them. A mansion block. It's Kim's earliest memory.'

'How can it be? She was far too young.'

'Not by the time they moved again, Frances. Peggy and Kim didn't settle in Crowhurst Green until Kim was three-and-a-half. The flats were condemned for demolition so Peggy applied to the council for a house in a more rural area. Why? What is bothering you, Frances?'

'Just something nagging at the back of my mind. Has Kim ever mentioned—' Frances paused. 'Has she ever mentioned Cheshire, George? The Wirral, particularly.'

'Never that I've heard. Why?'

'It doesn't matter.'

And Frances could not have said whether she was relieved or sorry that the mention of the Wirral in connection with a missing child failed to remind her husband of the Jarman murder trial.

✱

They were beginning to get a garden. Joan's activities might not have been quiet but they were efficient. Those builders with their jackhammers had been terrorized into getting the new patio down.

'What the hell do you think you're doing?' Joan demanded, not of the workmen but of Imogen, who was blearily carrying a tray over the ankle-turning chaos of clay and jagged concrete that had formerly been the path outside her kitchen door.

'They asked for another cup of tea, Joan.'

'Well, they can have their other cup of tea when they've finished digging up this bally concrete! And put the sugar in yourself, Imogen, one spoon each. Let this lot anywhere near that sugar bowl, and we'll have two coronaries and a diabetic coma before they've started on the pointing.'

By the first dress rehearsal of *Macbeth*, Imogen's woe-begone borders had been cleared of their jungly weeds. By the second dress, a patio of limestone slabs had been laid, pointed and swept, and Joan had softened its clinical precision by planting tiny drifts of lemon thyme in the interstices of the stones ('Interstices,' repeated Kim, making a mental note). By opening night they had hanging baskets high up on the back wall, blazing like chandeliers. Against a brand-new trellis, climbers were coming gloriously into bloom with papery purple flowers the size of plates. 'Until the snails get 'em,' warned Joan. 'They swagger out of the undergrowth and hunt in packs. If I catch 'em nibbling that clematis I'll chop their little legs off and pull their little teeth out.'

Kim had heard her discuss the planting with Sebastian, in a surprisingly genial conversation including a lot about Marrakesh, and the pros and cons of a growing technique called hydroponics.

'I decided against returfing the lawn,' Joan informed Kim. 'The whole concept of a perfect lawn is a triumph of hope over experience. I'll give this lot a haircut with a scythe – or machete and flamethrower – and then leave it to the rain of a good old English summer. Know how to manage a lawnmower?'

'I'll soon get the hang,' said Kim.

'In that shed there's a great steam-engine of a thing. Dates back to the year dot. Get 'em to buy you a new one. One summer of pushing that old soldier round the garden, you'll have the shoulders of a stevedore and a bust like a roll-top desk.'

The first night of *Macbeth* was Thursday. From the admittedly exhausted remarks made by the household, Kim gathered the problems that had so enriched everybody's vocabulary after the first tech had been patched up.

'I think we got a show,' Kim heard Sebastian telling somebody on the phone.

And on the Saturday, Imogen asked Kim to help them out as an assistant stage manager.

'No,' said Kim.

'The thing is,' Imogen's tone was threaded with panic, 'we're desperate.'

Someone called Janet had gone down with flu and a David had to rush home to Merthyr Tydfil for the funeral of an inconvenient grandmother.

'Please, Imogen, no.'

'I'm sure you have a natural aptitude. Given me and Douglas that's a biological certainty. Backstage must be in your genes.'

'But backstage is something you both learned,' contradicted Kim the scientist. 'Acquired characteristics are not inherited, Imogen. Honestly. It's Lamarckism.'

'What does that mean?'

'It means it's bollocks,' said Kim patiently. Monique gave a shout of laughter. 'Imogen, please don't make me do this. I'm thirteen years old. I'm supposed to be in bed by ten. I don't know anything about backstage and the only time I set foot in the Questors I didn't understand a word anybody said to me all afternoon.'

'All we're asking is that you look after the prompt-side tabs cued by the DSM.'

I rest my case, thought Kim, remembering a favourite expression of Sebastian's.

'Tabs are curtains,' explained Monique, who Kim had expected to back her up. 'So are legs. Prompt-side is the wing on the left. Off-prompt is the other side. The deputy stage manager coordinates the show from a desk, talking through headphones like air traffic control. When she waves her arm, you pull the curtain back.'

'The only problem I foresee,' said Imogen, 'is your height. You're not tall enough to hold the tabs free of the scenery when it's being wheeled off.'

Kim could foresee another one: she wasn't doing it. To Kim the theatre was utterly alien, and she had felt a fool there. Feeling a fool was new to Kim and searingly un-pleasant. At the memory of those carrying voices all the hairs stood up on the backs of her arms. She might have stumbled into a Brueghel scene of hell peopled with Frances Massinghams.

'If you don't do it,' said Sebastian, entering the conver-sation to Kim's further disgust, 'the actors will be fighting a twelve-foot length of velvet every time they leave the stage. We'll look like a bunch of wankers.'

'That might not be our best line of argument,' put in Monique, 'that Kim should spend Saturday night working a curtain to stop you looking like a bunch of wankers.'

'Please don't make me, Imogen. I don't want to do it. Imogen, please don't make me.'

'I'll show you the ropes,' said Daphne, the stage manager.

On hearing they were to be helped out by a daughter of Imogen St Clair she had rolled her eyes and said something about the devil and the deep blue sea, but faced with Kim herself Daphne was pleasantly surprised. So was Kim. Tacked up beside every prop table was a list, beside every rope-and-pulley an instruction sheet. Even better, shortly after Kim arrived Daphne called her crew together and issued them with tasks in a no-arguments style more usually associated with Japanese POW camps.

Then she talked Kim through the basics. The audience wrapped much of the way round the stage, and the cast would seethe on and off from all directions, including the aisles 'and three voms'. It turned out that this was short for the unhealthy-sounding 'vomitorium', an opening off that semicircular walkaround through which Benjamin Sacks had taken Kim. From the voms the actors erupted on to the stage as though directly out of the audience.

'Then I don't see what's important about one particular curtain,' reasoned Kim.

'You mean the tabs? They're the least of our worries,' said Daphne. 'We need you trotting up the ladder into the flies, opening trapdoors and hiding under the table in the banquet scene to help Imogen swap the fruit bowls. You didn't volunteer thinking it would only be the tabs, did you?'

'Not really,' said Kim with weary acceptance.

'And you can help Gerry fly the scenery for Dunsinane. Like I said, I'll show you the ropes. They're tied up over here.'

Imogen had provided Kim with a set of 'backstage blacks' – including old black pants sawn off at the bottom. Naturally, they were miles too big, so Imogen took up the slack with a forest of safety pins.

'How am I expected to go to the toilet?'

'Oh God. Can't you keep it in till the show comes down at ten forty-five?' So Kim resignedly paid a last visit to the loo. Now, Daphne told her she would also need a hood ('It's OK, there are eyeholes') to black her out when she was working the trapdoors from underneath the stage. But at this Kim did baulk. Under the stage was a pit of gritty carpets and metal poles to concuss yourself on. Sitting in a dungeon with a hood over your head, decided Kim, had too much in common with prisoners about to be executed.

'You don't have a phobia about heights, do you?' Daphne asked, pointing up the vertical ladder to the blackness above.

'Would it make any difference?' responded Kim.

'Not tonight,' admitted Daphne.

'Then let's take it I don't.'

At seven thirty a woman named Sheila, at the desk with headphones on, called 'Going dark!' and started flicking switches. The hard white light around them was obliterated and Kim's eyes blinked in the low glimmer of blue performance lights. 'Silence, everyone, we're letting the house in.' To Kim she added, 'Careful what you do with your hands. Start waving your arms about and you'll have some poor bugger pulling ropes or swinging the tabs open and shut with the compulsion of a Pavlov dog.'

A beautiful woman in a trailing gown and hair to her waist whispered, 'Could you tell Ginny I found the missing glove?'

'OK,' said Kim. 'Who are you?'

'Good heavens, Kim, I'm Monique!' said Monique.

So Kim went off to tell Imogen – along with a warning that certain basic facts about their life had been suspended for the evening. Halfway up that ladder, Daphne had stopped dead, swinging from one muscular arm with the skill of a circus performer. 'You are sixteen, aren't you?' she said, her voice suddenly thick with anxiety. 'Please tell me I haven't got a child tugging ropes and shinning up twenty-foot ladders in contravention of every notice Ben Sacks ever posted on a wall!'

And Kim, who knew real need when she saw it, told the first serious whopper of her life, assured Daphne she was sixteen, and wondered whether that distant rumble was the prompt-side scenery dock or Peggy turning in her grave.

✳

Kim's first show at the Questors came down shortly before eleven.

She had enjoyed herself. And she was impressed. It had rapidly become clear that going live in front of an audience with forty actors, costumes, props, and an entire forest of scenery to be pushed on, pulled off and flown up and down, all with split-second timing, represented a triumph of hope over experience that even Joan would have jibbed at. Various catastrophes that threatened the evening had been reined in by the frantic resourcefulness of Daphne's crew, hurling themselves on runaway scenery or flying up ladders with gaffer tape.

By the curtain call the cast was transformed from terse and snappy animals with something psychiatric in their eyes, into human beings all laughing and floppy. Apparently it was a triumph. A famous West End critic was in the audience, and had been overheard raving about Monique and Sebastian. Kim had been shocked at how different they sounded onstage – she so full of herself, and him shorn of all his usual arrogance. '*And* he gets his comeuppance at the end,' Kim would tell Denise on the phone. 'The witches lull him into a false sense of security saying he can't be vanquished until Birnam Wood be come to Dunsinane, but the enemy soldiers camouflage themselves as trees, so he thinks the wood's moving. And soon afterwards he's a goner,' added Kim gleefully.

As the wings flickered back to life under the working lights, some man in a cravat strode past. 'Sebastian darling, what can I say, what can I *say*?'

'What's it got to do with him?' wondered Kim crossly, and made her way over to Imogen, who was scraping the inside of the glass bowl with a ladle, quietly mewing with repugnance.

19

The journey from Ealing Broadway to Ilford was not a difficult one; an underground train took her to Liverpool Street station in about forty minutes, after which she emerged via a series of escalators and stairs into the sooty echoes of the great Victorian station, and waited for a main-line train to Ilford.

Had she asked Kim, she would have known to avoid Liverpool Street altogether, stay on the underground until Stratford and simply cross over the platform for the connection. Save herself two sets of stairs. But Frances Massingham hadn't any intention of asking Kim. She hadn't even told her husband.

Wingfield Drive was nicely respectable, number 93 a two-bedroom house at the end of a terrace, with a separate garage and a garden that curved around the side. A dog was barking in it, an Irish wolfhound, scruffy and knock-kneed. Frances liked animals. She clicked open the gate, hushed the leaping dog, and rang the bell. The gate looked new, as did the paintwork. She sincerely hoped the owners weren't too new to help her.

'I apologize for disturbing you. I'm trying to trace a Mr

and Mrs Davis. They lived at this address some years ago.'

The woman at the door was in her thirties and carried a baby. 'I'm really sorry, but Mr Davis died in 1960. I know because the place stood empty for years and then went into the hands of the Treasury. That's who sold it to us. And an absolute tip it was too. Sorry,' said the woman again, 'I don't mean to be offensive.'

'That's quite all right. Do you think any of your neighbours might remember him well enough to help me? There was a wife. Her name was Margaret though she was known as Peggy.'

The woman looked across Frances Massingham's shoulder as if to reacquaint herself with the neighbourhood. 'Most of us are newish,' she said. 'Mr and Mrs McCrae are the only ones that were here in his time. They're at number 85.'

'Thank you,' said Frances.

'Sorry I couldn't be more help.'

Mrs McCrae was sorry too. 'I thought we'd finally heard the last of this mystery when the house got sold,' she said. The two women sat in her bright Formica kitchen with a pot of tea. 'When Sid died the place was crawling with lawyers and investigators trying to track Peggy down. When was the last time we saw her? Did we have any clue as to her whereabouts? It was Sid's will, you see. Obviously he didn't change it when Peggy left him, and then he goes and dies, and along come the sharks.'

'And this was 1960?'

'Or thereabouts. Peggy must have gone off three or four years earlier.'

'I'm afraid I know nothing of this,' explained Frances. 'My interest in Peggy is entirely personal. She herself died last March, and I'm trying to help out a friend.'

'So Peggy Davis is dead. I'm sorry to hear that. She was a decent soul. Not that we were ever close. She kept herself to herself.'

'What happened about the sharks, I mean the investigators?'

'Well, they never found her that I heard. There were adverts in all the papers: the locals, the nationals, everything.'

'How long did this go on?'

'Till they'd frittered away the entire estate on fees, no doubt,' said Mrs McCrae. 'By the time the legal eagles finished their fun and games the residue probably amounted to fifty quid and a bath plug.'

'I hadn't the least idea. My understanding was that Peggy left this address and moved to a block of flats, probably in 1956. But I don't have that address, and anyway I understand the flats have since been demolished.'

'She could of done, I suppose. But not here in Ilford, definitely, or somebody would have found her, there were enough looking. Anyway, I can't think of any blocks of flats being pulled down.'

Peggy's likeness lay between them on the table, a photograph of a photograph. Kim had no faith in the Miss Unsworths of this world tracing her papers, and was naturally reluctant to hand over all she had left of her mum, so Colonel Massingham arranged to have a couple of them copied. The resolution was surprisingly good. This one was mid-1950s and Peggy in her mid-forties stood by a garden fence, probably the same fence Frances had just been standing by.

Frances remembered her first sight of Kim's photograph collection, the brief sense of bewilderment, of the world shifting a click or two on its axis. I would not have called myself a prejudiced woman, thought Frances, yet unthinkingly I took the meagre facts available to me about Peggy – domestic cleaner, accent like Kim's, heart of gold – and constructed a cartoon charlady, with a weather-beaten face and round-shouldered under the wraparound pinny. I even wrinkled her stockings and knitted her a woolly cardigan, Frances taunted herself, whose own cleaner was actually twenty-five and a platinum blonde. The real charlady, photographed here full length, was a woman well turned out in the fashionable dress of the Fifties: tight jumper and A-line skirt, her waist tiny and her bust high. Peggy hadn't Frances's plump femininity, and certainly didn't share Imogen's angelic fragile beauty, but when Frances showed the photographs to George he said, 'Good Lord, she's an It Girl.' And never mind that this picture showed a woman in early middle age, the It was not doused, the face and figure, the sex appeal. Peggy Davis had been a smasher.

'She had a baby in September 1955,' continued Frances to Mrs McCrae, 'but the poor child didn't survive. Did you know of the tragedy?'

'Well, we did and we didn't. Peggy must of been six months gone before any of us guessed she was expecting, even.'

'I understand the baby was premature.'

'Was that it? Poor thing never even left the hospital, that was all we knew. She was no spring chicken. Forty-five? That's late for any woman. And very soon afterwards word got about that Peggy had upped and left him, and that was the last any of us heard of her.'

'I was wondering . . . was there ever a suggestion she had gone to Cheshire?'

'Cheshire?'

'Or anywhere in the north-west. Does that ring a bell at all? I'm sorry to press the point but it's important.'

Mrs McCrae was already shaking her head. 'We had no idea then and none now. Sid went downhill fast, that's all we knew. Drink. He was dead himself in a few years. He'd always been so particular, too, before she ditched him, the sort of husband insists his wife has a daily help so her nail varnish doesn't chip.' Mrs McCrae laughed. 'We could all do with a bit of that.'

'Might he have been a drinker before?' suggested Frances.

'I'm trying to think of why Peggy might have left him. Under normal circumstances you'd expect the death of a child might bring a couple closer together.'

'Would you?' said Mrs McCrae. 'I wouldn't. Not if one of them was more cut up than the other. Noel and me never lost one of the kids, thank God, but we did lose our little dog. I came *this* close to packing my bags. Look at me – I'm filling up just talking about it. No, I don't know anything about the Davises' marriage.'

'And when the Treasury's investigators came round, you don't recall whether any of them mentioned Cheshire? The Wirral, for example?'

Mrs McCrae said instantly, 'No, I'd've remembered the Wirral from that horrible couple in the child-murder case. Have you thought of going to Somerset House? That would tell you if she married again, and give you the address where she was living at the time. Noel always insisted Peggy must have gone off with some man. Except I think Peggy was too bloomin' sensible to make that sort of mistake twice.'

*

The same day, Kim arrived home to find that instead of the usual visitors to Mount Hill Crescent there was an unusual one – a reporter from the *Sunday Clarion*.

He had come to the door an hour ago telling Imogen he was preparing an article on the Questors, concentrating on 'those valiant workers backstage'. Sebastian would never have fallen for it, but Sebastian was somewhere in Chelsea spending Imogen's money. By the time Kim got back, the reporter had drunk perhaps fifteen cups of tea, and had a notebook chock-full with anecdotes about the Questors' production of Shakespeare's tale of murder, machination and maggots. Kim figured largely. 'Feisty teenager' was one of his many notes. By the time the feisty teenager arrived in the kitchen, the journalist was poring over her school report, to Imogen's gratification.

'So tell me,' he said as Kim slung down her school bag. 'How does it feel to find your real mum after all these years of pining?'

'Now why don't we all calm down?' suggested the reporter, sliding off Imogen's kitchen stool like a polar bear down a chute at the zoo.

'You inveigled your way into my house,' said Imogen. She was suffering one of her drenching blushes and looked about seventeen. 'We have a right to privacy.'

'Do you, love?' he responded in the same easy tone as before. 'To many people's way of thinking, you made a mint of money out of this little girl when you wrote your book, and another heap when you sold the film rights. The great British public had its appetite whetted and I'm performing a service by letting them know the story's got a happy ending. Am I right or am I right?'

'I think you're a horrid little man,' said Imogen.

'Imogen, this isn't helping,' said Kim. And to the reporter, 'All right then: you tell me what you're going to write and I'll tell you if I like it. And if I *don't* like it, I'll ring up one of your rivals and give them a better story than yours, including all kinds of made-up juicy stuff I've invented for the purpose.'

'We call that a spoiler,' said the reporter thoughtfully.

'Yeah? Imogen, it's better if you go in the garden and leave me and him to negotiate.'

20

On the Tuesday evening at six o'clock, Barry came to tea.

Imogen conscientiously welcomed any friends of Kim's, but her idea about people who attended summer fêtes was broadly based on Agatha Christie's Miss Marple. She made a pot of Earl Grey and served it with tiny cakes and a megalith of cucumber sandwiches.

She was surprised at how concerned Kim was about Imogen's own appearance.

'No, this one suits your eyes better,' Kim said of her choice of caftan. And 'Not the shells, Imogen, and not the bells either or you'll sound like a milk herd in an Alpine meadow. I'll lend you a crucifix.'

'And what are you going to wear yourself?'

'Makes no difference what *I* wear,' said Kim dismissively, which Imogen interpreted as indicating a profound lack of self-confidence, no doubt due to Kim's early discovery that her birth mother had abandoned her.

'Lack of self-confidence?' Sebastian had scoffed. 'I've never met anyone so bloody sure of herself in all my life!'

They had tea on Joan's patio, sitting on chairs of wrought iron at a wrought-iron table. Joan had lugged them through the house, scrubbed them down and repainted all the curlicues. 'And wrought the iron in her teeth probably,' added Sebastian. Behind them the house smiled comfortably, buffed and shined weekly by Mrs Harris.

'Well now, isn't this nice?' Imogen poured tea in what she believed was the vicarage-garden manner, pot held high. The golden stream hit the base of the cup, splashing like a water feature. 'I understand you're involved with Kim's church?'

'I'd prefer to call it Jesus's church,' contradicted Barry through a mouthful of fondant fancy.

'Yes, of course,' murmured Imogen.

'Will we have the pleasure of seeing your good self in our congregation one of these Sundays?'

Quickly before Imogen could say no, Kim put in, 'She is deeply spiritual.'

'I'm interested in Buddhism,' Imogen explained with a smile, 'and Scientology, and Sufism.'

'Sufism,' repeated Barry.

'The selfless experiencing and actualization of the Truth,' elucidated Imogen. 'Through love and devotion. By the spiritual path or *Tariqat*.'

'But she's been baptized and confirmed and everything,' apologized Kim. 'And you never forget, do you? Like riding a bike.'

'I was once a choirgirl here in Ealing,' Imogen told him. 'But that was all organ and old-fashioned hymns. I know you and Kim belong to the modern camp.'

'We are all one camp in the Christian church, Miss St Clair,' said Barry, reaching for another cucumber sandwich.

He wasn't behaving like the same man Kim had shared a car with that day of the fête, easily confident, comfortably bumptious. Yet he had been the same man when Kim answered the door, the same man as she led him through the house, and in fact right up until the moment he clocked the sight of Imogen, perched prettily on the pretty chair, her hair like barley sugar in the sun. At which point Barry's easy manner rolled up with a *snap!* like a spring-blind. He sat stiff at the table, his scurf glittering in a sunbeam, an arch tone to his every utterance, and on his face the lemon-sucking look of a seaside landlady confronting a resident who has failed to flush the loo.

That a man might react to the power of Imogen's beauty by loathing her for it on sight was beyond Kim's ken. Kim could only conclude it was her hippy-ness he disapproved of. Well, so did Kim. It could be overcome. In fact, it must be overcome: the more Kim learned of Barry the better he looked as a catch. Barry was a pharmacist and owned a chain of chemist shops. He had a three-bedroom house on Eaton Rise with a vegetable garden whose marrows were awarded silver medals. Imogen was asking whether as a Christian he tithed his capitalist income to the poor, and Barry was telling her he was a Christian not an idiot, and Kim, in an effort to head Imogen off before the pass, asked him what he thought of Joan's garden.

'I would say your lawn is in rather desperate need of its own spiritual path or *Tariqat*,' said Barry tartly.

Joan, true to her word, had scythed the grass leaving a tundra of brown to await the rejuvenating properties of the next downpour.

'It used to be overgrown till we got a gardener,' explained Kim. 'In the winter she's going to have it all lit up.'

'Lit up?' queried Imogen.

'That's what Joan said. I heard her telling Sebastian how grass matures quicker in the dark and then goes to seed which ruins your quality, so next winter we're having lights on all the time to slow it down. Clever, isn't it?' continued Kim. 'She said so long as we can keep the mites off we'll have the best grass this side of the San Andreas fault.'

✳

'I don't fucking believe it,' shouted Sebastian. 'At this rate we'll end up blackmailed by half bloody Ealing!'

'Of course he won't blackmail you,' returned Kim. 'Barry goes to church.'

But she was shaken. In Kim's view Barry's behaviour was a far cry from any Christianity Peggy would have recognized. Against a salvo of Imogen's desperate diversionary fire, he had shot a few fast, pertinent questions at poor Kim before turning to his hostess. Barry then delivered an extempore lecture of such contempt, of such gloating condemnation, anyone would have thought he was leaping at the chance. To Kim this was so uncharitable as to outrank in infamy the crime of having a domestic greenhouse full of mind-bending drugs.

Even through her own shock at the discovery, Kim had found it in herself to be impressed by Imogen. Imogen didn't go to pieces. Quietly interrupting a speech about the criminality of cannabis alkaloids, she said, 'I'm afraid I don't know any words that long, Barry. Only Kim does, and in her case I think you'll find you are preaching to the converted.' She put a hand on Kim's shoulder and gave it an apologetic squeeze. 'I'm truly sorry, darling. Perhaps you would show your friend to the door, and then we can have a talk.'

'I will show myself to the door,' rejoined Barry huffily, and spoiled it by falling over his own feet and one of the wrought-iron chairs. 'And mark my words, you have not heard the last of this,' he barked at Imogen as he limped off, rubbing at his leg through his twill trousers.

Now Sebastian was flopped in an armchair, one hand over his eyes in an attitude of despair Imogen recognized. From a Terence Rattigan tear-jerker in last season's productions.

'That means the bastard is bringing the police round,' declared Sebastian in the voice of doom. 'One look at that greenhouse and they'll bust us for bloody dealing.'

Kim had quickly gathered from Barry's tirade that they

must indeed be bloody dealing. It was a pound to a penny Imogen would be dragged off to Holloway prison. Looked at logically, every word of Barry's could be defended as morally right. Yet all Kim could see was his look of fixed relish, and Imogen's quiet refusal to be intimidated. And all my fault for matchmaking, thought Kim, mortified.

'Barry probably will go to the coppers,' she concurred miserably. 'He was blathering on about them. I reckon you got to get rid of the evidence sharpish. Take the greenhouse to bits even, so it'll look like he made the story up.'

Imogen had been calmly pensive. Now she spoke. 'How about,' she suggested sweetly, 'we phone Joan?'

Kim expected Sebastian to rail at this, but he didn't. He stopped throwing his arms around and looked at Imogen from the corners of his eyes. 'Joan,' he repeated.

'I bet she could dismantle an illegal greenhouse in a jiffy,' continued Imogen offhand, her gaze fixed on nothing in particular. 'In fact, I bet she can even find a use for all that glass. Isn't there a huge garden at home? Room enough for several greenhouses, she told me.'

Sebastian was quiet another moment or two, then he said, 'Joan works at Kew Gardens, right?'

'Exactly,' replied Imogen. 'No doubt her ideas about operational scale are based on the Palm House. Shall I give her a ring?'

21

Frances Massingham had never used microfiche before, and by the end of the day she hoped never to use it again. Her eyes itched and she had cramp in her hand. There was a storm coming; the air was heavy; her armpits prickled with the heat, and she was dizzy when she stood.

'I think I've finished now,' Frances told the man at the desk.

'Worth the trip?' he asked. He was smiling at her. A pretty woman, even if knocking on in years. 'Find what you were looking for, like?'

'Yes, thank you. Far more informative than the Fleet Street papers.'

'Oh well, *London!*' said the man complacently.

She thanked him again and found her way back out to the daylight. There was something about the glow of the microfiche that gave her the feeling of a submarine, or somewhere deep and dead. Perhaps that's why they call newspaper archives the morgue, she thought. But even outside the sky had a sickly tinge; clouds the colour of oily rags lay low across Bridge Street and the mock-Tudor half-timbering of the Rows. The air smelled of exhaust fumes.

Frances felt the light strike her eyeballs, and registered with dismay that the right-hand side of her visual field was splintered with ziggurats. Migraine.

This was hideous. She was a taxi-ride away from Chester station, the journey back to Euston would take four hours and the Central Line to Ealing another hour on top of that. Frances estimated that she had about twenty minutes of relative cogency before she was blind and sick. Already, the rumour of pain was beginning behind her eyes. She stepped back into the offices of the *Chester Chronicle*.

'I'm sorry to be a nuisance,' she said, through a buzz as though a wasp were caught in her inner ear. 'But could someone be kind enough to call for a taxi, and advise me of a nearby hotel?'

＊

Colonel Massingham arrived shortly after ten o'clock in the evening. The storm still hadn't broken; the sky was lugubrious, the air thick and cloying. It had been a terrible drive and his own head ached.

The reception clerk tried to insist on calling up to Frances's room, subjecting her to the screaming ring of the phone. He was certainly not willing to let the man into his wife's room with the master key.

'It's more than my job's worth,' said the clerk chirpily.

'Then please let me talk to the manager.'

'Manageress,' corrected the clerk. 'And she's going to say the same as me. How would you like it if it was you staying here, and anyone that asked could get themselves let into your bedroom? Sir,' added the clerk belatedly.

'You can see from this telegram that my wife summoned me,' persisted Colonel Massingham. 'For heaven's sake, man, she must have sent it from this very desk!'

'Not on my shift she didn't.'

'What the hell has that got to do with it?' the colonel

demanded, to which the clerk replied, 'Language like that won't get anybody anywhere, will it?'

The wire that Colonel Massingham waved at the clerk read 'GEORGE SO SORRY POLEAXED WITH MIGRAINE STOP ADDRESS BELOW STOP EXPLAIN CHESTER LATER DON'T WORRY FRANCES'.

Eventually the manageress appeared from some inner room, took one look at the elderly man trembling at the desk and led him upstairs. 'I'll cut you some sandwiches, chuck,' she said briskly, 'and bring them straight up.'

*

After fourteen hours, Frances could open her eyes.

Of course she knew that her husband had arrived the previous evening; his hushed footfall had crashed into her head and his presence, sitting on her bed all night in a well-meaning dither, vivisected the raw membranes of her skull.

He was a dear man, but the last person on earth she wanted with her at the moment. His thought processes worked in forward gear only and what she needed now was somebody who could think sideways. It had been the manageress, not Colonel Massingham, who thought to put a cold flannel on Frances's forehead; the manageress, not Colonel Massingham, who came in at dusk to drape a cloth across the bedside lamp and soften its light. When Frances sent the telegram she had considered writing DON'T COME but rejected the idea, not because it was unkind but because it would be futile.

Now, her eyes open and uncontrollably streaming, she looked at those of her husband, rheumy from sleeplessness and popping with questions, and she knew she would be unable to dissemble or divert him from the truth. Nothing was within Frances's command, not even the withholding of information; this migraine-emergent state resembled the post-operative limbo of the recovery room. Her vulnerability was limitless.

'Water,' she said, trying her voice.

As her husband helped her sit up to drink, Frances felt his waves of unasked questions batting at her touch-tender skin like the wings of some predatory bird.

'George,' she said carefully, trying to estimate what it would cost her to speak another three syllables. 'Lynne Jarman.' Then she waited with an intolerable sense of help-lessness for the time it took him to register the name and understand what his wife was talking about.

'The child in the murder case?' He put down the glass on the bedside table.

'Stolen,' said his wife, the word thudding like a mallet.

'But the Jarmans were convicted.' Colonel Massingham looked at Frances with horror. 'You think their story was true? The girl was stolen while her mother was shopping?'

'By Peggy,' whispered Frances, and closed her eyes in the worst screaming pain she had ever known.

22

A day three summers ago. Kim and Denise were ten and would soon be eleven. This particular afternoon Denise's mother was off to town, '*On my own,*' she told a neighbour emphatically. 'The girls will be out at a party. I feel like a Victorian kitchen maid given a half-day.'

But when Kim and Denise got to the party they found domestic disaster – a burst water pipe and the birthday girl weeping over a drowned tea-table.

'Never mind,' Denise told Kim with uncharacteristic stoicism. 'There's games we can play at home.' The game she had in mind was a sophisticated version of 'house'. One with real furniture, which she and Kim could carry into the garden to create the Wendy house of their dreams.

'Your mum would go spare,' said Kim as Denise surveyed the garden with the eye of an architect.

'She won't, Kim. We were talking about it. It's not like we're taking the hi-fi and the telly.'

It is difficult to say how far Denise talked herself into believing her own fantasy. Certainly it was tricky for Kim. Denise's childhood boundaries were so different from her own as to be unfathomable: Denise watched TV programmes that were banned by Peggy beyond hope of argument, chose her own clothes, was allowed to stay up late whenever they had visitors and until *midnight* on New Year's Eve, and had never been to Sunday school in her life. Perhaps she was allowed to carry the furniture into the garden.

'All right,' said Kim, 'but no bedding, or we'll never get the dirt out.'

It was a grand little house. Between the dining table (a role enacted by the kitchen table) and the settee (a role enacted by a pair of kitchen chairs draped with bath towels), Denise's mother's china shepherdesses were displayed to great effect in the grass box of the lawnmower. Two framed reproduction Picassos (blue period) hung from the backs of more kitchen chairs, which served as walls. Behind them an armchair played itself, as did Denise's mother's vanity-table, while the smallest room was provided with a cased lavatory brush and bottle of bleach as set dressing. Indoors was divided from outdoors by the (true) garden path. The front path. The girls were in the front garden, not the back – the back was too cluttered with flower beds to accommodate a second house. Denise's mother got home at six o'clock and went mad.

Her fury wasn't confined to her own child. 'I thought you at least had more sense!' she yelled at Kim. Denise was sobbing into the bath towels. 'Look at the mess you've made of the lawn – holes dug in it and all the edges broken down. When her dad gets home he'll burst a blood vessel. And the toilet brush on display for the world to see from the road, have you both lost your minds?'

Then she phoned Peggy.

'Right,' said Peggy, arriving furious and out of breath. 'I'll deal with you at home, madam.'

'It wasn't my fault, it wasn't,' quavered Kim. She was seriously frightened. Kim had never seen Peggy in any emotional state more alarming than a snapping irritation born of overwork. Peggy's grip dug into her sensitive dermatographic skin like some metallic clamp.

'Denise said it was all right. Denise said—'

'Stop shouting in the street and drawing attention.'

By the time they got home the fear of crying made Kim feel sick. Her face was swollen and the colour of raw steak. Her breathing spat and spluttered like a clogged fountain. 'YOU'RE NOT F-FAIR!' she shouted. 'IT W-W-WASN'T—'

'All this screaming is upsetting Wilbur. Is that what you want?' This was Welly's predecessor. He was backed against the fridge, shrunken and scared, tail curled tight around his rump.

'You d-don't even love me anyway,' Kim shot at Peggy, her words completely breaking up. 'I'm not y-yours. B-boy at school is adopted and the others said said said those kids are different, their m-mums never love 'em like real ones. He—'

Peggy's face was already crimson. Now even her eyes seemed to turn the colour of blood. 'Upstairs!' she shouted. 'Up to your bedroom right now and stay there till I let you out!'

'I was going anyway!'

'Don't you ever come out with that again,' roared Peggy as Kim crashed and slammed her way upstairs in a house-rattling fury. 'Love is a gift from God. It isn't to be used as a weapon, not to me or anybody else. Love is sacred. Don't you dare twist it into emotional blackmail!'

'I don't even know what that means!' Kim shouted back, her final parry. But she thought she did know. And once the door hit the frame and she was left with the silence of her bedroom ringing like a Pyrrhic victory or a bad conscience, Kim couldn't rid her head of the picture of Wilbur by the fridge, frightened and whimpering, as if he was back in his previous life, his nightmare life before the cruelty people rescued him. And all because of her fit of temper and fling-ing out those horrible words. All her fault.

*

Imogen was right about Joan assisting them in their hour of need, she was round in minutes. As was Monique. By midnight Joan was driving off in a large anonymous van, and the plot on which the St Clair greenhouse had stood for all living memory was just an oblong of concrete, dirty and dead – and strangely much, much smaller than when it was an interior floor.

Kim watched the van drive away, and the sense of relief was delicious. Joan had taken not only the dismantled wood and glass but its contents 'for discreet disposal'. Kim had expected a bonfire until Monique pointed out that lighting a reefer three foot cubed and rendering the entire downwind population of Ealing stoned for days would be a bit of a giveaway.

Kim had decided what to do next. 'I'll go round to Barry's before school tomorrow and tell him not to bother sending the rozzers round.'

'But you leave at half six,' objected Monique.

'All the better,' said Kim.

'Our garden is clean as a whistle,' she told him as he stood there cross in his pyjamas. 'I'd say come and inspect, except you were so horrid to Imogen I wouldn't let you darken our door. Oh, and I'm joining another church,' added Kim as a final punishing swipe. But at this, Barry's expression changed and he smiled.

'Then we won't be expecting you on Saturday,' he pointed out slickly, 'for the house-to-house community singing to the bedridden.' He waited for his words to sink in and pointedly shut the door.

'Blast!' muttered Kim. Frustratingly she had forgotten all about the community singing, which she loved, especially when it was a bedridden audience: they stayed put. So when Saturday arrived Kim was at such a loss that she asked Imogen if she could help backstage for the last night of the Questors' production of *Macbeth*.

'Glad to see you back again,' said Daphne, who clearly was. 'OK for under the stage? The hood is in Wardrobe.'

When it came to the banqueting scene, sitting underneath the table, Kim was able to follow some of the story being enacted beyond her tablecloth. This was glued in sections across the complicated tabletop but fell in drapes around the sides. It was behind this obscuring valance that Kim waited for Imogen to emerge and perform her sleight-of-hand swap of the festive bowl for the maggoty one. Kim wasn't alone under the table. Banquo's ghost, aka Reggie, hunkered down with her before popping out to frighten Macbeth.

Around Kim and Reggie sat the Guests; legs and boots moved and swung, accessories to their dumb-show of party chatter. Sebastian talked urgently with the First Murderer. '*Is he dispatched?*' demanded Sebastian.

'*My lord, his throat is cut,*' was the reply, at which Reggie, whose throat they were talking about, mimed a slice across the windpipe with his tongue lolling. Kim stifled a laugh and nudged him in the ribs. Reggie mimed an old ham's death.

'Pack that in,' whispered Kim. 'You'll make me crack up.'

The Guests heard; legs twitched disapprovingly.

'*Safe in a ditch he bides,*' said the First Murderer. '*With twenty trenchèd gashes on his head.*'

Reggie clasped his own and rolled over backwards.

'Stop it!' said Kim, giggling. Reggie had progressed to miming an epileptic fit. And in the hilarity Kim failed to hear Imogen tap discreetly on the trapdoor before swinging it open from below.

Kim should by now have positioned herself upstage of the trap, ready to take the bowl. She hadn't. The door swung back and slammed down, dead-legging her. She dragged in her breath like a death rattle.

Imogen was crouched on the ladder, holding aloft a bowl

heavy with glass and six pounds of maggots. 'Take it from me!'

But Kim couldn't, not without being sliced in two by the half-down trapdoor, and she couldn't wriggle away without making a surprise stage début the other side of the table-cloth. Reggie had been crawling upstage, ready to surface as the ghost. He now scrambled back to relieve Imogen.

'Where do I put it, where do I put it?' There was suddenly nowhere; in front of Reggie Imogen was jammed halfway up the trap like a stuck cork. And if he placed the bowl down behind himself he'd block his own exit.

'Kim, take it from Reggie!'

'I can't.'

Guests' legs were kicking now in a fury of disapproval. Reggie tried to swivel round. *Clunk!* A medieval boot struck the side of the glass. 'Shit shit shit,' whispered Reggie.

'Oh God, is it broken?'

'Imogen,' whispered Kim, 'go back down and I'll do the swap.'

Imogen's hunchbacked figure reluctantly subsided. Kim swung the trap shut with a noise like a gun going off. A Guest's furious boot lunged at Kim's rear.

The swap could only take place while a particular actor was leaning across the table with his all-concealing cloak. Another minute and he would move away.

'*Here had we now our country's honour roofed,*' said Sebastian, '*Were the graced person of Banquo present.*'

'Fucking hell, I'm on!' said the graced person of Banquo.

'Back up first,' hissed Kim, '*then* put the bowl down!' She was trying to undo the flap in the table, scrabbling at the catch. Released, it swung down and cracked her on the funny bone. 'Ouch!' But at least it was still dark above; at least the audience wasn't looking at a sudden hole breaking open in the Macbeths' dinner table. Kim reached both hands through, got a purchase on the festive fruit bowl, manoeuvred it through the flap; set it down; reached for the maggot bowl. It should be on the floor. It wasn't on the floor. Reggie was still holding it.

His nerves in shreds, Reggie had just made an irretrievable mistake. He had never previously seen this ghastly prop closer than the other end of the table while he was busy terrifying Macbeth. Here, with the thing clamped in his arms, he had looked down at its hideous contents. Under a token barrier of cling film, an off-white mass seethed and bubbled like malignantly infested porridge.

A sickly tinge seeped beneath Reggie's stage make-up. Kim took one look and acted. Like lightning she reached towards the lip of the glass and ripped off the cling film. Then she held the bowl steady as Reggie threw up his dinner over the churning maggots. The Guests' boots froze for a brief moment in appalled disbelief. Then they swung like wrecking balls. When Reggie finished, Kim lifted the bowl up through the flap and on to the table. She'd done it.

'*Here's a place reserved, sir,*' said a Guest.

'Where?' demanded Sebastian.

'FUCK FUCK FUCK FUCK FUCK.' Reggie, still wiping his mouth, shot out from the top end of the tablecloth.

'*What is't that moves your highness?*' said another voice.

Kim heard revulsion ripple through the auditorium.

'*Which of you has done this?*' roared Sebastian. '*Thou canst not say I did it; Never shake thy gory locks at me.*'

Lucky Reggie's locks *are* gory, thought Kim. Nobody'll notice he wiped the vomit off his mouth with his wig.

23

There was no way Kim was going home to bed while every-one else attended the end-of-show party.

'It will be at least midnight before we even get started,' Imogen warned her.

'I'm not tired, Imogen, really.'

'Ginny, Kim won't turn into a pumpkin and a handful of white mice,' pointed out Monique.

'Stop fussing and let the girl stay,' said Daphne. 'She's earned it.'

By half past one, Imogen was exhausted.

'You look like death,' Sebastian told her casually. 'Why don't you go home for some shut-eye? We've got to be back here in the morning. It's the get-out. Oh, and Imogen – for God's sake take Kim with you. She's too young for all this. It's putting the dampers on everyone's revelry.'

Which was nonsense. Kim was onstage with Reggie, dancing under swirling lights care of Gareth the lighting director. They were not alone. Wife of Macduff, who was also wife of Reggie, danced with one of the soldiers still be-twigged in his Birnam Wood costume. 'The Ballad Of John And Yoko' poured from speakers that had earlier carried the howling winds of Dunsinane. Reggie was throwing Kim around in an energetic jive and Kim, laughing above the music, was telling him jive was uncool. As Imogen approached, Reggie swung Kim over one shoulder and offered to put her in a sack.

Monique sat at the edge of the stage, cross-legged and small and neat, her glossy Afro hair subdued from the nightly oppression of her wig. Except that she was smoking a cigarette, Monique might have been a child. 'Hi, Ginny, are you off?'

'I think so. I'm bushed.'

'I'll keep an eye on Kim.'

The Beatles track finished, sliding into the Edwin Hawkins Singers' 'Oh Happy Day'.

'You can't jive to gospel!' shouted Kim.

'I'll give you gospel!'

'*Put me down.*'

'I'll keep an eye on her,' repeated Monique with a smile. 'You go on home.'

Imogen turned away. It's just that I'm tired, she told herself. A vision had flashed into her mind of Charlotte: sweetly pretty teenage Charlotte with her waist-length hair and Imogen's eyes, the Charlotte Imogen had lived with year after year, watching her grow, listening to her laugh. I wonder what music Charlotte would have liked? she had thought, the question fully formed in her mind before she could suppress it. This is nothing but tiredness, Imogen told herself, but too late; she was choked with emotion, it took hold of her by the throat and shook her. It was a while before Imogen could move away from the stage where, just feet away, a girl danced and laughed, who had no more in common with this image of Charlotte than rock 'n' roll has with Tchaikovsky. Then Imogen waved a hurried goodbye and got herself out of the theatre as fast as she could.

* * *

Shortly before 3 a.m. Kim, taking a breather, became aware that somebody had hung up a sign on the entrance to the crawlspace under the stage: MEN WORKING. Kim walked over to the top step. The lights were out but there did indeed appear to be life down there. It laughed and sighed. It said, 'God, you're beautiful,' and 'Oh Sebastian, baby,' and 'Oh darling, yes, oh *yes*!' There were two of it.

Kim recognized the simpering voice; it belonged to a winsome blonde who played the Third Witch.

'Kim, what on earth are you doing?' demanded the director, next to her on the stage. It was mostly empty now, just Reggie and his wife slow-dancing to Fleetwood Mac. 'Bloody hell, that's a knife!'

It was actually a dagger; it could even have been the dagger Macbeth had seen before him. Kim was working it into the edge of the trapdoor. Squatting on the stage, she prised until she got the trap open. Gareth's swirling lights strobed across the gaping hole and lit the couple beneath. The eyes of the Third Witch stared up, appalled.

'Wha—?'

Kim turned to the prop beside her. She ripped off the cling film. Then with both hands she turned the bowl upside down over the open trap – and *shook*. The glass discharged its unspeakable load, a great tumble of white stuff and not so white, the snow ornament from hell.

In the perfect acoustics of the Playhouse, screams flooded the air.

'Oh my God oh my God.'

'What the fuck?'

'Oh my God – *help me*!'

Kim slammed the trapdoor shut. The voices now reached the theatre from the mouth of the tunnel: hysterical.

'HELP ME, FOR GOD'S SAKE!'

'JESUS!'

Somebody had burst into tears. Then Sebastian's voice carried across from the steps.

'*WHAT THE FUCK IS GOING ON?*' he demanded in his best back-of-the-stalls delivery.

The director had got to his feet. 'I'd say Birnam Wood be come to Dunsinane,' he called back, and wandered off to get another drink.

*

'You can't tell Ginny,' said Monique. 'They both believe in free love – no person owning another person and all that jazz. Leastways, Sebastian believes in free love and he's bullied Ginny into it.'

'Free licence to get his leg over, more like it.'

'No doubt,' agreed Monique. 'But the point is, as a philosophy it *sounds* fair and just. Ginny can't kick Sebastian out of the house for screw— for making love to another woman, not without looking like a complete hypocrite. And if you tell her, the knowledge will cause her a lot of distress.'

'He's a total bastard.'

'I know, darling, I was married to him. Oh Lord, what examples we're setting you. Couples coupling in the tunnel! Corrupted while in my care.'

'No fear,' said Kim with determined revulsion, ignoring the more uncomfortable feelings always stirred by anything to do with sex. 'Being squashed flat and steamrollered. I wouldn't fancy it myself.'

'Put like that it's a wonder anybody would,' murmured Monique.

This was the get-out, and they were meant to be breaking up a stage flat.

'No, no, no,' the director had reprimanded them. 'Don't stroke it with the hammer – swing the hammer and whack it. I said whack it. Look, if you can't manage that, try laying the thing on the ground and jumping on it.

Good gracious, doesn't either of you have any killer instinct at all?'

Earlier, he had quietly commanded Kim to clear up the mess in the tunnel. 'Much as one applauds the deed, I can't order the guilty parties to do it themselves because neither has put in an appearance. And we cannot expect the rest of the team to clear up a gallon of maggots and vomit.'

And you couldn't say fairer than that, conceded Kim, descending the steps with a shovel, a can of fly spray and a bucket of sand.

It was true that neither Sebastian nor the Third Witch had turned up. Sebastian, mumbling from a pillow, had convinced Imogen that his traumatized state was food poisoning – and therefore, as it was Imogen who fed him, it was entirely her fault.

The *Sunday Clarion* had given Kim's story double-page coverage with photographs. If she was expecting *Macbeth* to feature as background atmosphere, her first glance showed this was not the case.

> So when good-hearted Peggy passed away in a freak accident, this lonely lass thought she was an orphan. Until her best mate gave her Imogen's book.
>   'Soon as I saw the photos I knew I was the spitting Imogen,' quipped the plucky carrot-top.
>   She did some detective work and was soon knocking at the door of self-confessed unmarried mum Imogen St Clair.

'Why d'you say it was me gave you the book?' complained Denise when Kim got her on the phone. 'And why did you say terrible things about the Antrobus Motel?'

'I didn't,' said Kim. 'He made it all up.'

Kim confided her ordeal in the comfy kitchen of her new mum's spacious home in the leafy suburbs. It is a far cry from the orphanage where she cried herself to sleep each night.

'I yearned for my natural kith and kin,' Kim told me sadly.

Many a girl would have given in to cruel fate, but not this feisty teeny-bopper. After days of fruitless searching, the gutsy gal finally came face to face with her dazzling young mum.

'We are more like sisters,' said Imogen, 30, hugging her long-lost lovechild.

Imogen was not much older than Kim when she fell prey to the charms of the mystery man she has always refused to name. Kim pleads, but to no avail.

'I will never know my dad,' sighed the brave chit with a tear in her eye.

But even her daughter's anguish cannot persuade the sultry redhead to break a silence of fourteen years.

'Though he did me wrong, his name will never pass my lips,' said the auburn beauty as she poured me another cuppa.

'Tell me,' said Monique to Kim, 'what on earth was he going to print if you *hadn't* cooperated?'

'He was going to say where we live,' said Kim. 'Photograph of the house with the Roller in the drive and everything. It was blackmail basically,' she concluded crossly. Then she went out to find a call box to phone Denise a second time but in private. There was something else to talk about beside Sunday newspapers.

'Kim, listen a minute,' said Denise, crisply interrupting the wandering invective about Sebastian. 'Promise me you're not going to defy Monique and tell Imogen.' Kim was silent. 'Oh no, don't!' Denise cried out, and then hushed before her parents could hear and come hurtling into the hall. 'Imogen won't like you for it, Kim, people never do. They shoot messengers, don't they?' added Denise with a vague idea there was a movie coming out.

In the continuing silence Denise could feel her friend's pigheadedness as an actual physical force, batting at Denise's sensitive ear down the phone line. 'What would you even *say*?' she demanded, exasperated.

'How about "Either he goes or I go"?'

Denise jerked the receiver away from her ear and stamped round in a circle. The sitting-room door opened. 'What's all the noise, Denise?'

'Nothing, Mum.' But for once, the parental tone was an inspiration; it brought echoes of past tantrums and words that had stung like a beating. Denise clapped the phone back to her head and whispered urgently into the mouth-piece. 'Kim, you got to listen to me, you got to. People hate that more than anything else. They call it manipulative behaviour. It makes them go totally mad and hate you.'

But a different word was already tolling in Kim's head, one that she remembered hearing earlier in a different context. 'They call it emotional blackmail,' said Kim, deadpan and deadened. 'Yeah, I know.'

24

Expats and Visitors

Mother wrote regularly, typically a page of finger-wagging reprimand elicited by my 'cussed refusal to look reality in the face'. The face in question would be sunburnt and mildly equine, and belong to the latest Nice Young Englishman rounded up by my conscientious aunt and uncle. I had been sent out to Hong Kong as part of the 'fishing fleet', to catch a husband. Five years had gone by and I was still running around uncaptured, undomesticated and dangerous. If Mother's letters to me were censorious, God knows what she put in the mail to my aunt and uncle.

They did their best. I was introduced to nice young expat Englishmen at dinner parties, cocktail parties, days at the races, the Hong Kong Club, the Jockey Club, and innumerable ceremonial events that involved brilliantly coloured Chinese lions dancing to a percussion of cymbals. But in truth I wonder if their hearts were in it. Looked at in the right light, these social gatherings could be seen as nothing more high-handed than a family introducing their niece to a circle of potential friends. I suspect a reluctance to see me married young. Married off. I suspect serious subversion.

I read just one of Mother's instruction sheets to my aunt. This was my first summer and first typhoon, and I was clearing the balcony. Her letter was on the table, soggy from the humidity.

'. . . implore you to restrict any social contact with the inferior races. Imogen has never allowed us to know who fathered that child. Naturally, one fears the worst.'

Sadly for Mother, to my aunt and uncle an inferior race was one in which your horse fell at the first in Happy Valley. We had friends at every level of Chinese society. I didn't date them because I didn't date anybody. My heart belonged to a newborn baby girl with auburn hair and clutching fingers and little punching feet. But that doesn't mean I was having a miserable time. I was having a terrific time.

The apartment was high up the Peak, with red and green views across the reservoir and South China Sea. I had a secretarial diploma under my belt, and had got a job typing for the Director of City Services. It was interesting work: hospitals, public transport, traffic, the lifeblood of that jam-packed busy beehive of a colony. I would never progress beyond being a junior but, to be fair, that was partly because I would never be able to read Cantonese. I was *not* written off as 'too undisciplined to make a career', as my mother put it. 'It isn't as if you are the sort of girl capable of supporting herself, Imogen. A good match is imperative.'

Then one evening at the Jockey Club I met somebody I knew from Holbridge Manor.

I will call her Cecily. It was July. The evening was livid and smelled of storms, the sky purple, the gardens lime green and croaking with frogs.

'Cecily, this is Imogen St Clair. Imogen, Cecily arrived yesterday by P&O . . .'

Cecily's son was born a week before Charlotte; in our last heavy days we would sit together in the grounds, sluggish and puffy, reading aloud and waiting, waiting.

When the grown-ups wafted away I let my mask drop. 'How are you really, Cecily? Have you shaken off the smell of disinfectant?'

'I beg your pardon?'

'I meant Holbridge. I sometimes think I never shall.'

Cecily rose from her chair. 'I don't know what you're talking about. If we have met before I have no recollection. I never heard of Holbridge Manor in my life. Excuse me.'

And she left me on the veranda with the rich-smelling night and the busy cicadas and the tissue of lies that supported my life in Hong Kong.

25

The woman who came to the door seemed quite friendly, and there was even a dog, but she wasn't any help.

'I think you've made a mistake. It was a Mr Davis lived here, and he died in 1960. Are you something to do with the other lady that came round asking questions?'

'What sort of lady?' said Kim.

'Enquiring after Mr Davis. I directed her to Mr and Mrs McCrae at number 85, but I don't think they'll like me sending people over practically every other day.'

'Thank you anyway,' said Denise. 'We'll try number 85.'

But Mrs McCrae confused them further. 'Well, yes, that's Sid's wife,' she said as Kim handed her the photograph. 'Look, are you sure you're not anything to do with the other lady?'

'Must of been Miss Unsworth,' said Denise. 'What do you think, Kim?'

Denise was watching Kim, watching the colour well up beneath her freckles. It was what often happened to Kim in lieu of tears.

'The name wasn't Unsworth,' said Mrs McCrae. 'Elderly lady. Nicely spoken.'

'Must of been her,' insisted Denise.

'Look, I'm not deaf, dear, and I'm not daft,' said Mrs McCrae. 'Massingham! That's the name. Mrs Frances Massingham. She lives in Ealing.'

'Kim, you got to ask her and the colonel. You've a right to.'

They hadn't stayed long in Wingfield Drive. There was nothing to stay for. The girls were now back at Ilford station awaiting trains in opposite directions, Kim's westward to Ealing, Denise's eastward to Brentwood and Crowhurst Green. Beyond the smeary windows of the waiting room a grey evening threatened rain. They were tired. This was a Monday, there had been school all day, then the slog out to Ilford, and then this shock.

Denise recognized in Kim the same look she had worn at Peggy's funeral, her face tight, shut in upon itself. Denise had hated Peggy's funeral, hated the sight of Kim hating it, standing there between Mr and Mrs Antrobus all shrunken and tortured.

'Married,' said Kim now. 'How could Mum be married and never tell me?'

'She must of had a really good reason to keep it secret.'

'Yeah, well, it's some secret now!' said Kim bitterly. 'I should never of given them Mum's address. I wonder who else knows.'

A tingling vulnerability undermined Kim's sense of order. She had an image of the adult world alight with communications to which she wasn't a party, shared confidences, recounted secrets. Peggy's secrets.

'Talk to Mrs Massingham, Kim. You've got a right.'

'They both think I'm common,' said Kim in a monotone. Then: 'Davis, right? Sidney Davis.'

'That's what Mrs McCrae said, and your mum went off a few years before he died in 1960, which fits with when she got you. So maybe this Sid didn't want a baby and she left him cos of wanting to keep you. It makes sense, Kim. She chose you cos she loved you more.'

'Yeah,' said Kim, too crestfallen to register Denise's kindness. 'Well, we're stuffed now anyway. We'll never find the couple Mum got me from.'

'You don't know where her home was in Dagenham?'

'That was years and years back. Nobody there would know who she was cleaning for when I was a baby. Anyhow, I haven't got the address.'

'We can get it though. There'll be a marriage certificate, and I bet those things say where the bride was living. We'll track down someone that knew your mum in the old days, and just keep going till we find someone that knew her in the not-so-old days.'

But Kim saw nothing ahead but obstacles, interviews that might yield nothing, rebuttals from people like the Barbers in Australia, and all kinds of officials who would be uninterested in helping because she was only a child. The whole thing seemed endlessly wearisome.

'I'll send Dad off to Somerset House,' promised Denise. 'He'll do the hard graft for us.'

When Denise's train arrived Kim waved her off, and then stayed on the same platform staring at the fuming metal of the rattling tracks, as if her own onward journey was suddenly beyond the limits of her drained energy, the whole concept of a journey having taken on a different edge now she knew Peggy had lied to her.

*

'First it's the address of an author,' grumbled Denise's father. 'Then it's maggots, and now it's marriage lines.'

'Still, looks like I was right after all,' responded his wife. 'I always did think Peggy had a husband tucked away somewhere.'

'Funny she never got hitched again.'

'Funny?'

'I mean, what with Peggy being . . . well, not in later years of course but—'

'A sex bomb?' suggested Denise's mother drily.

'Well, wouldn't you say so?'

'All I'd say is this: I don't think you should go digging up her marriage certificate. That's a can of worms. If Peggy Tanner left her husband, my guess is he was better left.'

'I haven't got the time, anyway. Those girls treat me like I'm a cross between a private detective and the *Encyclopaedia Britannica*.'

'That's called parenthood,' said his wife.

'But Kim isn't even ours.'

'Makes no difference, not with girls, they're joined at the hip. I wonder how long before Imogen St Clair begins to wonder if she wasn't better off when her baby was still a pipedream.'

Her husband laughed.

'Actually,' she continued, 'it's no laughing matter. She's spent more than thirteen years dreaming about that kid, inventing a life for it as it grows up. Once the novelty wears off, how can little Kim match up to Charlotte?'

*

Kim shut her bedroom door and talked to Peggy.

She tended to rotate the photographs, and this time chose an early one. There were only ten that pre-dated Peggy's life with Kim, all of them black and white. Peggy in various degrees of girlhood always looked as if the camera had taken her unawares in the middle of some more compelling activity, even the formal studio photograph with the stiff pot-plant and button-back chair.

In the snaps of her as a girl, glimpses of the house suggested a neatly kept working-class home, an old-fashioned back-to-back with a yard and a washing line and an alley running behind. Dagenham.

The picture Kim held between her small fingers showed Peggy aged about forty in the garden of the Wingfield Drive house. She smiled into the camera easily enough: the lady of the house, the handsome, well-dressed wife of Mr Sidney Davis.

As if to mock her, the man's very name blazed across the pale underside of Kim's arm. Abstracted, on the train home she had etched it with a hairgrip. The initial white scratches quickly died away and for a while nothing happened, but then the thin red lines brightened and sharpened, around them a bleached outline like shadows in a negative. *Davis.* It would be there until morning.

'You never actually told me you *wasn't* married,' Kim said now to Peggy's image. 'But even so, Mum. Even so.'

'Marry in haste, repent at leisure,' Peggy used to say. 'From what I've seen of the world, Kim, I'd say there was never a truer word spoken.'

'Did you ever have boyfriends, Mum? Did you have a beau?' Kim had asked, seven years old and eager for romance.

'I certainly did. And very happy I might've been had I married a certain one of them. Billy, his name was.'

'Is he the Billy that died, Mum? I never knew you and him were sweethearts.'

'The silly boy let himself be talked into joining the Communists. And where did it get him? Killed in a fist fight, that's where. I've had no time for politics ever since.'

But had they really had that conversation? wondered Kim now. Certainly there was once a Billy, and there had been a boy who met his end in some politically motivated punch-up. And Peggy as a girl had had beaux; Kim knew it from twinkle-eyed stories of dance bands in dusty halls – dances to which a teenage Peggy had slipped out of the house via an upstairs window so her father wouldn't know, and from which she had returned at dawn up a drainpipe. But was this particular dialogue a true memory? It felt more like an illustration of Peggy. Still, as such it had a poetic truth.

'You could of hid the address from me, Mum, you could of done it easy but you didn't. So it was always on the cards I might find out about Sid Davis one day.'

Therefore she might have intended to tell me one day, realized Kim. When I'd grown up. But why wait, unless the story was too horrible to—?

'Was he bad to you, Mum?' And then, 'Well, he must've been, or you'd never have left a husband you were married to in the sight of God.'

Beyond the unyielding photograph, Kim could see the Peggy she knew – tucking her hair under her hat for church on Sundays; waiting at the gates of Kim's primary school to walk her home when Kim was ten and none of her friends had their mothers walking them home as if they were babies. She could see Peggy basting the Sunday roast on the hottest weekend of the year, her forehead trickling, cross with herself, taking it out on the clangy roasting tray. She could see her in front of the TV laughing, wiping her eyes with laughter, bent double with it, creased up over a joke, a sitcom, Benny Hill, the old Ealing Comedies, Kim and Denise infected and giggling, rolling on the carpet, rolling in a heap, shrieking and aching. And at the enormity of this idea, that a man might have so badly ill-treated Peggy that she ran away, changed her name and never mentioned him for the rest of her life, a sense of intolerable injustice swept through Kim's veins like fever, a protectiveness as sharp as if Peggy had been her child instead of her mother.

'Oh Mum,' she said and felt tears prick behind her eyes.

Instantly the pain was overwhelmed by a different emotion, something primal and ineradicable. Terror. It blotted out memory, and light, and sound; the skin tautened across Kim's face; along the length of her pale arms, the white hairs bristled, caught in a vicious rustling fear.

The same thing had happened at Peggy's funeral when they sang the 23rd Psalm, 'The Lord is my shepherd', and she felt the tears welling. A sense of dread.

'I don't understand what's going on, Mum!' said Kim aloud, in a voice that sounded to her own ears like an infant's. 'I don't understand.'

26

It was not until the Saturday evening, the second day of her migraine, that Frances Massingham had allowed George to drive her home. Her skin was still raw and resented every jolt of the car, but she wanted to be home among her cool French chintzes and her own crisp linen sheets.

The journey took six hours and drained her; there was no possibility that she could undertake a discussion of the Jarman case until Sunday, and by sheer wretched luck Colonel Massingham had a long-standing and unbreakable appointment. Monday he was in court. The house felt airless, stuffy with waiting secrets.

It was now late Monday evening. The rain that had swollen the Ilford skies above Kim and Denise had blown west and now pattered on Frances's clean windows.

'Are you certain of these terrible facts?' asked her husband.

'No,' she said. 'I've no actual evidence that links Kim, Peggy Tanner and the Jarmans. It's guesswork and circumstantial things. I hope to God that when I speak them aloud the whole construction will look so insubstantial that it vanishes, like confiding a nightmare by the light of day.'

'Tell me about the circumstantial things.'

'First, the Jarman girl's name was Lynne. Peggy apparently told Kim she used to be called Linda.'

'But surely, on the contrary, that's evidence against.'

'George dear, you asked me and I'm telling you.'

'I'm sorry.'

'Secondly, Lynne Jarman was adopted, and the Jarmans had a child of their own shortly afterwards. Exactly the background story Peggy gave Kim. It really was shortly afterwards. The mother was already pregnant when they took on the new baby, and although at the trial the Jarmans swore they had known for weeks and were delighted at the prospect of two children instead of one, it patently wasn't true. Olivia Jarman wouldn't be the first woman to be five months pregnant before she recognized it, particularly if she had long ago given up hope. The prosecution argued that Olivia developed a deep resentment of the first child, the adopted baby.'

'But it isn't uncommon for adopting couples to go on to have a natural child. That could easily be coincidence.'

'It could all be coincidence, George. For example, Lynne Jarman had red hair. I remembered that. The case was one of the first things I thought of when Imogen came home from Hong Kong and we learned she had a baby girl at sixteen and gave her up for adoption. After the shock subsided, I remembered the Jarmans.'

'Good grief, did you really, Frances? It never crossed my mind.'

'It crossed mine to hope Imogen would never hear about it. Presumably she didn't, not in Hong Kong. But of course I couldn't remember exactly how old Lynne was, and I don't suppose I had ever known her precise date of birth. And I couldn't find it in the archives in Fleet Street.'

'But you've found it now? And it's the same as Kim's? As Charlotte's?'

'Yes. September the second, 1955. I got that from the *Chester Chronicle*.'

'I remember the case was tried at Chester Assizes,' said Colonel Massingham. 'Olivia and . . . William, wasn't it? William was a lawyer with a thriving practice in Liverpool.'

'But they lived the other side of the River Mersey,' Frances reminded her husband. 'The Wirral. The Jarmans preferred an address in rural Cheshire rather than industrial Lancashire. These were very status-conscious people, if you remember.'

'And is there anything to link Peggy with the north-west?'

'Nothing that I know of. I caught a train to Chester on intuition, hoping that when I searched the newspaper archives the dates wouldn't match. There is nothing else, nothing beyond the coincidence of their birthdays and the adoption, and her colouring. And the part-coincidence of their names. And the extraordinary secrecy surrounding Kim's sudden appearance in Crowhurst Green with no papers, no family and no traceable background. And round about the time of the trial. The case was heard in April and May of 1960. Lynne had disappeared in November 1959.'

'But, Frances, the dates don't fit at all. Peggy took on Kim as a baby. Lynne Jarman disappeared as a four-year-old.'

'Peggy *told* Kim she took her on as a baby. But, well, she would say that, George. If I am right, Peggy was forced to concoct an entire false history.'

Her husband was shaking his head. 'But we do know Kim was three-and-a-half when they arrived in Crowhurst Green. Which would make it spring 1959, six months before Lynne Jarman disappeared.'

'Again, we only have Kim's word for it, George. She was far too young then to verify the date now.'

'What about her photographs? Surely there are pictures of her as a baby with Peggy?'

'No. That is one of the things that has worried me all along. There's nothing whatsoever earlier than 1963 when Kim was eight, which is surely unnatural and suggests some serious degree of secrecy.'

Colonel Massingham walked to the window. Beyond it, the front garden sloped away in perfect emerald stripes of lawn. 'I'm at a loss,' he said. 'I simply haven't one earthly idea of how to proceed.'

'I know, dear. That's why I was so reluctant to tell you.'

Her husband turned back to her. 'Neither William nor Olivia is still ... I remember she was sentenced to life imprisonment but died. It was a few years ago.'

'She died in 1965 in Holloway prison.'

'So she had served five years.'

'Stubbornly maintaining her daughter had been stolen from her baby carriage outside a dress shop while she was inside complaining about a faulty zipper.'

'Oh God,' said Colonel Massingham.

'The worst of it is, George, perhaps we will never be able to set our minds at rest. I keep thinking of Mrs McCrae's accounts of those probate investigators. With all their resources they were unable to track down an address for Peggy. That tells us how desperately she did not want to be found.'

'But we can't attribute her disappearance to the Jarman case, Frances. Peggy left Wingfield Drive shortly after she lost her baby. Mrs McCrae confirmed that, and that gives us a date around September 1955. Lynne Jarman disappeared nearly four years later.'

'Oh yes, Peggy was running away from Sidney Davis. And no matter how respectable the neighbours thought him, he must have been some monster that she couldn't even face his executors; that he could still frighten his poor wife from beyond the grave. But the fact remains, if a team of investigators with police assistance failed to unearth an address for Peggy when it was still fresh, how can we do so more than ten years later?' Frances paused. 'And would we consider involving the police?'

She saw her husband recoil. After a moment he said, 'Need we involve anyone, Frances? If Peggy did live on the Wirral she must have left some record. The investigators weren't looking there, after all. We could find a trace if we searched.'

'And if we do find a trace?'

'If we do,' finished her husband, rubbing his eyes, 'then it will be one coincidence too far. William Jarman . . . I can't remember where—'

'Manchester,' replied Frances. 'Strangeways prison, July 1963. William Jarman died of a perforated stomach ulcer while serving a seven-year sentence as an accessory to murder.'

'And we're sitting here discussing the possibility that Lynne is not only alive, but that I'm her legal guardian,' said Colonel Massingham.

27

'*Peace, peace! he is not dead,*' said Mick Jagger, '*he doth not sleep, He hath awaken'd from the dream of life.*'

Denise, who had been sobbing on and off ever since Thursday when Brian Jones died, gave a yelp of delectable grief.

'Shush up, Denise, I'm trying to listen.'

''*Tis we, who lost in stormy visions, keep With phantoms an unprofitable strife.*'

'Christ, but his delivery is *terrible.*'

'Sebastian darling, please.'

Immediately around him, a rippling current of censure trembled through the multicoloured installation that was the crowd.

'I've heard better intonation from bingo callers!'

'Hey, cool it, yeah?' admonished the young man on their right. He had a guitar slung across his back. As he turned to Sebastian, its head twitched at Denise's handkerchief.

'It's like listening to Shelley regurgitated by an adenoidal barrow-boy.'

'Oy!' One of a group of greasers on their other side leaned across to him. 'You. Shut it!'

'Sebastian,' suggested Monique languidly, 'may we please spend one day in a public place without your so incensing those around us that they threaten to fell you with a left hook?'

They weren't even supposed to be here as hoi polloi, but backstage with the rest of the elite. Lenny Dunk-a-Doughnut had promised passes and let them down, so here they were with perhaps a thousand people between them and the stage, and possibly half a million around them, a vivid sprawl across Hyde Park, lapping around the trees, packed along the lake. Welly, bored and mystified, had been fast asleep for hours.

'Oh look!'

Billows of white were exploding from the stage; thousands of cabbage-white butterflies streaming upwards like tickertape catching the wind. Across the sea of people, arms waved.

'How mind-bogglingly crass,' said Sebastian.

'What's with the bad vibes, man?' demanded the guy with the guitar. 'If you don't dig the scene, keep cool while the rest of us dig it.'

'Well, *there's* an original slice of vocabulary.'

'Sebastian, you are going to get laid out,' said Imogen.

'What, by this wet jelly?'

'No, mate, *this* wet jelly.' An arm of studded leather formed itself out of the human mass, and clamped its hairy hand on Sebastian's shoulder.

'Oh super,' said Monique.

The Hell's Angel, who looked surprisingly breezy in unseasonable leather and a badge-laden hat, gave Sebastian's shoulder a casual thump like somebody setting a top spinning, and turned him round. 'I don't want to kick your teeth down your throat,' he said reasonably, 'not when we got kids looking on.'

'Please don't mind us,' said Kim.

'So I'm telling you: shut up and listen to the man on the stage.'

'Right,' said Sebastian.

'Out of respect for the dead,' he continued, his tattooed swastika twinkling in the sunshine.

By now the men on the stage were well into their first number. The Hell's Angel took himself off, and Sebastian stared unfocused into the distance with an air of intellectual derision. Unhappily for his dignity it took him a minute to notice that everybody around them had sat down.

'Imogen?' piped up Denise. 'Imogen, is it all right if I freak out please?'

'Let's both freak out,' suggested Kim, where Denise had expected her to say, 'You'll only make a spectacle of yourself.'

The Stones launched into 'Jumpin' Jack Flash'. The girls scrambled to their feet and Denise indicated a willowy young woman with a dragon painted on her cheek, who writhed and waved her arms above her head, snakelike.

'OK, I can manage that,' said Kim.

The greasers also got to their feet. In unconscious comic synchronization they put their hands on their hips; they twisted to the left and one-two, twisted to the right and one-two.

Kim shouted across to them, 'Let it all hang out!'

'Well, who'd have thought it,' said Monique.

A month ago Kim had refused to accompany everyone here to see Blind Faith. Today here she was in clothes she had spent an hour deliberating over in Granny Takes a Trip – a short white frilly dress worn over trousers; pretty much the same as Mick Jagger was wearing, in fact – and now singing along to 'Honky Tonk Women' word perfect. Earlier in the day, at the conclusion of a set by King Crimson, Kim had been leaping up and down with the frenzied spectators, shouting, 'Sock it to me, that was *outasight*!'

'She's a sweetheart,' said Imogen to Monique. She raised a long-fingered hand and affectionately rubbed Kim's calf. 'A sweetheart,' repeated Imogen.

When the day was over, everyone collected the trash; the entire crowd, as it spread and thinned, collected the trash.

'There's still stuff in this one!' announced Kim of a discarded soap-bubble can. She would blow bubbles all the way home on the Central Line. When eventually they made their way towards the gates, an arm-waving woman in the distance resolved into somebody Imogen knew from the Questors.

'Marjorie! Hello. And you, Christopher. I didn't know the Stones were your bag.'

From their dress neither would anybody else have known. In the teeth of one of the hottest days of the decade Christopher was in a shirt and tie, and Marjorie in a sweater and woollen kilt.

'Matter of fact,' said Christopher, 'we hadn't the least notion there was any sort of concert going on today. We often come up to Hyde Park of a Saturday for a stroll.'

Denise and Kim were now some distance away, chatting to a couple in matching frocks and headbands while Welly tugged at his lead.

'My daughter,' said Imogen.

'Yes, we heard,' said Marjorie. 'This is the baby you wrote about in your . . . er . . . memoirs. It must take some adjusting to.'

'You can say that again.'

'Yes, we've heard she's not exactly what one would expect.'

Imogen stopped walking. 'Not what who would expect?' The warmth had gone from her voice.

'Well, by all accounts she's a funny little thing.'

Christopher tried to clarify. 'My wife only means the girl was a bit of a shock to everyone at the theatre.'

Monique had joined them. She looked questioningly at Imogen.

'Kim has been a godsend at the theatre,' said Imogen.

'Oh certainly, certainly,' agreed Christopher. 'Quite a brainbox, I'm sure.'

A few yards ahead, Kim and Denise were doubled up with laughter at something their new companions were telling them. 'Right on!' shouted Kim. 'You must of got it then. You must of.'

'We only meant people were surprised she wasn't more *comme il faut*.'

Christopher was vigorously nodding. 'Only because the girl hasn't been used to polite society. No doubt your influence will set her straight.'

Across the grass, Kim's voice carried back to them. 'Me neither,' she was saying with loud emphasis. 'I don't dig that grot, but Denise does. Yeah, you do! You do! You're mad, you do!' The girls shoved at each other, giggling.

'Kim!' called Imogen peremptorily. 'We're ready to leave.'

Kim was still laughing. 'You're mad,' she shrieked at Denise, 'you know you are!'

'*Kim! Here!*'

Both girls stopped dead.

'We're leaving,' repeated Imogen, moving off at a pace. The girls, subdued and confused, left their friends and followed her but Imogen didn't look at them. As they all trailed away from the park, minuscule black figures swarmed across the distant stage, dismantling the day.

Imogen hardly talked all the way home. Jammed against the door in the crowded carriage she snapped at Kim to stop blowing bubbles, though their fellow passengers, all in Hyde Park clothes, were evidently enjoying it, pawing dreamily at the glistening evanescent globes as if catching butterflies. At the reprimand Kim spun round, startled as a smacked toddler. Monique didn't like this, didn't like it at all.

Evening was well advanced by the time they trudged up Eaton Rise. The air smelled of lavender and grass cuttings and the spent fuel of suburban lawnmowers. Monique could feel exhaustion dragging at her own spirits.

'I'm going to leave you now and go home,' she said. 'My poor feet are older than all of yours.'

'What, all of ours put together?' suggested Kim perkily. 'That's four times thirteen is fifty-two, plus two times thirty is one hundred and twelve plus—'

'Kim, please,' said Imogen.

'Have an early night, all of you,' advised Monique. 'You too, Mr Bigfoot,' she told Welly.

Waving her off, they reached the gate before it was clear they had a visitor. Somebody with a head of chestnut hair sat cross-legged on the tiled path. As Sebastian clicked open the gate, she jerked to her feet as though on strings. She was young and strikingly pretty with heavily lashed dark eyes in a pale face, and hair to her waist. She looked straight past Sebastian to Imogen and her eyes stretched wide and imploring.

'Oh golly!' she said and proceeded on one breath and a rising inflection. 'Now you're actually here I've no idea where to begin, my name's Sukie Sandeman and the thing is I'm adopted and my parents got me in 1955 and my baby hair was ginger like yours and I'm the daughter you gave up for adoption,' said Sukie. 'I'm Charlotte!'

At which she threw her arms round Imogen and burst into tears.

28

It got worse by the minute. Sukie's alternate sobs and laughter rang unheeding across Imogen's confused mutterings and Kim's horrified silence while Sebastian, a look in his eye that Denise registered with profound misgivings, unlocked the door and herded them all into the kitchen. After which he actually put the kettle on.

When eventually the girl told her story ('She never even asked who I was!' Kim would later complain) they learned that Sukie Sandeman lived in rural Oxfordshire – she, Mummy, Daddy and a pony named Twinkle. It was only recently that Sukie had read *Starched Linen* – under the bedclothes because Mummy was very sensitive and her feelings would be hurt. 'She and Daddy are such *fabulous* parents and it would be so *hideously* unfair if they thought I wasn't grateful and everything.' Whenever Sukie's gushing torrent glugged itself out, Sebastian threw in a helpful word, in a far friendlier tone than he had used all day.

Sukie was vague about the circumstances of her adoption; when she had tried to confirm with her parents that she did indeed come from the Holbridge Manor named in *Starched Linen*, her mother had become overtly upset.

'Which is quite telling, don't you think?' said Sukie. 'I suppose she and Daddy knew all about your book and recognized themselves from your description of Collection Day and were *deathly* scared I would put two and two together and find my natural mother, because, you see, it would break Mummy's heart.'

'Hasn't stopped you, has it?' pointed out Denise.

Her birthday was 2 September. Sukie ventured this information with a terrified expression and a trembling lip, and then instantly read in their faces that the date was Charlotte's. 'I JUST *KNEW* I HAD THE RIGHT BIRTHDAY!' shouted Sukie in ear-splitting triumph. 'I KNEW IT, I KNEW IT!'

'Sukie, I think I should explain—' began Imogen but Sebastian cut across her.

'How did you find the address?'

'I can tell you that,' said Kim. 'She got it out of an old phone book. Just like I did when I tracked Imogen down.'

Sukie turned her deep-lashed gaze on Kim. 'Oh!' she squeaked. 'Are you—? Golly. I would hardly have thought—'

'Kim found me last April,' said Imogen gently. 'So—'

'So provisionally we accepted the possibility that she might be Charlotte,' interrupted Sebastian. 'We took her under our wing primarily because Kim was orphaned and homeless.'

'I was *not* homeless, if you don't mind!'

'But she would be the first to agree her claim is based on hardly more than the date of birth.'

'Sebastian, that is misleading,' said Imogen.

Sukie's puzzled expression was still fixed on Kim. 'Did your parents adopt you from Holbridge Manor?' she asked.

'That's the sticky thing, Sukie,' answered Sebastian. It was clear to everybody that her arrival had bucked him up no end. 'Unfortunately, Kim's early history is shrouded in mystery.'

'Ooh, he's a poet and he doesn't know it,' said Denise

acidly. 'Actually, Sukie, Kim is practically Miss St Clair's daughter by law. The courts gave her to Miss St Clair's god-father who's a colonel and a magistrate.'

'Which hasn't the slightest bearing on Kim's actual parentage.'

'Sebastian, let me handle this,' Imogen cut in. 'Sukie, we're all rather tired, it's been a long day. If your mother doesn't know where you are, and I gather from what you've been telling us that she doesn't know, she must be worried.'

'Oh no, Miss St Clair. I went to the Stones' concert with my best friend Tonya, and—'

'The Stones finished hours ago,' said Denise. 'Hours and hours.'

'Yes, but I'm staying with Tonya for the night. She lives in Barnes in this *fabulous* house overlooking the common and they—'

'Then it is Tonya's parents who will be worrying,' said Imogen briskly. 'Sebastian can walk you to Ealing Broadway station. I'm sorry you're disappointed, but we've accepted that Kim is my daughter.'

At which Sukie burst into tears afresh.

'And by the time we did manage to sweep her out,' Kim told Joan bitterly the following day, 'Sebastian had got a complete set of details including her address, the address of this best friend Tonya, her phone number, Tonya's phone number and the address of her school. And her shoe size too, probably.'

'And Twinkle's shoe size, no doubt,' added Joan thoughtfully.

It was Sunday morning. Denise had tactfully disappeared indoors, leaving Kim to confide in Joan. Even through her own unhappiness Kim felt for Denise; it was like being present at a family bereavement when you hadn't brought anything black to wear. Joan was a good confidante – digging, clipping and weeding with occasional sympathetic grunts; she didn't embarrass Kim by looking her in the eye.

And if anything, she was even more scandalized than Kim and Denise. 'You say her name is *Sukie?*' Joan had demanded. 'What is she, a chihuahua?'

Kim's one comfort was the garden itself, transformed and glorious. I found Joan, I did this, she could tell herself with watertight justification. And, most importantly, Imogen loved it. Instead of the stodgy angularity of the neighbouring gardens' straight edges and uncompromising concrete paths, Joan had created an arc of stepping stones and great sweeps and curving borders from which *Alchemilla mollis* spilled over on to the lawn. There were fragrant herbaceous rockeries and borders in sweet-pea pastels – temperate, uninsistent, English.

'Won't the plants get caught up in the mower?' Kim had suggested, meaning the alchemilla.

'No need to mow right up to the edge, what?' responded Joan, sweating in her corduroys.

'Won't the borders look sort of frayed?' persisted Kim.

Peggy's idea of a garden was to plant her daffodils in rows. A little leeway was allowed when it came to the summer bedding plants, but only because the baked Essex clay had to be broken up with a hammer before there was any hole to put them in. In wet summers her geraniums would have passed a military inspection. To Kim, the idea of buying beautiful plants and then letting them overhang the lawn was analogous to having expensive rings on your fingers and biting your nails. But Imogen shared Joan's artistic vision, and that was what mattered.

As she picked distractedly at the nibbled leaves of a hosta, Joan's conversation progressed seamlessly from slugs to Sukie as though the girl were at one with her garden's slimy predators. 'I think we should expect Sukie Sandeman to make a reappearance sooner rather than later.'

'What chance have I got now?' said Kim. 'Dropping my aitches and a face like a slapped weasel. I'm stuffed.'

Joan straightened up. She dragged a crumpled

handkerchief from one of the bulging pockets of her trousers, wiped her brow with it, and shoved it back. A blot of soil on her forehead was now distributed right the way across like war paint. 'Oh, I'm sure we can find a way to spike her guns. Sukie doesn't know if she comes from Holbridge Manor at all. And I'd say she can't have done. She told you Mummy and Daddy chose her from a line-up of cots because she was so delectable? Well, that doesn't fit with what Imogen says about the system at Holbridge.'

'But it's not the system anywhere else either, Joan,' explained Kim in deep dejection. 'That's just the story parents always give adopted kids. It makes them feel special, Imogen said. Anyway, there can't have been that many homes for unmarried mothers. This was before England joined the promiscuous society.'

'Dozens!' contradicted Joan. 'Heaps of the horrid things all over the place. Look, we'll bally well have to track your own history back to Holbridge Manor. *Nil desperandum!*' proclaimed Joan, waving a garden fork. 'We'll just have to find out who Peggy got you from, and take it from there.'

29

It was not difficult for Colonel Massingham to reacquaint himself with the facts of the Jarman case; he found all he needed in back issues of *The Times*. And most of those facts were extremely odd.

That it ever came to trial at all was at face value extraordinary. William and Olivia Jarman were highly respectable, in fact they were from the same stratum of society as the judge who tried them. The prosecution's evidence was entirely circumstantial: there was no proof that serious harm had come to anyone at their hands. Nothing was certain except that their four-year-old daughter was missing. Put like that, it seemed astonishing that the police charged the parents with murder, and incomprehensible that a jury brought in a verdict of guilty.

In fact, there was legal precedent for a murder conviction in the absence of a body, but really the Jarmans convicted themselves – by lying their heads off to the police, changing their story twice under cross-examination, and coming across as deeply unpleasant people. Juries do not like hard-faced women. Mothers do not fare well when they appear dry-eyed and toffee-nosed. And, finally, critically, Lynne had been ill-treated.

The narrative begins, appropriately enough, on Friday the thirteenth. Friday 13 November 1959 was Olivia Jarman's forty-eighth birthday, and she and William threw a party, just a small gathering: Olivia's sister and her husband, and those few of their neighbours with whom the Jarmans had not fallen out. They were a very odd pair, and falling out with people was virtually a hobby.

The weather was fine, and they rounded off the evening with fireworks in the garden, standard family fireworks of the sort every household in the country had bought for Firework Night on the 5th. The guests would later give evidence that Lynne was 'unwell and lethargic' but livened up later for the fireworks, laughing and clapping.

The Jarmans' house on the Wirral, that prosperous slice of headland opposite the River Mersey, was a large detached property beside a quiet road, with a country lane winding behind. There was always a car or two in the lane en route to the country pub; there were generally one or two pedestrians strolling or exercising their dogs, the gentlemen raising their hats whenever they passed a lady.

On the Sunday after Olivia's party a retired headmaster named Nicholas Bennett, who was taking his constitutional at around three in the afternoon, heard 'whizz-bangs' coming from an upstairs window of the nearby house. The driver of a family car also witnessed the commotion, which he described as 'violently flashing sparks and high-pitched cries'. He kept going but Bennett, who was at a loose end since giving up work and was more than glad to be of assistance to somebody, turned on his heel and made it to the Jarmans' front door in three or four minutes. The house was now quiet.

It was Olivia Jarman who opened the door. She was holding a small girl. The child didn't fit Lynne's description, and the Jarmans' defence never tried to claim she was Lynne. This was the Jarmans' natural daughter, Marianne. Olivia told Bennett, 'We accidentally exploded a firework upstairs,' but she insisted nobody was hurt.

What struck Bennett was the quietness of the house: there was none of what he called 'the purposeful scurrying about and calling up and down stairs' that characterize domestic accidents. And the mother's behaviour was distinctly strange: she talked casually about exploding fireworks indoors as though she were explaining that the puddle on the front path was due to yesterday's rain. But clearly Bennett's assistance was not wanted so reluctantly he went on his way.

After dark a neighbour, calling for her cat, heard William Jarman's car screaming out of the driveway. No witnesses ever came forward who saw him between this time and his reappearance the following morning, pulling up at the house around eight o'clock just as everyone else in the road was leaving for work. Another of the Jarmans' neighbours watched him take a large suitcase out of the car and go into the house; William's appearance he described as 'dishevelled, and looking as if he'd been up all night'.

William eventually arrived at his office in Rodney Street, Liverpool, more than an hour late, something that had never happened before. He was in a clean, pressed suit, but his staff reported that his manner was distrait all day. When the secretary enquired whether he was feeling unwell, he bit her head off. The police had no difficulty extracting these potentially incriminating reports from either William's neighbour or his staff: he was a man most people disliked. So much for William.

The autumn day was crisp, clear and warm. In the middle of the morning Olivia left the house to walk to the local shops. She was pushing a double pram, one of the large, old-fashioned sort with a hood at each end and sprung like a royal carriage. Both its hoods were pulled up. Olivia's principal destination was a dress shop, where she intended to have a row about a skirt she had bought the previous season, claiming its zipper was faulty. She got there around half past eleven, and went inside leaving the pram on the pavement – and, according to her account, leaving Lynne inside it.

This in itself was neither unusual nor suspicious: no mother manoeuvred a pram or pushchair in and out of shops, it was not acceptable; unless there was actually a blizzard she left the child outside. It was the pram itself that was peculiar. Lynne was already four, and Marianne just a few months younger. Their baby carriage hadn't seen the light of day for years; Olivia always took the girls out in a double pushchair. And although an entire host of witnesses could swear to having seen Marianne variously riding and trotting by her mother's side, not one of them had seen Lynne. It was also notable that while leaving the pram outside the shop, Olivia took Marianne in with her.

At eleven forty Olivia emerged into the High Street. She sorted out her bags (the brave assistant had refused to give in about the skirt), reached for the pram and disengaged the brake. Then, according to Olivia's own account, she registered that the weight was wrong, checked the blankets and screamed the place down. Witnesses confirmed that she screamed the place down.

The police mounted a search that began with Cheshire and Liverpool, and then fanned out across the country. Every national newspaper covered it; child abductions were virtually unheard of. Because the Jarmans were comparatively wealthy, one obvious possibility was that Lynne had been kidnapped and a ransom note would follow. When it didn't, the police became interested in various discrepancies in the parents' accounts: that pram, for a start; William's night-time drive with suitcase; the odd tale of the witness Nicholas Bennett. Forensics made short shrift of confirming that the bathroom had recently been the site of some pyrotechnic spree, which scorched the ceiling and floor, the bathtub and tiles. In explaining the various oddities, the Jarmans' story changed by the hour. They were arrested, and the case was tried the following spring, April and May 1960.

The prosecution's version of events was as follows: the Jarmans perpetrated this outrage on their adopted daughter as punishment for some childish misdemeanour. However outlandish, it was consistent with previous ill-treatment. They shut her in, lit the touch-paper and retired, no doubt not intending a fatal outcome. But this time they had gone too far. That night William disposed of the terrible evidence. You can cover a great many miles if you drive all night. The following morning, Olivia acted out the pantomime with the pram.

At the heart of the Crown's case were Lynne's medical records. There had been far too many broken bones. In brief there was a history, and Lynne Jarman should have been removed from that house long ago.

She very nearly had been. Even in that reserved and reticent community, somebody made anonymous calls to the child-welfare officer. He in turn was sufficiently alarmed that he recommended Lynne be removed to a place of greater safety. The advice was overruled by his superiors. Perhaps the Jarmans spun a plausible story but the most significant factor was their social status. Everyone knew that domestic violence was a lower-class phenomenon; only blue-collar workers and the unemployed hit out at their children, usually while brawling drunkenly with their wives. The Jarmans belonged to the world of quiet wealth and clipped hedges. And William was himself a lawyer. He knew his rights. It would have taken more than the reports of one Cruelty Man to remove William Jarman's daughter from his house. According to the prosecution's account, that overruling was fatal.

But even if this was accepted, it wasn't *a priori* murder. Under English law an unlawful killing is not murder unless the Crown can prove death was intended, or at least that its probability was foreseen – malice aforethought, *mens rea*, intent. Otherwise the crime is manslaughter. Yet it was for murder that Olivia went on trial, and when it was over she was sentenced to life imprisonment and William to seven years as an accessory after the fact.

It was in the context of Lynne's history of abuse that the prosecution put its case, that to detonate an explosive device in a closed room demonstrates such reckless indifference to a child's safety that the perpetrators must have foreseen a probability of grievous harm. And that, in law, is enough. That, in law, is murder.

But only just. Although this was a capital charge, Olivia was not sent to the gallows. By 1960 the movement was gathering steam for outright abolition of the death penalty. In fact, some makeshift and ham-fisted limitations had already been brought in. These would still have allowed the judge to pronounce the death sentence, but only if he was determined. He wasn't.

So the Jarmans were imprisoned – and forgotten. There was no outcry, no petition, no journalistic books asking what really happened in the Jarman case. The public was too disgusted with the pair of them to care. Until the Jarmans came along they too had believed it was only the drunken dregs of society who deliberately hurt their children. The same photograph had been carried by one newspaper after another: the Jarmans standing before their luxurious house, their smugness as unmistakable as a sneer, William with a pipe in his smiling teeth and their natural daughter in Olivia's arms, not little Lynne, the adopted child, the alien. That said it all, decided the public.

But there remained the possibility that no matter what other lies the Jarmans had told, Olivia's story, of Lynne being stolen from outside the dress shop, was God's honest truth. And if it was true, then perhaps Lynne was not merely alive and well, but had recently turned into a teenager.

30

Joan had guessed right: Sebastian had made arrangements for Sukie to come back. The following Saturday.

Imogen lost her temper. 'You had no right!' she shouted, raving up and down the kitchen. 'I might remind you this is my house, Sebastian.'

'Do you know why you're so upset?' he challenged her. 'Because deep inside you *know* Kim's a mistake and Sukie is Charlotte.'

'Rubbish!'

But Kim, who had been halfway down the stairs when the row started and had listened to its development from the hall, felt that he had a point.

Even Monique was unable to cheer her up. 'There have been dozens of claimants,' she said. 'I sometimes think every girl-child born in Britain in 1955 has turned up in Mount Hill Crescent at some stage. Until you came along, Ginny never accepted anyone for more than a day or so.'

'But most of them got the birthday wrong,' Kim reminded her glumly. 'And Sebastian wasn't rooting for them, I bet.'

Monique cupped her hands around Kim's face and tilted

it towards her. 'You've got me rooting for you,' she said. 'Sit tight.'

But Sebastian's campaigning took a disturbing turn. He stopped shouting and bullying. He started to work on Imogen with quiet reasonableness.

'Listen to me,' he said, his voice soft, beautifully modulated, an actor's calculated tone of persuasion. Even his timing was good. Imogen had just left her typewriter, having manoeuvred Amelia into a Punjabi wedding ceremony engulfed in gaiety and flowers, actually *enjoying herself* for once. It was a major breakthrough.

'I admit I'm partisan,' began Sebastian. 'I've never taken to Kim so I can't help but welcome Sukie. *Mea culpa*, Imogen. But it's not my feelings that matter here, only the truth. If you refuse even to countenance Sukie's claim, you do injustice to the very essence of your love for Charlotte. And Sukie's *is* a weighty claim, darling. She has Charlotte's birthday and Charlotte's looks.'

'But not Douglas's dermatographia.'

Now Sebastian's voice dropped, low and thrilling. 'Are you easy in your mind about that? Your baby really had skin you could write on? So how come you never left marks when you stroked her little face, squeezed her tiny fingers, tickled the soles of her baby feet? That precious atom in your arms, Imogen, wouldn't you have noticed marks of trauma?'

'Perhaps I didn't try scratching her, Sebastian.'

'Imogen, if there's a mere scintilla of a possibility that Sukie is your daughter, don't you owe it to Charlotte to judge the facts on their merit? That sweet vulnerable little baby you last saw being swept away by strangers when she wasn't even weaned?'

'You carry on with your soliloquy,' said Imogen, 'I have tea to prepare for my unwanted guest.' And she was past him and out of the room before Sebastian was able to evaluate how much of this was bravado and how far he'd rattled her. But he knew damn well he had.

Sukie wasn't returning here unarmed, she was bringing my-best-friend-Tonya. So Kim brought Denise. It was like seconds at a duel. But Denise couldn't wriggle away from her parents before the evening so Monique took Kim into the West End to spend the day with her at Shash Books.

'It'll act as a counter-irritant,' said Monique.

The shop was double-fronted with recessed doorways and old-fashioned windows, the watery imperfections of its thick old glass reflecting the street in great moving swirls of colour: the tomato-red buses and Mini Coopers in yellow and lime green; the purples, marigolds, saffrons and magentas, Indian-bazaar colours of the new youth.

Shash was located just off St Martin's Lane. It had moved there in 1967, taking over the property from a theatrical costumier whose closing-down sale clothed half of Swinging London in the summer of love.

Monique encouraged the costumier's ghosts to haunt the place. In the midst of the books making up the window display were a tailor's dummy and medieval pointy-toed boots in primary colours. The ceiling of the ground floor was painted with figures from the stage: gentlemen in doublet and hose flanked by bespangled showgirls and Arthurian damsels, a vast and impossible chorus line. It was one of the shibboleths of the counterculture to understand this connection: one did not enquire why a bookshop would display pantomime boots in its window any more than one asked whether the 'hash' in Shash was intended. Which of course it was.

The premises were long and deep, with a rather grand spiral staircase of white cast iron leading to an upper storey, and echoey concrete steps leading down to the enormous basement. The steps reminded Kim of her earliest memories, Peggy's Ilford flat with its resonant canyon of a stairwell. All three floors of Shash were walled with books, their massed spines like several thousand brushstrokes of colour.

Kim liked the smell of books, and in Shash this mingled

with coffee; customers from the café next door would wander in, mug in hand. And cigarette in the other hand, most of them: the first thing Kim did was to check the position of the fire extinguishers.

'I'll help at the cash register if you show me how,' she suggested, looking at an old-fashioned silver till that crouched on the counter. So Monique introduced her to a young woman called Sagittarius Sal, dressed entirely in black including her lipstick, whose job it was to ring up the purchases. When Sal drifted away for some unfathomable monotone of a reason, Kim took over. The first altercation began within minutes.

'You've short-changed me.'

'I haven't,' said Kim.

'I gave you two pound notes.' He was holding out a hand in which the copper coins of his change glinted dully under the strip lighting. 'Do I have to call the manager?'

'If you want,' said Kim agreeably. 'Then we can all have a chat about that copy of *Rolling Stone* you stuffed in your carrier when you thought nobody was looking. I've took the price of it out of your change.'

Kim was amazed to discover that the phone rang all day long. She answered it herself just the once, to be involved in an angry and mutually baffling exchange about *Fuck You* magazine. But the majority of callers were nothing to do with the book trade: people phoned Shash to ask advice about drug problems or police busts or unwanted pregnancies; they phoned Shash for directions to Glastonbury or to ask where they could get their poetry published. They phoned Shash to ask whether the shop was expecting a visit from Paul McCartney during the coming week and if so, please could someone take down the following number and give them a call the minute he appeared? None of this shocked Kim as much as the handwritten notice glued to the counter beside the phone: **NEVER FORGET THIS LINE IS TAPPED.**

'You think we're paranoid?' said Monique. 'Sweetheart, one Saturday I got Sebastian to phone this number with details of a completely fictitious demo in Soho Square. Within an hour you couldn't see the square for police horses. Take it from me, we're tapped.'

Among the wall ads was a sheet of instructions: WHAT TO DO WHEN YOU'RE BUSTED. This finished with advice ringed in red:

DO NOT LAUGH AT THE POLICE.
NOTHING MAKES THEM MADDER THAN
OUR REFUSAL TO TAKE THEM SERIOUSLY.

Sagittarius Sal scoffed at Kim's disbelief. 'I suppose you still call them bobbies and ask them the time?'

'If you kept your eyes open instead of coming it with funny quips,' retorted Kim, 'you might notice the bloke in the green suit just slipped two books under his jacket. Hey, you! Yes, you, the leprechaun with the ponytail.'

In the middle of the morning, the manager of the café next door came in to round up some of his missing coffee cups. 'Shash and me have got this symbiotic relationship,' he said. 'My customers come in 'ere with the mugs they nicked from me, and Monique's customers come in my caff with the books they nicked from her. Between us we're stocking the kitchens and bookshelves of half the bleedin' underground.'

'I know how you could stop customers pinching your china,' said Kim.

'Attach 'em to the table with chains?'

'The mugs or the customers?' put in Monique.

'No, I mean it,' said Kim. 'You just make the china unusable outside your café. Get your mugs specially manufactured cone-shaped. Then you put holes in all your tables for the cones to sit in. You can still have a handle and they'd hold coffee just like normal ones. But they won't be any use when some sticky-fingered klepto takes them home.'

Sal hooted. 'Unfortunately the cost of producing that little lot would exceed the profits of his café for the year!'

But the manager was looking hard at Kim. 'I don't think we've been properly introduced,' he said, extending a hand. 'I'm John McKinley, generally known as Jack the Mack. Who are you? And however much Shash are paying you I'll treble it.'

The day picked up after that. Kim's vigilance managed to reduce the deluge of casual pocketing to a trickle of resolute theft.

'What I'll do next time,' she told Monique, 'I'll bring Welly along and stand in the exit. That'll scare the buggers.'

When Kim got home in the evening Denise hadn't yet arrived. Imogen had cut a vast, tottering pyramid of sandwiches and was now juggling with a plate of shop-bought confectionery. A teacake with a cherry in the middle like a nipple slipped off the edge to splodge on the floor.

'I didn't invite Sukie, Kim,' she said. 'And I've been trying to un-invite her. Sebastian refuses to give me her phone number or address.'

'I know, Imogen.'

'I love you.'

'I love you, too. Imogen, you're covering me with icing sugar.'

'You need sweetening up.'

'Five boxes of cakes. Is Sukie's best friend a gannet?'

'It wouldn't surprise me.' Imogen was distractedly buttering both sides of the sandwich bread. In fact they were rather low on supplies, Mrs Harris having thrown out Imogen's rancid margarine and two lightly poisonous loaves. 'I can't even remember the wretched girl's name. Tango? Tin-tin? Tonto? Damn!' added Imogen, slicing off the end of a white-painted fingernail.

When Tonya and Sukie turned up on the dot of six thirty, Kim's immediate thought was that Tonya was exactly what every pretty girl needed to have in tow. She was bespectacled, befreckled and beefy. She rolled up the front path with a sailor's gait, one plump hand clamped possessively around the slender arm of Sukie Sandeman. Her thirteen-year-old face wore the expression of a night-club bouncer on the lookout for riffraff not on the invite list.

When Imogen opened the door Sukie was already effervescing like a sherbet fountain. 'This is my best friend Tonya Shilling. She's been mind-blowingly supportive and encouraging through all this,' babbled Sukie, as one acknowledging the help of loved ones during major surgery.

'Yes. Well, come in . . .'

Imogen's voiced trickled away across Sukie's groundswell, and Sebastian appeared from another room 'showing all his teeth like a Labour councillor up for re-election', as Kim would tell Denise. He ushered Sukie and Tonya outside, where he proceeded to show them round Joan's garden with the proprietorial air of a Capability Brown. Sukie's voice soared insistent and shrill, like the peacocks in Holland Park.

'Oh *look!*' she exclaimed over a bed of common pansies. 'Don't you just adore their smiley faces? Our garden is *brimming* with flowers. Daddy is a wiz with chemicals. He says it's his ambition to completely eradicate insect life across the whole of Oxfordshire. Do you spray yours?'

'Those are snapdragons,' said Kim crossly. 'Spray them for what, lockjaw?'

With an air of rescuing Kim, Imogen turned to Tonya. 'Do you have a garden?'

'Yes but it's not as nice as Sukie's,' replied Tonya flatly.

'Well, perhaps yours has merits of its own.'

'Not as many as Sukie's,' said Tonya.

'Shilling is a nice name,' persevered Imogen. 'Is Tonya short for Antonia?'

'No. Short for Toinette,' expanded Tonya, cornered. 'It's only a nickname.'

The doorbell chimed. Denise. 'I'll get it,' said Kim and Imogen together, and together ran back to the house.

On the thyme-fragrant patio, they sat around the same wrought-iron table at which the ghastly Barry had brusquely derailed the teatime pleasantries just three weeks ago. Now it felt like months. Imogen produced the fairy cakes, Sukie reacting as if they were the fabled first banana after the war, and Tonya tucking in with a zeal not otherwise evident in her temperament. Sebastian watched over the proceedings with a massive air of patrician expansiveness.

Welly lay across the stones. Sukie, inevitably squealing, had asked if he was a pedigree, to which Kim, without batting an eyelid, replied that Welly was a rare long-haired Antarctic Eskimo dog, bred for rounding up penguins.

'You have a birthday soon, then, Sukie,' said Sebastian with bright artificiality.

'So has Kim,' said Imogen and Denise in unison. Imogen turned to the taciturn Tonya. 'When's yours?'

'February,' said Tonya in a voice gluey with marzipan.

'Aquarius?'

'Tonya's on the cusp,' said Sukie.

'So was Hitler,' said Denise.

Kim hiccuped a fine spray of cake crumbs.

Sukie asked of the assembled company, 'Don't you find astrology is simply marvellous for helping us understand our place in the universe?'

'No,' said Kim.

'Absolutely,' said Imogen at the same time.

They sat a moment in a silence reigned over by Sebastian's knowing smile.

There was no doubt about it, Sukie was a very pretty girl.

She shared with Imogen qualities that were as foreign to Kim as if they actually belonged to a separate race: Sukie nibbled her lip in the same way and twiddled her long hair just as Imogen did; even that breathy, little girl's voice was Imogen's with seventeen years surgically removed. As the evening proceeded in a clunky sequence of stops and starts, Kim could no longer understand how she had ever believed she belonged here among the plummy accents and hippie ideals, the natural offspring of a woman whose looks turned people's heads when she crossed Ealing Broadway.

Sukie's eyes hadn't left Imogen's face since they all sat down at the table. Their expression said, Now it all makes sense, now I know who I am. But who am *I*? cried Kim in silence, that most devastating of human questions, the subject of Greek tragedy, Oedipus's terrible question. Who am I?

As Sukie watched Imogen, Tonya watched Kim, in fact so hard she stared her out of countenance. She's thinking the same as me, Kim told herself, that someone like me can't possibly be the child of someone like Imogen.

'We met at Guide camp, actually,' Sukie was saying of Tonya, in the shy tone of a bride recalling the moment she was introduced to the groom. 'I was supposed to be cooking but I've always been *hopeless* at it and suddenly all the sausages exploded and I sort of jumped and the trivet collapsed and Mrs Heddingly-Jones was yelling at me, and suddenly there was Tonya being just wonderful, trying to beat out the flames and telling Mrs Heddingly-Jones the inferno was her fault for building a campfire too close to the communal tent in the first place. Are you in the Guides?' she asked Kim.

'Was,' said Kim shortly.

Imogen explained. 'When she moved here to live with me, Kim sacrificed a number of things from her old life.'

'But only temporarily because of the distance,' put in

Denise. 'Kim's going to be a Queen's Guide. She's so good at it.'

As Denise continued her damning recital of Kim's competence in all the areas where Imogen and Sukie shared an ineptitude that bordered on the life-threatening, the last of Kim's hope dribbled away. Beneath the tearless surface of her apparent equilibrium heaved a swollen sea of grief.

Kim heard Sebastian chat to Sukie, friendly and insinuating; she watched Imogen, luminous and increasingly troubled, trying to curb Sebastian with pretty frowns and the hand gestures of a gentle Buddha. Kim had a vision of her own career as a Brownie and Girl Guide, a long-winding sequence clicking through her life like the shifting patterns of a kaleidoscope: Peggy checking Kim's needle-work when she sewed the first badge on her Brownie uniform; Peggy at the ceremony when Kim the tenderfoot jumped the Toadstool; Peggy helping her pack her duffel bag for camp the summer when it poured for three days and they were flooded out and Peggy had to ask a neighbour to run up there in the car and bring her home.

The drive back was awful, the neighbour grumpy and driving too fast, Kim silent in her steaming uniform and sodden shoes. When their car pulled up outside Peggy was at the window, one arm fidgeting at the net curtains. Then the lace fluttered back and the front door opened.

'Good Lord, girl, I thought you'd drowned!' she said, and squeezed the bedraggled Kim against the soft eiderdown comfort of her ample bosom.

I want to go home, thought Kim now, impossibly. I want my mum.

And then Tonya suddenly spoke up, hooting across her fuddled misery like a foghorn. 'People think adopted children aren't allowed to trace their real mother,' she announced, 'but it isn't true, it's the other way round. The children can apply to the courts as soon as they turn eighteen, they have the right to apply for permission to see their adoption file. The courts nearly always say no to protect the secrecy but I bet they won't this time, not now Sukie and Imogen have found each other already and it's not secret any more. I bet Sukie only has to wait and she'll have the papers to say she was born Charlotte St Clair. Won't that be nice?'

31

Colonel Massingham accepted a cup of tea from Mrs Antrobus and hoped the wobbling sofa would survive the additional weight of the china cup.

'I'll leave you both to it,' said Mrs Antrobus. 'Shout if you need anything.' And she melted distractedly back to a distant kitchen and the twin-tub washing machine.

Colonel Massingham addressed her husband guiltily. 'When I said this was urgent I would have waited for the weekend, you know. Please tell me you haven't taken a day off work.'

'My employers are used to it,' replied Mr Antrobus, which they were. He was an intelligent man, an accountant who might have made chief accountant one day had it not been for these requests for mornings off, plus all the emergencies his employers were resigned to, for which he would go speeding home to arrive shortly after the police or ambulance or fleet of fire engines. 'And from your voice I judged that the problem needed immediate attention,' he added.

'The problem is a dashed nuisance,' responded Colonel Massingham. He sipped the scalding tea. Around him the house complacently hummed with the activities of the distant kitchen. This was the Motel's only sitting room, but like the many bunk-bedrooms and the garden with its goat, it was designed around children. The books on the shelves, the board games and boxes of toys, even the creaking utilitarian furniture, were at odds with the two huge men who sat there now, Mr Antrobus with his shiny bald head and indefatigable smile, and Colonel Massingham with his 1920s moustache and air of ingrained anxiety.

'I'd say Kim landed on her feet,' said Mr Antrobus. 'She writes to us, you know, most weekends, like a dutiful child away at boarding school. It's rather touching.'

She had also paid them a visit, a month ago. Outside with Welly and the goat, Kim had described the garden in Mount Hill Crescent. Ostensibly the principal character in this monologue was somebody named Joan, but Imogen's name was all over it like daisies in a meadow. '... and Imogen won't even let her poison the snails in case hedge-hogs eat them and die and Imogen can't bear the idea of innocent creatures suffering and every time next door's cat gets a mouse we bury it quick before she sees and gets upset cos Imogen's so sensitive and she ...'

Colonel Massingham said, 'I have to confess Frances and I have not succeeded in breaking through Kim's reserve. No doubt we appear as old fogies, but even allowing for that, Frances, rather bluntly, says she has a chip on her shoulder.'

Mr Antrobus smiled. 'Your lady wife is probably right. Kim has always been uneasy outside her familiar environment, and she's a little inclined to suspect people of looking down on her. I don't think you should worry about it, Massingham. She is obviously happy with Miss St Clair. Her letters read as if she were talking about a kid sister.'

'I'm afraid there's a lot of us who treat my goddaughter that way. Frances regularly ticks me off about it. But it isn't Kim I want to talk to you about, it's Peggy Tanner,' he said. 'I need your opinion.'

When Patricia Kim's birth certificate (and death certificate) had eventually arrived, Colonel Massingham phoned the Antrobus Motel to let them know the baby was not Kim after all, but he hadn't recounted the facts about Peggy's marriage and the death of her daughter. He did now. 'I take it this is news to you.'

'Yes. Peggy was never the sort of woman to confide in her neighbours. But I'm not astonished to hear her history included a tragic marriage. Peggy would dust herself down, pick herself up and start all over again. Besides, it helps explain why she was on her own. I don't know if you're aware of this, but Peggy Tanner was an attractive woman. Not to put too fine a point on it, there were husbands in Crowhurst Green making fools of themselves from the day she moved here.'

'I rather guessed, yes.'

'But there's more, isn't there? You haven't come all the way here to tell me about Peggy's marriage.'

'There is indeed something more. My wife and I are struggling to eliminate one dreadful possibility that would explain Kim's appearance out of nowhere.' And he told him about the Jarmans. 'You see our dilemma,' concluded Colonel Massingham. 'This is based on nothing except a handful of facts that might be coincidence.'

'You are hoping I have some information to indicate where Peggy was living at the time of little Lynne Jarman's disappearance. I haven't, I'm afraid. If she ever mentioned Cheshire I don't recall it. But if your worst assumptions are correct, she would have taken care to hide the fact.'

'That is true.'

'But perhaps what you are really asking is whether the Peggy Tanner I knew was capable of stealing another couple's child, and holding on to her while an innocent woman stood trial on a capital charge.'

'I suppose that is what I'm asking,' said Colonel Massingham. 'How ghastly it sounds.'

'She was absolutely trustworthy. It is inconceivable that Peggy would allow harm to come to anyone who was innocent.'

'Forgive me, Antrobus, but that remark has the feel of an evasion.'

'Yes. You're familiar with the medical evidence, of course. Lynne was in hospital purportedly after a bad fall down the stairs, which was grossly suspicious. On another occasion the child was taken to the Casualty department with a fractured arm, then a week later this had to be reset after some apparent further accident in which the arm was twisted behind the child's back in its plaster cast.'

'You remember these details.'

'Am I right in believing you were never involved with the Children's Court? We have seen so many of them, my wife and I, victims of neglect or brutish maltreatment. Very often there is a docility about them. While healthy children play and shout and cry and fight, they will sit where you put them, silent and hunched. At the Jarmans' trial the child welfare officer, the Cruelty Man as we call him around here, said Lynne was sitting in a corner like something that had been left out for collection. After the trial he was the subject of wide public sympathy, while his superiors who ignored the warnings fared very badly at the hands of the press.'

'I remember now.'

'Treatment such as Lynne Jarman endured certainly can prove fatal,' continued Mr Antrobus. 'Anyone who saw how Olivia was treating her adopted daughter might have been tempted to act. Peggy always maintained she lived her life in Essex. We have no idea whether she ever set eyes on Lynne Jarman. But if she did, I would bet a lot of money it was Peggy who made those calls to the Cruelty Man. And when they failed, I would trust her to get the child out of that house.'

'Should I pursue this at all?' asked Colonel Massingham, unhappily. 'I have nightmares about the yellow press. You know they ran a nauseating article recently about Kim? Imagine them getting hold of this. The Jarmans are dead. Even if they were innocent strictly speaking, they were still monsters. Is there a moral imperative to clear their names posthumously?'

'Unfortunately it is never only the dead. There are always family and friends whose lives are contaminated. If the Jarmans didn't murder Lynne there are people who deserve to know.'

In the kitchen, Mrs Antrobus hauled washing from the tub with steaming tongs. The smell of hot wet laundry was everywhere. She started the tumble drier and the house juddered. This upset the goat and its angry complaints set off somebody's dog. The air was full of animal noises and agitation.

'So I must take my conjectures to the police,' said Colonel Massingham. 'I won't be welcomed with open arms,' he added with sudden realization.

'No.'

'I fear that the connection between Lynne Jarman and Kim simply can't be established and we will live with this dreadful possibility always.'

'Surely if the two girls are one and the same it can be verified in a trice,' said Mr Antrobus. 'From the medical records.'

'We keep coming back to those medical records. Doesn't it seem astonishing that the Jarmans could talk their way out of it with the Social Services?'

'I have known other cases,' said Mr Antrobus. 'And they came close to talking their way out of it at the trial. The jury took three days to bring in their verdict. It must have been touch and go.'

'Forgive me,' said Colonel Massingham, 'but I am astounded that you should remember quite so much detail of a case that's nine years old.'

'I haven't been entirely straight with you. I didn't

remember them. After Kim came to us I looked them up.'

Colonel Massingham stared at him. 'Are you telling me you had the same suspicions as Frances? Good God. And I didn't. Have I been immensely dense?'

'Not at all. It seems that each of us recognized a different detail, and it is only when they come together that the case is substantial. For example, I had no idea Lynne Jarman's birthday was the same as Kim's. But there are three things you couldn't possibly know, Massingham. First, the story Peggy gave Kim doesn't add up. Of course, until she died we all believed Kim was Peggy's natural daughter, so there was nothing to question. Not until Kim dropped her bombshell. According to Kim, Peggy's secret arrangement with the adoptive parents succeeded because the couple immediately moved away – and so did she. Peggy moved to a block of flats, where they stayed until coming to Crowhurst Green when Kim was three. But my wife and I remember Peggy and Kim arriving. It was June 1960, no doubt about it. Which means Kim wasn't three, she was four and three quarters, and it was seven months after Lynne Jarman disappeared.'

'And the trial was over by then,' added Colonel Massingham, 'so the Jarmans were no longer on the front page of every newspaper.'

'Of course, that could just be Kim misremembering. But has she ever talked to you about the block of flats?'

'Only that they're her earliest memory. A galley kitchen and a view across rooftops.'

'Quite. Kim paints a picture of one of those pre-war mansion blocks, you know the sort of thing, pokey apartments giving on to an enormous communal stairwell. But I'm familiar with Ilford, and there has certainly never been anything like that there. London's East End, yes, but not Ilford.'

'And not the Wirral either, of course,' said Colonel Massingham thoughtfully. 'But the port of Liverpool must be full of them.'

'Quite,' said Mr Antrobus again.

'That makes two things. You said there were three.'

'The first visit Kim made to Miss St Clair – when she came home I heard a word I had only met once before in my life. The Jarmans' defence counsel argued that Lynne's skin trauma, documented by the Cruelty Man, was nothing to do with ill-treatment but resulted from a congenital condition. The medical men have a Greek name for it – dermatographia. It stuck in my memory. I am sorry, Massingham,' he said. 'That day when you phoned to say Miss Unsworth had established that Kim was Peggy's daughter after all, I was relieved.'

32

Kim was dreaming. She dreamed she was flying off a wall.

Her dream was in colour, a warm jade canvas in which Kim was flapping her arms because they were wings and she was a bird. The sky was iridescent; she soared into it, free, streaming upwards to its glassy floors. Of course! thought Kim, you only have to find the floors in the sky, and glide.

She was skating across the marble flooring of a magnificent hall of cumulus, a cloudscape with great whipped, vanilla-flavoured towers reflecting the sun. And she wasn't alone. The birds flew in pairs – because they were lovebirds. Hand in hand with her bird-partner, Kim's contentment was euphoric. Like that Damascene revelation of how to fly, she suddenly understood the key to absolute happiness. It was here, here with her soulmate, the light of her little life. This bliss was like coming home at last. But then Kim saw her partner's face. Tonya's. The lovebirds were Tonya and Sukie.

Kim crashed to earth, flat out and broken, her wings concrete heavy, concrete grey. She needed to run but her stone limbs dragged her down. She jerked and jolted, frantic and whimpering. Eyes watched, furious, incensed by her uselessness, her sickliness, her pathos. And now she wasn't flailing on the ground but in the sea. Wet and loathsome.

Kim thrashed at the pillow and woke with a shout. Welly groaned and shifted. Then Kim knew why she was wet. The bedding was soaked. With a sense of unutterable shame she understood that she had wet the bed.

*

Monique sat in the airless outer office. The carpet was electric and crackled. As each slow minute passed, the hands of the clock juddered and wobbled on a strange, numberless clock face that was part of the panelled wood of the wall. It seemed to Monique that even the wood sweated.

She had been here an hour, her confidence wilting with her Afro perm. The uncomfortable chair was plastic and looked glutinous; when she moved it became all too evident that she was stuck to the seat. With one eye on the secretary at the desk, Monique peeled a bare thigh away from the plastic. It made a noise like ripping tape but the secretary didn't pause at her clacking typewriter. She had the air of a woman who could work undisturbed by the sound of flesh being flayed. She had the air of a woman who could work undisturbed in a sealed tank.

As Monique reached towards her bag for a cigarette, an intercom machine on the desk gave a painful buzz.

'Mr Rowe will see you now, Miss Shashkova,' said the secretary.

Monique re-stowed her cigarette and made her way across the fizzing carpet.

'Monique!' said Mr Rowe. 'How the hell are you? It must be, what, ten years? More? Take a seat.'

'More,' said Monique. 'You've done well. Company director.'

'Amazing what a hefty mortgage and a third child can do for a man's ambitions. No more travelling round in rep and paying for two lots of rent, me in smelly digs and the family renting two rooms while they waited for me. You've travelled a bit yourself – I understand you're responsible for supplying London's intelligentsia with most of its reading matter. Didn't I also hear that you married?'

'This isn't about me, Douglas. Probably you don't read the Sunday scandal-sheets.'

'I read that one. Could hardly miss it, could I? There was Imogen's name splashed across the front page.'

'Yes, it was pretty grim. But at least that means I don't have to fill you in on the background. You know that a girl called Kim Tanner appeared at Ginny's door a few months ago and it looks very much as if she is her baby. But of course we can't be certain. Which is why I'm here. I've come to ask you a favour, Douglas. I want you to give a blood sample.'

'Monique—'

'It's simple and painless. And it's our only possible hope of determining whether—'

'Please stop,' said Douglas.

'I think you're a louse if you don't,' finished Monique with spirit.

'You think I'm a louse anyway, you always did.'

Which was true enough. Monique could see Imogen at fifteen, breathily nervous, smiling in admiration at something he'd said. Monique had wanted to throw herself bodily between Imogen and the danger like a hero on a grenade.

'Look,' Douglas was saying, 'I'm sorry about what happened with Imogen, I've been sorry for more than fourteen years. But to publish that bloody book and make the whole story public property—'

'I hardly think that's fair! Ginny didn't write one word that could lead anyone to you.'

'It made my position damned uncomfortable, Monique.'

'Really? How too awful for you.'

There was the silence of impasse. Then Monique said, 'I'm not going to get dragged into a messy argument about the past. I'm convinced Kim is Imogen's daughter and yours. She looks like you both, and has your skin and so on. And she's very likeable. Lovable. But now another girl has turned up and it's pulling the rug from under her. All I want is for you to have a blood test. We'll be entirely discreet.'

'No.'

'But *why*? Ginny has never made any demands for all these years—'

'And she isn't making any now, as far as I can see. If everyone's so positive about Kim, why is the newcomer a problem?'

'It's making waves. The girl is middle class and ravishingly pretty, and in her own scatterbrained way she has the sticking power of a limpet.'

'What you mean is that Imogen's taken a fancy to her. This is not my problem. I can't even see why it's yours.'

'Don't you feel the slightest responsibility, Douglas? You got an underage girl pregnant and she behaved with such fantastic integrity that she wouldn't even name you to the registrar.'

'Oh leave off, Monique. If it hadn't been me it would have been someone else.'

Monique had been reaching for another cigarette. She froze. 'What?' she said.

'Look, I've got teenage daughters of my own. Decent girls. And it's a sight more difficult to be decent nowadays given all this free love and love-ins and dolly birds with hemlines up to their knickers. If my girls behaved the way Imogen did, their mother and I would chuck them out of the house.'

Monique sat motionless, her cigarette packet in one hand with its top flipped back like a gun at half-cock.

'The birth certificate doesn't name the father,' concluded Douglas. 'And as far as I'm concerned, that is how it stays.'

'Good God, you are a bastard.'

'So you said at the time. At least we are both consistent.'

'Douglas, one thing please. Your arms. Kim is double-jointed in her right but not her left. Are you?'

'No, Monique, I'm not. And now, if you don't mind, I want to wind up the day. Our youngest just finished her exams, and we're celebrating. The Compleat Angler at Marlow. Do you know it? A real beauty spot. No need to close the door behind you as you leave, I could do with the air.'

33

The following weekend, Denise had to tell Kim they would be doing their own research at the Public Record Office. Her father could not be persuaded to take a day off work and go to Somerset House for them; there were limits, he said.

'It's OK,' was Kim's response. She was beyond expecting any good luck.

They were indoors because there was a crowd outdoors, not Sukie and Tonya for once, only the counterculture, sitting on the lawn ranting about Vietnam and getting between Joan and some serious hoeing. Denise had stood to attention goggle-eyed as Imogen introduced Lenny's entourage, which today comprised a smart-suited gallery owner, an artist named Miss Muffet in floor-length flowery satin and an eye patch, and three saffron-robed monks.

'I like that underground poet,' said Denise to Kim, pronouncing the words with a degree of awe. ('Imogen has friends in the underground scene,' she said at least once a day at home.) Denise had learned the hard way that most of those friends thought villages were all pitchforks and pig manure, but on the contrary this poet had rested a hand on her shoulder and said, 'I'm so grateful to you country people for looking after the sheep and cows, otherwise they'd clog up the traffic in Chelsea,' which Denise intended to quote all week.

'How about him as a husband for Imogen?' she now said.

'You mean Lenny Monkey-Nuts?' said Kim. 'Useless.'

'Lenny what?'

'They've all got barmy names. If somebody isn't called Mercedes Benz they're called Hoot or Zoot.'

Yesterday in Shash Monique had introduced her to Peter Brown, actually right-hand man to the Beatles, but Kim assumed that with a name like that he must be some dowdy relative up from the sticks.

As long as the hordes were outdoors Kim was happier indoors, and Denise could work her way through Sebastian's record collection.

'Help yourself,' he told her graciously because Imogen was looking and his stock with Imogen was low. 'What's your bag?'

'West Coast,' replied Denise promptly. 'The Doors, the Airplane, not so crazy about the Grateful Dead.'

'The Dead are better live.'

'Right on.'

'What's your mood?'

'Mellow. Where can I find Love?'

'Between Led Zeppelin and Mahler.'

'I dig it.'

So the girls were now sitting on beanbags with Love's *Forever Changes* on the turntable and an attractive scattering of albums around them on the carpet. But nothing could thaw Kim's ice-bound unhappiness.

It was to get worse. Once the crowd left, Kim found herself in an unsatisfactory conversation with Imogen. About Sukie, of course.

'You can't help wanting to see her,' said Kim. 'Sukie's got more chance of being Charlotte than I have.'

Imogen reached out a hand to stroke Kim's hair. 'And who says I want to see her? This is you speaking. I never said it.'

'You're only human, Imogen.'

'Nonsense. Wonderwoman, me.' But she couldn't make Kim smile. Imogen knew about jealousy, and you can't make it smile. 'Sukie isn't coming back. I told Sebastian that if that girl and her sullen, podgy little friend turn up at my house again I won't let them in. I give you my word.'

Kim knew this already, as did Denise. And the neighbours too probably: the row had smashed through the quiet of the small hours. 'But, Imogen, that's worse for me,' she began. Brought up by Peggy, Kim had had no practice in mining her emotions and analysing them. If Sukie was banished from Mount Hill Crescent Kim would feel worse, not better, but she struggled to explain it. 'Either Sukie is Charlotte or she isn't,' said Kim. 'It's not like it will go away. You'll find out the truth from the courts. You know what Tonya told us.'

'That's years away,' said Imogen.

'Exactly. So . . . so it's like when the baddie is offstage in the wings,' said Kim, inspired. 'The demon king. He's much more scary when you can't see him.'

And Kim truly was unnerved, as if there were literally a baddie in the wings. She had not suffered a repeat of that nightmare with its horrifying corollary ('Kim, you don't have to do your own washing,' Imogen had said innocently, coming on Kim huddled over a spin cycle at breakfast) but most nights brought the tattered rag of a half-dream, rank with the odours of some formless peril. She dreamed of being shouted at, a furious female voice slapping at her like a bully with a wet towel.

She was derailed by everyday trivialities. Yesterday it was the radio, and a breathy-voiced Marianne Faithfull, all feminine vulnerability. It was as if the appearance of Sukie and Tonya had muddled up Kim's head and made her into a nonsense – knocked the breath from her skull, the hearing from her eyes, the eyesight from her finger ends. It must mean I'm terrified of Sukie taking my place, decided the rational Kim. And Mum always said fears are worse when you don't face up to them.

Imogen considered the girl sitting across the patio table, her hair on fire in the sun, hair which might, despite Sukie, be Imogen's, and her jaw stubbornly set, a jaw that might, despite Sukie, be Douglas's jaw. I never really knew Douglas, thought Imogen for the very first time. Not well enough to judge, at this distance, whether Kim really is like him. And Sukie is too wretchedly pretty and appealing for anybody to judge whether she is really like me. The un-certainty subverted Imogen's every waking moment: it was like vertigo.

I was only eighteen months older than Kim when I fell in love with him, Imogen thought. But how significant they are, those eighteen months. Kim's age is a quaking hinter-land, shifting and unstable as the breaking voice of an adolescent boy.

'Imogen, I'll get even more upset if you lock her out,' insisted Kim.

Could that be true? wondered Imogen. Should I take Kim at her word? Certainly she deserved to be believed. Yet how dreadful, how unfeeling, to be taken at one's word.

Kim resorted to the safety of a Peggy-ism. 'Absence will only make the heart grow fonder,' she said. 'Let Sukie and Tonya keep coming round. I give it a month before they drive you so far up the wall you chuck them out voluntarily for the sake of staying sane. Like I said, Imogen, you're only human.'

34

Chief Superintendent Collier considered the file in front of him, and with a thick, spatulate finger turned over a page. He had not been chief super ten years ago. The Massinghams' suggestion that the force had made a terrible mistake was irritating but it didn't have the power to incense him. It wasn't he who had sent the Jarmans down for murder.

'Here it is,' he said. 'Dermatographia. The family doctor was a witness for the prosecution, not the defence. Dermatographia wasn't a diagnosis of his, he just gave the term to Olivia Jarman when *she* told *him* Lynne's skin was prone to welts. Justice Wetherby referred to it in his summing up. I have it here. "As for the suggestion that Lynne's welts, as witnessed by the Child Welfare Officer, were in fact due to an unusual skin condition, we have only her parents' word for this, unconfirmed by any of the various clinicians who attended the child." Personally I've no doubt the girl's skin showed welts. Her mother had hit her.'

'Yes, I've read the summing up,' said Colonel Massingham. 'Nevertheless, it is a most uncommon word.

Surely the very fact that the term was mentioned is rather too coincidental—'

'In cases of assault, it's not unheard of for the defence to claim the victim's marks were due to some innate skin problem.'

'How about photographs? Does Kim look like Lynne?'

'Unfortunately, the Jarmans didn't go in much for photographing Lynne. There's nothing later than baby pictures, and they're not close-ups. Our experts say the evidence is insufficient for a comparison but in my experience that is hedge-betting expert-speak for "No, they are not the same girl." '

Frances said soothingly, 'Mr Collier, please understand we will be delighted if you can dismiss our fears. The last thing in the world we want is to hear that Kim is really Lynne Jarman.'

'That makes three of us, Mrs Massingham. But let me move on. The dental records don't help either because there's not enough to go on, but the medical records are a different kettle of fish. They were part of the prosecution evidence, including Lynne's X-ray films and her records from the family practice. We've also got hold of Kim Tanner's. There is nothing that dovetails. One of my men even had a discreet word with the Tanners' doctor in Crowhurst Green, who all but laughed in his face. Said Kim never suffered an injury in her life, and the idea that she arrived there traumatized by cruelty was the silliest thing he'd ever heard. *And* he's a Cheshire man himself, born in Stockport. Said he would certainly have recognized the accent. Kim was broad cockney.'

'That doesn't help us, you know,' argued Frances. 'Kim didn't arrive in Crowhurst Green until nearly seven months after Lynne disappeared. That's more than enough time for a four-year-old to pick up Peggy's accent. And the only way the Tanners' doctor could be certain Kim never sustained any injuries would be if he had her X-rayed – which he didn't, because Kim never sustained any injuries.'

'Mrs Massingham, with respect, I'm a policeman. I can only deal in facts. I can't speculate on the possible significance of evidence that doesn't exist.'

'The chief superintendent is right, my dear. We can't interpret a negative as though it supported the opposite argument.'

'But if we're talking about speculation, wasn't the entire case a matter of speculation? Mr Collier, doesn't it worry you that ten years have passed yet the body has never come to light?'

'Mrs Massingham, whether it worries me is immaterial. The Crown Prosecution Service could have decided the case shouldn't go to trial in the absence of a body. They didn't. The jury could have concluded that in the absence of a body there was reasonable doubt. They didn't either. The evidence was enough to convince a jury of the Jarmans' peers, and the judge who could have directed them to acquit but didn't, and the Home Secretary who turned down the Jarmans' appeal.'

'Nevertheless, their story *could* be the truth. It *could*.'

'Again with respect, Mrs Massingham, no it could not. That rocket, for a start. The Jarmans came up with six different explanations. Six. Eventually they said in court that Lynne herself got it out of the firework box, took the thing upstairs and lit it. How? The Jarmans' party guests saw William return the unused fireworks to a cupboard above the kitchen cabinets; they remembered asking if it was safe and William said he wanted them to last until Christmas and the garage was too damp. Besides, that cupboard is where the scene-of-crime officers found the box. We know Lynne was under the weather. She could not possibly have climbed up there, even if she'd been a climbing sort of child, which she wasn't. It didn't happen, Mrs Massingham.

'Then comes that famous baby carriage. Mrs unearths a pram that hasn't seen the light of day for years and takes it out with both hoods up. First she tells the police the pushchair was broken, which it wasn't, then that she'd lent it to a neighbour, which she hadn't, and finally that the pram ride was Lynne's own idea, for a treat. Meaning what – the kiddie wanted to bounce along in it? We're talking about a four-year-old, remember. We have witnesses who saw this expedition, both in the Jarmans' own road and also the High Street. And the only child they saw was the sister. The reason for that pram was to hide the fact there was one child instead of two.

'And then the dress-shop farce. We have witnesses who saw the pram. We have a witness who saw the sister. What we don't have are witnesses who saw Lynne. At all, let alone being abducted. So we're talking about a four-year-old being hauled away by a stranger in a busy high street without creating the slightest disturbance. Then William swears blind he hadn't left the house all night and the neighbours that saw him in the car were lying out of spite, because of a dispute about garden fences. Mrs Massingham, I've been in the force twenty-seven years and I've heard some codswallop if you'll pardon my French, and the Jarmans' stories are right up there to win the pom-pom. Take my word for it, that poor little lass will turn up one dark day – she'll turn up in the woods or on the heath or even, heaven forbid, on Saddleworth Moor. And when she does, every copper in the north-west will be at her funeral.'

With the mention of Saddleworth Moor, Frances's previous assertion rang in her ears, that the last thing in the world they wanted was to hear that Lynne was still alive and well. She felt ashamed and rather sick.

'And I take it you had no joy placing Peggy Tanner in the area,' suggested Colonel Massingham.

'You take it correctly, Colonel. At the time, Olivia Jarman's daily help was a Mrs Amy Mortimer of 14 Linley

Gardens, Birkenhead. She was actually in the house cleaning while Olivia was making that journey to the shops. Amy wasn't called to give evidence at the trial but the police interviewed her – at home with her husband and teenage son. She wasn't your Peggy Tanner in disguise.'

'Do we know how long she had worked for Olivia Jarman?'

'Long enough for the Jarmans to be paying the veterinary bills for the Mortimers' dog.'

'Dog?'

'Believe it or not, it's here in the interview notes. "I won't hear a word against Mr and Mrs Jarman. Last week our Labrador got hit by a car and they've been good enough to shell out for his operation."'

'Good Lord.'

'Even Hitler liked dogs, if I remember correctly. Mrs Massingham, I agree it's a peculiar story, Kim Tanner's. If you find out where she was prior to turning up in an Essex village in June 1960 I'd be interested to know. But she wasn't living on the Wirral under the name of Lynne Jarman.'

35

On the subject of the moon landing they were split, the counterculture. Monique, for example, could give anyone half an hour on the immorality of squandering billions of dollars on a status race against the Soviets while half the world was starving. Even one of the broadsheet newspapers carried a cartoon of skeletal children beside a mud hut saying they hoped the astronauts would find the moon was made of green cheese after all, and bring some home to eat. But mostly people thought it was absolutely bloody marvellous.

The moon landing also triggered bizarre domestic arguments. Families fell out over what went on round the back of the moon, was the dark side really dark, and what was the difference between a new moon and no moon and a lunar eclipse. They fell out over gravity, moon boots and weightlessness; and whether some putative monster moon-mobile, running into you full pelt, would hurt as much as it would have done on earth.

In Mount Hill Crescent, an over-excited Denise nearly fell out with Kim, who was wearily trying to explain, to a household that generally held to a belief in the age of Aquarius, that the female menstrual cycle was *not* related to the cycle of the moon. This was a lot of Earth-mother mythological tosh. For a start, the cycle of the moon was not 28 days; it wasn't even 29½ days; it was approaching 30. And most importantly, the cycle of the moon was predictable to the nearest split second, in flagrant contrast to that notorious wandering star the menstrual cycle, whose average length varied between 25 and 33 days from one woman to the next. The much-quoted 28 days was a convenient estimate based on averaging cycles across several thousand woman-years, in a goodish number of which it was erratic, unreliable and guaranteed to let you down. At which Sebastian said the thought of several thousand woman-years made his stomach queasy, and he would prefer to get through Sunday lunch without menstruation *if* Kim didn't mind.

Imogen set aside her deep qualms and gave Kim the benefit of the doubt, so on Sunday they were joined once more by Sukie, and therefore by Tonya. Sukie's illustrious school was already out for the summer, and although Tonya's wasn't she was Sukie's alibi. The Sandemans believed their daughter was spending the historic weekend in Barnes: a fictional visit to the London Planetarium had been cited for good measure. And so here they all were, all staying over because Imogen was the only grown-up who would raise no objection to the girls' being up most of the night. Not to mention the colour TV.

Monique breezed in mid-evening.

'Monique, I thought you said the moon mission was a disgrace!'

'It's appalling. But it won't become less appalling by my ignoring it. Oh hello, Sukie, Tonya. It's a full house again then?'

And getting fuller by the hour. Gareth from the Questors was the next to turn up and ask if he could kip down on the sofa. 'My telly's on the blink,' he told them. 'What time are things hotting up?'

It was now half past eight in the evening; the landing was due around nine o'clock, and the actual walk not until about three in the morning. They were in for a long night.

Inevitably, Sukie made it longer. Her father worked for the BBC, so they were all used to 'Daddy knows him *ever* so well and says he's absolutely *super!*' Tonight the house was half expecting Daddy to know Neil Armstrong, but instead Sukie babbled about a forthcoming children's series featuring long-nosed animals that lived on the moon and conversed in squeals like a Swannee whistle. 'They're *pink*,' said Sukie delightedly, 'and they're *knitted*.' And Gareth, who maintained that the entire Apollo programme was an elaborate conspiratorial hoax, suggested the astronauts were probably using the same studio, and to look out for pink knitted whistling animals edging into view every time Neil Armstrong's camera wobbled.

It was a lovely evening. Irrationally leaving both TV sets on indoors 'just in case', the party took Imogen's transistor radio outside and sat on Joan's patio listening to the BBC. Through the crackling static and ear-piercing bleeps, the hissing and chugging and one-note hum, came various voices, all of them cheerful and all of them male, and some of them apparently talking inside a bread bin.

Joan herself was uncharacteristically dawdling over her newly created shrubbery. 'Might have to work late into the night,' she told them. 'Get this alchemilla back out before it seeds and takes over the bally garden. It's a pretty little thing in June and a pest by August.'

'OK, Joan,' said Monique. 'Ginny will let you stay over and watch the moon landing in colour.'

'Righty-ho,' said Joan, instantly putting down her shovel. 'I'll pack up.'

She collected her tools, tidied up, housed the wheel-barrow, pulled off her gloves, changed from boots to shoes and disappeared indoors, to make for the front door, her car and her overnight bag.

There was nobody about in Mount Hill Crescent when Joan stepped out on to the front path in the warm mothy evening. The bluish flicker of TV sets was visible through uncurtained windows. The rising moon was half full, or half closed, like a frozen winking eye. Joan tugged a couple of weeds from the delicate tiling of the path. Straightening up, she heard a mechanical swish, a likeable and friendly sound, the sound of a bicycle. Then the scuff of feet, followed by the tick-tick-tick of the bike being walked towards the gate. By a helmeted policeman.

'Good evening, miss,' he said, politely touching his helmet. 'Do I have the right house for Kim Tanner, daughter of a Miss Peggy Tanner of Crowhurst Green, Essex, also known as Mrs Sidney Davis?'

*

Colonel Massingham was out of his house and across Ealing to Imogen's at a speed unusual in a man of retirement age.

'I would hardly call this a job for the uniform branch,' he said.

'Oh, we do get roped in sometimes, sir, when it's a sensitive matter. Between you and I,' added the officer with a confidential air, 'I think the boys down the station are tuned in to the wireless for this moon landing.'

So, probably, was Frances. A meeting of the local Women's Institute had been due to finish three quarters of an hour ago. Presumably they wouldn't drag themselves away from the news coverage until the *Eagle* had landed.

'There isn't a soul about, sir,' said the officer contentedly. 'Just my luck to be on the beat tonight. Though I don't suppose I'll be bothered much by way of crime.'

'Good,' said Colonel Massingham. 'I'm a magistrate, you know.'

'Yes, I did know, sir. I was just wondering,' continued the

officer, 'while you're perusing the letter, would it be possible to just . . . I heard your wireless as I came in. It should be coming along a treat by now,' he added, as though the Apollo moon mission were a Victoria sponge.

'Of course,' said Imogen, jumping up. 'Everyone is out on the patio. Please be my guest.'

'That's very accommodating of you, madam.' And he was already in the hall, his heavy tread retreating towards the rear of the house.

The letter in Kim's hand was from somebody called the Treasury Solicitor. Colonel Massingham had explained that this was the person who took over an estate when the beneficiary of a will could not be found.

> It has been brought to my attention that Mrs
> Davis, who reverted to her maiden name of
> Tanner, is herself recently deceased, leaving her
> estate to Miss Kim Tanner. If Miss Tanner pres-
> ents herself to these offices with proof as to her
> identity she will learn something to her advantage.

'Kim my dear, I'm so sorry,' said Colonel Massingham. 'The fact is, Frances and I knew Peggy had been married, and we chose not to tell you.'

'It's all right,' said Kim. 'I went to Wingfield Drive myself. I talked to the same neighbour as Mrs Massingham did.'

Imogen was looking from one to the other. 'Have I got this right?' she said. 'Both of you, independently, without telling me . . . ? Kim had every right, I can see that. But you, Uncle George?'

'It seemed to Frances and me . . . it seemed the right thing to do at the time.'

'Then you were wrong,' said Imogen simply. 'May I ask if we're any nearer to solving the mystery of Kim's background?'

'We only know Mum was married,' said Kim guiltily. 'To the bloke in the letter.'

Colonel Massingham added, 'Who presumably didn't change his will when Kim's, er . . . Peggy, when she . . .'

'When she left him,' completed Kim.

'Yes, and therefore Peggy remained his beneficiary. And when she died you, Kim, were Peggy's beneficiary, so it passed to you.'

'Do we know what became of Peggy's marriage?' asked Imogen.

'No,' said Kim.

'No,' said Colonel Massingham.

'But I've seen the house where they lived,' said Kim, still not able to look Imogen in the eye. 'The woman that's there now said it was a right old tip when she moved in, so I don't expect it was worth much. I don't expect there's a lot of money due.'

Certainly not enough to justify missing the moon landing. From the back of the house came ragged applause and a lot of whooping. Kim could hear Welly joining in, no doubt while whirring round in circles as if to drill a hole in the patio stones.

'Anyway, when you inherit houses you pay tax, don't you? *And* I bet they get their money twice, once for Mum and again for me.'

'Indeed,' said the colonel. 'Two lots of inheritance tax.'

'Tell me, Uncle George,' said Imogen with an edge to her voice, 'have we an explanation for how the Treasury Solicitor managed to know all this? How he knows about Peggy's marriage, her alias, her relationship to Kim, and the address where Kim could be found now? Because as I see it, there is only one possibility: someone in authority dropped that particular combination of facts into the waters like a message in a bottle to see where it washed up. Someone whose authority is so high that he has contacts even in the

Treasury. So who? And who provided those facts in the first place?'

Colonel Massingham had little experience of lying. He ran a hand across his hair in a gesture that dated from the days when he had enough hair to justify it.

But Kim was already answering the question. 'I suppose those neighbours in Wingfield Drive got in touch after we'd all been round, and then he linked it up with the piece about me in the *Sunday Clarion*,' she said with a shrug. To Kim, it was just typical grown-up behaviour: i.e., all-powerful. The Treasury Solicitor had conjured a rope by which she was lashed to Peggy and Peggy to Sid Davis, and simply reeled her in on it.

Imogen, however, was looking hard at her godfather. 'I'm to accept that explanation, am I?' she asked icily.

'Oh, my dear,' he said and passed a hand over his eyes.

Kim was having a more practical thought. 'The bit about proof of identity,' she said. 'Does that mean they need my birth certificate?'

'No, no,' Colonel Massingham assured her. 'You are already accepted as Peggy's beneficiary.'

Across his mind ran words as black as oil: I'm sorry, Kim, but Peggy not only made a bad marriage, she also had a baby who died, a baby girl with your name. And the Treasury Solicitor knows all those facts because Frances and I have indeed been talking to somebody in authority. We've been trying to convince a chief superintendent of police that your beloved Peggy was a child-snatcher.

36

Kim knew it would be difficult waking Denise, but she also knew that if she failed Denise would refuse to speak to her for days.

She herself hadn't slept. She never did with Denise here, for fear of a recurrence of that unmentionable accident. Kim would doze fitfully, and wake whenever she was sinking into dreams. At half past two she got up, turned on the TV and settled in front of it, ready to hoik Denise from under the blankets once the spacemen stopped nattering to Houston and got on with the job.

From the kitchen, Kim could hear the muffled shuffling and sharp clangs of someone half asleep trying to make coffee. She slipped quietly out of the door and down the stairs, to get to the kitchen herself before you couldn't move for the lolloping Welly and a galumphing Tonya.

In the bedroom next door, Tonya herself was going through similarly frustrating emotions about Sukie. Past experiences of trying to wake her were not happy. There had been an elaborately planned midnight feast for which she had been unable to get Sukie out of bed and over which Sukie had sulked very prettily for days, her eyes haunted by hurt bafflement. Now, calmly, Tonya considered her practical options.

Her uncle was a doctor; from him she knew about techniques to test the responses of an unconscious patient, which basically were procedures so painful only the brain-dead could withstand them without flinching. Some were not applicable to a sleeping Sukie: grabbing a testicle and wrenching, for example. However, Tonya remembered another one where you draw a metal object sharply across the very base of the thumb nail, and then dodge out of the way in case the patient sits up and punches your lights out. Nevertheless, she was disinclined to use it on Sukie without a rehearsal. Earlier, Tonya had been down to the kitchen and made two cups of tea. Now, she heard Kim softly closing her own bedroom door. Tonya waited for Kim's slippered feet to descend to the hall. Then she picked up Sukie's cup and took it in to Denise. In her other hand was a fish knife.

Downstairs, Imogen, in a trailing dressing gown that had once been Guinevere's cloak in the West End production of *Camelot*, perched on the edge of the table and watched Joan preparing breakfast. It had started the other way round. Joan watched Imogen preparing breakfast for about three minutes before wresting it from her. Now Joan slapped butter across sliced white bread and layered it with bacon rashers.

'Dead pig between slices of spun tissue,' said Imogen over her bowl of muesli. She kept forgetting there was a cupboardful and buying more, so Mrs Harris lined up all the packets in date order.

'Might do you some good,' suggested Joan. 'Put colour in your cheeks. Anything happening yet?' she hollered in the direction of the hall.

'BBC bloke said they might be another hour,' Gareth called back.

'Typical!' tutted Joan, who held to the view that if you wanted a job done properly you got a woman on to it, not a couple of overgrown schoolboys on the jolly of a lifetime. 'Any ketchup in the house?' asked Joan, ransacking a cupboard.

'*Wha'?*' Denise snapped upright in bed like a marionette. '*What is it, what is it?*'

'Only me,' said Tonya. 'I've brought you a cup of tea. The astronauts will be off on their moonwalk soon.'

Woozily, Denise struggled up in bed.

'Sugar?' said Tonya.

'Nice bloke, Gareth,' Joan was saying to Imogen as she shook the sauce bottle. Then, hardly lowering her voice, she added, 'Queer, of course. Had a humdinger of a bust-up with his other half last week. Did you know?'

'No,' said Imogen, surprised. 'I wonder why he didn't tell me.'

'Ah well, you're his ideal, aren't you,' pointed out Joan without resentment. 'Your sort always attracts his sort. Look at Judy Garland's funeral,' she continued with mystifying logic. 'And speaking of pretty faces and cry-babies, I can't say I'm much taken with that Sukie.'

'She's Sebastian's protégée rather than mine,' said Imogen.

'Protégée?'

'I think he's grooming her as a potential actress,' invented Imogen tactfully. Imogen wouldn't discuss Kim's business, not even with Joan.

'Sebastian's grooming her all right,' said Joan shortly. 'To usurp Kim as Charlotte. You should put your foot down. Tell the simpering little miss she's not welcome here any more, let alone that Tonya, mooching about like a hippo with a hangover.'

'Joan, I would have done exactly that but Kim wouldn't countenance it. It's Kim who insists they stay. That is the truth.'

'But something's happened this weekend. I'm not talking about that peculiar letter from the bally Treasury, Lord help us, I mean your attitude to the whole box of tricks. I've been watching you. You've changed your mind and decided Sukie is Charlotte after all. And I think it's rotten of you,' continued Joan. 'There we are, I've said it. Straight from the shoulder. Kim's had a rum deal losing Peggy, she's a good kid, and she deserves better than you're giving her.'

Imogen had finished her muesli. She carried the bowl to the sink and made a meal out of rinsing it. Then she set it on the draining board and turned to Joan. 'You're right,' she said. 'And I hate myself.'

'Well, a fat lot of use that is!' responded Joan. 'You know the right thing to do: boot them out.'

'And suppose Sukie *is* Charlotte?' said Imogen. 'Suppose the simpering little miss, as you call her, is in fact my flesh and blood, the baby I held in my arms when my heart was breaking? My daughter. My child.'

'A month ago you were convinced Kim was! What's this latest one got that Kim hasn't, apart from a dolly face and a voice like a squealing piglet?'

'She has provenance,' said Imogen. 'To my woe, Joan. Believe me, I didn't take on Kim carelessly, I wouldn't hurt her for the world. But I was wrong.'

'What do you mean, provenance?'

'I'm trying to tell you. Tonya might not say much but when she does it's to the point. She did some detective work and yesterday she told me the results.'

'Detective work?' repeated Joan with disgust.

'Look, you have to understand that Tonya doesn't merely adore Sukie, to Tonya Sukie is life lived vicariously. You know what she's like; people don't take to her very easily. Tonya has a serious stake in Sukie being Charlotte and the subject of a bestselling book.'

'So? So?'

'So she chatted to Mr and Mrs Sandeman, scrutinized

the family photo album and so on. And last night she had a quiet word with me. The facts fit, Joan, and they're facts I didn't put into *Starched Linen*.'

'What sort of facts, for heaven's sake?'

'Devastating ones. Starting with detailed descriptions of the parents.'

'You only saw them for a matter of seconds, in a state of emotional chaos.'

'The father was ginger. So is Sukie's.'

'Well, one of the two had to be, Imogen, because Sukie herself was ginger as a baby. You said yourself most parents refuse point blank to take on a red-headed child because they can never pretend it's their own, so the agencies always offload them on to—'

'And they drove away in a black Wolseley car. I didn't imagine that, and I didn't put it in the book. Tonya says there are photos of a Sandeman picnic with Sukie as a babe in arms and the car in the background.'

'Tonya says. I bet you mentioned the Wolseley to other gals at the mother-and-baby home, and I bet word got round when you published the book. It all sounds deuced fishy,' continued Joan. 'All this secrecy. Mummy and Daddy would be heartbroken if they knew their little girl was looking for her other mummy. Perfect set-up if you ask me. Sukie and Tonya get insider information and cook up the whole show between them, with an eye on the fame. Or even the money – you're a rich woman, Imogen. And no way you can check out a word of it.'

'I thought of that. But there's something I never told a soul, not the other girls at Holbridge Manor, not even Monique. The licence number of the car. I was keeping it back in case the day ever dawned . . . Well, it has dawned. Among other things, Tonya made a note of the Sandemans' licence plate: 40 ALM. That was the black Wolseley that took Charlotte away from Holbridge Manor.'

'Tonya says,' repeated Joan. But she was clearly distressed.

'Joan, the only way Tonya could know is by seeing the car in the flesh or in a photograph. Any other theory is just too implausible.'

'Snooping and prying,' said Joan. 'Typical.'

'Yes, I don't like her either. People don't. That's why she needs Sukie and Charlotte and the whole exciting story. But knowledge is enough for her; Tonya has agreed not to breathe a word of this to Sukie for the time being. She's the first to admit Sukie would never keep it quiet, she would tell Kim, and Mummy and Daddy, and they'd be round here like a shot and . . . Oh, all hell would break loose. Tonya understands that.'

'In other words, you and Tonya are in cahoots to keep a secret from Kim.'

'You think I'm comfortable with this? Having given Kim a home, welcomed her as her mother? Only to discover three months later that she's nothing to do with me at all? That brave, clever little Kim isn't my baby, my baby is spoiled, pampered little Sukie?'

In the hallway Kim turned silently back towards the stairs. She didn't immediately climb them but stood there staring blindly at the silk hangings, the sculptures, the delicate pattern of the stained glass.

It was nearly four o'clock before Neil Armstrong stepped on to the ladder and activated the camera for the telecast. At which point it became clear that the colour sets of Imogen's household were *de trop*.

'It's in black and white!' wailed Gareth and Joan together, from above another round of bacon sandwiches. 'What a swizz!'

Even Tonya was wondering why she'd suffered a hot night in a bed with Sukie when she could have got the same picture quality at home in Barnes.

Although Kim had her own set, they all ended up together in the sitting room, drawn by Joan's endless rounds of food and tea, and the camaraderie common to persons sharing the pre-dawn when lesser mortals are asleep in bed.

'Well, of course it's black and white,' scoffed Sebastian, whose camaraderie had a short lease. 'You've seen the size of colour transmission cameras. How were the astronauts supposed to pack one of those into the lunar module?'

'But they'd be weightless. I call it a shame.'

'Look, last night you heard Buzz Aldrin tell Houston the surface was grey on one side of the module and very white chalky-grey on the other. If he'd said it was all heliotrope and psychedelic orange, you'd have cause for complaint. Now can everyone please put a sock in it, or we'll miss the action.'

'I wanted to know what colour the sky was,' grumbled Joan.

'That's one small step for man,' announced Neil Armstrong with his dustbin-lid acoustics. 'One giant leap for mankind.'

'Huh?' said Imogen and Denise.

Kim, silent on a beanbag, watched the grainy images and battled against a misery that threatened to swamp her. She imagined herself telling Imogen that she knew. Imogen would cry, and Kim, who hadn't the ability to cry, would bleed inside, and at the end of it she would still be Colonel Massingham's ward, with none of the major decisions of life her own to make. And unless she was prepared to move in with the Massinghams, there wasn't a roof in this world under which Kim had the right to shelter. The powerlessness of childhood would keep her here with this beautiful woman who had made a well-meant but catastrophic blunder.

'It's Michael Collins I feel sorry for,' said Denise, sucking her thumb. For some reason the nail throbbed as if she'd slammed it in a door.

'I know,' said Sukie, sucking her own thumb. 'Fancy being stuck up there going round and round while your friends get to land on the moon! If it were me, I'd sulk all the way home.'

'Yeah, you would,' agreed Tonya.

In this new grief, Kim's unnameable fears were swept away, nullified, obliterated, like an effect of theatrical lighting. Having nothing more to lose she had nothing left to fear. She sank deeper in her beanbag, broken and defrauded and bereft.

Somebody opened the curtains. The monochrome moon-world was being imitated in the quiet suburban street, a threadbare daylight and a lifeless sky. On the TV, something new was happening.

'As you talk to us from the Sea of Tranquillity,' said the voice of the President of the United States, 'it inspires us to redouble our efforts to bring peace and tranquillity to Earth.'

'Peace and tranquillity?!' shouted Monique, who never shouted. 'The man is secretly bombing the shit out of Cambodia!'

'That's news to me,' said Joan.

'With B-52 bombers, virtually daily since March.'

Sebastian groaned. 'Oh, don't get her started.'

'I've got a tape of broadcasts by Cambodia Radio. They're in French. I'm half French, I know what they say.'

'Monique, not now.'

'Sebastian, since when did you want to listen to Richard Nixon?'

'Since he was on the phone to a man on the moon! Belt up, Monique.'

Suppose Gareth is right, thought Kim, and this whole thing is one big lying scam. Suppose Monique's Cambodian tape is the truth. Suppose she, Kim, hadn't been given away to Peggy by a mystery couple in Ilford? Suppose nothing anywhere was really what it bloody well seemed. She floundered out of the room, slamming the door behind her. She was up the stairs, and into her bedroom.

'*Kim?*'

'No, Ginny,' said Monique quickly. 'Leave her alone.'

'Well, I'm off for a bath,' said Sebastian. 'I've had enough history for one morning.'

There was a general restlessness. It was daylight. The TV was replaying earlier footage. Sebastian was right, they had all had enough history.

'Know what I can't believe?' asked Sebastian.

'That flag?' suggested Gareth. 'Fluttering in the breeze on a windless moon?'

'I can't believe Neil Armstrong,' said Sebastian. 'He has just one line to deliver to the largest audience in the entire history of the planet. And he fucks it up.'

With which Sebastian went upstairs.

37

Peggy's was not the only death of Kim's experience. She had lost Wilbur, her first dog. Peggy woke her at half past seven, and Kim knew instantly from her face.

'Mum?'

'I'm sorry, love. I've been up all night with him. He's got a lot worse. I'll wait another hour and phone the vet at home, ask him to come round. But, sweetheart, Wilbur's very poorly.'

'He isn't going to die?'

'He is, lovey.'

'You said he'd be all right,' protested Kim. 'Just a bone he'd eaten or something. Too much Christmas dinner.'

'I was wrong. But it wouldn't've helped if I'd known. I reckon it's parvo. That's a bad illness dogs get and there isn't a cure.'

'The vet might say there is.'

'Kim,' insisted Peggy gently, 'we're going to lose our poor Wilbur. You'll want a bit of time to say goodbye to him. Put on your dressing gown and come downstairs.'

The vet said, 'Rotten way to finish Christmas.' And then, 'Yes, it's parvovirus, I'm sorry to say, third case I've seen this month. Mrs Tanner, shall we have a quiet word away from the little one?'

'Thank you but we're a family,' Peggy replied politely. 'Kim understands it wouldn't be fair to let him linger. We'll both stay here and talk to Wilbur while he goes to sleep.'

Later they were on the settee in front of the TV when somebody rang the doorbell. It was Mr Antrobus, standing on the step in the cold, his big round face pink and his breath a restless white smoke.

'I've just heard,' he said. 'Peggy, I'm so sorry. Hello, Kim. Poor old Wilbur.'

They sat in the front room amid the tired detritus of Christmas, the wilting paper chains and deep shadow of fallen pine needles beneath the twiggy tree. On the side table was a round of turkey sandwiches Peggy had made but neither of them could eat.

'Tasted like chaff,' she said sadly.

'Mind you, so do our turkey sandwiches,' said Mr Antrobus with a wan smile. 'Wilbur wasn't even very old, was he?'

'We're not exactly sure. Got him from Battersea Dogs Home and he was no puppy then. A rescue dog,' added Peggy shortly.

She had a tight arm around Kim, who was suffering one of the episodes Peggy called 'crying panics', her poor little frame trembling, her misted eyes stretched open so far Peggy was half afraid they would pop.

'What a marvellous change for him then,' said Mr Antrobus. 'Coming to live here with you. What a smashing life he had.'

'We know,' said Peggy gently, squeezing Kim.

'Actually, there's an ulterior motive to my visit,' continued Mr Antrobus. 'Please slap me down if this is insensitive. Jill and I know of a young dog that's in trouble.'

He paused. Kim hiccuped.

'Go on,' said Peggy.

'Another cruelty case,' said Mr Antrobus in a matter-of-fact tone. 'Needn't go into details. Nice nature, though, probably about three months old. Trouble is, he looks like he's going to be a big boy. Huge great feet like wellington boots. Puts a lot of people off. And he has this habit of spinning round in circles. A family bought him for their children at Christmas and changed their minds on Boxing Day. Second time that's happened. His future doesn't look rosy.'

'Do you hear that, Kim?' said Peggy. 'It sounds like there's someone might need us.'

'What about Wilbur?' demanded Kim sullenly. 'He'll think we've forgot him. He'll think we just traded him in for a new one.'

And Mr Antrobus, nodding that he understood, talked to her for a long time about grief, and feelings of guilt, and the redemptive powers of loving care both for the giver and the receiver.

38

The office of the Treasury Solicitor was in Petty France, on the edge of St James's Park. Its workers didn't look as if they had been up half the night to watch men walking about on the moon. To Kim, innately suspicious of anything associated with the government, the Treasury's suited gents and tailored women looked as if their natural habitat was circa 1938 and they were still sniffy about those newfangled aeroplanes.

She and Colonel Massingham arrived early. They wandered up the Mall, the colour of cinder, towards Buckingham Palace, before veering off to dawdle in St James's Park with its ornamental fruit trees and self-important ducks, and its views of the Admiralty buildings like a medieval encampment beyond the summer greenery.

Frances had declined to accompany her husband. 'That poor child is slightly less overwhelmed by you than me,' she said, and packed him off alone. Now, for something to talk about, Kim asked Colonel Massingham whether Monique could be right about Cambodia. He didn't ridicule the idea; he was quiet a moment and then said, 'I don't think so, Kim. The leader of the free world would never involve himself in such a despicable act. But this isn't what is making you unhappy, is it, the war? Has something gone wrong?'

'Gone wrong,' repeated Kim. And she heard herself tell him about Sukie and the black car of Holbridge Manor.

'But this is atrocious,' said Colonel Massingham.

'It's not Imogen's fault. Just bad luck.'

'Nonsense. She should never have allowed herself to be confidante to this Tonya Shilling. Tonya? It isn't even a proper name,' he added, crossly irrelevant.

'It's short for Toinette.'

'Well, that isn't a proper name either,' snapped Colonel Massingham.

Kim continued dismally, 'You don't have to be my guardian any more if you don't want. Now it turns out I'm not really Charlotte, I can go back to the Antrobus Motel.'

'The deuce you can!' he responded. 'This is unforgivable of Imogen.' When it came to self-analysis Colonel Massingham wasn't a great deal more practised than Kim, but he understood that the true identity of Imogen's Charlotte was no longer of anything but academic interest. Moreover, he was damned if he could see why it still mattered to Imogen. She had yearned for a daughter. Well, she'd found a daughter. Case closed. As far as Colonel Massingham could see, Imogen had no more right to appoint a new Charlotte than to renege on any other contract. 'I shall take her to task the moment we get home.'

'Oh, please don't, please.' In her distress Kim reached for his sleeve. 'Imogen doesn't know I know. Please, Colonel Massingham.'

The girl was so upset that eventually, deeply uneasy, he promised not to tell Imogen. That still left the question of where he would find the courage to tell his wife.

When they were called into the solicitor's office, a man who introduced himself as Mr Cavanaugh asked whether they had tuned in to watch the moonwalk, adding that it was a splendid technological feat, all praise to the

Americans. He went on to examine the documents relating to Colonel Massingham's guardianship.

'These appear to be in order,' said Mr Cavanaugh and smiled at Kim. 'I won't beat about the bush. At the time my office wound up Mr Davis's estate it comprised some sixty-five mansion blocks, all of them in and around the East End of London. He was landlord to much of Bethnal Green and Hackney.'

'Good God,' said Colonel Massingham.

'Yes indeed,' agreed Mr Cavanaugh. 'And it appears that Mr Davis was a man who believed in keeping his money rather than spending it. Shall we cut to the chase? The estate is valued at a little over five hundred thousand pounds.'

'*Five hundred thousand?*' repeated Colonel Massingham. 'Good Lord, man, that's half a million! Are you sure of your facts? It's, well, it's *excessive!*'

Kim, so composed that she almost looked bored, glanced briefly at her guardian.

'It is indeed a substantial inheritance,' agreed Cavanaugh cheerfully.

'Bethnal Green and Hackney,' repeated Kim. 'One of them slum landlords, was he?' she suggested, her grammar out of the window.

'Oh, well now, I couldn't—'

'Village I grew up in in Essex, lots of people come from the East End. I heard stories,' she continued darkly.

'Sidney Davis,' said Colonel Massingham slowly. 'In the '50s I used to come across the name Sid Davis. Exorbitant rents and bully-boy tactics. Hackney and Bethnal Green. Both Sid and Davis are common enough names but the facts would fit. The Ilford neighbours didn't know, but maybe he took pains to protect the illusion of respectability.'

'Slums for immigrants?' asked Kim.

'Yes, from the West Indies mainly. Not unlike Peter Rachman in Notting Hill. Except Rachman was a flamboyant individual: owned night clubs, friend of the Kray twins, that sort of thing. Davis was a far more shadowy character. One way or another the police never managed to get a case against him.'

'A sorry business, Rachmanism,' said Cavanaugh.

'Then I can tell you why Mum left him,' said Kim. 'And why she was waiting till I was older before she told me. *And* why she never chased up his money when he was dead. So I won't have it either, if that's all the same to you. Can I turn it down?' she asked Cavanaugh.

He answered instantly. 'Not until you're an adult,' he said. 'With this new law that's going through, that will be on your eighteenth birthday. Then you can do as you wish.'

Colonel Massingham turned to her worriedly. 'Kim, there is no moral case to answer. The money is yours by law and by right.'

'Yeah,' agreed Kim. 'Blood money.'

What was it about this child, wondered Colonel Massingham, that fate succeeded in putting a damper on every turn of good luck that crossed her eccentric path? She couldn't have her background investigated without turning up a secret life her mother never told her of, not to mention a dead baby. Couldn't find her birth mother without some other contender appearing within weeks. And couldn't get herself adopted without being landed with the Jarmans, he added to himself, the chief superintendent's opinion notwithstanding. And now she couldn't inherit a fortune without its turning out to be the ill-gotten gains of one of the worst landlords of post-war London.

'What's happened to them now?' asked Kim. 'His tenants. When the flats was sold off to wind up the estate?'

'I'm afraid I've simply no idea,' said Cavanaugh.

'The law changed,' said Colonel Massingham. 'Because of the likes of Rachman and Davis. Parliament outlawed the practices that had made them rich.'

And which therefore made Kim rich. The men were

quiet. Outside in Petty France the traffic stopped and started, clotted and spurted, the silted arterial circulation of overcrowded London. Below Cavanaugh's window a lorry stood and throbbed, its low-frequency vibrations barely audible but sickening. The glass trembled. Then the traffic flow was released again and the lorry was gone.

'And now to practicalities.'

Cavanaugh clicked open a box file and began peeling papers from beneath the snapping jaw of its lever arch. 'Colonel Massingham, perhaps you would be good enough to examine these, which relate to the sale . . .'

39

'But why that ordinary house in Wingfield Drive? And however could the neighbours not have known? Mrs McCrae—'

'The man was a miser, Frances. The legal team recovered nearly £50,000 in coins and small-denomination notes, stuffed into boxes in the loft.' He hadn't recounted Kim's other news, about Sukie Sandeman. He simply hadn't the bottle.

'But how did the man escape notoriety?'

'Rachman was not the only slum landlord in London. If you remember, he only came to public notice because he got himself tangled up with a national scandal – Rachman was involved with the call girls from the Profumo affair. There were others. You see, the majority of London landlords refused to house West Indians, and it cleared a golden path for the racketeers. It's only by chance that I know the name Sid Davis. One of his thugs ended up in my court in the late '50s. I never met the man himself.'

'Presumably that was why Peggy ran away from him.'

'That's what Kim said.'

Then, 'No,' continued his wife, contradicting herself.

'We're getting muddled. We know from Mrs McCrae that Peggy walked out on her marriage soon after losing her baby. I'm convinced that baby is key to everything, not just to Peggy but to Kim.'

✳

Imogen was shocked and thrilled, and Kim saw in her re-action relief. If I'm rich she doesn't have to feel guilty about me, thought Kim miserably.

'I don't even want it,' she said, cutting off Imogen's bubbling congratulations.

'Don't be so tiresomely righteous,' Sebastian told her. 'All money is blood money if you dig deep enough into its antecedents.'

The transistor radio was playing a Beatles' flip side from a couple of years ago: 'Baby You're A Rich Man'.

'This God of yours has a sense of humour,' said Sebastian.

✳

'I take it you've heard the latest from the Tanner/St Clair household?' said Denise's father.

'Kim and that money, you mean?' His wife was stirring the gravy. The kitchen was full of steam and the smell of grilled chops. 'Denise told me, soon as she got in from school.'

'Bit of a turn-up for the books. She seems pretty dis-missive about the whole thing.'

'I think that's because Kim is.'

'Wouldn't you have expected her to be a bit more . . .? I don't know, a bit more something, anyhow. It isn't as if Denise was the sort of kid that takes the unexpected in her stride. Think what we put up with when Kim first announced she was moving to Ealing. And now the girl's inherited a mint we get told as calm as custard.'

'It's not envy Denise suffers from, it's jealousy. Kim could go and buy herself a yacht and Denise wouldn't turn a hair. But if she took the rest of the class sailing in it, we'd get the mad scene from *Lucia di Lammermoor*.'

'Who?'

'Anyway, Kim says she doesn't want the money and Denise can have it soon as they turn eighteen.'

'Oh good,' said Denise's father. 'It'll come in handy, half a million. She can buy me a motorbike. I've always wanted to race on the Isle of Man.'

'Over my dead body,' said his wife, and dished up the dinner.

*

It was the last week of school, and the sheer routine was keeping Kim together. She dreaded the start of the holiday. Yet when the weekend arrived it was rather good.

It was free of Sukie and Tonya for a start, the former being at a gymkhana with Twinkle, and the latter not actually having the gall to turn up in Ealing on her own.

On Saturday Kim went into Shash with Monique, and spent the day standing guard at the till – with Welly. He had only to jump up with his head and paws looming over the counter to persuade exiting customers to shell out for the books under their jackets.

'I'm a cat person myself,' said Sagittarius Sal snootily, though later Kim found smears of lipstick on Welly's woolly head. Black.

Then the owner of next door's café appeared and handed her an envelope containing two crisp five-pound notes. 'Reward,' explained Jack the Mack, 'for what your hippie friends would call creative input. The tables with holes in will be ready August and I've got a potter down in Devon doing me the mugs.'

'But Sal said it was a stupid idea,' objected Kim.

'Well, if it turns out Sal's right, I'll be round your house demanding me ten quid back,' said Jack the Mack, and left Kim to sort out one of Monique's customers who was in the process of stealing two copies of *Last Exit to Brooklyn*.

And on Sunday, the next production got under way at the Questors, with the read-through for J. M. Barrie's play *Mary Rose*.

'Kim!' said Daphne with such evident delight that Kim flushed. 'I hope you're signing up full time. You are? Wonderful! Know what a prompt book is? Let me show you.'

They were upstairs in the Georgian house, Mattock Lodge, in what had once been a bedroom and was now a rehearsal room named after Michael Redgrave. Kim liked its vestigial domesticity and open rafters, its curtained windows looking out towards Walpole Park. She was even more delighted when Reggie walked in, lovely Banquo's-Ghost Reggie of the celebrated maggot bowl.

'*It's Kim!*' he roared and chased her round the Redgrave Room like a Spanish bull with all the chairs flying and Welly barking with hysterical ecstasy.

Welly was very tired and very clean. It had started with one of Kim's overzealous walks, evolved into a long inexplicable spell of standing outside Ealing Studios while Kim imagined rolling cameras and Peter Sellers, and culminated in a bath. The bath took place in the garden, but it was in Imogen's hall that Welly shook himself dry and ruined all the wall hangings.

'Hello, everyone,' said the director, sailing in with a wave like royalty on a balcony. 'Oh hell, some other production's left their bearskin on the . . . *Christ!*'

'OK, Welly,' said Kim. 'It's all right.'

'What's it doing, what's it doing?'

'Just spinning round. All right, Welly, the director

isn't going to hurt you. The director isn't going to hurt any of us.'

When they got down to work he filled in the cast about background. 'The play can be read as a very saccharine bit of melodrama. Rest assured, our production will be neither saccharine nor melodramatic.'

'Do you see it primarily as a ghost story?' The question came from someone named Giles. Very young, very good looking.

'No, I see *Mary Rose* primarily as a study of loss,' said the director.

Then the cast began their read-through. As the afternoon warmed up so did the lino floor, its plasticky smell reminding Kim of hot afternoons at school. Kim liked hot afternoons at school. She liked the Redgrave Room. Unfortunately, she thought the play was a lot of fey baloney.

Mary Rose certainly was a ghost story – it opened and closed in a house where no one would live because it was haunted, the rest of the action being flashback. Mary Rose herself was the unhappy phantom, but even in merrier days before she was dead the girl had a penchant for the supernatural. She went in for disappearing acts. The final one lasted a full twenty-five years until Mary Rose suddenly turned up again, unchanged and uncomprehending, to the shocked dismay of the family that had lost her – and who did not welcome her return after all these years.

The play moved backwards and forwards, and characters talked about other bits of the past that you never got to witness for yourself. Kim, who had seen *Peter Pan* and frantically clapped her hands to show she believed in fairies, could detect here no glimmer of that author's genius. Perhaps it was like the Beatles' film of *Yellow Submarine*, she thought: perhaps no matter how clever you were you could still lay the occasional egg.

Sebastian was playing Mary Rose's boyish husband,

Monique the middle-aged mother, and Reggie the father. Giles was Mary Rose's baby, grown up all these years later when she's a lost ghost. And there was the actress playing the lead. A pretty girl of twenty who went by the silly name of Tish, she had nothing to say until page 30. And then Kim's contentment trickled away like mist through a sieve. Tish was all little-girl-lost, all gasps and simpering side-glances. In other words, she was another Sukie. Imogen had been dragging a huge wicker basket across the threshold while Tish was reading some winsome lines about hiding up an apple tree. Kim saw Imogen stop dead. Daphne, walking in behind her, kept going and slammed into Imogen's rear. It's the Sukie-ness, it's turned her heart over, thought Kim, who was not often given to neologisms. Her own heart ached.

Later, Daphne beckoned Kim out to the landing and they discussed her role. Daphne explained the rehearsal process, how important her notes were.

'Don't be scared – pipe up and tell the director he's wrong and that's not what they thrashed out last time. Directors can never remember what they decided half an hour ago. And as for *actors*, you're lucky to get one with the memory span of an over-excited toddler.'

'So how do they learn their lines?'

'Fear,' said Daphne. 'They suddenly realize that one evening soon they will be standing on a stage in full view of human beings who have paid to get in, and if they don't know what they're supposed to say next they are going to look a complete moron. Oh, and only ever use pencil. It gets changed a dozen times in rehearsal, and once they're in the theatre they discover none of it is any good anyway because all the action's taking place in shadow. There's a major panic and the entire play gets reworked the night before the first dress rehearsal. Theatre is not for the faint-hearted,' added Daphne. Then she looked Kim in the eyes. 'You're not as happy as you used to be,' she said bluntly. 'All the sunshine's gone.'

'I'll be OK,' Kim assured her. 'I won't let you down.'

For an instant, Daphne's eyes filmed over. 'Heavens, girl, I didn't mean it like that,' she said, and Kim was reminded of Imogen all those weeks ago when she first moved to Ealing.

40

They got home at half past eight – and Tonya *was* there.

At least she had the grace to look sheepish. Even Sebastian, champion of Sukie, said, 'What the hell is she doing here?' when they turned in at the gate to find Tonya sitting on the front path, exactly the attitude in which they had first come upon her friend.

'You weren't expecting to see me,' she told them accurately. 'Please can I come in for a moment? My family sent me round.'

'Brought them too, have you?' said Kim.

Imogen barely disguised her weariness. 'It can only be for a moment, Tonya. We're all tired.'

'Yes, so am I,' agreed Tonya. 'I've been waiting five hours. Joan left a few minutes ago.'

'You've been indoors all that time?' Kim had a panic-stricken vision of a snooping Tonya with the run of the house.

'No, Joan made me wait out here on the front path,' said Tonya in a rather different voice. 'She insisted you'd all be home any minute and then you'd disappear off again so I'd miss you if I tried leaving and coming back later. She kept saying so all day long, every time she came out to get some-thing from her car.'

Good old Joan, thought Kim. And she *never* trotted back and forth, garden to car. Good old Joan.

'Your poor bum must be numb,' said Imogen, swallowing a smile. 'I'll make some tea.'

It was hot in the house, a stuffy, draining heat. Tonya padded into the kitchen with her flat feet and flat voice. 'I've come to say sorry,' she announced to everyone's further shock. 'My family said it wasn't fair on Kim, Sukie and I bursting in here from out of the blue. They sent me round to apologize.' Nobody could think of a thing to say in reply. Unperturbed, Tonya asked Kim, 'School finished yet?'

'Yeah.'

'Do well in your end-of-term exams?'

'I came top,' said Kim.

'Congratulations,' said Tonya. 'So did Sukie.'

'Kim is expecting to go to Cambridge,' said Imogen.

'Congratulations,' said Tonya again. 'So is Sukie.'

Kim was not only hot and fatigued, she was suffering the anticlimax of being home after the rewarding bustle of the Questors. She wanted a bath and a good book.

'Anyway,' continued Tonya, 'I was wondering if Sukie and I could make it up to you by helping look for your adoptive parents. Denise told me Peggy's Wingfield Drive address was no use so you were going to Somerset House this week to get hold of Peggy's marriage certificate from when she was Sidney Davis's wife in case it tells you where she was living in Dagenham at the time.'

'I wouldn't of, Kim. It's only because she got me when I'd just woken up. You know what it's like when you've just woken up. Your resistance is low.'

'Not that low,' said Kim. 'What else did you tell her?'

'Nothing,' responded Denise too quickly.

'*What else, Denise?*'

'I don't know, I might of told her all kinds of anything.' Her voice was a wail. 'She wouldn't give over asking questions and I was trying to keep schtum but I couldn't stop stuff slipping out. It was three o'clock in the morning!'

Kim held the phone receiver away from her ear and mimed throwing a fist at it. From within the earpiece a tinny voice quacked on, traduced to the blustering of a cartoon character, a squeaking fairy, an elf. Kim burned to slam the phone down and cut her off, squawking.

'All right, Denise, listen,' she said instead. 'We got to get moving before Laurel and Hardy beat us to it. That means tomorrow. I want you with me outside Somerset House nine o'clock tomorrow morning.' Denise didn't reply and Kim found that her fingers were trembling. 'OK, forget it,' she said. 'I'll go on my own.'

'Whereabouts is Somerset House?' asked the small voice of Denise.

*

But it was not that simple. You went up the steps and through to an impressive hall, then up to a counter where four officials were answering queries from behind a grill. The girls stood in the queue and heard the enquiries:

'I'm looking for the birth certificate of John Howard Anderson, born 19 August 1925 in the parish of St Nicholas, Kelvedon Hatch, Essex.'

'You'll find 1925 up one flight of stairs, second gallery on the left.'

'Death certificates, please. Mrs Florence Maud Grundy who died at St Mary's Hospital, Paddington, on 5 January . . .'

The girls had no date, no address, no parish. The man behind the grill barely looked up. 'I'm sorry,' he told them, 'but I don't think you grasp the magnitude of your difficulties.'

Outside again, the girls trudged sadly along the Embankment, only too well aware of the magnitude of their difficulties. The day was overcast, the sky low, grey and oily, the River Thames cold, grey and agitated. A dreary wind blew the smell of salt and diesel fumes across the banks exposed by the low tide. Denise was as miserable as Kim. Over the past weeks, she had noticed with consternation the cracks in Kim's former infallibility. That appalling wrong-headedness over Barry from the fête, for example, and the near-suicidal plan to tell Imogen she'd caught Sebastian with that actress. Perhaps Kim's very stubbornness led to tunnel vision, thought Denise now. In which case, maybe Denise's own unruly imagination offered certain advantages. 'Kim, I been thinking,' she said. 'We got to go back to the one good lead we ever had. Mr and Mrs Barber in Perth.'

'Can't. Mrs practically told me to eff off. What a joke, eh?' said Kim, acid with despondency. 'Half a million quid and I'll probably never be able to jump on a plane to Australia because I can't get a passport.'

'True,' agreed Denise calmly, 'but if *I* had half a million quid, I wouldn't slog all the way out to Australia. I'd sit at home in an armchair and phone them up.'

Imogen and Sebastian were both out, so the girls got the phone to themselves: no Lenny Plink-a-Plonk carrying it up and down the hall while he raved for an hour at a publisher in West Berlin or woke up all his friends in Greenwich Village because he'd forgotten that over there it was the middle of the night. Two operators later, and Kim had the Barbers' phone number in Perth.

But with Lenny in mind they first had to check out the time difference, and that took a great deal longer – and got them three different answers, including a refusal by Denise's mother to phone Denise's father at work and get him to find out for them. Eventually Kim decided from her atlas that even if Sydney was tucked up in bed, Perth was still awake and answering telephones.

'Hello.'

'Is that Mrs Barber?'

'The Barber family are not at home. Can I take a message?'

'Oh,' said Kim. And then, 'Are you their daughter?'

'Miss Cathy is out too. This is Mary speaking, the maid.'

Kim clamped a hand across the receiver. 'They got a *maid*,' she told Denise.

'A *maid*?'

'I'm phoning all the way from London,' said Kim. 'It's like an emergency. I need to get in touch with somebody who lives near where they used to in England. Can you tell me their address before they emigrated, please?'

Down the phone line was the humming silence of ten thousand miles, an ocean and a continent. Mary's voice came back, distant and pleasant and useless. 'You'll have to phone again tomorrow and ask Mrs Barber,' she said. 'You really calling from England?'

'Isn't there an address book you could look up?' suggested Kim.

'I'm a maid, I ain't a secretary. Phone back tomorrow.'

'Kim!' put in Denise, wildly signalling. 'Mention Fairlop and Barkingside. Ask if the Barbers ever talk about living there.'

'I bet they sometimes talk about the place they came from, though,' said Kim in desperation. 'It was Fairlop, wasn't it?'

'Well, sure they talk about the place they came from,' said Mary. 'Everybody knows where they came from. Same street as John.'

'John?'

'You should hear Miss Cathy on the subject. Mr and Mrs Barber lived there right through the war watching the city on fire every night from Hitler's bombs, and then the same month the Beatles get into the hit parade they catch a ship to Australia. They lived in the same street as John Lennon. You should hear Miss Cathy on the subject,' said Mary again, happily hooting. 'She *cries*.'

41

It took Frances nearly three days of searching, of taking down one heavy leather-bound ledger after another and scanning every entry. And serve me right if I get another migraine, she told herself. But at the end of it she had the certificate recording the marriage of Sidney Davis, businessman, to Margaret Mabel Tanner on 24 June 1933 at Dagenham Parish Church. She was twenty-three and he thirty-six.

'Spinster,' read Frances, 'of 21 Cold Gate Lane, Dagenham.' And then, 'Businessman. Yes, well.'

But all her hard work got her nowhere. The houses of Cold Gate Lane had been destroyed in the Blitz by a combination of bombs aimed at Dagenham's factories and others dropped short of London's docks. Nobody living in the ugly new houses had ever heard of the Tanners.

So Frances went back to Somerset House, this time downstairs to search the death certificates. Again she proceeded ledger by ledger. There were continual interruptions, other people needing to look up a name in the volume she was monopolizing. But by the Monday morning that nearly brought her slap bang up against Kim and Denise, she found another. Craig Arthur Davis, stillborn 18 December 1949.

'Two children, Frances! She lost two.'

'We don't know how many she lost, we only know how many I found.'

'Sid Davis employed thugs,' said Colonel Massingham.

'You're wondering if he was one himself and it was his thuggery caused the poor woman to lose her babies.'

'We might be jumping to conclusions, Frances.'

'We might. But I have a feeling we're not,' said Frances Massingham.

*

'Miles of it,' said Kim, looking down at the map. 'Miles and miles.'

'Makes more sense though,' said Denise. 'I mean if John Lennon's road is miles long, then *hundreds* of people live in it.'

To the girls' request that they urgently needed the home address of John Lennon before he was a star, Monique had responded rather well. She looked hard at them, picked up the phone, got rid of the incoming call and started dialling.

'Go next door and ask Jack to give you a coffee,' she suggested. 'This shouldn't take long.'

Kim was grateful for coffee. She hadn't slept again, sharing a bed with Denise. Kim no longer doubted the maid's story, though initially she had assumed they were at cross purposes.

'The operator must of give me the wrong number,' she told the phone. 'I wanted Mrs Hazel Barber of 115 Sandy Point, Perth.'

'Well, who do you think you got?' the maid had returned, surprised.

So the Barbers came from Liverpool. They had never

lived in Ilford. It was in Liverpool that Peggy had done their cleaning. And she had never said a word. All these years of Beatlemania, 'Mersey sound', TV comedies with Scousers and Liver birds, Lime Street and Scotland Road, yet Peggy had never said a word. As a secret it was awe-inspiring.

Yet that it was a secret fitted with other facts. That night, Kim had taken out Hazel Barber's letters to Peggy and read them through. There were fifteen, dating from 1962. And as a collection they were oddly incomplete. References were made to other letters, letters that weren't there. Nothing strange about that per se – but not one of those that remained contained a reference to the Barbers' former home. Not a single instance of 'I had a card from Mrs X who you'll remember from Y Street,' or 'We were sorry/delighted to hear that Z school/hospital/library has been pulled down/expanded/awarded a prize.' Not a whisper by which a reader could identify the locale, even though it was the only locale wherein the correspondents had ever known each other. It looked suspiciously like deliberate processing, as though Peggy had retained only those letters that gave nothing away. And that same logic meant there was something to be given away. Something to hide.

'OK, I've got it,' said Monique. '241 Menlove Avenue, Woolton. John's Aunt Mimi moved to Bournemouth four years ago, so there's nobody in Woolton now in case you planned to camp out on the doorstep.'

'Thanks, Monique.'

'You owe me.'

The girls were sitting in Jack the Mack's café with two coffees and the map they had bought en route to Shash. After which it hadn't taken long to find Menlove Avenue because there were a couple of miles of it. Tracing the road to its western end they found one they had heard of, called Penny Lane.

'Well, your mum didn't get there on the bus from Ilford,' said Denise flatly. 'I suppose we could go up ourselves,' she suggested. 'Knock on doors. Ask around. Or even,' continued Denise with heavy nonchalance, 'we could try Bournemouth. I mean John's Aunt Mimi might remember Mr and Mrs Barber, Kim. She might.'

'Denise, we're trying to find the other family Mum cleaned for, remember? We're looking for my legal parents.'

'Oh yeah,' said Denise defeatedly, staring down at the map. Denise was unhappy about that map. Whereas the city itself was depicted as a dense mass of white-lined streets and blue-lined docks, when it got to Woolton the colours turned green. There were woods and open spaces. A picture inset boasted of public gardens with a floral clock. It was a cuckoo clock.

'Well, the Barbers must be a bit posh,' pointed out Kim when Denise objected. 'What with having a *maid*.'

'It wasn't the Barbers I was thinking of,' said Denise, who had vaguely assumed John Lennon was the rebellious street-tough child of a Scottie Road slum. This Woolton stuck in her throat. Floral clocks. *Cuck*-oo! Denise felt her underarms prickle with embarrassment.

'What we got to do,' said Kim, 'is find where Mum lived, and then see if there's still neighbours around who knew what families she cleaned for.'

'Liverpool's ginormous,' said Denise. 'People with enough money for a cleaner probably live all over the place.' Denise looked down at the map, west, away from Woolton's mortifying cuckoos. 'That bit looks green, too. Birkenhead. Oxton. Wirral.'

'*The* Wirral,' corrected Kim automatically.

'It just says Wirral here. Kim? What's up?'

'I need the loo,' said Kim, and was on her feet, past Denise, bumping the tables and stumbling across careless bags and careless feet, breathless, winded with fear. She was through the door marked Ladies and standing at the basin with her hands over her ears. Blocking the people in her head who shouted in Daddy's voice, shouted that Mummy didn't do it, it was an accident. Who shouted, 'Liar!'

42

To Write a Book

We were in a Soho café, full of arty types and woollen stockings and in the background the laboured snorts of the espresso machine.

'Just look at you!' proclaimed Ursula as if offering me to the customers. 'And golden bronze to boot, like a model in a fashion plate!'

It was wonderful to see her.

'Just the tropical sun,' I said, shyly pleased. 'And the sea and the fresh air. Oh, and the parties.'

She laughed. 'So whyever did you come back, you eejit?'

Mother died first, then Pa followed her unquestioningly as he had done for more than thirty years, that was why I came home. The more pertinent question was why I hadn't hopped aboard the next P&O sailing east before the lilies had even wilted in the funeral wreaths. I didn't yet understand how mean and unworthy were my motives for staying in my childhood home – to live there and run it in my own slapdash fashion, thereby spiting Mother's memory. But Ursula's question had been rhetorical; she was already retrieving a spring-clip file from a rather serious-looking bag at her side.

I had recently joined our local theatre group, and for a startled moment I thought this was the prompt book for some play. No. These were research notes. It seemed Ursula had spent the last few years gathering information on mother-and-baby homes. A mass of documents and correspondence shared her overcrowded bag with a colour photo of her son Roderick (now a strapping seven-year-old at school) – and surprisingly my own letters to her, with their long set pieces describing Hong Kong.

'. . . a true gift for portraying atmosphere, Ginny, and that's exactly what this project needs, a human touch.'

'Project?'

'You said you're just after getting a job.'

'Yes, secretarial, I've—'

'Secretarial hooey. Write a book. Get your story down in black and white. Our story. The publishers will beat a path to your door. Out there in the colonies did you read *The L-Shaped Room* or see *A Taste Of Honey*? Both about girls thrown out of the house for being pregnant – and both made into huge box-office films. There's a mass audience out there, Ginny.'

Irish Ursula pronounced it fillums. Both made into fillums. But unfortunately Irish Ursula was always very quick and sharp. She clocked my reaction immediately.

'What's the matter? Were their scenarios too squalid for your refined taste?'

Yes. Squalid indeed. Tales of the backstreets and the dole, of 'Never darken my door again' and cramped rooms with bedbugs. 'Of course not,' I said lamely, 'it's just—'

'Listen to me. Our situation wasn't exceptional, there are thousands of vulnerable young women locked up, denied their legal rights and treated sadistically by the self-righteous. Tell your story for their sake, Ginny. See this?' She waved a clutch of letters at me. 'Girls at this one are paraded through town on foot every Sunday morning so the locals can gawp at their shame. Scrubbing and cleaning are the most common themes, as are bullying and coercion. Read these, they're witness accounts of outright threats: "Sign the papers or you'll be locked away as a moral defective"; "Sign the papers or Baby will be forcibly removed to an orphanage". I have stories from girls whose babies were literally pulled away from their nipple as they were breast-feeding. All to maintain a supply of nice white well-matched babes for nice white middle-class couples who can't have their own.'

'Ursula—'

'And as for all that crap about how we would end up destitute if we attempted to bring up Baby ourselves? Rubbish! The mother-and-baby homes might be medieval but the law isn't. Financial assistance has been available to single mothers *since 1948*! There's even a National Council for the Unmarried Mother and Her Child, which exists precisely for the purpose of giving advice and assistance!'

'Ursula, they're not all bad. I've heard—'

'True, some are perfectly humane. Unfortunately, some others are completely unspeakable. Generally it's a case of the more religious, the grimmer the conditions. You must have heard rumours of the Magdalene laundries. But you thought they were confined to Ireland? Oh no, Ginny, you have Magdalene laundries right here in free, fair England, the girls virtually slaves, washing and scrubbing and fed on gruel, not supposed to speak except in prayer, not allowed friendships, not allowed to *leave* until the nuns say so. For some it is lifelong incarceration.'

I have never dealt well with embarrassment, skin prickling and cheeks flushed and a wash of feeling akin to shame. Oh, my poor Ursula! I knew my friend's antipathy towards her native Catholic church, knew it of old, we all did; the very mention of the word 'nun' would earn you ten minutes on the iniquities of life as a convent girl in County Cork. However astute on other matters, Ursula was the perfect dupe for exaggerated tales of Dickensian horror in any establishment run by nuns. I squirmed for her well-intentioned gullibility. Constant prayer and *gruel*? Surely even Ursula should have jibbed at *gruel*.

She closed her file and set it down on the table. 'Holy Mother of God,' she said with singular inappropriateness. 'You don't believe me.'

'It *is* a little Gothic.'

'It is indeed. Indeed it is, Ginny.'

Shortly after that Ursula gave up, and got up, and went, my attempts at conciliation rebuffed. She could see my petty rebellion for what it was. I would never set aside my bourgeois upbringing and tell the world I was one of those girls, the girls in mother-and-baby homes, a moral defective, oversexed, damaged goods. I would keep my shame to myself. That was how the system survived to bully and incarcerate others. I was a collaborator. If she'd had her way, Ursula would have seen my head shaved.

All of this I was explaining the next day to another friend over another cup of coffee, instant this time, in a quickly swilled mug and the dressing room of a North London theatre. I will call her

Dominique. An actress, she was making up in preparation for a matinee performance, in which she played the northern mother of a pregnant teenager in – *A Taste of Honey*. Ursula had been absolutely right, it was everywhere, that and *The L-Shaped Room*. She wasn't wrong about the market. Nevertheless—

'*Me*. A *book!*' I said. Then, disapproval still rankling, I went on to recount her gory stories. Dominique didn't say much in reply, and then there was a knock on the door for her five-minute call.

It was a couple of weeks later that she phoned and asked me to drop in again. Once I was installed with the obligatory mug and the Nescafé Dominique brought somebody in to meet me.

'Kathleen, Ginny,' said Dominique in introduction. 'Ginny is the one who doesn't believe the stories about the Magdalene laundries.' At which Kathleen turned round and without a word pulled her T-shirt over her head.

Beneath an awkwardness so acute I felt faint, my colour was rising. Then my colour ebbed away. Kathleen's young back was a screaming mess of puckered skin and ridges. Not merely cicatrized but calcified. It looked like a scaled-down model of a field of mud with tractor tracks. I couldn't speak. After a moment Kathleen did. She reorganized her blouse and turned to me.

'The first time I tried to escape they caned me. The second time they caned me every day for a week. So in the laundry I threw scalding water across the wounds. I knew that would frighten them into sending me to the hospital. They did. And that's when I escaped.'

I heard my own voice ask, 'But your baby? What happened to your baby?'

'No idea. None of us ever knew. Our babies were just taken away.'

And then she checked her face in the wall of light-bulb-lined mirrors and smiled an ordinary smile and left the dressing room, quietly closing the door behind her.

43

The specifics of Kim's panic in Jack the Mack's café didn't recur. Once the terror subsided and some days had passed she even tried to recapture it, needling her pain masochistically like tweaking a sore tooth to make it twinge. Those words 'the Wirral' meant nothing to her now, and when she tried to replay the man's voice in her head it was as if her memory had dug itself into a bunker and she could not reach him beyond the sandbags.

But it was inescapable that Peggy's secrets were disturbing her at a profound level. All kinds of other things crept up to scare Kim, to fill her with a similar gaping dread. It happened all the time, incidents invisible as piano wire, as if her world were cross-strung with snares. Booby-trapped. Like something is wrong in my brain, she thought with a brief fear of tumour and surgery. The following Sunday morning Kim came out of the bathroom and ran full pelt into Tonya, who gave the impression of creeping about the place like the ghost in *Mary Rose*. The collision frightened the life out of Kim, the sudden closeness of another person's skin scent, intimate and insistent, muscling in on her personal space like a threat. She shrank from the girl and ran headlong down the stairs, falling towards that sunless pit of memory like an unstrung climber from a mountain ledge, unable to rid her nostrils of the smell of Tonya's clean-washed hair.

Kim, who had always seen life as simple and distrusted complexities, was aware of an internal tug of war. She desperately wanted to know, to understand, to remember. Yet she could not bear to remember, would fight any slithering demon that threatened to emerge from the deep alleys of her mind.

Her relationship with Imogen had been edgy ever since the night of the Treasury Solicitor's letter. They were polite to each other. Kim didn't want to be polite, she wanted the nudging and childish banter of their former life.

'You're terribly jumpy,' Imogen had said at breakfast. 'I know it's because Sukie is coming again today. Sweetheart, you hate it. Let me stop her coming round. You're my number one priority.'

Imogen had said this also to Joan.

'And your feelings about Sukie?' countered Joan.

'Chaotic,' returned Imogen. 'At least Sebastian doesn't know, or he really would put me through hell.'

And Kim wasn't supposed to know either, but she did, and couldn't tell Imogen she did, couldn't tell her how her heart was broken. So many lies, so much pretence, so many secrets.

'You can't stop Sukie coming,' Kim told Imogen drearily. 'Tonya will find a way of getting her in.'

'It's nothing to do with Tonya.'

But it was. The girl was now central to their lives: one word from her about that black Wolseley and an hysterical Sukie would hurl herself on Imogen howling. One word from Tonya and the house would be full of weeping and wailing. At least it would serve Sebastian right, thought Kim.

'You can't un-invite Tonya,' she said. 'It's like with

vampires. It's too late once you've let them into the house.'

'Lucky you've got the crucifix,' said Imogen. But she couldn't make Kim laugh.

And so Sukie and Tonya were here again, and on Sunday afternoon Daphne had more help than she could handle.

'They will all behave themselves,' Imogen promised her. 'If they don't we just boot them out.'

'Personally I won't make so much as a *squeak*,' said Sukie.

Kim saw Daphne do a double-take at Sukie. 'Good,' she said eventually. 'Because you'll find neither the director nor the cast take kindly to squeaking.'

It was the start of the third week of rehearsals. Denise was here, thank God, but Tonya had turned up with Sukie, who predictably thought it would be perfectly *super* to come along to watch the actors.

The first scene had Sebastian and the prissy Tish as a young married couple. They were picnicking on holiday in the Hebrides, and reminiscing about the birth of their son, 'all coy glances and euphemism', as Daphne put it. The rehearsal schedule had to jump about a bit, making use of whoever was around. Next week they would be losing both Imogen and Sebastian, who were off to America for some kind of pop festival.

'Not me, I'm too old to sleep in a field,' said Monique.

'Never,' whispered another of the actors to her, Giles, the one who was twenty. Until Kim remembered the age difference she actually thought he and Monique were flirting.

In mid-afternoon Daphne sent the girls off to the property store ostensibly to find a picnic basket, but clearly to get rid of them for a space. Normally Kim would have been happy as Larry heading up any expedition in the theatre, particularly as Daphne had allowed her to know where all the various keys were kept 'in case of emergency', giving Kim an authority that made her glow. But she had a profound distaste for being in any confined space with

Sukie and Tonya; just the thought of it gave her the heebie-jeebies, and as confined spaces went, the Questors' prop cellar was a corker. Reluctantly Kim led the girls round the side of Mattock Lodge and down a crumbly set of steps. Then she unlocked a thin white door, and reached inside for the light switch.

'And whatever you do, don't shut it,' said Kim of the door. 'It doesn't unlock from inside.' She went back out for a brick to prop it open.

Affectionately known as Aladdin's cave, the cellar comprised a confused chain of tiny rooms at different levels and with different ceiling heights, most of them low, all alcoves and shelving, chock-full of props, and seriously tidy. Moving carefully through the interlinked passages and cubby holes, up steps and down steps, the girls passed rows of lampshades lined up in size order, paintings covered and labelled, Virgin Marys gesturing towards heaven. This was the last place anyone would want to be with a Sukie, who cried, 'Oh, look what I've found!' every time they came upon a fluffy toy. But then: 'Actually, it's all a bit creepy,' she added.

More than a bit. The prop store had started life as a coal cellar, and had also served as an air-raid shelter during the Blitz. Many an evening performance had moved down here to continue in an atmosphere of cheerfully stoic determination until the sirens sounded the all-clear. But somehow that gritty wartime spirit had not survived VE-Day. The place had a churchly silence and the damp green smell of a recent flood. Its contents wore the forlorn air of jettisoned belongings, which was what they were. Dolls lolled lifeless in frilly frocks. A couple of dozen telephones stood on a shelf, the old-fashioned candlestick style with an earpiece on a hook. Their ropey old cords hung rheumatically stiff, fingered by people long dead. It was impossible not to imagine the absolute horror if one of them should ring.

'I could never stay in here alone,' confessed Sukie. 'Like

poor Jane Eyre in the Red Room. Have you read *Jane Eyre*?'

'Yeah,' replied Kim shortly, who a month ago had believed she had been named after its author. 'Look, we're supposed to be collecting stuff for Daphne.'

But they weren't having any luck. Edwardian toys, clockwork toys, clockwork clocks . . . The girls ducked under a low joist into one of the coal holes. Around them now were various glimmering surfaces. Something in the shape of a snout was reflected back and forth. An entire row of snouts. Attached to heads. Skull-heads with snouts and dead eyes.

Kim and Tonya jumped, so Denise jumped and Sukie screamed, like a domino effect. The four of them spun round and were jammed together trying to get out of the narrow entrance.

I'm going mad, thought Kim. I'm cracking up. 'Stop it!' she said in a massive effort to calm her own nerves. 'It's just gas masks. Stop it!'

'Oy!' A voice called from the doorway, peremptory and authoritative, familiar as school. 'I thought you'd all fallen down a well. The picnic basket's right here by the hatboxes.'

'Sorry, Daphne,' carolled Kim, pushing past the others, out to the daylight.

For one shocking moment Kim had seen Tonya as though in double exposure, her eyes as dolls' eyes, cold and sinister, fixed on a world of the dead and the dank. They were the selfsame eyes that chased Kim through her nightmares. And Kim knew that if her guard slipped, if she relaxed her watch for one moment, her memory would build a face around those eyes and give it a name.

It didn't help that *Mary Rose* was a ghost story. When the girls returned to the Redgrave Room, the cast had reached the scene in which Mary Rose is spirited away from the Hebridean island of her holiday picnic, to vanish for twenty-five years. Kim was glad of the cup of tea at the break.

Tea was served downstairs. Sukie took a copy of the script

with her, and rapidly polished off the play. 'That's horrible,' she said, snapping the book shut. 'All those years, and then when Mary Rose finally comes back they don't want her! And that final scene when she's a ghost is *so* sad.'

'The ghost is incidental,' said Kim, remembering the director. 'It's a play about loss.' But as far as Kim was concerned it was a play about a load of old tripe.

Sukie went off to get more tea from the kitchenette and didn't return for ten minutes. 'Guess who I've been talking to!' she demanded excitedly when she came back.

'Jim Morrison?' suggested Denise without looking up.

'No, a *black man*!'

'What – here?' said Kim, surprised.

'Don't worry, he's very respectable. A doctor, actually. He's just moved to London and joined a family practice in Acton. I do hope people go to see him and aren't put off by his colour. I said so actually, and he told me I was very kind.'

'You said so,' repeated Denise.

'Is he here with someone?'

'Actually,' said Sukie, dropping her voice, 'he was talking to that other foreign-looking man in the dismal corduroy suit.'

'That's Benjamin Sacks, the stage director!' objected Kim protectively.

Denise put down her tea. 'Hang on,' she said. 'I'm going to have a look myself.'

'How did you get talking to him?' asked Tonya.

'Oh, you know, I just went up and introduced myself and said what one always says to put strangers at their ease. Actually, I asked him about himself. I asked him his name and how long he'd been in England and if he was married and whether he had a job. Which is actually when he said he was a doctor.'

'And did he tell you his name?' pursued Kim. 'Actually?'

'Dr Robert Yelland. He was born in Jamaica but studied medicine over here – at Oxford, in fact. And he's a widower, isn't that frightfully sad? No children, though, which I said must be a big relief to him. He's just joined the Questors to get involved in community life. I think that's so brave.'

'Isn't it just,' said Kim thoughtfully. 'What does he look like?'

Sukie's eyes widened like saucers. '*What does he look like?*' squealed Sukie, incredulous.

Denise was back. 'She's right and all,' said Denise. 'There's a black man in there, drinking a cup of tea.'

'What does he look like?'

She shrugged. 'Mid-thirties. Tall. Quite slim.'

'*What does he look like, Denise?*'

Denise thought for a moment. 'A bit like Sidney Poitier in *To Sir with Love*,' she decided.

The girls looked at each other.

'Good,' said Kim. 'OK, break's over. Let's ask Daphne what she wants next.'

44

'I'm not going,' said Imogen. 'Sebastian doesn't mind.'

No, I bet he doesn't, thought Kim. A music festival and a field full of American girls. 'But you've already bought your airline ticket.'

Imogen made a 'throw it over my shoulder' gesture. 'I'm staying here with you,' she repeated. 'We'll go to the King's Road and spend loads of money.'

They did better than that: the day Sebastian flew to New York Imogen took Kim to Kensington where an acquaintance was in the process of moving Biba to glamorous premises in the High Street. It was an anthill of busyness, of women with notepads and men up ladders. Everything was shining black: floor, walls, counters, ceilings. Workmen in overalls grunted, 'Excuse us, love,' as they lugged gilded mirrors across the burnished floor. It was backstage in the Playhouse, gone Art Deco chic.

'Barbara, it's fab,' said Imogen.

'See our new logo? We've moved into the thirties.'

'Kim and I should get out of your way.'

'Come with me.' Barbara led them into a vast back room full of satin and velvet and feathers. Rails on castors were run together, their hanging garments lined up with the angular neatness of suspension files. 'Take one outfit each,' said Barbara. 'I have to get back to check where the men have put that mirror.'

'But, Imogen, we can't,' whispered Kim.

'Of course we can. She asked us to. How about this?'

An hour later they were in a trendy café with the only new Biba bags in London and a lot of autumnal crushed velvet.

'I'll see you at the opening,' Barbara had said to Imogen. 'You won't recognize us.'

'How are you lighting it?'

'Hardly at all. Deep and dark. Opulent gloom.'

'I wouldn't if I were you,' piped up Kim, 'or the shoplifters will be hoiking your stock out the doors quicker than you can shout "thieving hippies". I know what I'm talking about.'

Later, over coffee and cheese sandwiches, Imogen asked Kim to talk to her and Kim told Imogen she had overheard her conversation with Joan about the black Wolseley.

'Oh Kim!'

'Yeah.'

'I am so sorry. I am *so* sorry.'

'I don't think I ever really believed I was Charlotte. Not inside. It was Mum who was convinced.'

'I was convinced too. I wouldn't have done this to you for the world.'

'I know.'

Imogen looked across the table and saw for a moment the buoyant clear-complexioned Kim of a few weeks ago in Questors' backstage blacks, and then this one, bleak, shivery and introverted, acne breaking angrily through the skin of her forehead and chin. How could I do this to a child? she asked herself, ice around her heart.

'Still,' continued Kim, 'you did find her in the end. Charlotte, I mean. You must be a bit pleased.'

'Why? I went through it already, back in April. Something like that doesn't happen to a person twice.'

'Doesn't it?'

'Kim, I don't like Sukie as much as you. Do you believe me?'

'Well, yeah,' responded Kim, surprised. 'She's like the treacle sandwiches Mum used to pack for rainy-day picnics. One's all right but any more and you'll feel sick till Tuesday.'

Imogen snorted into her coffee.

'I've been thinking about boarding school,' continued Kim, dry-eyed and practical.

'Oh Kim,' said Imogen again. 'I don't want you going away.'

'Well, don't worry cos I don't see how I can. Not unless there's a school that'll let me take Welly along.'

'He'd be an asset to the netball team.'

'But I can't keep living with you, Imogen. I can't. It's like . . .' Kim ransacked her imagination. It was like continuing to live in the same house as a lover who has broken your heart by finding somebody new. But that couldn't be said. 'What I need is to get my bearings, find out who I am and where I come from. Find my legal parents. They might even want me back. Stranger things have happened. What I'm saying is—'

'That you need a new start. That this was a false start.'

'Yeah,' said Kim and turned sadly back to her coffee.

Imogen was quiet a while. Then she asked, 'Have you made any headway?'

Kim told her about the Barbers.

'Liverpool! That's a good result.'

'Know what I think?' continued Kim. 'I think I've got to employ a private detective.'

'You're joking.'

'We do have them over here, it isn't just Humphrey Bogart in the movies. And so what if they charge like sin? I've got half a million quid.' A number of heads turned in their direction. 'Though I'll have to talk to Colonel Massingham to get at it. Imogen, it's not your fault,' added Kim. 'Sukie, I mean.' Another Peggy expression popped up in her mind. 'It's like London buses: you wait all this time for one and then two come along together.'

But Imogen heard Joan's voice: It's rotten of you. Kim's had a rum deal, she's a good kid and she deserves better than you're giving her.

'Do you want any help, Kim? Maybe I could ask around about suitable detectives.'

'Denise and I already found a couple in the phone book. I'll give them both the once-over. You know, interview them,' concluded Kim with one of her shrugs.

Her resourcefulness and courage were always a shock to Imogen. Just like Douglas, she thought before she remembered. 'Perhaps I could talk to Uncle George about the trust fund,' she suggested forlornly.

'Let's wait till I've sorted out a detective. Remember, I've already got that bit of money you put in my savings account.'

'That isn't much. Look, I can—'

'Plus what Monique's been paying Welly and me to stop the customers bleeding her white at Shash, plus the bonus from Jack the Mack for my creative input.'

Imogen laughed tearily and shook her head and lit a cigarette. 'The world is full of Sukie Sandemans but there's only one Kim Tanner. You'll always have a home with me if you want it,' she added. 'Always.'

'I can't leave you yet anyway,' said Kim. 'There's still a couple of things to sort out.' She looked pointedly at the cigarette.

Imogen smiled. 'A couple? What's the other one?'

'That would be telling,' said Kim.

Dr Robert Yelland had joined the backstage crew for *Mary Rose*. And Sebastian was away an entire week.

*

'She's telling you true,' said Denise. 'It's not a wind-up.'

'I never thought it was,' said the detective. His name was Peter Ford. He sat across the desk in a small office that also had a kitchen and a lady named Mrs Sutton who made them all a cup of tea.

He had started by explaining that detective services are expensive. In response, Kim took a wad of five-pound notes from her handbag and ran a thumb along their crisp edges like a card sharp flicking through a deck. 'There's plenty more where this came from,' she told him. 'But it doesn't mean you can take me for a soft touch.'

'I wouldn't dream,' said Peter Ford, amused. But the amusement faded as Kim's story progressed.

Kim had brought with her a praiseworthy inventory of facts, dates and general background. She expected some probing questions. But Peter Ford's struck her as peculiarly tangential, off the wall: 'Can anyone in Crowhurst Green remember the date you moved there? What's your own earliest memory? Can you read out this list of words I'm writing down? Good. Did you realize that you say "singging" and "ring-ging"? No? Do any of these place names mean anything to you? Please think hard.'

They were on the Wirral.

*

Kim was dreaming of Peggy.

'Safety first,' she was saying. 'In this house we hold to the motto of safety first.'

They were in the flat, in the tiny slit of a kitchen with its green pull-across curtain and everywhere the smell of gas fires, sickly, like anaesthetic. Images of danger were being projected on to a screen, warnings of a careless world, scissors left on chairs, saucepan handles sticking out instead of tucked to one side. Dish cloths hung above the cooker ring, wafting gently in the rising heat.

Kim's teacher was outside on the landing, trying to catch Peggy out by lighting a bonfire. 'Not us,' Peggy was arguing. 'We go into London and watch the displays, safe and sound. You ask the doctors up the hospital. Every Firework Night kids get brought in blinded or with their skin burnt off. We leave it to the professionals and watch from a safe distance.'

The teacher was Mrs Kennet from Kim's first year of school. Kim was five. Proper Firework Night was tomorrow, but a girl at school was having some in the garden. Peggy thought Kim was just going round there for tea.

And now Kim was dreaming, screaming.

'MUMMY NO MUMMY NO MUMMY MUMMY MUMMY'

The dream air was on fire, her dream head full of bangers and Jumping Jacks, whizzing sparks and fiery trails exploding in her dream eyes.

'Lovey, it's all right now,' said Peggy. 'I'm here. It's all over. The horrid things can't hurt you.'

'Kim! Wake up, you're having a nightmare. Wake up.'

Kim was tearing at her hair, frantically thrashing at the flames. 'Mummy!'

'Your mum's here, sweetheart, and it's all over. Let's get you home.'

'I'm not a liar, Daddy. Help! Help! *Lyndee*,' she screamed. '*LYNDEE!*'

Peggy's voice was sharp. 'Not Lyndee. You wasn't Lynne or Lyndee, you was Linda. But we don't say that either, do we? We don't say Linda or Lynne or Lyndee.'

'Oh Kim darling, please wake up!'

Kim flung herself upright in the bed, still jerking as though galvanized, excruciating cramp in her feet and hands. Her hair was stuck to her head with sweat. 'IT'S ALL STUPID,' shouted Kim at Imogen. 'I *LIKE* FIREWORKS!'

45

Mary Rose wasn't being staged in the Playhouse but in the Stanislavsky Room, a big empty box of raw brick. 'Our more experimental space,' explained Daphne. 'The atmosphere is mostly sound and lighting effects.'

'One day I'd like to do the technical stuff,' said Kim.

'Stick to lights. The worst you can do is plunge the stage into blackout till someone flicks a wall switch. With sound cues you can cock up an entire play. "Ah, here comes the train." *Clip-clop clip-clop.* "Is that the phone?" *Mooooooo.*'

But for now, Kim was happy to be a runaround. With Dr Robert Yelland.

She needed this project to stay sane, and luckily he was a keen student. 'May I bother you for a moment?' he would ask, smiling. 'Would you talk me through the prompt book?'

And it never entered Kim's head that such requests always came when she was standing by herself with her guard down, her usual briskness wilted and a look on her face of a lost and frightened child. One evening Imogen was out with her publisher and Kim found she enjoyed having Dr Yelland to herself. His presence soothed her.

Because the Stanislavsky Room really was a big empty

box there was no backstage until stage management created one by constructing a screen, and no audience seating until Daphne's helpers lugged it in. Meaning Kim and Dr Yelland. While they slogged back and forth, Monique was in the corridor smoking cigarettes with Giles. The two were so deep in smiling conversation that Monique didn't even look up at Kim and say hello.

Kim, always one to do her homework, had checked Sukie's account of Dr Yelland. He had indeed joined a general practice in Acton, and had lost his wife. But not recently. A decade ago. She particularly liked the man's voice, its Balliol-modulated tones being softer round the edges than most she heard hereabouts, warmed by the last traces of his Caribbean upbringing. Kim rather wished he hadn't lost any of it; the fewer people who sounded like Frances Massingham the better. Dr Yelland didn't seem to mind when she asked him, 'If I do get to Cambridge, will I have to polish up my voice, same as you did?'

'The polishing wasn't conscious on my part. Not affectation but protective coloration,' he smiled. 'No pun intended. But, Kim, the pressures on me were far more daunting than anything you will encounter.'

'Yeah?' In all seriousness she said, 'There were many charladies' daughters at Oxford, were there?'

'Ah. Touché,' said Dr Yelland.

Mary Rose was to have no actual set beyond simple chairs or a tree – or an isolated stair-less banister suspended by rope and raised into the darkness of the Stan Room's mansard roof when the scene moved to that Hebridean island.

'Banister rail?' queried the cast. The elderly building behind had a steep narrow staircase. The designer intended to unscrew the entire banister and hang it over his set, leaving the stairs unprotected and lethal.

'It will be your balls hanging over the set,' said Sebastian. 'Ben Sacks will string them up.'

'Ben will be on holiday that week, Sebastian. Most unfortunately.'

The production was using music by Pink Floyd, reworking eerie drones from the album *A Saucerful Of Secrets*. This should have reminded Kim of Denise but all she could hear was the word 'secrets' hissing from some inner world of lies and lost memory. It isn't fair, shouted Kim's head, me and Mum aren't the types for secrets. It was a form of showing off to have secrets in your past. That Pink Floyd's mystical mantras could be her own theme music cut through Kim's sense of solidity. Whenever the album was mentioned, she determinedly changed the title in her head. 'A bowlful of maggots,' she chanted to herself. 'A bowlful of maggots.'

Gareth was glad of a break from rigging heavy lanterns. Over a cigarette he talked to Kim and Dr Yelland about lighting, how metal stencils create dappled sunlight or foliage, or the shadow of a backlit window projected across the stage. *Mary Rose* would have more projections than actual solid matter. The only awkwardness came when he explained about colour gels. 'The mainstay is called Bastard Amber,' said Gareth – and instead of moving tactfully on, gave them an entire lecture on the subject. 'I didn't know where to look,' Kim told Denise.

When they finished hauling in the tiered rostra and stacking the chairs on them, Kim said, 'Imogen's here tomorrow. You can check the furniture together.'

'But there's hardly any furniture.'

'I mean the props,' improvised Kim.

'But there are hardly any props.' Dr Yelland smiled at her, and Kim felt herself blush. 'One can't help noticing how you throw us together,' he told her, adding, 'almost like a matchmaker. Am I wrong?' He looked amused.

'Yeah, all right,' said Kim. 'I think you'd be really good for her.'

'Yet Miss St Clair already has a romantic attachment.'

'You mean Sebastian? Oh, you don't want to worry about

Sebastian. He's completely useless or I wouldn't be planning to chuck him out and get her a new one.'

'And you have set your heart on me. How very flattering. But may I ask why?'

Kim thought about it. 'Promise you won't tell?'

'Tell whom? I won't tell Miss St Clair, certainly.'

He has lovely eyes, thought Kim, to whom eyes had become totemic. He must be a good doctor; you could imagine telling him anything.

'I do promise,' he assured her, smiling.

'Well, it's like this. You know how Imogen's been looking for Charlotte all these years? What I think is, she'll never find her even now she's found her.'

'I'm afraid that's too deep for me.'

'Charlotte's grown up now. She isn't the same as in Imogen's dreams.'

'Yes. I see.'

'I reckon Imogen'll never be happy till she's got a new baby. It'll be best if it's a boy so he can't be compared to Charlotte, but nobody can guarantee that, so the next best thing is to go for a kid that's nothing like Charlotte – *on account of being a different colour*. See what I'm getting at? The minute I heard about you I could see you'd fit the bill,' said Kim. 'My mum always said, "Don't leave things to good luck, leave them to good planning."'

✳

'Oh Kim,' said Monique.

'I don't even want him to go out with Imogen,' said Kim. 'He was absolutely horrible.'

'But, sweetheart, the man had the right to be.'

Kim's lips were trembling. She kept biting them.

'Please don't do that, Kim, you'll draw blood!'

In some odd ritualistic compulsion Kim had made fists of her hands and was banging her knuckles on the table. Is she just too proud to cry? wondered Monique. Even in front of me?

This was the following day, in Jack the Mack's café. Last night, Kim had been too mortified to tell even Monique, besides which Monique had gone off somewhere with Giles.

Dr Yelland had not been horrible, as Kim asserted. He had merely gone very quiet, and then, 'with his voice turned all ice and Oxford', as Kim put it, suggested to her that his colour and background were precious to him, and if Kim wanted to order them as commodities like gifts on a Christmas list, perhaps she should open an account at Harrods. Monique, suffused with dismayed sympathy, spluttered her coffee across the table. Then she did her best to explain.

'Suppose you were in Jamaica and a man wanted you to marry into his family, not because of any actual qualities of your own but merely because you were white English. Wouldn't it make you feel like just a baby machine?'

'Being white English *is* one of my actual qualities.'

'Darling, that's rather what I meant.'

'Anyway, wanting to be English isn't the same thing.'

'There speaks the voice of Empire,' said Monique Shashkova. 'Let me put it another way. Suppose they wanted you as a kind of pet because you were brought up as working class. Now do you see? Kim, my love, you meant well but it was blisteringly tactless and caught him on the raw. You did a Sukie, sweetheart.'

A retort percolated up through Kim's mind like rising damp. Somebody wanting me as a pet cos I'm working class? thought Kim. That's not doing a Sukie, it's doing an Imogen.

46

'Imogen, come here quick, it's Sebastian, he's on TV!'

He was, too. On the news, drenched and bedraggled, his talking head robbed of its habitual hauteur, his lean jawline wrecked by a straggly three-day beard. With one sopping sleeve Sebastian was trying to polish the rain from his black-framed glasses.

'. . . And the authorities' response, closing the roads, is all too typical of a climate where the administration is unleashing B-52 bombers on—'

'Yes, thank you, we certainly hope you get home safe to London, England. This is Johnnie Biedebecker reporting from upstate New York.'

Imogen scooted in from the kitchen and just caught the camera panning back. The scene was one of wet tarmac and soaked fields, and hell's own traffic jam. Cars, station wagons, vans painted over with love slogans and flowers, the whole lot apparently enchained, snaked across the landscape in a twenty-mile clutter of immobile metal. And beside and around them, mile after mile, trudged dripping lines of humanity like refugees.

'What's going on?'

'It's that festival, Imogen. Seems they got half a million people turn up and another million trying to get there. And it's been pissing down with rain for days.'

'Oh God!'

'Yeah, what a bugger. Bet it's a hell of a concert though,' added Kim brightly.

'But what was Sebastian saying? And who was there with him, did you see? Was Lenny with him?'

But Kim had noticed only one person close to Sebastian, a brunette edging her photogenic profile into shot. The phone rang.

'Ginny, we've just seen Sebastian on the ITV news.'

So had everybody else from the Questors. The phone rang all evening. But only from the Questors; the rest of Imogen's friends were in upstate New York themselves. And somehow they managed to make it to Woodstock.

'Yo!' announced Lenny Tonka-Toy, striding into the kitchen the following Friday in plenty of time for lunch. 'Kim, yo!'

'Pardon?'

He was followed by the usual crowd: an elderly poetess with a lot of recklessly applied perfume and a cigarette holder, a college professor in crimson satin and his boyfriend, a film-maker who had tagged along to ask Imogen to finance a project that intercut erect penises and bullfights. 'I know how it sounds,' Monique had already told Kim, 'but Zuzu really is a genius, and this is a work of art, not pornography.' But Kim was accustomed to Lenny's lot with their relentless pornography. What disgusted Kim were the bullfights.

'Please keep the noise down,' urged Imogen as she made them all coffee and checked the fridge for food that had not been condemned by Mrs Harris. Could all seven sirloin steaks really be earmarked for Welly? 'Sebastian's in bed with the most frightful cold.'

He had eventually fallen in through the door an hour ago,

feverish and half-dead. It wasn't his first contact with home: Sebastian had phoned from a Manhattan hotel in the small hours of Wednesday morning reversing the charges, to demand that Imogen wire him some money. The airline had taken one look at his filthy, disintegrating clothes and streaming nose, and refused to let him board the plane.

Lenny and friends were hooting. 'Baby, that guy should keep out of beds. If he wasn't so obsessed with beds, maybe he'd have made it to Yasgar's farm for the festival.'

'Obsessed with beds, Lenny?' asked Imogen.

'Baby, she was the cutest little chick you ever did see. Worth missing any amount of music for. Hey, don't take it like it's a drag, Ginny. Free love is freedom of the soul. Exclusivity isn't love, it's ownership. Jealousy is to true love what an occupying army is to ... Hey, Clytemnestra darling!' he called to the poetess. 'Go find some Hendrix in Seb's collection, would you?'

The doorbell chimed. Oh *no*, not Sukie and Tonya, thought Kim. They had been even less tolerable than usual yesterday, sitting at Imogen's feet and gazing at her. And Imogen, presumably in a well-intentioned effort to boost Kim's standing, blabbed a whole heap of stuff about the private detective and John Lennon's road, to which Sukie responded by nearly bursting Kim's eardrum.

But the doorbell was Frances Massingham.

'Let me in please, Imogen,' she said on the doorstep. 'George has just told me about Sukie Sandeman. It appears that he kept it to himself because he knew how I would react. Well, I'm here now, reacting.'

Kim had been getting ready to go out to help set up a jumble sale at her new post-Barry church. But at Frances Massingham's advent she stopped where she was, and watched astounded as the woman made mincemeat of Imogen's guests.

'You'll take yourselves off to another room, if you please. And as for that incompetent cacophony,' added Frances, pointing towards an immortal Hendrix guitar solo, 'I'd be obliged if you'd replace it with somebody who knows how to play a musical instrument. Are you staying, Kim?' she asked as Lenny *et al.* actually retreated, silenced, to the sitting room.

'Er, not really, Mrs Massingham. There's this um ... I promised ...'

'That's perfectly all right.'

Imogen turned urgently to Kim. 'Could you leave Welly with me?'

'No, Imogen, he's—'

'Please, Kim.' The look in Imogen's eyes was plaintive. 'I'd really like him to stay here with me.'

So Kim left Welly sitting at Imogen's feet in the kitchen, to be clutched at like a comfort blanket.

'How long will you be gone?'

'Um, not sure, Imogen. Might be a while. Bye.' And she was out the door.

Kim's new church was a mile's walk from home. The day was muggy, the cloud cover low, the air heavy. Headache weather, Peggy would have said. Kim turned out of Mount Hill Crescent. Halfway up Eaton Rise, a car pulled up.

'Hello, Reverend. On your way to the church hall?'

'On my way back, sad to say. Mix-up with the keys. It will be four o'clock before we can get started. Want a ride back home? Hop in.'

But in Kim's mind was an image of Mrs Massingham. A talking image. 'Thanks, but I think I'll go for a wander,' she said.

'Happy wandering. See you at four.'

'... any concept of responsibility, Imogen. The child is an orphan without ...'

'Aunt Frances—'

'... any known relatives in the world. You went into the enterprise like a bull in a china shop. Anyway, I want to talk to this Sandeman girl myself, and settle it once and for all. Please give me her phone number.'

'But Sukie doesn't know. We haven't told her she's the true Charlotte.'

'Then it is high time somebody did. I want the girl here by the next train. This whole thing is far too devious. All these secrets, and "please don't check my story with Mummy and Daddy" and clunking great clues fed to this Tonya person who adores her. Has it not occurred to you that beneath her engaging exterior might be a calculating young woman who is duping the lot of you?'

'Hi, Denise, it's me. No, I'm phoning from a call box. Imogen's got Mrs Massingham doing a rant in the kitchen. Can you get up here, give me some support? Yeah? Say an hour and a half? I'll try to time it so I don't get back till you arrive.'

'What are you talking about?' Frances Massingham set down her teacup. There was something quite different in her voice.

'I think it's very enterprising of Kim,' responded Imogen, rallying. 'She and Denise took all the information they have, and—'

'And set a private detective to uncover Kim's background? Oh Imogen,' cried Frances. 'Why in heaven's name couldn't you discuss this first with George and me? You cannot begin to understand what you have started, where this could lead.'

'You're quite wrong, it's leading somewhere rapidly. It turns out Peggy wasn't living in Essex after all but Liverpool. The detective phoned last night to say he's got a lead from Birkenhead on the Wirral.'

47

A very smart young man in uniform told Frances they were flying Chief Superintendent Collier down to London by helicopter.

Frances was staggered.

'If the Americans can put a man on the moon, madam, I'm sure the British can fly a policeman a hundred and eighty miles,' he told her complacently. But somebody had been pulling his leg. Chief Superintendent Collier caught the train at Chester station like anybody else and changed at Crewe. By the time he reached London the police in Australia had already interviewed Hazel Barber.

It was the business about a private detective that made it all so urgent. And also led to a great deal of shouting down a phone. Kim's Peter Ford gave the police a maddening lecture on client confidentiality before eventually admitting that yes, his research did suggest she was Lynne Jarman, and the inquiries had also stirred up a lot of suspicion on the Wirral. He wouldn't be surprised if the lid were about to blow, exploding the story across the media. He doubted that they had twenty-four hours. Frances was afraid they might have even less. Imogen had told this Sukie and her Tonya about Peter Ford and the Wirral, and Frances's opinion of the unmet Sukie was that she wouldn't trust her not to call a press conference.

Frances envisaged the skies cross-hatched with phone calls: she had phoned her husband, who put a call through to Collier, who phoned New Scotland Yard, who simultaneously phoned the private detective and the Western Australia police, who phoned the Barbers, in a sequence of connections as sharp as a reflex. And in a very short time, on opposite sides of the world, surprisingly senior officers were standing at suburban doors while men in uniform waited in marked cars with the engine running. And a finger poised over the siren, probably, thought Frances, shaken.

Hazel Barber didn't even try saying she refused to get involved; she confirmed that Peggy Tanner had worked for Olivia Jarman, who had sacked her a few weeks before Lynne's disappearance, 'Because Peggy was sticking her nose in where it wasn't wanted.'

Hazel believed she was Peggy's only confidante. Sid Davis was a wife-beater.

'He was one of those men who marry a woman because she's a stunner and then drive themselves insane with jealousy because of it. Nothing she did was right. He'd insist Peggy kept herself looking good – hairdresser every week, manicure, the lot – and then accuse her of dolling herself up for a lover. They'd go out for the evening so he could show her off as a trophy, and soon as they got home he'd beat her black and blue for letting other men look at her.'

Violence was a skill at which Sid Davis was accomplished. 'Learned his techniques off his bully-boys. Peggy's injuries never showed, not when she was dressed.' And like many another violent husband he was always at his worst when his wife was pregnant. 'He'd pretend the baby wasn't his and use it as an excuse to knock her from here to next week. The truth was, Sid was jealous of Peggy's babies even before the poor things were born. Three she lost.'

Why didn't she leave him earlier? 'Because his henchmen would have tracked her down, that's why. Sid's property empire was spread all over the place, and he made bloody certain Peggy was never sure exactly where. He knew how to keep a wife in line.' But after Patricia Kim died, she took the risk and fled. 'Even if he found her and killed her it was no worse than the life she was living. Not just her own life, either, there'd have been more pregnancies, more dead babies.'

Sid had never mentioned connections in Liverpool, and being a port it had a large migrant population in which Peggy could try to lose herself.

'Peggy was clever but she wasn't qualified for a job. Of course Sid never allowed her to go out to work. In an *office*? Where there were *men*? But she was never afraid of hard graft,' added Hazel, her phrase an echo of Peggy herself. She answered ads posted in shop windows, and the wife who had never been allowed to do a hand's turn in her own home was soon working as a cleaner five days a week at houses from Knotty Ash to the Wirral. And in the wealthiest of them she found a child who had been thrown down the stairs.

'Peggy took one look at the poor little beggar and knew,' said Hazel.

She called the welfare services and the Cruelty Man did go round, but nothing seemed to come of it. 'Lynne wasn't taken away, all that happened was Mrs Jarman realized who had made the phone call and packed Peggy off without even a day's money in lieu. And no, before you ask, I didn't guess Peggy had stolen her. Peggy had much too good manners to burden me with that kind of knowledge. But I'm bloody glad she did. Good on her.'

For Kim to be formally identified as Lynne Jarman they would need to take X-rays. As Mr Antrobus had pointed out, that the two girls were one and the same could be verified in a trice. And then the case against William and Olivia would go to the courts so that the verdict could be quashed.

'And a royal pardon issued,' elucidated the commissioner of police. They were in his office at New Scotland Yard awaiting the arrival of Mr Collier. 'We talk about unsafe verdicts. Well, finding the murder victim full of beans ten years later is about as unsafe as it gets.'

Had I known I was going to meet the commissioner of police, thought Frances Massingham distractedly, I would have come out this morning in my green silk instead of a cotton sundress. And then, Of all aspects of human adversity and how it takes one unawares, the question of being caught in the wrong frock has probably received the least attention. Frances had a fleeting image of Jackie Kennedy going through her wardrobe and deciding disastrously on pink.

Imogen had been deeply shocked, but she didn't doubt what Frances told her. As soon as the Massinghams left with the police, she jumped into the Rolls to fetch Kim and break the news as best she could. Outside the church hall one of the vicar's sentries explained the delay, so now there was nothing anyone could do until Kim drifted home. When Denise turned up in Mount Hill Crescent in mid-afternoon, both she and Imogen were surprised Kim hadn't returned. Surprised but not alarmed. Not yet.

The commissioner was talking to the Massinghams. 'I must impress upon you both the extreme sensitivity. On the one hand we can't inform the Jarmans' surviving family until we have absolute confirmation from Kim's X-rays. It's a question of protocol: however slim, there is a theoretical chance this could turn out to be some abysmal coincidence. But it's unthinkable the family should hear of it via the press.'

It would be Chief Superintendent Collier's job to talk to

the Jarmans' relatives. But first he had to face Frances Massingham.

'It seems you were absolutely right and I was absolutely wrong,' he said.

Colonel Massingham sketched a bow. 'You had your reasons, Chief Superintendent. And we still have no idea what actually took place. My wife and I are certain Kim has no inkling of her past. Probably she has never even heard of the Jarman case.'

'No reason why she should.'

'Which means, I suppose, that we will never be able to piece together precisely what happened.'

'Fiddlesticks,' said Frances. 'We can piece together some of it here and now. Now that our minds are not fogged by doubt.'

'Frances?'

'That baby carriage, for instance, George. How stupid of us all not to see this before. Olivia was pushing Lynne in a pram because the girl had been injured the previous day, that ghastly business with the firework. She couldn't risk anyone seeing the child injured yet again, particularly not like that. Burns are graphic. So Olivia dragged that huge old-fashioned double carriage out of the attic and tucked her sick daughter into it with both hoods up.'

'But Frances, Olivia could simply have left Lynne at home.'

'Not that day. It was you, Mr Collier, who provided us with the reason why not. Olivia's new cleaner was in the house.'

'It's certainly a possible explanation,' said the chief super-intendent, expressionless.

'And as for William's driving off with a suitcase,' continued Frances, 'perhaps that was nothing more than a marital row, possibly in the wake of his wife's atrocity with the firework. He storms dramatically out of the house, but like most husbands he can't survive so much as one single night on his own and next morning he's home with his tail between his legs and—'

'Frances, my dear,' said Colonel Massingham, 'we mustn't abuse our position. If a supposition is obvious, the chief superintendent probably worked it out for himself before his train reached Crewe.' He turned to Mr Collier. 'If we can get Kim X-rayed tonight, will you speak to the relatives tomorrow?'

'That is my intention, yes. There's only Olivia's sister. William didn't have anybody close. After the Jarmans' arrest it was the sister who took in their natural daughter, Lynne's sister Marianne.'

'I keep forgetting about Marianne,' said Frances guiltily. 'She must have been, what, coming up to three years old?'

'Older,' said the chief superintendent. 'Nearer four – the Jarmans were already expecting when they adopted Lynne, though they didn't know it. I shall speak to the family as soon as we get young Kim sorted out.'

'I do feel for you. And for them, naturally. The shock.'

'It will be all of that, Mrs Massingham. We've got a child psychologist on stand-by. It turns out the daughter Marianne has never managed to rise above the disgrace, so to speak. I read the file while I was being driven here from Euston station, and it made grim reading. Pity. Pretty little thing she was, by all accounts. She kept in touch with her mother in prison. Sometimes they do, sometimes they don't. I can't help wishing she hadn't. Olivia died in 1965 when Marianne was nine, and basically they haven't had a day's joy of her since.'

'You mean the child is . . . depressive?'

'I mean she's a nutter, Colonel Massingham. I beg your pardon, Mrs Massingham. It's like all the grief about her father's death never hit her till her mother died, and then the whole lot came down like a ton of bricks and she became convinced they were innocent all along. Started acting like a one-person campaign. We were getting a dozen letters a week about the case, all from her, all under different names, all railing at us.' The chief superintendent pulled himself up. 'Yes, well, rightly as it turns out. Every miscarriage of justice has victims beyond the central ones.'

Frances said, 'But surely there was never any question of Marianne being convinced or not convinced. She would know it of her own knowledge. The girl was with her mother when Lynne was stolen from the pram.'

'She wasn't even four years old, my dear,' said Colonel Massingham. 'Does one's memory go back that far?'

'Good gracious, George, it does for a catastrophe on that scale. Marianne witnessed her mother flying into hysterics, screaming that Lynne had been stolen. This is the child's sister we're talking about. Passers-by had seen Marianne riding in that pram at one point. She knew her sister was lying asleep or groggy under the blanket. And more to the point, she would remember the terrifying incident of the firework explosion, and how Lynne was alive at the end of it.'

'That would all fit, certainly.'

'Suppose she blames Kim for what happened to her parents?'

'I assure you, Mrs Massingham, she blames the Cheshire county police. You should see our mailbag.'

'But that's recent. That's only what her head tells her, not her heart. In 1959 Marianne was far too young to understand about the police, she only knew the catastrophe started with Lynne. And she was bound to believe Lynne was a bad child anyway – she would have learned that from her mother. Mr Collier, suppose she came across Kim knowing her to be Lynne?'

'Now that *is* improbable. That would require a massive coincidence, Mrs Massingham.'

'Coincidence doesn't come into it. You say the girl is obsessed with clearing the Jarman name. Obviously the only way is to seek out her sister. And from within the family she'd have all manner of facts at her fingertips to help her, so . . . Oh God, you said the child was a pretty little thing. Mr Collier, did she take her aunt's surname? What name is Marianne using now?'

Colonel Massingham said quickly, 'There's a girl called Sukie Sandeman, Chief Superintendent. She suddenly appeared out of nowhere and we know nothing except—'

Frances stood up. 'I've had the most terrible thought. Yesterday Imogen told her all about Liverpool and the private detective. Mr Collier, if that girl is Marianne Jarman and she has some twisted vindictive plan, she knows she has to get on with it today before the news breaks and her identity is blown!'

'Not Sandeman,' said the chief superintendent, cutting her off. 'Please calm down, Mrs Massingham. Her surname is Shilling. Calls herself by the nickname Toinette. From Marie Antoinette, I suppose. Not the best of jokes, considering what happened to the lady,' added Chief Superintendent Collier.

48

'Tonya!' said Kim, surprised.

'Hi, Kim.'

'Something up?'

'Not up, just urgent. I've been following you ever since Mount Hill Crescent. I need a favour.'

'Yeah?' said Kim dismally. There were few things she wanted less than to be derailed from her day by Tonya and Sukie. 'Where's Sukie?'

'No idea. You know this project I have to do for the summer school?'

'No,' said Kim. 'What summer school?'

'I have mentioned it, but I suppose you didn't bother listening. The thing is, it's history and I need to check a couple of facts.'

'I'm not best at history, Tonya, I'm—'

'Please hear me out. The information I want is at the Questors. Nineteenth-century military helmets. There's a hat box in the property store. R. S. Grant of the Royal Engineers, 1830. I distinctly remember.'

This was surreal, decided Kim. She was halfway up Eaton Rise being waylaid by Tonya with talk about military helmets. And there was something peculiarly businesslike about the girl in the absence of Sukie's usual bubbling Greek chorus. Barely tolerable at the best of times, Tonya authoritative and bossy was the rock bottom. She made all the hairs prickle on the backs of Kim's arms. It was like seasickness, the pitch and yaw of her disquiet, yellow like fear. 'There'll be nobody at Questors, Tonya. It's Friday daytime.'

'But you know where the spare keys are. All the spare keys. You said.'

'Look, I'm really busy—'

'You're not actually, Kim, I heard the vicar. All I want is two minutes in the prop cellar and then I'll be out of your hair. Shall we go?' said Tonya.

*

'She's still just a thirteen-year-old kid,' insisted Sebastian, sneezing into a handkerchief. 'Even if she is the Jarmans' daughter.' But he was trembling.

Imogen wasn't. Sheet white, she was on her feet making phone calls. To one person after another she said, 'If you can check the streets around you I would be so grateful.' Then down went the phone and Imogen dialled the next number.

The chief superintendent had talked her through the situation with professional precision before handing the phone to Frances Massingham. But it was he who made the call, not Frances. With the name 'Tonya' hardly out of her mouth, Frances had reached across the desk, which was actually the commissioner's desk, for the nearest of several phones and started to dial. With unhurried authority Collier set his finger on the cradle to cut her off, unpeeled her fingers from the receiver, and moved the entire apparatus out of her reach.

'I'll do this if you don't mind, Mrs Massingham, and we'll use another phone. Miss St Clair's number is—?'

Later, Frances would wonder whether it was the Prime Minister or Her Majesty the Queen whom she had so nearly talked to.

Imogen briskly evicted Lenny and the hangers-on. Monique and Sukie turned up at the door together, and Imogen immediately organized Monique to sit beside her with phone numbers at hand and a notepad. Then she dealt with Sukie.

'Stop crying and start thinking! Tonya's your friend, you know what she does and where she goes. Where would she take Kim? For once in your life, Sukie, try to be of some use to somebody. Oh hello,' she said into the phone. 'This is Imogen St Clair and it's an emergency. Listen . . .'

Then two plain-clothes detectives arrived to interview everybody. They started with Denise, who had been chafing in the kitchen for an hour now. 'And Kim would normally stick to an arrangement to meet you? I see.' Then they turned coaxingly to Sukie. 'You are our best bet, Miss Sandeman. Put yourself in Miss Shilling's shoes. Where would she take Kim?'

'It's all an hysterical storm in a teacup,' said Sebastian. 'So Kim's with Tonya. So what?'

'For God's sake,' shouted Imogen. 'Kim was due back here more than an hour ago, Tonya left home before lunch with a story about the library, the librarian denies she was ever there, and the local vicar saw a girl of her description with Kim in Eaton Rise. And no one has a clue where she went after that, only that she's deranged and dangerous.'

'Imogen, nobody says she's deranged and dangerous except Frances Massingham, and Frances Massingham would lock up the Beatles as deranged and dangerous!'

What the police had said was, 'We have to be alarmed that Marianne has sought out Kim. She is known to have an obsessive interest in her parents' history.'

'Obsessive,' repeated Sebastian smoothly. 'So tell me, what would count as *normal* interest in the fact that your father and mother died in jail for a crime that never actually took place?'

∗

The area at the bottom of the cellar steps rustled with leaves. Every rainstorm or windy day sent them blowing across from the mature plane trees in the front garden of Mattock Lodge, to settle in trapped drifts around the cellar door and die there, browning and curling on the mildewed concrete. Kim crunched her way to the narrow white door and unlocked it.

'I don't even remember any helmets,' said Kim. She reached a hand around the wall and clicked on the lights.

Dank inside. The doughy smell of an untenanted basement. The prop cellar was always dingier than Kim remembered, and more complicated: the ups and downs of its ceilings and floors, the whole shadowy layout with its bricked-up alcoves and sudden inexplicable bunkers honeycombing through what you had assumed was a structural wall.

'Over there,' announced Tonya, shepherding her. Then she added, matter-of-fact, 'Wouldn't it be horrid to be locked up? Somewhere like this. Locked up for something you hadn't done?'

She was too close. Tonya's skin scent slammed into Kim's senses. It rocked her. Turning, Kim was looking into Tonya's eyes. And she knew them. She had always known them, and could no longer pretend she didn't.

It was like brickbats. It was like a shelf collapsing with her beneath it, heavy metal objects rolling off and striking her face, her arms, her knees. Kim actually ducked down with her arms over her head, which cricked her neck, the muscle spasm burning like a hot poker. She wasn't cringing from Tonya, Tonya had gone already, striding off to leave her locked in here alone in the dark. Kim was frantic to prevent this raining blizzard of memories striking through the membranes of her mind and revealing tissue that must not be touched, must not be exposed to the light, must not be breathed upon.

By the time she heard the door slam she had wet herself.

49

Frances Massingham was crying. Her manicured fingers clutched with unconscious compulsion at the stuff of her summer dress.

'Please, gentlemen, do not patronize me,' she implored them. 'I need to have some context in which to understand the danger Kim is in. What do we know of Marianne's life before the Jarmans were arrested? Are we certain she wasn't ill-treated like Lynne?'

'As certain as we can be, Mrs Massingham. The parents doted on her.'

'Doted on her. Right. But her sister was being hurt before her eyes. How did that affect her at the time, do we know?'

'We do not. Nobody thought to interest themselves in Marianne's state of mind until she was nine and starting to show signs of disturbance. Which were put down to her mother's death and belated reaction to her father's.'

'And she was close to her mother?'

'According to the file, yes. Naturally, Marianne was too young for prison visits but they kept up a correspondence.'

'And do we know whether Lynne's abuse had been systematic? I mean continual cruelty?'

The chief superintendent hesitated.

'You don't want to tell me,' said Frances promptly. 'Does that mean the answer is no? The police knew Olivia's ill-treatment was confined to some isolated instances? Which of course was not how the evidence was presented at the Jarmans' trial, therefore—'

'Frances!' interrupted her husband. 'We don't have the right to browbeat Mr Collier like this. Whatever went on in that godforsaken house, there was an injured child in it, and two fully grown adults who were responsible.'

'But I will answer your question, Mrs Massingham. There were stories at the time. There are always stories. It seems that Olivia Jarman occasionally blew her top and went for the child, generally when Lynne was under the weather or wetting the bed. That sort of thing. Olivia wasn't good at coping. And we know more now from talking to the aunt, Mrs Shilling, after Marianne started plaguing us. It's all in this file I mentioned. It had started slowly but was picking up steam like many another vice. But there was no question of us believing the Jarmans were innocent. A few isolated incidents of throwing your small daughter down a staircase? That does not constitute normal maternal be-haviour. And until today everyone, but everyone, believed William Jarman drove off in that car with his little daughter's body inside his suitcase. Olivia's own sister believed it, Mrs Massingham. Even she.'

'So why? Why did Olivia hurt the child?' demanded Frances with revulsion. This was *Kim* they were talking about. *Kim.*

'That's just what the defence counsel asked at the trial,' answered the chief superintendent. 'Meaning – look, these are respectable sober people, and respectable sober people don't beat their children. And anyway there was a second kiddie who was alive and well. The Jarmans' counsel argued that people do not abuse one child and love the other. It was an ill-judged defence because some people do exactly that.

And anyway the prosecution made great play of the fact that Lynne wasn't their flesh and blood. Worst of all, they couldn't even pretend she was, not once they had Marianne just months later. There was still quite a stigma about adoption back then, not least because a lot of people believed illegitimate children would inherit bad blood and loose morals from the unmarried mother. William and Olivia were horribly status-conscious. They made sure they got a baby they could pass off as their own – William was ginger, remember, and so was Lynne – but then bingo! along comes Marianne and a difference of not much more than six months between the two kiddies.'

'Most of us have known some couple who adopted and then had a child of their own,' objected Frances. 'They don't ill-treat the first one! And anyway, those proceedings take time to complete. Olivia must have known about her condition before the adoption became legally binding. The Jarmans could have said, "Sorry, we've changed our minds," and handed Lynne back.'

'Not if the girl had already sustained some injury that was identifiable, Mrs Massingham.'

'Even when she was still—?' Frances put her hands over her eyes.

'Like I said, Olivia Jarman wasn't a coping sort of woman, and no spring chicken either. Forty-five when she fell for her first baby, and unwell from Day 1, according to her sister. And then two little ones to look after. The sensible thing was to employ a nanny, but she was too scared of having anyone else around in case they witnessed . . . well, call it a vicious circle. And Mrs herself had been ill-treated,' he continued. 'We knew that at the time of the trial but neither the defence nor the prosecution thought it would help their case. Again the perpetrator was the mother, and again the behaviour was only ever directed towards one of her two children. Olivia's sister was cherished while Olivia got knocked about. One story says the mother locked her in the garden shed for two days and nights until the neighbours intervened.'

'Good God,' said Colonel Massingham.

'What's the line by that poet Auden? "Those to whom evil is done do evil in return." We see a lot of that in the force. But if you ask me, explanations just make simple things complicated. Some people lash out, and some parents channel their violent behaviour towards the one kid while its brothers and sisters never feel the back of a hand in anger. That's just how people are.'

50

It was like freefall. Freefall with your clothes on fire. And in the dark; the lights had gone out just before the door slammed shut. The voice that issued from her own mouth did so without her full consent, and some of its sounds seemed not to belong to her. Except the crying. She knew that was hers.

Mustn't do it, mustn't. She hates me when I cry. 'If you don't shut up, I'll give you something to cry about!' Put my hand over my mouth, thumb in my mouth, keep quiet. Not frightened of the dark, don't mind the dark in Mummy's cupboard, not as long as I keep still, as long as I don't move then nothing will fall on me, rolling off the shelves, bang! bang! bang! Nothing to be scared of in the dark. It's daylight I'm frightened of.

She even knew why, though gauzily, in flashes of unjoined-up memory. They could never be called scenes. She never would remember them as scenes. Yet true scenes had underlain them.

There was the time she wet the bed and went straight to the cupboard of her own volition, like Silas Marner's Effie in the tole hole. It was Mrs Tanner who found her there with her arms around the Hoover.

'What's all this?' she demanded in that bright voice with its strange sounds. Sometimes Lynne didn't understand a word she said. Mummy told her it was because Mrs Tanner was common. 'Game of hide 'n' seek, is it?'

Mummy was there instantly as if she'd come shooting up through the floor. 'Oh no, what now? All right, Mrs Tanner, I'll take her. For God's sake, you're wet *again*.'

Lynne was swept away, up the stairs. But it would be all right. Mummy didn't get horrible when Mrs Tanner was here. The Hoover noise would start soon, growling like some huge friendly animal, guarding her against hurt.

They were on the ferry. She woke groggily. It was the tail-end of mumps, her residual swelling like an injury on the mend.

'It's all right, dear. We're having a day out.'

'Where's Mummy?' she asked in panic. 'Mummy and Marianne?'

'They're coming along a bit later, lovey. It's an outing.'

Outing? The word meant nothing to her. The only time Lynne had been away from her mother was in the hospital. But Lynne hated the hospital.

A light drizzle was blowing on deck. A gust blew at her scarf and she tugged it off her head. Her scalp itched. The firework had scorched her hair; it had come away in blackened handfuls like chaff blowing off a bonfire.

'No, no,' said Mrs Tanner, anxiously retying the bright silk. 'We got to keep it hid till we get indoors.'

'My head's sore,' said Lynne.

'I know, lovey. Soon as we get inside I'll take the scarf off of you and have a proper look-see.'

Have a what? Spray mingled with the drizzle. It was chilly. November.

''Fraid I have to stay up on deck, rain or shine,' said Mrs

Tanner. 'It's cos I suffer with seasickness. Even a short hop like this turns me up. Aren't I a silly billy?'

'Yes,' replied Lynne politely.

None of it meant anything to Lynne. Besides, grown-up persons didn't often address her in a tone of apology, not even the doctor when she had her vaccination.

'This is going to hurt a little bit,' he had said with brisk authority, so Lynne had braced herself, cowering, stiff and solid. Everyone laughed.

'Well, Mrs Jarman, anybody would think the child expected a beating!'

After the ferry they caught a bus. Lynne knew where she was: this wasn't the first time she had travelled by bus through these teeming streets; it wasn't far from Daddy's office. This place was called Toxteth. Liverpool people called it Tocky.

'Well, aren't you clever?' exclaimed Mrs Tanner. 'Fancy knowing that.'

Fancy knowing that. It might have been a foreign language, so instead she answered the first part, which was a question. 'No,' said Lynne.

'Sorry?'

'Yes, I'm sorry,' agreed Lynne immediately. 'Marianne's clever,' she added.

When the bus turned a corner that Lynne didn't know, she spoke again. 'Are we going to Daddy's office?'

She would like to go to Daddy's office; she didn't see much of him. And he only shouted at liars.

'Mummy did it. On the stairs.'

'If you ever say that again, the police will come and take you away. They'll lock you up. That's what happens to little liars, the police put them in prison. Do you hear me?'

But the next time it happened her parents took Lynne away themselves. They took her to hospital. She had never before spent a night away from her mother; she was lost and frightened, aching for home and her own bed.

Lynne woke in the night to the funny smell and the lights on.

They had put her in a room off the surgical ward. There were two beds, and in the other was a girl named Jennifer, a big girl of seven but she cried all night, a desperate sobbing that made Lynne's tummy ache and churn for fear they'd think it was her and come at her for it with a slap.

In the daytime Jennifer acted as if she'd never cried in her life. 'I'm in for tonsils,' she said proudly. 'They're giving me an operation. I heard the nurse say you went downstairs arse over tit. What are you, a spastic?'

After her operation, Jennifer was brought back to her bed still sound asleep, with something in her mouth like the stopper of a hot-water bottle. Two men in navy blue wheeled her in. A bit later the nurses took out the stopper and Jennifer dribbled in a way that would have earned Lynne a smack.

The middle of the night and two nurses were in the room. They spoke in Scouse accents, deep and nasal. Speaking in Scouse was common too, but unlike Mrs Tanner's manner of speech Lynne could at least understand it. Except she couldn't.

'Fell downstairs my foot.'

'Abused, you reckon?'

'Or I'm one of the Everly Brothers.'

All double Dutch. And what was a bused?

'Nowt you can do, is there?'

'We've the Cruelty Man coming in for a baby on Lister Ward. I can have a word with the doctor.'

'Oh aye? You take care. Her dad's a solicitor on Rodney Street.'

'I don't care if he's the King of Ruritania. That kid should have the Cruelty Man.'

After they left, Lynne lay in a state of terrified despair. She actually cried, nothing she could do to stop it, soaking the hospital sheets and shaking. He hadn't come by the time dawn arrived, followed by a breakfast Lynne was too frightened to eat. Not eating was a serious dereliction in hospital, one for which the day nurse gave her a fearful telling off. But then the cavalry arrived.

'I'm not being a liar, Mummy, please, Mummy, I heard.'

She was home within the hour, discharged by her mother and carried out of the ward in her nightie. Home, and safe from the Cruelty Man.

Last night Daddy and Mummy were shouting at each other. They had never done that before. The quarrel started about the firework but got very muddled until Daddy was yelling that he couldn't stand it any more.

Marianne cried and cried, and held on to him. He stormed down the hall with his suitcase, trying to shake her off like a man with a terrier on his trouser leg.

Now they were in a huge old block of flats. Lynne was fascinated by a line-up of enormous grey dustbins along the outside wall. There was no door into the building, just an open hole giving on to an echoey stairwell with walls painted peely green. Lynne walked up the first flight herself but Mrs Tanner carried her the rest of the way, getting slower and slower, resting on the landing of the third floor puffing and red. At the next one they stopped for good and Mrs Tanner unlocked an ordinary door. The flat was tiny. Lynne asked her where the rest of it was.

'I haven't got any toys,' Peggy admitted sadly. 'Wasn't expecting you, you see. Not till I suddenly come on you, there by the shops. Thought it was a baby in a pram, went over to chuck it under the chin, and there you was! And your poor hair burned off. But you can play with anything you want, even the bits and pieces of china. It doesn't matter what you break.'

'Please,' said Lynne in a small voice. 'Please may I play with the Hoover, Mrs Tanner?'

Peggy applied Savlon to her scalp, which made the

remaining hair stick up in bristles. It wasn't sore for long. After a funny meal of fish pie, Peggy washed Lynne's face and hands, and told her she was a good girl.

'You've ate up all your dinner,' she said. '*What* a good girl!'

Lynne hung her head.

'What's the matter, lovey?'

It took a lot of coaxing before Lynne would reply. 'I'm not a good girl,' she whispered so low Peggy could hardly hear. Peggy was about to contradict with a grown-up's bright dismissal when she took in the child's motionless posture, her head hanging as if her neck were broken. Peggy kneeled down beside her.

'What is it, dear?'

'I'm a nuisance,' breathed Lynne.

Peggy was quiet until she could trust her voice. 'Well, never mind,' she said carefully. 'Being a nuisance doesn't matter any more. We'll still love you.'

But the girl wouldn't move.

'I'm sure you're not trying to be,' continued Peggy slowly. 'Not on purpose.'

Lynne shook her head.

'Then it's just an accident and doesn't count. I tell you what – we could turn you into a different little girl. Would that help?'

Lynne thought about it. Then she nodded hard. To be turned into a different little girl. What an idea.

'First we have to find you a new name. You can choose. What's a nice name for a good girl?'

'Marianne,' said Lynne.

'Yes, but that's your sister.'

'Olivia.'

'Can you think of a special name just for you?'

Lynne cast about in her mind. 'Kim,' she decided.

Kim. Patricia Kim. Peggy felt the excruciating spasm of a wound unhealed and unhealable.

'That's a nice name,' she said eventually, 'I used to know

a Kim. She was a lovely little thing. We'll call you that if you want. Do you know somebody called Kim?'

'Mrs Mortimer's dog,' said Lynne. 'I like him. He's a Labrador.'

By the evening, when Mummy and Marianne still hadn't come to collect her, Lynne was desolate. She ached from the strangeness and the separation. Homesickness thrummed through her tiny bones and shook her. Peggy's kindness meant nothing, the offers of cake and stories, the hugs. She was adrift.

'I want my mummy.'

'I know, lovey. Soon.'

'Where's Mummy and Marianne?'

Lynne heard the whine in her voice and the threat of tears. She bit her lip to stop it.

She slept in Peggy's bed. When she woke in the night knowing she had wet it, Lynne lay there soaked, silent and paralysed, expecting Peggy to wake and give her a slapping. But Peggy didn't wake until morning, and then she just said, 'Oh dear,' with cheerful acceptance. 'I should of thought of that and put a nappy on you. Aren't I a silly billy?'

After a couple of days, Peggy started going out and leaving her. She would be gone long hours in which Lynne mostly slept, half-dead with malaise, to wake up lost, whimpering for home. Peggy would bring her picture books and soft toys of crackling Bri-nylon. Lynne ate cakes and chocolates while Peggy read her stories about talking animals that lived in a river bank.

If there was any pattern to her new existence, it was beyond Lynne. 'Are you going out today?' she would whisper with sick dread. And sometimes the answer was no, not today, sweetheart, I'll be here with you all day long. And sometimes it wasn't.

But Lynne didn't go out, didn't leave the flat, week after week, for months. Not until it seemed as though outside didn't exist, that the universe had contracted to this tiny place with its smelly gas fire and chimneyed rooftops beyond the cold-glinting glass of the window. For exercise they played games of tag, skidding over the carpets and clunking their shins and elbows, until there wasn't an ornament left in the flat.

Lynne had her own camp bed. She no longer slept the whole day long but her poor pasty skin developed pimples and then eczema. Peggy coated her in calamine lotion so the child looked like some flaking ghost. Next she developed boils.

'Better get you out in some fresh air before it's rickets,' said Peggy, standing beside a second-hand pushchair. 'Let's put this pixie hood on, to hide your red hair.'

They would trundle up and down the heaving streets of Toxteth or along the docks, Peggy pushing her whenever her small legs were tired. Sometimes men would look at Peggy, eyeing her up, but nobody greeted them, nobody knew them. They varied the location every time and kept themselves to themselves.

Winter turned to spring and spring to early summer. They were on a train heading south. 'It'll be lovely,' promised Peggy. 'We can go out every day.'

'Yeah? Up the shops?'

'The park even, now it's nice and warm. Feed the ducks.'

'I can talk duck language!' shouted Kim. She jumped up and down on the seat, excitedly quacking at the scenery and the flying railway lines.

'Steady now.'

'Can we have a doggie and take it for walks up the park? Can we?' pleaded Kim. 'Can we have a doggie, Mum?'

And her mother, gently sitting her down again, promised they could have a doggie.

51

It would be all right; somebody would come for her. She would be missed. Perhaps even the keys would be missed, the keys still jangling in her hand but useless from the moment Tonya slammed that door. And even if they didn't guess, if Tonya fobbed them off with a story that directed searchers elsewhere, some unsuspecting Questors person would come to the prop cellar on business of their own. It would be all right.

The floor was peeling, cold and leprous and clammily damp like the walls of Peggy's long-ago stairwell, but it was less frightening to crouch here in the dark than feel her way towards the door and the light switch. Mummy's cupboard under the stairs had acted as store for all kinds of household equipment. Moving always dislodged things; the coalmine blackness would fill with creaking and shifting, grinding and resettling, the tectonic plates of Lynne's miniature world. Once, the carpet sweeper toppled over to strike her shoulder blades like a kendo pole, and a steel rule rolled off the shelf and hit her plump knee sideways, dislocating it. She howled with pain. Mummy opened the door like a hunter springing a trap.

'They'll say I did it!' she bawled at her. 'You stupid child, you'll get me locked up.'

Not that Kim could put names to any of this. Their images floated wordless in time and space. But she knew her own name was Lynne. It took longer, much longer, to understand that Tonya wasn't Mummy.

'And my name is not Shilling,' decided Kim with absolute certainty. Then: but how can I know? Through the chaos in her mind Kim fought to hone her thoughts. Any memory of the name Shilling would have dissipated over the years from workaday use: that'll be six shillings, please; to you, madam, two shillings and sixpence. But Kim's brain, tingling, raw and reeling, still said, 'My name is not Shilling.'

And I am at the Questors, not in Mummy's cupboard.

Standing up, her knees shook. Her shoes were in a puddle. Disgusting. She edged away, kicked off the wet shoes and struggled out of her sopping knickers and slip. Her skirt was mostly OK. She was able to dry herself a bit with an unsullied corner of the slip. She was Kim again and decent, not Lynne, smelly and damp and in danger of a slapping.

On legs full of air Kim picked her way in the direction of the door. So many things to bump into and steps to trip down.

She reached a hand to the light switch. Thank God this wasn't a fluorescent tube that flickered into life; she could not have tolerated on-off-on-off strobing in this room of gas masks and dead-eyed dolls. Luckily the illumination had no atmosphere, cast no spooking shadows. The place could be seen as a banal storeroom. Almost.

Standing in front of the door was Tonya.

∗

Frances had been crying gently into a handkerchief. Suddenly she caught her breath. 'Oh God, oh God,' she cried out, 'the firework!'

'Mrs Massingham?'

'Oh God, it has never made sense before. Mr Collier, you say Olivia used to lash out when she couldn't cope. Yet we're supposed to believe she suddenly launched herself on imaginative forms of torment with fireworks. It's nonsense.'

'What are you saying, Frances?'

'Marianne learned literally at her mother's knee that her sister was worthless. That's enough to seriously warp any child. And small children are much more resourceful than we give them credit for. Of course Olivia wasn't responsible for that rocket, it was Marianne! *She* shut her poorly sister in the bathroom and let off a firework out of sheer spite.'

'Mrs Massingham, I must intercede. Continue down this line of thought and we'll frighten ourselves catatonic.'

'*Why can't you see?* It could only have been Marianne – and that's what she was capable of as a small child. Now she's half grown-up and with a grudge that has festered for years. What in God's name might she do this time?'

*

'I don't understand,' she said. The vowels were Lynne's. 'Mummy and Daddy both died? Both? How?'

'Oh, for God's sake, they were sent to high-security prison, not health farms! And Daddy already had an ulcer. You think *you*'re scared, locked up in here with me? You think you were frightened when the lights went out? Then start imagining Daddy shut in a cell with a couple of violent men and an overflowing slop bucket, and sentenced to seven years of it. Even guilty inmates have abnormally high levels of acid gnawing away at their guts, let alone innocent men wrongly convicted and terrorized by every monster that can get his grubby hands on them. The prison population suffers what is called an excess of deaths, because of stress. What's the matter?' she continued. 'You thought I didn't know anything about anything? Poor stupid Tonya, the lump of lard?'

'Did they . . . was Mummy—?'

'Hanged? So you are following the plot, then. You've registered that Mummy was convicted of a capital crime, all because of you. No, she wasn't hanged, though there were plenty crying out for it. Sometimes she wished she had been. You in your protected little life wouldn't know how child murderers are treated in prison.'

'Was it because of Mummy hurting me?'

'You can shut up about that! Shut up!' shouted Tonya, suddenly a thwarted infant. Which was much easier to deal with, because it turned her back into Tonya instead of Mummy. And another small bulb was lit in Kim's head.

'Listen,' she said. 'I remember going on the ferry with . . . with Mrs Tanner. I knew her already, she used to come to our house, and did the hoovering. It's all muddled up, but I've always remembered the flat. Perhaps that was where—'

'Yes, she stole you. And you let her. So the police—'

'But I was so young. How could I know?'

'You didn't need to know. All you had to do was to tell someone your name! *Anyone*.'

'I think . . . I don't think there was anyone to tell. She locked me away, I suppose.'

'Oh, don't give me that! You wanted to stay with that filthy Peggy, or you'd have run off and told someone who you really were.'

'Marianne, I was so little.'

'Not by the time they died you weren't. When Mummy died you were nearly ten. What kind of monster lets her mother stay in jail to die?'

'Marianne, I didn't have any memory of—'

'Shut up! I mean it, Lynne, shut your fucking mouth. You say one more time that you can't remember, and I won't be responsible.'

'Look, when did you say the trial was? April 1960?'

'Soon after my fourth birthday. That's when I became the daughter of infamous child murderers.'

'Then so am I, Marianne. Why can't we be in this together?'

*

There had been people crying out to have Mummy hanged. A bag over the head, a lever pulled. A trapdoor. Kim thought of the trapdoor beneath the banqueting table on the Playhouse stage. Banquo's ghost. *Thou canst not say I did it. Never shake thy gory locks at me.* Take that accusing look off your face, I've never seen a child look like that, it isn't natural – stop looking at me!

'You have Mummy's eyes,' said Lynne. 'Oh God, I must have been dreaming of them ever since you first—' Ever since Tonya had come rolling into her life like a grenade. Mummy's eyes chasing her through those fulminant nightmares. 'How did she die – what from?'

'From a broken heart! Two years after Daddy. She had a thrombosis, if you must know.'

'And Daddy was jailed, too, for—?'

'For driving away with your dead body in a case. Your dead body, Lynne, get it? This body standing in front of me now.'

'And everyone believed it was true because ... That means everyone must have known Mummy was hurting me. Well, if they knew,' said Kim with a show of spirit, 'why didn't anyone bloody stop her doing it?'

52

The doorbell chimed. Imogen dropped the phone and ran. It was Dr Yelland.

'I don't have news,' he told her immediately. 'Daphne phoned me. I'm here to offer my services,' at which he stepped gently past Imogen and into the kitchen.

The detectives eyed him suspiciously.

'I'm a local doctor and member of the same theatre as Miss St Clair and Kim.'

Sebastian said, 'Good of you to come round, Yelland, but I don't see—'

'Please tell me: does this girl Tonya bear Kim a grudge?'

'Terrible grudge,' replied Imogen. 'Infinite.'

'Can you tell me why?'

'Unfortunately not, sir,' began the detective inspector.

But Imogen was saying, 'Does the Jarman case mean anything to you? No, nor me but we seem to be on our own.' Imogen gave Dr Yelland the facts.

'And Tonya is – the sister presumably.'

'Marianne, but she changed her name to Toinette. It's a sick joke about execution. Back in 1960 we still had capital punishment and this was a capital crime. And frankly the joke alone scares me half to death.'

'Has anybody checked at Ealing Broadway station? In case—'

'That would be routine, wouldn't it?' said the detective inspector. 'Sir.'

'The police have checked the station, Dr Yelland: ticket office, porters, newsagents. The girls haven't been there.'

'In which case they are at the theatre.'

'Yes, sir. That was the first place our men looked, sir. And they haven't turned up a dickie bird.'

'Then they haven't looked in the right place. Did they have a site plan and an experienced Questors person to lead them round? Well then, of course they haven't found the girls. Miss St Clair, may I phone Benjamin Sacks?'

＊

The chief superintendent was on his feet. 'If you are right,' he said, 'we are looking for an enclosed space. Can you think of anywhere Kim could be persuaded—'

'The Questors Theatre,' interrupted the Massinghams in unison.

'That's where they are.' Colonel Massingham rose in his turn. His joints felt stiff. 'It's in Mattock Lane, Ealing, chock full of lockable rooms. Hand me the phone, Chief Superintendent. I'll get the stage director to meet your men there with a site plan.'

＊

'I kept asking to go home,' remembered Lynne. 'I kept asking where were Marianne and Mummy.'

'Liar!'

Liar! It was an accident. Do you hear me?

Not a naccident, Daddy. Mummy did it. It was Mummy.

'I think she must have kept me shut away for so long I started to forget. I even forgot Mummy hurting me.'

'Shut up saying you forgot. I don't want to hear it!'

Stop that bloody crying, I can't stand it, I can't stand it, I can't . . .

Stop lying! If you tell lies about Mummy, the police will take you away and lock you up.

Please help, Daddy, help!

'We were both tiny, Marianne. You still talked like a baby and called me Lyndee.' Kim's voice trembled. Peggy had said she used to be Linda. Half-truth. A half-truth that fitted snugly into some crevice of her blighted and wrecked memory.

'I hate you,' said Tonya. 'I'll never forgive you. I wish it was you that was dead.'

'Oh bloody brilliant,' said Kim, exasperated. It was the petulance that released her from fear. There was never anything petulant about Mummy. 'So what are you going to do – wallop me with those medieval swords? Batter my head in with a stuffed stoat?' Kim looked around her for inspiration, at the sad Edwardian toys. 'Rocking-horse me to death?'

'I hate you!'

'Yeah, you said. Look, we've found each other now. So we can go to the police and tell them what really—'

'And Mummy and Daddy's names will be cleared? We're part of the language, *Lyndee*. The Jarmans. Child murderers. Part of English national culture like the World Cup win and the Beatles. We're indelible. You and your filthy Peggy even robbed me of my own fucking *name*!'

*

'Dr Yelland, would you come too?'

'Of course.'

'Nobody's coming except Miss St Clair,' said the policeman.

'I want Dr Yelland with me.'

'All right but stop arguing and go!' This was Monique. 'Go go go!'

Even Joan had come screaming up in a taxi.

Denise had been crying quietly for the last hour. Sukie of course was in floods. 'I knew Toinette was only a nickname and her parents had died, but I never guessed . . . I can't even *think* what Mummy and Daddy will say. If they'd had one *inkling* of who Tonya was they would never have allowed her in the *house*.'

'Then we don't have to look far to see why the child bears a grudge,' said Joan.

'It's all so *sordid*. How could Peggy carry on hiding Kim when the real parents were on trial for murder?'

'Sukie, for God's sake leave it alone,' barked Joan.

'Shut up, Sukie, or I'll clock you one,' echoed Denise.

'I don't see why you're all taking it out on me.'

'Because we're at our wits' end.'

But a minute later Sukie was at it again. 'I suppose Tonya only made friends with me hoping I was Charlotte.'

At this Monique snapped, 'Oh, for God's sake! Why the bloody hell would Tonya care a fuck whether you were Charlotte?'

'Monique,' said Joan in gentle reproach.

'Can't you see, you silly girl? Tonya made friends with you in case you were *Lynne*. She knew her sister had been stolen, and it followed that she was probably still alive somewhere. Then one day at Guide camp she meets you. God, what a blinder that must have been. I've no doubt that within three minutes of saying hello you'd gabbled your entire life history at her, including the fact that you were adopted and your date of birth. Tonya had probably been sniffing for clues like a bloodhound ever since her mother died and suddenly – kapow!'

'Oh,' said Sukie.

'Wangled an invite to your home, did she?'

'Ever so soon after we met. Tonya was so *gooey* about everything. Oohing and aahing over our family album. I thought she loved me,' finished Sukie in a small voice.

'I suppose she was checking out photos of you as a baby. Which of course proved you couldn't be Lynne after all. Lynne was abducted as a four-year-old.'

'Odd though,' said Joan. 'When she realized Sukie wasn't Lynne, why didn't she just, well—'

'Just dump me,' finished Sukie. 'Go on, say it.'

'Perhaps she did love you,' put in Denise surprisingly. 'Does, I mean. Perhaps she does, Sukie.'

But Monique, worried sick, wasn't going to allow Sukie her soothing balm. 'You were useful because you could be passed off as Charlotte,' she said. 'Whether you turned out actually to *be* Charlotte was peripheral. You were Tonya's pretext for coming here and meeting Kim.'

'But how could Tonya know Kim was Lynne Jarman anyway?' asked Denise. 'Nobody else knew. I didn't and I'm her best friend. Imogen didn't, and she's—'

'Kim's story had just made the front page of the *Sunday Clarion*,' Monique reminded them. 'That article was full of proud mentions of Peggy Tanner. Tonya recognized the name because it was a name she knew, the name of her late mother's cleaner.'

'How would Tonya remember the name of her late mother's cleaner?' demanded Joan. 'She wasn't even four years old.'

'True. Well then, her aunt remembered. The aunt is Olivia Jarman's sister.'

'I've got a sister myself, but I don't know the name of her charwoman,' responded Joan bluntly. 'It isn't good enough, you know. You're saying that after all these years Olivia's sister not only remembered Peggy's name, but it was so indelibly carved in her mind that she recognized it the moment she saw it in a Sunday scandal-sheet. *And* she knew it must be the selfsame Peggy Tanner that used to do

Olivia's cleaning – *and*,' continued Joan, '*and* therefore this must be the woman who stole Lynne from the pram, and therefore Kim was really Lynne Jarman. It's not as if the Jarmans ever suspected their cleaner of stealing her. If they had, they would've set the police on to Peggy as soon as the gal went missing. It won't wash, Monique,' finished Joan. 'I don't see how Tonya could have worked out Kim was Lynne.'

Sebastian was slumped in a chair, sneezing and wheezing. Now even he found ten cents' worth to throw in against Monique. 'Joan's right, it's garbage. Yeah, Tonya might have started off thinking Sukie was Lynne, until the family album showed her she was wrong. And eventually something happened that demonstrated that Kim was Lynne, and then Sukie was a godsend. But she didn't figure that out from seeing Peggy's name in the newspaper.'

'I don't understand about the newspaper,' said Sukie in a whine. 'The article only happened this summer. But Tonya gave me *Starched Linen* to read yonks ago, saying I might be the baby Charlotte. Yonks and yonks.'

'So it was Tonya who encouraged you to believe you might be Charlotte?' said Monique. 'Well then,' she began and then petered out.

Joan tried again. 'We mustn't forget that Tonya turned out to be correct. I mean, not about Sukie being Lynne, obviously. But her next guess was that Sukie was Charlotte. And she was right. That must be central to something.'

'How was she right?' demanded Sukie.

'How was she right?' demanded Sebastian.

'Oh no, not now!' said Monique. 'It feels disloyal to Kim.' She closed her eyes. 'I'm sorry,' she said. 'That's irrational.'

'Sukie,' said Joan, 'there's something you don't know. You too, Sebastian. Kim isn't Charlotte after all. Sukie is. You're Imogen's daughter, Sukie. When Tonya was checking out your background certain facts stuck in her memory. The weekend of the moon landing she tried them out on Imogen, who confirmed they fitted with Charlotte. Your father's car, for example, the black Wolseley. Tonya saw it in one of your family photos, number plate and all. Those details were never in *Starched Linen* and Imogen always kept them to herself.'

'And Imogen didn't tell you because . . .' Monique stopped. 'Oh God, I can't remember why.'

'That was Tonya yet again,' said Joan wearily. 'She talked Imogen into keeping it from you.'

'Cos you'd've blabbed to all and sundry,' said Denise. 'And so would you, Sebastian. Imogen wanted to protect Kim from knowing, as long as she could.'

Monique said, 'What we didn't realize was Tonya had a vested interest in keeping the info under her hat. She knew damn well you would both spill the beans to Kim, and Tonya dare not lose her. Kim was her target.'

'Poor Kim,' said Joan. 'Poor little Kim.'

'I don't know what you're all talking about,' said Sukie, her voice skidding up the scale towards hysteria. 'My father drives Jaguars. He's always driven Jaguars. In British racing green. He wouldn't be seen *dead* in a black Wolseley.'

53

'Wait a minute, Joan,' said Monique.

'No, I think I've got it. Listen. We accept that Tonya's target was always Kim. Never mind for a minute *how* she knew Kim was really Lynne. Or how she knew the Wolseley's number plate – maybe she got hold of that from one of the other girls at Holbridge Manor. The point is, the information about the car was gold dust. It was Tonya's key to Imogen and therefore to Kim. But only so long as she could persuade Imogen not to tell Sukie. Sukie would have blown it sky high instantly, and everyone would know she wasn't Charlotte at all, and then Tonya would no longer have any right to be in Mount Hill Crescent.'

'One minute, Joan. Why did Tonya give Sukie a copy of *Starched Linen* in the first place?'

'To groom her as Charlotte. I suppose she figured that with Lynne having the same birthday as Charlotte, then one of these days—'

'No, Joan,' interrupted Monique. '*Starched Linen* doesn't give Charlotte's date of birth. It doesn't give any inform-ation that could possibly suggest a connection between Lynne Jarman and Charlotte St Clair. How could it? There isn't one. Sukie isn't Charlotte, remember? So the only connection is Tonya herself.'

'Unless there's a very simple connection,' said Denise, ''cos they are the same person. We now know Sukie's not Charlotte after all. Why are we still assuming Kim isn't, either?'

'Kim is Charlotte. Kim is Charlotte.' Monique could not stop repeating it. 'My instincts were right all along. Kim is Charlotte.'

'And . . . and Tonya found this out?' said Joan.

'Must of,' said Denise.

'I can't see how.'

'Perhaps—'

'Wait, Monique, let me think,' said Joan. 'Tonya's aunt worked it out! Yes! She read *Starched Linen*. She recognized Holbridge Manor as the place her sister Olivia adopted the baby and everything else slipped into place.'

'Forget the aunt,' said Monique grimly. 'The book hit the shops in 1965. I can tell you who recognized the baby was Lynne. Olivia Jarman. She read *Starched Linen* in Holloway prison and there in front of her was the story of her terrible doomed adoption. It's all there, the October day, the panicking girl on the gravel shouting, "I've changed my mind, they can't have Charlotte," even the feather in Olivia's bloody hat. Didn't the police tell Imogen that Olivia kept in touch with Tonya in prison? With Marianne, I should say? So she told her. Or alternatively she told her sister, the aunt, who passed it on.'

'Of course,' cried Joan. 'That's how Tonya knows the number plate of the Wolseley. It was *their* car. The bally Wolseley is in the Jarmans' family album, not the Sandemans'.'

'Exactly.'

'Can we go back a step, Monique? Tonya grows up knowing her sister was stolen and might well still be alive somewhere. She learns that Lynne was born Charlotte St Clair, the baby in *Starched Linen*. She keeps a lookout. She meets Sukie and Sukie goes jabbering on about her birthday and being adopted so Tonya thinks she's Lynne till the family photos show Sukie in bootees and christening gowns which means she can't be, as Lynne wasn't stolen till she was four. So then Tonya changes tack and starts grooming her as a pretend Charlotte. But what use was a pretend Charlotte?'

'It gives Tonya the entrée to Imogen. The entire English-speaking world knows Imogen St Clair wants her daughter back. Tonya knows that when she finds her, the girl she finds will be Lynne Jarman.'

＊

'I must have blocked it out of my memory because it was just too terrible to—'

'Shut up about that!'

'For God's sake, Marianne, you know why I blocked it out! You know what Mummy did.'

'Shut up!'

'Remember my plaster cast. A great heavy white cast dragging down my left arm. This arm, see? It isn't double jointed any more because of the break. Remember Lyndee's plaster cast.'

'That was an accident. You fell off the wall.'

Stop these lies! It was an accident.

No naccident, Daddy. Wasn't a naccident.

'Forget the wall. This was a different time.'

'Lynne, you broke your bloody arm falling off the wall of the sunken garden because you were trying to fly like a bloody bird!'

'I know, I know, I remember, we were both doing it, and I fell off! But I'm talking about a different time. I suppose it was the same break but later on. My arm was in plaster and throbbed all day and night, so badly I couldn't stop crying. Mummy could never stand me crying.'

No naccident. Daddy, help. Please help, Daddy!

'She came thundering into the bedroom and lunged at me . . . '

No naccident. Mummy did it.

'. . . wrenched my arm and then threw me across the bedroom.'

Mummy did it, Daddy.

Marianne, how many times? Stop these lies! Your sister had an accident, she's always having accidents, she's a clumsy bloody child!

No, Daddy, Mummy threw Lyndee on her broke arm. Her poor broke arm. Cross the bedroom. Please help, Daddy!

Shut up, Marianne, you little liar!

Behind them in the alley were voices. A key turned in the door. Lynne yelled out, 'NO! Don't come in! Leave us alone!'

'Kim?'

'Go away, go away!' She turned back to her sister. 'Remember Lyndee's firework box! You fetched me a rocket, a wonderful rocket, you climbed up all those cupboards to get me the biggest firework in the box. I'd caught your mumps and was still feeling rotten and you knew how much I loved the firework box. We hadn't the skill to strike matches so I told you to find Daddy's pipe. *Think*, Marianne! Every night Mummy put us in separate beds, but you had nightmares about her hurting me so you'd snuggle up in mine and we'd cuddle each other to sleep. For God's sake, this is your Lyndee!'

'And you deserted me! You went away and never came back, and when I found you, you'd forgotten I existed! How could you? How could you forget me? How could you just go away and never come back and forget about me? How could you?'

54

They took Kim from the prop cellar wrapped in a blanket. It was Benjamin Sacks who wrapped her in it and Dr Yelland who carried her as if she weighed no more than a kitten. But she didn't want to go. She was shouting, 'What are you doing? Don't hurt my sister!'

As soon as they were out of sight of Marianne, Kim started weeping. Now she was unable to stop. She lay across Imogen's sofa in the huge candlewick dressing gown like a swaddled doll, gulping until her jaw ached and her ribs ached and her face was swollen, red as road kill.

Frances Massingham called the family doctor, Dr Bayly, a stocky, no-nonsense man who raised his eyebrows at the sight of Dr Yelland. When he approached Kim with a soothing phrase and a syringe, she flew from the sofa and was halfway out of the door before any one of the five men in the room managed to catch her. Then she was dragged back to the sofa, gibbering and incoherent.

'It's all right, girlie,' Dr Bayly told her. 'Just a little prick with the needle. Keep your arm still and it won't hurt.'

'Wait, please!' It was Dr Yelland. 'One moment. I would like a word with your patient.'

'Actually, I'd rather you didn't, Yelland, not right now. Come on, girlie—'

But Dr Yelland was on the sofa – and Kim didn't shrink from him, an observation that further irritated Bayly.

'Kim,' said Dr Yelland gently, 'the injection won't hurt you in any way. On the contrary, it will allow your mind and body to rest.'

'No!' shouted Kim.

'Can you help me understand why not? You see, in your place I would welcome a break from this distress.'

Kim hiccuped agonizingly and her frame shook.

'For God's sake, Yelland—'

Stammering and furious, Kim shot the words out. 'Will it muddle my head up?'

'Temporarily, yes.'

'Then no! No! No! No!'

Imogen, frantic, turned to Colonel Massingham. 'What's best for her?' she cried out. 'Tell me!'

'Get this charlatan out of my way,' snapped Bayly, 'and let me attend my patient!'

But the charlatan was still trying to get to the bottom of the problem. 'Was an unmuddled head your protection against harm, Kim? Was that how you survived, by keeping alert and using your wits?'

Kim shook her head, back and forth like somebody shaking a rag doll.

Dr Yelland tried again. 'No? Can you tell me—?'

'Dangerous!' The word shot from Kim's heaving chest. 'Crying. And stuff. She'd hurt me.'

'So – if you couldn't control your tears or . . . or other functions, if you lost control there was a danger she would hit you.'

Kim shrank further into herself but didn't contradict him.

'And of course, being weak and muzzy meant you couldn't stay alert. So she would hit you when you were ill or off your guard.'

Still sniffing and trembling, Kim said, 'Don't make my brain go muddled up.'

Dr Yelland turned to Dr Bayly. 'We're not in the business of kicking away a patient's psychological support,' he said. 'Colonel Massingham, as Kim's guardian will you back me up? I move that before we resort to drugs, we try comforting Kim in the more traditional manner.'

'And what tradition do you propose?' demanded Bayly, bitingly. 'Voodoo perhaps?'

Kim's ribs were heaving but she got a sentence out. 'If you lot want to comfort me,' she told the packed room, 'you can let Welly back in for a start!'

55

There had been a funeral: across a gently rising belly of earth the flowers were arranged, lilies and chrysanthemums, little white cards. It was nobody Kim knew.

Peggy had never liked chrysanths, which she said smelled of crematorium services on a wet winter Wednesday. Instead Kim had brought anemones, out of season and expensive, deep purple and floppy in their glass jar.

MARGARET MABEL TANNER (Peggy)
13 March 1910 – 2 March 1969
Beloved mother of Kim
The day Thou gavest, Lord, is ended

Now Kim sat with her companion on the slatted wooden bench and looked between the yew trees across the hedges to the surrounding fields, ploughed into great loopy stripes of coffee and chocolate. Birds wheeled over them, their cacophony retexturing the air. Every now and then one of them would upset Welly and he'd offer a disgruntled bark.

Kim was comfortable here in this borrowed cameo of time. To be away from Mount Hill Crescent felt like respite:

the place still had a niff in the air of various betrayals, which would disperse more easily if Kim and Imogen kept from analysis and dissection. Let the wound heal a while. Kim wanted this time with Mr Antrobus.

'I can't make it fit the Mum I knew,' she told him. 'Once Mummy and Daddy went on trial everyone knew about the Cruelty Man's report. They wouldn't have sent me back home. But Mum let the trial go on.'

'Answer me something,' said Mr Antrobus. 'Do you accept what Olivia's sister said – that your mother's outbursts were getting more frequent?'

'If she says so. I can't count the number of times or sort them out in my mind.'

'Because if she is right, Kim, Peggy probably saved your life. Had you been left with Olivia, she might well have killed you.'

'I suppose so,' said Kim. 'If you keep throwing kids about, one day you'll kill them. But people only go on trial for murders they *have* done, not for murders they might do.'

'Perhaps Peggy, as a battered wife, saw her options in a different light.'

On the advice of the police, Kim had made no effort to keep Peggy's medical records out of the newspapers. They shocked every household in the country. Peggy had not returned to Essex until the early summer of 1960, when the same newspapers that provided daily coverage of the Jarman case also carried notices in their personal columns: *Will Mrs Margaret Mabel Davis, widow of the late Sidney Davis, or anybody knowing of her whereabouts, please contact* . . . According to Hazel Barber, that was when Peggy left Liverpool. It would remain for ever between Hazel Barber and her conscience whether she suspected that Peggy had with her a small red-headed child.

The word ironic was being thrown about 'like confetti at a wedding', complained Kim. Olivia Jarman had perpetrated all those outrages against her adopted daughter but she went to jail for the one incident she hadn't engineered. And had the judge so decided, she might have hanged for it. Not only were the children themselves responsible for that firework accident, but had it been anything but a firework the spectre of the death penalty could never have been raised. A couple of years earlier the Homicide Act 1957 restricted the use of capital punishment to a narrow range of crimes, which included murder by shooting – or explosion. 'There should be a law against flogging the word ironic to death,' suggested Kim.

Peggy's history incited public sympathy but— 'But I bet people don't think that it excused Mum staying silent,' said Kim. 'Even if they don't care about Mummy, I bet they blame her for Daddy. Mummy would've gone to jail anyhow for hurting me. But Daddy wouldn't of. And Mum, Peggy, let him be locked up as an accessory.'

Mr Antrobus was flooded with affectionate bewilderment. He had known Kim since she was four, had lived with her a month in the Motel. She was perhaps the least liberal child he had ever come across. Kim Tanner would probably have advocated chopping anyone's hands off who failed to return their library books on time. Yet here she was in an agony of conscience over the man who allowed his wife to break her bones. It always astounded Mr Antrobus, the capacity of human beings to give their heart to those who do them most harm.

'I know what you're thinking,' said Kim without rancour. 'But this isn't just about me. There's what it did to Marianne. You have to understand, it was just as bad for Marianne as for me. Having to stand by helpless when Mummy . . . She loved me. I was her Lyndee. Her nightmares got so bad she was frightened to go to sleep unless I was cuddling her.' And cuddling Marianne kept me from wetting the bed, realized Kim for the first time. 'And I abandoned her. Then Mummy and Daddy were taken away. And then they both died—' Kim's voice trembled so she had to stop. Crying was one luxury she would never have. 'And now look at her!' she concluded.

Because Tonya was underage, a writ had been slapped on the media to stop her name being published. She was now being reassessed by a child psychologist in light of the over-turned verdict, to show that 'she's not obsessed and loony', as Kim put it, but haunted by her knowledge of what had actually happened.

Kim had refused to see the aunt and uncle, Mr and Mrs Shilling; she had no memory of them and no interest; if they suspected what was going on in that house then they were blameworthy themselves. But in Tonya Kim could still see the little sister who adored her, the soulmate of Kim's flying dream.

Actually, what Kim *saw* in Tonya was their mother. Marianne had grown up with too much of Olivia's mouth and black-button eyes. From that first evening Tonya appeared in Ealing with Sukie, Kim's memory had been nagging for attention, insistent as a rattling door handle. But close to, Kim's sister smelled the same as always, that skin scent that had wafted through her infant sleep. Its sudden reappearance one Sunday morning on the landing had nearly sent Kim reeling down the stairs.

And now there were photographs too. At the sight of Marianne as a toddler Kim's heart ached. Such a lovely child, as the chief superintendent had said to the Massinghams. Before she uglified herself into Tonya, victim of bungled justice.

The facts, confirmed by Olivia's sister, were pretty much as Joan and Monique had thrashed out in the kitchen. Olivia read *Starched Linen* in Holloway, and immediately recognized her own experience collecting Lynne from Holbridge Manor. She had felt so ill that day. In fact she hadn't been well in months. But nobody guessed why.

The sister said, 'Olivia had a lousy pregnancy that was mistaken for early menopause, and then post-natal depression. In prison she confessed that she first hit Lynne as a baby, and it scared her so much she pulled herself together. She couldn't love the girl, but it was a long time before she hurt her again. Even so, it was true what she said about Lynne's skin. Those welts were not Olivia's doing. Lynne had German measles and nobody could stop her scratching. Her skin went into welts on its own.'

German measles was the first of a long sequence of childhood illnesses. The girls contracted one after the other, and that was when Olivia's self-control began to disintegrate. It would be Marianne who caught the infection first, followed by Lynne, but Lynne was always the more ill of the two. By the time Olivia finished nursing Marianne she had no emotional stamina to deal with a second bout. One day when Lynne had crawled out of bed and wet the carpet Olivia cracked and lashed out and Lynne went flying down the stairs.

'The trouble was,' continued the sister, 'she now hated Lynne for turning her into this monster, and hit her for that. Just like our own mother. And God forgive me,' she added, 'but I believed she had killed her. When Olivia kept changing her story I believed she had gone too far and Lynne had died. And later I thought Marianne's memories were just fantasy.'

Olivia wrote to Marianne about *Starched Linen*. Probably she was deliberately planting the seed: Olivia had a serious emotional stake in her daughter's continuing to believe she was innocent, and Charlotte St Clair was such a high-profile baby, Imogen's search might one day lead everyone to Lynne, alive and well. As Marianne grew up she threw herself into the hunt. No doubt Marianne's motives were as chaotic as anybody's who has suffered in extremis: she wanted to clear her parents' names, but most of all she wanted her Lyndee back.

Sukie was a perfect decoy, a gift from heaven, to be deployed one day as an intro to Imogen St Clair, with whom

Tonya could sit and wait for the real Charlotte to come a-knocking. And then, one weekend, Tonya read in the newspaper that it had already happened, and a girl called Kim Tanner had moved in. So Tonya promptly got herself established in Mount Hill Crescent too. When Sukie jeopardized the plan by seriously irritating Imogen, Tonya fed Imogen the stuff about the Wolseley. But Denise had been right that day in the kitchen: there was another reason Tonya stayed with Sukie even when it became clear that she wasn't Lynne – Tonya loved her. Sukie was everything she wasn't, all shiny sunlight to her own misery and brooding. The warmth of the friendship reminded her of Lynne.

And little by little Tonya wheedled out of them all the details of Kim's mysterious background, mostly from the hapless Denise. But it wasn't conclusive, the whole thing might have been a mistake, with Kim not really Charlotte and therefore not Lynne. Until Imogen told them about the Liverpool connection. Then there could be no doubt. As Colonel Massingham had said, months ago, that would be a coincidence too far. Kim had to be Lynne Jarman.

Marianne had spent years searching for her sister Lyndee but the girl she found was Peggy Tanner's Kim. And Marianne now knew that she had not merely been deserted, but utterly forgotten.

'What *are* you on about?' Kim had demanded crossly of a particularly high-ranking detective. She was exasperated at the failure of so many intelligent adults to grasp a perfectly simple story of pyrotechnics, self-protective memory block and locking up your long-lost sister in a theatre property store. '*Of course* Marianne wasn't going to hurt me. She was going to yak at me. She locked us both in so I couldn't escape it!'

Once Marianne was in Mount Hill Crescent, the nickname of Toinette and its mutation into Tonya turned out to be useful as an alias just in case the name Marianne jogged some vestigial memory in Kim. But the idea that this was a sick joke was rubbish: yet one more example of adults adding two and two and getting ninety-nine. Marianne Toinette was just the standard laboured pun of the classroom.

'At my school we've got a Jim Bull who we call Canni-Bull,' said Kim. 'But that doesn't mean he really eats people!'

And lastly, there had been one other woman who read *Starched Linen* and recognized a connection. Peggy. Mr Antrobus said to Colonel Massingham, 'You know, it always worried me, why Peggy was apparently so adamant that Kim was the baby in *Starched Linen*, based on nothing more than the cover photograph of the author. That sort of slapdash thinking was unlike Peggy, particularly about something so portentous for Kim.'

'You think she had inside information?'

'Peggy worked for Olivia Jarman for a couple of years. I would guess that in that time she heard a mention of Holbridge Manor, or maybe even something more specific. Poor Kim recalls Olivia in one of her rages screaming that she, Lynne, wasn't theirs at all but some other woman's bastard. I wonder whether Peggy overheard a more detailed reference to her parentage, perhaps an hysterical teenager bawling at them on the gravel like some madwoman. Certainly, I would guess that a few years later, when half the females in this country were reading *Starched Linen*, there was something in Imogen's story that stopped Peggy dead in her tracks.'

Now, in the quiet churchyard, Mr Antrobus was talking to Kim. 'If Peggy had not abducted you, Marianne might have watched her beloved Lyndee being thrown down the stairs to her death.'

'But Mum always said two wrongs don't make a right,' insisted Kim stubbornly. 'And anyway, Daddy still wouldn't have been guilty.'

'Let me put something to you. In my youth, there was a fashion for debating the moral rights and wrongs of fictional scenarios. There would be a young heroine who suffered one thing after another like the Perils of Pauline. I seem to remember there was always one crisis that involved taking her clothes off. The recital concluded with her turning to a friend – who let her down. We would argue into the small hours about who was most to blame for her plight. And eventually we judged that the most culpable was the friend. Because she trusted him, he was the last person she could turn to for protection, and he turned away. In your case, that was your daddy. He was all you had, you and your sister. And he made the moral choice to turn away.'

'Only cos he couldn't bear to believe Mummy was doing it.'

'That is a moral choice, Kim.'

'But what Mum did, it mucked up Marianne something rotten.'

'You know, it's an interesting comparison. Two girls, both with traumatic childhoods. One of them forced to watch her mother mistreat her sister, and then she loses that sister and both parents. And, as you say, now look at her. Then there's a second girl, ill-treated by her mother, then abducted, stolen away from her beloved sister and her home. And look at you. Of course,' he said, 'these comparisons are never quite fair. But nevertheless, I think the woman responsible for bringing up Kim Tanner deserves credit. In fact, credit enough to ring all the church bells across the south-east of England from now until Michaelmas.'

'Right,' said Kim.

'I'm a good churchman myself, aren't I?'

'Yes.'

'I couldn't care less that William Jarman went to jail. There.'

'Thanks,' said Kim. 'Thanks, Mr Antrobus.'

They sat quietly for a while, listening to the breeze and the distant cars and the ordinariness of other people's day. In a neighbouring garden somebody lit a bonfire. Great black smuts flew upwards and caught the wind, flapping like crows. It was only the second day of September, but the air smelled of autumn.

'When do you start the new school?' asked Mr Antrobus in a changed voice.

'Next Monday. We're later in London, don't ask me why.'

'A whole week of freedom then, to celebrate your birthday.'

'Now I know you're having a laugh,' said Kim. '*Mary Rose* goes up next week. I'm DSM. Tonight's the first tech, right? Well, we're still two flyers short, the hardboard's only rough-laid, and Nigel's mist machine is lying upside down in Jim's workshop with a split right up its pipe.'

'Up its pipe, eh?' said Mr Antrobus. 'Tricky.'

Kim looked at him and laughed. 'I'm sorry. You don't know what I'm on about, do you?'

'Not entirely,' he admitted. 'I only know that somehow, some way, it will be all right on the night.'

56

'Imogen?' shouted Sebastian. '*Imogen!*'

'Sebastian, what on earth—?'

'You stay out of it. This is between me and her.'

'And the rest of Ealing by the sound of it. We'll have the police back.'

'*IMOGEN!*'

'Oh, for heaven's sake.'

Kim had just got home from school and was in a hurry to change before the theatre. She pushed past Sebastian on the path and put her key in the lock. It didn't fit. Kim looked at it. The lock was new. The lock was changed.

'Imogen?' shouted Kim and Sebastian together. '*Imogen!*'

Above them a window opened. A head appeared. Kim didn't ask, 'What's going on?' Every household in Mount Hill Crescent realized what was going on, even those who didn't have a view of the front garden strewn with male clothing.

'Kim darling, I'm sorry but I can't let you in or he'll slip past us through the door.'

'Look, you silly cow, where am I supposed to go? Tonight's opening night. I'll be in the theatre all evening. *Then* what am I supposed to do?'

'Don't know, don't care. Kim, can you get yourself fish and chips and then go straight to the Questors?'

'I'm still in school uniform.'

'I'll bring your backstage blacks to the theatre.'

'But how are *you* going to get out without him getting in? Soon as you open the front door—'

'Joan's bringing a ladder at seven. Sebastian will never shin up a ladder. He'd die the death.'

'Oh. Where's the Roller?'

'Garaged.'

'That car is mine, you rotten cow.'

'Not according to the registration documents. Kim, are you OK with that? Fish and chips, and see you at the theatre?'

'I suppose. Imogen, what's he done wrong? I mean specifically? To trigger getting actually chucked out.'

'You might remember the Second Witch in *Macbeth*.'

'Do you mean the Third Witch?'

'No, the Second, the dark one. I caught him in bed with her this afternoon. Here. Our bed.'

'*So?*' demanded Sebastian.

'And her sister.'

'*So?* Free love is freedom of the soul, Imogen.'

'And the First Witch.'

'Exclusivity isn't love, it's ownership.'

'And *her* sister.'

Kim took this in. 'Welly's all right, is he?' she asked.

Imogen's demeanour was extraordinary. She wasn't distraught, in fact she didn't even seem particularly flustered. Then Kim was visited by an image of the house that day, *the* day, the day of Marianne and the prop cellar; she saw Imogen in a room full of men, all of them tall, two of them handsome, but only one in command, one on his feet calmly bringing order to chaos while the other sneezed and shivered in a corner, his opinions vacuous, his contributions futile, his authority obliterated. Perhaps, thought

Kim, when you are that particular sort of bastard you can't afford to look a useless twerp, or your pulling-power dribbles away like dishwater down a plughole. It was a most reassuring thought.

The useless twerp was still shouting at the window. 'Sole possession isn't love, Imogen, it's property rights.'

'I won't forget your clothes, Kim,' promised Imogen.

'OK, I'll go to the chippy and then Questors.'

'Love is not love that alters when it alteration finds, Imogen!'

'See you later.'

'See you later.'

'Jealous ownership is to true love what . . . what the Dow Jones is to poetic creativity!'

Kim paused en route to the gate. 'Pardon?' she said.

But Sebastian was staring, frantic and desperate, at the window. Imogen had shut it.

∗

When the run was over, the end-of-show discussion was led by the theatre critic Michael Billington.

'With just a few square feet of bare theatre and a forty-year-old play,' he told them, 'you have succeeded in showing us what is meant by human loss.'

He also said the ending was a stroke of genius, but to Kim it was no more nor less than a metaphor for her own story. That last scene was shiveringly atmospheric, with Mary Rose as a lost ghost searching for her lost child in a cold house – portrayed now by just that eerie suspended banister electrified under Gareth's crackling white light. But at the very close of the play she was finally at peace. And instead of ending with conventional blackout, the actors walked straight off the glacial stage and out of the building, and then two things happened: the thin screen that hid the backstage crew rotated until it was end-on to the audience

– so that it effectively vanished – then all the lights came on at once, mundane workaday light exposing everything: brick walls, audience, stagehands moving quietly in their blacks, the light-and-sound operators up their makeshift tower. All theatre tricks over and ghostliness expunged. Daylight let in upon magic. Let in upon nightmare. No more secrets.

Of course, it hadn't been quite that simple. During a night-long technical rehearsal the usually sanguine Gareth threw a hissy fit, shrieking and arm-waving like some barking Nazi on benzedrine. Then the stagehands lost control of the rotating screen, which lurched around the stage flailing up and down like one of those doomed early flying machines until finally thrashing itself to death. The weeping designer had to start carpentering a new one at four in the morning.

But by the time the show went up, Kim understood the play. In the penultimate scene Mary Rose's parents have grown old. It is twenty-five years since she disappeared. And they have survived. The father, lovely Reggie, talks sadly of the passage of time.

'*I suppose anyone who came back . . . however much they had been loved . . . should we know what to say to them?*'

But Mary Rose does come back, and she now has a loss of her own. '*Where is my baby?*' she wants to know. '*Where is Harry?*' But Harry is no longer a baby.

The last scene is in that same house some time later again. Mary Rose's parents are themselves dead, and she is a ghost, still searching. Harry has come back to see his childhood home. It is here that Tish, with her kittenish innocence, was surprisingly touching as a lost and frightened phantom, too dog-tired even to remember what she was searching for.

'*I don't know you, do I?*' she whispers to Harry, con-fidentially.

He says of her, '*There are worse things than not finding what you are looking for; there is finding them so different from what you had hoped.*'

Watching this through at the second dress rehearsal, Kim felt her stomach give a lurch and she spun round to check on Imogen, Imogen who had searched nearly half her life for Charlotte. But Kim saw that Imogen was unconcerned, nodding her approval of the scene, ticking off her notes. Harry's words don't apply to Imogen, realized Kim. She hasn't been disappointed in me. She wobbled a bit now and then under all the emotion, but when the evidence told her Sukie was her daughter and not me Imogen wasn't relieved, she hated it.

Then Kim's mind moved to the Redgrave Room, the smell of hot lino, the plane trees beyond the open windows. Sunday afternoon, and Tonya was there, confronted with this scene, Marianne searching for a Lyndee who no longer existed.

There are worse things than not finding what you are looking for. There is finding them so different from what you had hoped. Kim was swamped by a sense of desolation. It was only because of me that Marianne was at the rehearsal at all, thought Kim. It must have felt as if I was rubbing her nose in it.

Kim was not the only one watching the play in distress. When Mary Rose's father spoke his line, that if the dead came back we would have nothing to say to them, Dr Yelland closed his eyes in pain.

After the end-of-show discussion they all chattered off to the Grapevine bar. Reggie chased Kim in there, waving a pair of antlers he had found lying outside the Stan Room for the next production, for the disappearance of which Daphne was giving someone a bollocking that could be heard in Acton. Her sister would be joining them for a drink.

'Name of Joan,' said Daphne. 'Gardener at Kew. Doing extraordinarily well for herself, can't think how. She's just bought a sports car.'

Giles joined in the chase for Kim. 'I've caught her!' he called. 'And I think I might keep her.'

'No, don't, I'm ticklish!'

Giles set her down, wriggling and giggling, on a bench seat where the two happily wrestled.

Imogen laughed. 'I suppose there are going to be other twenty-year-olds chasing her. Kim is growing up.'

'Yes,' said Monique. She watched them a while, and turned away. She was still smiling as she approached the bar and asked for a whisky and soda.

57

As Safe as Love

I knew about love already. I loved Charlotte's father.

Winter evenings and Saturday afternoons lazing in his room – all slopy ceiling and brass bedstead. For me it had the magic of Rodolfo's garret in *Bohème*. It also had much of the inconvenience. The window didn't fit the frame. We sealed the gap with gaffer tape. This also sealed in the fumes of the gas fire; I fell asleep to groggy nightmares and woke to visions of a snake pit, inspired by the writhing cracks in the ceiling above the bed. I remember a day coming up to Christmas, the half-hearted twilight of three o'clock; he lay asleep, and gazing at him I thought my love would fill the room, fill the day, light up the darkling sky. So I already knew about love when Charlotte was born.

'May I see her? Please. Please let me see her.' My throat was sore. My body wasn't sore, it was stunned.

'All in good time. The midwife is making sure everything's in working order.'

'Why – what's wrong?'

'Nothing's wrong. You've waited nine months, another couple of minutes shouldn't tax you too severely.'

And then Charlotte cried.

'There, you see? A lot of fuss about nothing. Tidy yourself up, now. And put those legs down. You'll embarrass the doctor.'

They knew at the hospital, of course, they knew what I was, no ring on my finger and brought in from Holbridge Manor. The midwife did finish eventually, after long terrifying minutes of cries and silence. And eventually my baby, wrapped in a blanket, was put into my arms.

She was more blanket than baby, nothing of her but fists and mouth, balled fists, wet mouth, wet and working, mobile as a globule of oil in water.

I suppose I had expected a tiny mite; I was surprised at her size, the length of those arms, the girth of her head, amazed. Suddenly her hand closed tight about my little finger. The grip was so strong, so unexpected, I jumped. At that, her wandering eyes found me and stared, challenging, into mine.

'She's looking at me!' I said, awestruck. 'Hello. Hello, little one.'

'Baby's eyes can't focus. Not for weeks.'

'But they are, she is! And they're ink-coloured. How can that be?'

'All babies' eyes are blue until . . . Whatever do you think you are doing?'

I was unwrapping the blanket. 'I want to see her.'

'You want to . . . ? You silly creature, she'll catch cold! She's only just come out of your tummy!'

'I've got my arms around her and anyway this room is like a furnace. Her limbs shouldn't be restricted so tightly. Let her move.'

And there she was, all of her. Not rosy and sweet like

babies in pictures. Creased. Crusty even. Mottled with lavender patches. But entirely perfect: her legs moulded and bendy like something compact that could be folded away, the heart-rending vulnerability of the wet mouth and the soles of her punching feet, the tiny intricacies of her open lap, her conciseness and her complexities. Then I put out my index finger, slowly inching the tip into that moving sea-urchin mouth. And she sucked me.

Nothing I had ever thought about love had prepared me for this. I was drowned in it, drenched in it, damp and oozing and leaking with love.

'Miss St Clair, either you wrap that child in the blanket or she goes straight to the nursery for her own safety and protection. Really! The sooner Holbridge finds your poor baby a proper mummy the better!'

58

1977

Kim ordered another coffee and a cheese sandwich, and then turned back to the window. The view gave her Trinity Street in both directions, glimmering harsh and brittle under a low sun. But no Sukie.

It was Sukie's idea, this coffee bar, and was therefore the sort of place where they made you choose from an entire list of coffees, and the cheese sandwich would turn up on a lettuce leaf. Typical, thought Kim. And of course Sukie was typically late.

Open on the table was a hardback copy of Fieser & Fieser's *Advanced Organic Chemistry*, its white spaces obliterated by notes. Kim's marginalia had begun at school, and by now there was a hint of palaeontology about them, a suggestion of strata: different pens and evolving hand-writing. It was January 1977 and this was Cambridge. Kim had arrived at King's College in October 1974, among their third ever intake of female students. She had now completed Part I of her natural science tripos with first-class honours, and was well into her Part II.

'Be there!' Sukie had demanded on the phone, as if it were Kim rather than she who was temperamentally incapable of turning up on time. 'And just you, Kim. I want to tell you on your own before we break the news to Denise and Tonya.'

'What news?' Kim had demanded. Then, 'Denise and Tonya are spending Saturday sorting out the party disco.' Which was funny really, as both had urged Kim to keep Sukie out of the way. 'Or we'll *never* get it sorted,' they had chorused in unintended unison.

Marianne had sloughed off the Toinette nickname with childhood, but they all forgot sometimes and Tonya'd her, to the incomprehension of newer friends. Sukie was at Girton College reading English, and she too had done all right in her own Part I. They were all of them doing all right, and had stubbornly stuck together, Denise and Marianne both at the nearby polytechnic, Denise studying sociology and Marianne psychology.

'Who better to dig into the recesses of the mind?' she said to her school's careers adviser, who coughed in embarrassment and hastily moved the conversation on.

It wasn't only the careers officer she had to fight. Marianne came to Cambridge against opposition from her aunt and uncle, who forcefully predicted a breakdown under the pressures of higher education. And of course they were not swayed by Kim's opinion that her sister was happiest channelling her obsessive energies into something constructive. The aunt and uncle never did take to Kim or she to them. But Kim was right, and Marianne was happy here, relatively, much of the time.

Even so, she would never be up to facing an entire hall of residence, so Kim bought her a flat in town. She bought it for her outright, but originally intended that they live there together. It was Marianne herself who talked Kim out of the idea.

'You mean you'll live outside college instead of in a room

up an ancient windy staircase overlooking a quadrangle, with the whole medieval scene of porters and bedders? And it's me that supposed to be crackers? Anyway, who says I want to live with my big sister – yes, I know I'm twice your size but still. You go off to your feudal system, Miss Clever Clogs. I'll be fine.'

So Miss Clever Clogs did. And for her sister's sake she even kept up the friendship with Sukie. Tonya would always love Sukie. And to be fair, Sukie wasn't quite as irritating at twenty-one as she had been at thirteen going on fourteen. Or perhaps it was just that Kim had mellowed and was more tolerant of her.

They had all come through, the only fatal casualty being the movie of *Starched Linen*. Imogen would never see herself on the big screen played by Julie Christie. The circumstances were much too dark, decided the production company. Kim had been right that long-ago day with Mr Antrobus: a great many people blamed Peggy for William Jarman's imprisonment.

In September 1973 Kim had turned eighteen, and immediately applied to the Registrar General for her original birth certificate. At that time it was a step seldom used and not often successful, but the authorities did not refuse her. Shortly afterwards Kim had a copy of the paper that formally bound her to Imogen. For a brief droplet of time she had been Charlotte St Clair.

Nevertheless Kim's legal name was Lynne Jarman; it was as Lynne Jarman that she was required to register at Cambridge. Kim then applied to the courts again, this time to change it by deed poll. The following summer, when she took her exams, she did so under her real name. Lynne Jarman was merely a nightmare that seemed to belong to somebody else, a shadow that even Marianne had shaken off eventually, mostly, almost. Perversely, the arrival of that definitive birth certificate had allowed her to understand the true answer to the question 'Who am I?' She was Kim Tanner. She was Peggy's daughter.

On the subject of Sid Davis's money, Kim had never wavered. She didn't want it. Under pressure she agreed to wait until she turned twenty. But then Kim simply gave it away.

'And why shouldn't she?' demanded Imogen of a nearly distraught Frances Massingham. 'If Kim keeps this up, she will probably leave Cambridge with a starred double First! Let her make her own way.'

So the profits of Sid Davis's racketeering, minus only the cost of Marianne's flat, went to various reputable charities for housing the homeless.

'She will regret this bitterly, Imogen.'

But Frances, who had been so utterly wrong about Marianne, was wrong about this too. Kim never did.

And then English law changed to the tune of the Children Act 1975. All adoptees, on attaining the age of eighteen, had right of access to their birth records. It was at last accepted that it is a deep-seated human requirement to know who you are. When the change did come, the consequences were often explosive: most adopters and birth mothers had been given the assurance that the child's natural parentage would never be disclosed.

'It's been *such* a thorny decision. Poor Mummy and Daddy will be absolutely *desolate*,' Sukie told Kim as she wrote off for an application form just hours after the Act came into force.

It would be another few years yet before a further Act of Parliament outlawed the style of private adoption used at Holbridge Manor, which went ahead without any formal vetting of parents. Nevertheless, most of the mother-and-baby homes had already been swept away, the sort that had incarcerated and bullied Imogen, and lied to her, and allowed her baby to be handed over against her will. By 1975 even the English middle classes no longer locked up their pregnant daughters.

The new law might have been revolutionary but it wasn't quick. An entire new bureaucracy had to be set up and its machinery oiled. Once all that was in place, Sukie was required to undergo consultation with a social worker, who pointed out the possible dangers and disappointments. But Sukie was an adult now with the legal right to go at things bull-headed. At the end of the interview she was handed the name of her natural mother and father, after which she had to apply for a copy of her original birth certificate. All this had taken place before Christmas. From the ear-splitting phone call of last night Kim deduced that the birth certificate had arrived.

Sukie eventually blew in through the door of the coffee bar, an hour late and her hair inexplicably full of leaves in January. Heads turned when she tripped over a chair and then stayed turned because of her looks.

'Hi, Sukie, I'm here.'

'Kim! Oh Kim, wait till you hear this!'

'Yeah. Sit down first. Want a coffee?'

'What a turn-up for the books, it's simply mind-blowing.'

Kim waved over a waitress and ordered a cappuccino for Sukie, who was rummaging in a huge bag of tooled leather. Her hand emerged flapping an envelope. Kim reached out to take it.

'Wait wait wait,' said Sukie. 'The names won't mean anything to you. I have to explain first.'

Comfortably, Kim snapped shut her copy of Fieser & Fieser. 'I'm all ears.'

'*Well*,' began Sukie, 'the birth certificate arrived Tuesday and I did some research. I already had my parents' names. My mother's is Ellen Endicott, which is rather super, isn't it, having a name that alliterates?' said Sukie Sandeman. 'Anyway, the birth certificate gave an address in Kensington, which is also where the adoption agency was, a proper one and *frightfully* posh, no shady deals with mother-and-baby homes for Ellen's daughter.'

Kim smiled.

'*So* I skipped lectures and caught the next London train.'

'Sukie, you are not supposed to make contact without first—'

'Listen, listen. It turns out Ellen moved to France a couple of years ago *but* guess what: she was an actress! Actual Hollywood.'

'Marvellous,' said Kim politely. 'Oh, well done, Sukie.'

'I still haven't finished. This will just blow your boots off. At exactly the time I must have been conceived, she was in the States making a film called *Three Tall Men*. Just a small part, but still. Now read the birth certificate. Look at my name.'

Kim unfolded the paper. Mother: Ellen Endicott. Father: Marswell Verne Johnson, and an address on Laurel Canyon Boulevard, California. A baby daughter, named . . . 'Tara,' read Kim. 'Beautiful. That's fantastic, Sukie.'

'And guess who starred in *Three Tall Men* – Clark Gable.'

'Better and better,' said Kim.

'Wait, wait, you haven't heard the rest. The whole thing's a clue. That name – Marswell Verne Johnson. In 1953 Clark Gable played a character called Victor Marswell and in 1940 he played someone called André Verne and in 1941 somebody called Candy Johnson.'

Kim, dimly recognizing the blind alley down which Sukie was flying without a crash helmet, closed her eyes.

'And everyone in the wide world knows that Tara is Scarlett O'Hara's home in *Gone with the Wind*!'

'Oh Sukie,' said Kim wearily.

'Ellen didn't want to embarrass the real father by—'

'Sukie.'

'What?'

'The movie your mother was working on—'

'*Three Tall Men.*'

'My point exactly. Clark Gable wasn't the only guy on that picture, was he? How about the other two?'

Sukie's eyes flashed. 'I knew you'd be like this. Tara *and* Marswell *and*—?'

'But given that Clark Gable must have played dozens of characters in dozens of films,' began Kim gently.

'I knew you'd be like this,' said Sukie again.

Kim sipped her coffee. 'Did you say *Candy* Johnson?' she asked mischievously. 'That doesn't sound very butch. Was it a gay character? How fantastically brave of him.'

'Go ahead and scoff!' snapped Sukie, throwing her arms wide in a gesture of despair. The sugar bowl hit the wall flying. 'I am the lovechild of Clark Gable!'

Any heads that hadn't turned already did so now.

'OK, Sukie,' said Kim pacifically. 'Good luck.'

'When I meet Ellen I'll suddenly drop his name into the conversation and watch her face.'

'OK, Sukie,' said Kim again. 'Good luck.'

They were quiet after that. Sukie huffily drank her cappuccino and Kim looked out of the window at the street abuzz with shoppers and students. Saturday. This time next week they would be getting Denise's rooms ready for her twenty-first party. Her actual birthday was Wednesday, for which she was being hauled home to Crowhurst Green. 'Cousins, aunts, grandparents. And my great-grandparents probably, dug up from the graveyard,' groaned Denise. But on Saturday, well, that was her own and it would be a party to remember.

On the subject of home, Kim had spent a very happy Christmas in Ealing. Imogen still lived there. Joan's garden had endured, which Kim would for ever see as one of her own triumphs: beautiful even in December with its dogwoods and blazing berries, it had been at its very best – rambling roses and deep, rich purple borders – when Kim achieved her greatest triumph of all. Imogen and Robert Yelland had married in 1970. And they had decided to live in Mount Hill Crescent because Robert believed the continuity would be good for Imogen – and that the house deserved to see a happy ending. And happy they were. Joan was married now with frighteningly healthy twin toddlers, but Mrs Harris was still there, maintaining the house in a style Peggy would have approved of.

Monique had joined them for Christmas. She had sold Shash in 1971 and disappeared for a while to India, but was now home again and working with the celebrated Erin Pizzey at London's first women's refuge. Being Monique she did it thoroughly, made a success of the job and managed to enjoy herself.

Frances Massingham would never mellow, and would always put the fear of God into Kim, but Kim knew how to be grateful. Of Frances's husband she had become very fond. Colonel Massingham had at last retired from the bench, and kept himself fit going for long walks with another old man. Welly. He was going grey too, but he still rolled over smiling, hoping to have his tummy rubbed. If he had any memory of the cruelty of his own early years, it was gauzy and insubstantial. They had all come through.

The Questors was now regularly putting on plays in the Stan Room, calling it the Studio. In total, the previous season had mounted no fewer than thirty-three productions, including some world premieres – and in the Studio something called *The Twelve Pound Look*. It was by J. M. Barrie.

Mr and Mrs Antrobus's own children were at university now, so they simply upped the number of foster children in the Motel and bought a second goat. And Lenny Hanky-Pank, who was actually the acclaimed poet Leonardo Høeg-Petrarch, had joined the faculty of Berkeley where at least once a week wide-eyed students looked up from Lenny's deathless verse to ask if it was true he had inspired 'Norwegian Wood'.

And Imogen had finally quit smoking – three years ago when she and Robert had their daughter Naomi.

'You'll be at my side for the birth, won't you, Kim?' Imogen had urged her. But the concept was rather too hip for the conventional Kim.

'I can have the baby at home, can't I, Robert?' she had said, at which, as a medic and a man who had lost his first wife and baby in childbirth, Robert fretted silently until: 'Joan says she can have larchlap screens constructed for privacy, and I've ordered a paddling pool.'

'For what?'

'So I can give birth in the garden, of course.'

At which he set about dissuading her, and Imogen had their baby in the maternity unit of the King Edward Memorial Hospital while Kim waited in the corridor in a worse fever of anxiety than would ever attend her Cambridge exams. And when a beaming nurse opened the door and invited Kim inside, there was Robert looking trembly and quite stunningly handsome and there was Imogen, her magnificent hair in damp rats' tails and her skin speckled with tiny petechiae like a rash, but tiredly calm.

'Come in, sweetheart. You have another sister. No, better not say anything to Robert,' she added, squeezing his hand, 'or he'll burst into tears.'

Kim leaned gently across the bed. Without squashing the little creature lying extraordinarily content in Imogen's arms making sucky noises, Kim hugged her mother.

And Sebastian? He was on TV twice a week in a blindingly successful detective serial. But you can't have everything, thought Kim.

'Oh Kim!' In one of her typical about-turns, Sukie set down her cup and threw open her arms in a gesture to encompass the universe. 'Isn't life just wonderful? That you can wake up on an ordinary winter's day and by the end of it you're intricately linked to Laurel Canyon and *Gone with the Wind*. Isn't life absolutely heavenly?'

'Absolutely,' agreed Kim. She envisaged her friend as a young girl again, in the early autumn of 1969. Sukie had accepted that she wasn't, after all, Imogen's daughter Charlotte and the subject of a bestselling book. They had just been listening to a pre-release acetate of the Beatles' new album, *Abbey Road*.

'Oh Kim, isn't life absolutely heavenly!' she had suddenly cried out. 'Virtually every couple of weeks there's something fabulous from the Beatles or the Stones or Jimi Hendrix or Bob Dylan or *all of them*, and supergroups being formed, and men walking on the moon, and if it's not an historic concert in Hyde Park it's Woodstock – and we're still only fourteen! We might live another sixty years with this type of brilliant stuff coming along week after week, year after year!'

But it doesn't, realized Kim now. That rollercoaster stopped with the decade. And then: I didn't join in until it was nearly over. But at least I had the tail end of the sixties in Mount Hill Crescent. Nobody can say I wasn't there.

'Fancy a walk?' she suggested, stowing Fieser & Fieser into her shoulder bag.

'OK. Oh hey, I didn't tell you.' Sukie sorted out her own bag while Kim paid the bill. 'I ran into the utterly scrumptious Adrian again.'

'I thought you were potty about Patrick.'

'Patrick's passé. *Tragically* obsolete.'

'I thought you were in love.'

'Who knows where one will find love?'

'Filed between Led Zeppelin and Mahler,' replied Kim crisply. Sukie didn't think to ask after Kim's own nice boyfriend, a rather brilliant theoretical physicist named Justin. It was expected that everything was fine as always. And she was right, it was.

Kim pulled open the door. Outside in Trinity Street cyclists swept past, college scarves streaming behind them.

'Which way?' asked Kim. 'Left? Right?'

'Frankly, my dear,' said Sukie, 'I don't *give* a damn!'

And there in the doorway, doubled up, their laughter buffeting from one to the other in waves that wobbled the passing cyclists, both young women realized they truly didn't give a damn whether they turned left or right. Either direction was bound to be absolutely heavenly.

ACKNOWLEDGEMENTS

I am grateful to NORCAP (112 Church Road, Wheatley, Oxfordshire, OX33 1LU) for answering all my questions about adoption and pointing me towards other helpful organizations and publications. By lucky chance, the excellent book *Love Child* by Sue Elliot (Vermilion, 2005) hit the shops three days before my final draft was due with the copy-editor, and not three days after. I also recommend Polly Toynbee's *Lost Children* (Hutchinson & Co., 1985) as a clear, thoughtful and humane account of adopted children and relinquishing mothers, while Peter Mullen's film *The Magdalene Sisters* (2002) remains the best though devastating account of the so-called Magdalene laundries.

For anyone interested in 1960s London, Barry Miles's *In the Sixties* (Jonathan Cape, 2002) is the best there is – oh, and I borrowed some elements of his Indica for my Shash.

Then there's the Questors Theatre. First I must thank Alex Marker, general fount of knowledge, for his enthusiasm, his patience – and for spending more time than he probably wanted to in the prop cellar.

I can't thank everyone I've worked with on every show or

this will read like an acceptance speech at the Oscars, so I'll just thank those I've worked with most closely, most recently: John Horwood and John Wibberley, Claire Whitely, Sally and Joel Schrire, Karen Milburn, Lubna Malik, Annabelle Williams, John Dobson, Michael Smith, Ian Buckingham, Freddy Henry, Melanie Short, Jo Matthews, Clare Watson, Perri Blakelock, Tom Butler, Tessa Vale, Mark Lucek, Charlie Lucas, Nigel Worsley, Martin Choules and Peter Salvietto. And Robbin Pearce, Alison Winter and John Pyle. And Jim Craddock. And Anne Gilmour. I must stop. And Martin Stoner.

Neither can I include all the people we have lost, but Brin Parsonage was there with every reference to the DSM desk, whenever I mentioned set design I remembered Kris Collier's amazing exploding set for *Accidental Death of an Anarchist*, and I thought of Richard Murphy with everything I wrote about everything.

That just leaves all the people who turned this from a typescript into a book. Véronique Baxter and Diana Beaumont are my agent and editor extraordinaires who keep me on the straight and narrow. Grateful thanks also to Deborah Adams, Prue Jeffreys and everyone else at Transworld for making the process so pleasurable.